RUTHLESS

Annie Carter should have demanded to see their bodies lying on a slab in the morgue, but she really believed the Delaney twins were gone from her life for good. Now sinister things are happening around her and Annie Carter is led to one terrifying conclusion: her bitter enemies, the Delaney twins, didn't die all those years ago. They're back and want her, and her family, dead. This isn't the first time someone has made an attempt on her life, yet she's determined to make it the last. Nobody threatens Annie Carter and lives to tell the tale...

RUTHLESS

RUTHLESS

by

Jessie Keane

Magna Large Print Books
Long Preston, North Yorkshire,
BD23 4ND, England.

British Library Cataloguing in Publication Data.

Keane, Jessie
Ruthless

A catalogue record of this book is
available from the British Library

ISBN 978-0-7505-3849-7

First published in Great Britain by Pan Books
an imprint of Pan Macmillan, a division of Macmillan Publishers Ltd.

Copyright © Jessie Keane 2013

Cover illustration © David Thrower by arrangement with
Arcangel Images

The right of Jessie Keane to be identified as the author of this work has been asserted by her in accordance with the Copyright, Designs and Patents Act, 1988

Published in Large Print 2014 by arrangement with
Pan Macmillan Publishers Limited

All Rights reserved. No part of this publication may be reproduced, stored in a retrieval system, or transmitted in any form or by any means, electronic, mechanical, photocopying, recording or otherwise without the prior permission of the Copyright owner.

Magna Large Print is an imprint of Library Magna Books Ltd.

Printed and bound in Great Britain by
T.J. (International) Ltd., Cornwall, PL28 8RW

Cliff, this one's for you…

ACKNOWLEDGEMENTS

To all the usual suspects – you know who you are: love & thanks for your support, laughs and general cheerleadership.

Also to Andy Woodward, External Communications Manager of the Cessna Aircraft Company, for the advice.

1

London, 1980

Annie Carter swept into the Ritz Hotel in Piccadilly with a determined stride and a face like thunder. Heads turned and conversations stopped mid-sentence. She was wearing a black power suit, big gold earrings, shoulder pads out to here, and killer heels. She was tall anyway, but the heels took her up to six feet. Her thick chocolate-brown hair was bouncing loose on her shoulders and her eyes, dark green and flashing with barely repressed emotion, said *Don't fuck with me.* Her red-painted lips were set in a grim, irritated line as she was led in under the high gilded cupola of the Palm Court by a doorman dressed in a brass-buttoned tailcoat and white tie.

Dolly Farrell, former Limehouse madam and currently manager of the Palermo, one of three clubs owned by Max Carter – Annie's husband – was already waiting at their table. Dolly saw her old mate sweeping in like the wrath of God and thought that you would never know in a million years that Annie Carter had come from nothing. Now, she looked rich to the tips of her fingers. She also looked seriously pissed off.

Uh-oh, thought Dolly. *What now?*

She half-rose from her dainty gold Dior chair, the words of greeting dying on her lips as Annie walked straight up to the table and slapped a brown envelope down upon the pristine napery, rattling the glasses and knocking the cutlery askew.

'Well, there it is then,' said Annie, planting her hands on her hips and glaring around as if she was mad at the entire world. Which she was. Mad enough to *spit*. 'That's it. Done. *Finished*.'

Dolly looked from Annie's face to the envelope and back again. Slowly, she sank into her chair.

'The decree absolute?' she guessed.

'No, I've won the pools. Of *course* it's the decree absolute. I am officially, as of this moment, divorced from Max bloody Carter.'

'If madam would care to sit?' asked the waiter, pulling out a chair for her.

Annie sat down. He placed a napkin in her lap and discreetly withdrew. The other diners averted their eyes, resumed their conversations.

'Get me some champagne or something,' moaned Annie, slumping with elbows on the table and head in hands. 'Let's celebrate.'

Annie dragged her hands through her hair and looked up at her friend's face. Her mouth was trembling. Dolly thought that if this was any other woman of her acquaintance, they would break down and cry their heart out at this point. But not Annie Carter. Tough as old boots, that was her. Impervious to hurt. Ex-madam, once ruler of the streets around the East End, once true Mafia queen. Now a divorcee.

Dolly gazed at her. 'You don't like champagne,' she pointed out. She knew Annie didn't drink alcohol or have any tolerance for it. *And you know what? You don't look much like celebrating, either.*

'No?' Annie gave a harsh laugh. 'Well, maybe it's time I started.'

The waiter returned.

'Tea for us both,' said Dolly, and he went off to fetch it.

Annie was staring at the envelope. 'I can't believe it,' she said faintly.

'I thought it was what you wanted,' said Dolly.

No, what I wanted was for him to stop behaving like a jealous manipulative arsehole, thought Annie. *And instead, I got this.*

'So what happens next?' asked Dolly when Annie didn't answer. She had watched this, the war between Annie and Max, escalating over several years. The arguments, the confrontations, then the courts, the decree nisi. Now it looked as though the final shot had been fired.

'He's moving out,' said Annie, struggling to keep her voice steady. 'He's at the Holland Park house as we speak, getting the last of his things together.'

'So you're keeping the house?'

'Of course I'm keeping the house. It's *my* bloody house.'

'Where's he going then?'

'He's got the place in Barbados, he'll go there.'

Dolly nodded. Their tea arrived, along with scones, jam, cream, tiny chocolate cakes, finger sandwiches and raspberry Bakewell tarts. Annie looked at it all, so lovely, so appetizing, and felt sick.

'I never wanted this,' she said, poking the envelope with her finger. 'I just wanted...' she faltered to a halt.

'What?' prompted Dolly.

Annie shrugged. How could she bear to go over it all again? To explain that her visits to Annie's nightclub in Times Square, New York, had been viewed with extreme suspicion by Max. She'd been so proud of the club, so pleased with it, it was *hers* and hers alone. But he had killed her pleasure in it. Every time she went over there, he behaved as though she was betraying him in some way and was cold to her for days after. It was maddening. *He* travelled on business, and you didn't catch *her* behaving like a moron.

'You know what finally finished it for me? He had me followed,' Annie said. 'It was this time last year.'

Dolly stared in surprise. 'What? You didn't tell me that.'

'I'm telling you now. It was in New York. I had a feeling I was being watched. Then I caught this bloke trailing me. I grabbed him. It was a private detective, Max had hired him. He *seriously* thought I was having an affair.'

'For fuck's sake,' said Dolly, too fascinated to even start in on the cakes. Her eyes narrowed. 'Oh, wait. Not ... Alberto Barolli?'

Annie nodded and heaved a sigh. 'Yeah. He thought I was having an affair with Alberto and he had some private dick trailing me, for God's sake. I was that mad at him, Doll. I'm his *wife*. If he couldn't trust me, what was the point? So when I got back to England, I faced him down about it. And I totally lost it. I said if he couldn't take my word as the truth, we'd better end it.'

'Shit.'

'And you know what that son of a bitch said to me?' Annie's eyes were flaring with temper. 'He said, "Fine. Then you'll be free to fuck whoever you damned well like."'

Dolly winced in sympathy. 'And what about Layla?'

Annie gulped. This was the most awful part. Layla was a daddy's girl, she adored her father. She'd always run to Max rather than to Annie, which hurt. But Layla's schooling at Westminster was at a crucial point and she couldn't relocate to Barbados with her dad, it just wasn't practical.

'Layla's staying with me,' said Annie.

'And how does she feel about all this?'

'How do you *think* she feels?' snapped Annie. Then she shook her head. 'Sorry, Doll. Didn't mean to take it out on you. It's just been so hard. She's devastated. Of course she is. And I'm public enemy number one as far as she's concerned. Her dad can do no wrong.'

'She'll come round,' said Dolly, reaching across and patting Annie's hand.

'I don't know. All I know is I couldn't go on that way. What did he want to do, keep me in a cage or something? I have *business* in New York.'

'But Alberto's there,' said Dolly. And she knew – *everyone* knew – that Annie and the Mafia boss Alberto Barolli went way back. There had been times when Dolly herself had wondered about the closeness of their relationship. Not that she would ever tell Annie that. 'Have some tea,' she said.

'Why not?' asked Annie, although she thought it might choke her.

She had an hour to kill, and then he'd be gone.

Then she'd go home, wait for Layla to come in from school, try and console her – if she could. And somehow, after that, she was going to have to carry on, to salvage something from the train wreck of her life.

2

Talk about the best-laid plans, though. Her *plan* had been to meet Dolly at the Ritz as arranged, give it at least an hour; that would be ample time for him to get the hell out of her house. But no. When she opened the front door at Holland Park, there was Max's overnight bag and suitcase still in the hall – and from the study, there came the sound of Layla crying.

Annie closed her eyes and leaned against the door. *Please, no more,* she thought.

But she pushed herself upright and walked over to the study and eased the door open.

Max was there, leaning on the desk. Layla, wearing her school uniform of plain skirt and white blouse, her dark hair pulled back into a pleat, was holding on to him and sobbing.

Fourteen years old, thought Annie. *God, what are we doing? What are we putting her through?*

Max looked up at his ex-wife as she stood there. Annie felt her guts constrict as he stared at her. Her husband. Correction: *ex*-husband. He had chipped away at her love for him remorselessly, but still – even now – she found him physically almost irresistible with his black waving hair, his tanned skin, his predatory hook of a nose, his dense, dark navy-blue eyes. Even if they were looking at her with something close to hatred, right this minute.

'Layla?' said Annie hoarsely. 'What are you doing home? You're meant to be in school.'

Layla said nothing, just shot her a tear-stained glance and cuddled closer to Max.

Max cleared his throat. 'She was afraid I'd be gone before she got home, so she told them she felt ill.'

'Well, she shouldn't have done that.' Annie'd had no education to speak of, and she was always determined that Layla, who was very bright, should not be raised the same way. Layla's schooling was of the utmost importance.

'I don't want you to go!' shouted Layla, and started sobbing again. 'Please, Daddy, don't go.'

'We'll still see each other. As often as you want. I'll come to London to see you, and you'll come out to see me,' said Max, rubbing his daughter's back soothingly.

'It's not the same.'

Annie could only stand there, feeling sickened and powerless. This was a bloody disaster. Max was supposed to have been gone before Layla got home – to avoid a scene. Only it was all going wrong, pulverizing her afresh with the pain. She hated what they were doing to Layla. But it was done. And it was best now – wasn't it? – to just get this over with.

Max straightened, seeming almost to read her thoughts.

'I'd better go,' he said, easing Layla away from him.

'No, Daddy, please don't,' she wailed.

As if she was four, not fourteen, thought Annie in anguish, feeling Layla's torment as if it was her own.

'I'll call you,' said Max, kissing Layla's cheek. 'Very soon. OK?'

Layla nodded dumbly, crying more quietly.

Max moved away from her, came towards the open door where Annie stood. He paused there, and their eyes met. If she reached out to him now, said, *Let's talk, let's not do this,* would he stay?

She almost did it, but her pride stopped her.

Then the moment was gone. Max brushed past her, walked across the hall, picked up his suitcase and bag, and left.

Annie gulped hard, trying to compose herself. It was finished. Leaving her with a heartbroken girl to look after. It didn't matter how *she* felt, she had to focus on Layla. She walked toward her. Layla's sobs had died away to hitching little gasps.

'Honey, why don't you go and find Ros–' she started.

'Don't you come near me,' yelled Layla suddenly, stopping Annie in her tracks. 'This is all your fault. All you had to do was *be* here, but you always had to be running around doing your stupid *business.* I *hate* you.'

She ran past Annie, shoving her aside. She flew across the hall and up the stairs.

Annie stood there, feeling sick with hurt, and heard the door to Layla's room slam shut. She closed her eyes and took in a deep breath. The silence of the house enveloped her. She was alone again.

On shaky legs she walked over to the leather-tooled desk and sat down behind it, slumping there in exhaustion and despair. She didn't even know who she was any more. She took the decree absolute out of her pocket and put it on the desk and stared at it.

Well, I'm not Mrs Max Carter, that's for sure.

God, she was tired. Too tired to think, but still it all spun around, unravelling in her tortured brain – losing Max in Majorca, believing him to be dead. Then her involvement with Constantine Barolli, Alberto's father. All the troubles and the dangers she had endured to come to this point.

Was it worth it?

Ten years ago she had been an underworld power to be reckoned with, running the streets of Bow. Until Redmond and Orla Delaney, the psychotic twins who'd ruled Battersea with an iron fist, tried to kill her. And that had ended in their deaths, organized by her Mafia contacts.

So much trouble.

So much pain.

The attempt on her life had caused her to step away from all that. She'd thought she could leave it behind her, sit back and enjoy the good life – but it hadn't worked out that way.

Annie gazed around her at the empty, opulent study with its tan Chesterfield sofas, its walls lined with books, the costly Aubusson rugs on the floor. She had everything ... and she had nothing at all. She'd lost her husband, and her daughter hated her.

Raindrops pattered against the window panes. She stared out of the window at the darkening sky, and wondered how the hell she was going to come back from this. She'd fought so long and so hard, but all she felt was *defeated.* She was too worn out even to try any more.

Annie sat there and thought of old friends, old enemies, her weary mind a tangle of jumbled images. Two faces emerged from the fog in her brain and she shuddered.

The Delaney twins.

She could see their faces, their cold, pale green eyes, their red hair. Those twisted, horrible bastards.

It was raining harder now and she was dimly aware that she was crying. She *never* cried. *Dig deep and stand alone,* that was the motto she'd always lived by. And she'd never been more alone than she was right this minute.

Well, that was one thing she no longer had to worry about. The Delaneys were gone. And she couldn't help thinking that, perverted as they were, evil and vindictive and out for her blood as they had always been, the Delaney twins were the lucky ones. She was here, alone and suffering: Redmond and Orla Delaney had been fortunate in comparison.

They were out of it.

They were dead.

3

Over the Irish Sea ..., 1970

Orla Delaney had always been a nervous flyer. She was nervous *anyway,* on this flight – for it was a flight in every sense of the word. Along with her twin, Redmond, she was fleeing for her life in the Cessna 210, knowing that London was over as far as they were concerned. Orla's only comfort was the knowledge that, before their crime empire had collapsed, they had finally got rid of Annie Carter.

Barumph!

The wind buffeted the small plane with a vicious swirl and she clutched harder at her seat, stifling a scream as the four-seater rocked from side to side and then plummeted, dropping like a stone, leaving her stomach somewhere up on the padded ceiling. She wondered if she was about to be sick.

'Rough night,' said Fergal the pilot, a big grey-haired Irishman who sat unperturbed at the controls.

Orla was reassured by Fergal. He'd worked for the Delaney firm for years, ferrying illicit cargoes – drugs, arms, people – in and out of Britain. He boasted he could land the Cessna on a gnat's tit, he'd been flying it for so long. Orla believed him. He'd been a British Airways pilot once, then he'd done a stint crop-dusting in Kenya before Redmond had recruited him into the far more lucrative family firm.

She glanced at Redmond. He seemed calm. He half-smiled, squeezed her hand briefly. It was only *her* who was panicking.

It felt like an eternity since they'd left the airport. After a wild drive down to Cardiff in the dead of night, Fergal had flown them into the tumultuous skies unauthorized, with no co-pilot, no mechanic, no clearance. They were in violation of air traffic safety guidelines and aircraft operation rules. But Fergal didn't give a shit about any of that. Neither did either of his passengers.

Orla glanced at her watch and saw that they'd only been aloft for ten minutes.

Whumph!

Again the wind tossed the plane, batting it almost playfully around the blackening sky. Night was coming, the moon was up and full, scudding clouds drifting across its face. Even in big planes, she was nervous. In a miniscule Cessna, a fluttering stomach and a chest tight with fear took on a whole new level. She prayed for dry land, for the lights of the airport. Peering out of the window, she saw only the dark sea below them. No lights. No *ships,* even: in weather like this, any sane captain would put in to shore, ride out the storm.

But not them. If they'd delayed getting out of England by so much as an hour, the police would have shut down their escape.

They'd only just made it.

Orla stifled her nerves. It was OK. They'd got away. Soon they'd be in Limerick. She could see it now in her mind: the old farm on the banks of the Shannon, the Delaney family home. From there they could go anywhere, anywhere in the world. All would be well. She breathed deeply, told herself, *calm, be calm.*

'What the f–' said Fergal.

'What is it?' asked Redmond.

The pilot was tapping one of the dials in front of him.

'Fuel reading's low.' He tapped it again. 'Should be showing nearly full.'

Orla felt the fear erupt, break out of its cage. Suddenly she found it hard to catch her breath.

'How low?' asked Redmond.

'Ah, don't worry. Must be a malfunction, we've only just filled up,' said the pilot comfortably, not answering the question. 'It's nothing. Ten minutes, we'll be there.'

Ten minutes, we'll be there.

Fergal had hardly finished uttering the words when the engine started to sputter. Orla saw – she didn't want to see but she couldn't help it – she saw the damned propeller falter and stop turning.

No, this can't be happening, she thought wildly, clutching at Redmond's hand.

But it was.

She watched Fergal fighting the controls, trying to keep the nose up when there was no power, nothing to stop the inevitable. And finally, horribly, it happened. The tiny plane stalled in midair. Then it plummeted like a stone into the cold embrace of the Irish Sea.

4

The stunning, mind-numbing impact as the plane hit the water nose-first blew in the windscreen. Icy water instantly surged into the cockpit like a burst dam. The water enveloped Orla, whipping all the breath from her body with the intensity of its coldness. As the nose-cone dipped, she saw Fergal, still strapped into his seat at the controls, his arms flailing against the force of the inrushing water.

As their pilot vanished beneath the churning foam, Orla felt movement beside her as Redmond tugged at his seat-belt release.

'Christ!' he was shouting as the sea battered them, swirling up around their chests, snatching the air from their lungs.

This couldn't be happening, it was a nightmare. Reeling with shock, Orla reached down with rapidly numbing fingers and tried to free her own seat belt.

The water was rising fast, too fast.

She was fighting against the strap, panicking. She couldn't get it undone.

'Don't lean forward, you're jamming it, try to relax...' Redmond yelled as waves rose up around his mouth.

Orla couldn't. Had he got his free? She couldn't tell, couldn't see anything, couldn't do anything above the hysterical fear that the water was coming in, *pouring* in, and they were going to drown. It was up around her neck now, and her fingers were struggling, she couldn't get the clasp free.

She was going to die.

Redmond was surging up out of the water, he was half-standing, getting above it, but it was still coming in, it was rising all the time and *she couldn't get free.*

'I can't–' she shouted, her teeth chattering with cold.

Redmond took a breath, and plunged down under the swirling waves.

Orla was alone with the rising sea. The airplane was groaning, the fuselage popping and shuddering with the pressure and weight of the sea water as its interior filled up.

'Redmond!' she shrieked.

There was no answer.

She was alone. She was going to *die* alone.

Then suddenly he appeared beside her, spluttering, coughing, his face shockingly pale in the half-light, his red hair flat to his head.

Her belt was loose. He'd done it.

'We have to get–' he started.

His words were cut off as the plane lurched sideways.

Orla screamed. Redmond lost his footing and fell against the bulkhead, his forehead striking metal. His eyes rolled up. He collapsed into the water and disappeared from sight. Then the tiny battered plane gave one last deathly groan, and sank further beneath the waves.

'Redmond! *Redmond!*' Orla cried, frantically

reaching out, trying to find him.

Her hands were numb, like her legs. She was freezing, she was dying. She knew it. She scrambled around, sobbing with terror. He was gone. He must have been swept out of the hole made by the blown-in windscreen and into the sea.

Then her hand touched cloth.

His coat.

He was still in here, in this coffin that was now swirling downward, spiralling deeper into the icy waters, carrying them to their graves. She found a reserve of strength from somewhere and grabbed the cloth and hauled it up.

Redmond's face appeared above the surging waters, his eyes flickering open in panic, his mouth open too, whooping in a mouthful of air. He was shivering hard, and bleeding. Orla pulled him toward her.

'Oh, holy Christ, Red–' she sobbed.

The water was lapping over their mouths and they were slipping, sliding sideways as the plane descended into icy blackness. The aircraft tipped sharply again and Orla's feet slid from under her. She tried to hold her breath, but her lungs were bursting with the effort and with the fear that at any moment she was going to die. She couldn't get her balance. She floundered, stretched, grabbed Redmond's arm and hauled herself up, coughing, choking.

The cockpit would soon be completely full of water, and what would they do then?

They would drown.

There was only a tiny air pocket left to breathe

in, under the roof of the cockpit, and they were huddled there, gasping, as the waters rose and rose around them.

'We have to get out,' said Redmond.

Orla clutched at the roof and shook her head.

'Before it sinks too far down,' he insisted.

There were trenches in the Irish Sea thousands of feet deep. Long before they reached that depth, the water pressure would kill them. He was right. They *had* to get out.

'Through the front. It's the only way. The windscreen. Come on.'

Not giving her time to answer, Redmond took a couple of deep breaths and plunged under the black churning water.

Orla was left there, alone, the water lapping around her face. Terrified, she didn't want to move. But she was alone here. She would *die* here. Redmond was gone.

She took a desperate, despairing breath and dived.

5

Orla swam, lungs bursting, pushing herself along to the front of the little cabin. In horror she saw with salt-stung eyes the dim outline of Fergal in his short-sleeved white shirt, his arms floating aloft, his hair billowing around his shocked, bug-eyed dead face. He was still strapped into his seat at the controls. She saw the hole where the windscreen had been. She couldn't see Redmond.

She wanted, so badly, to breathe. Her head felt like a balloon, pumped full of air she ached to release. Just to inhale one wonderful mouthful of air ... only she wouldn't. If she breathed in, she would draw the savagely cold salt water into her lungs and that would be the end of her.

Somehow she reached the windscreen. Fighting against the downward plunge of the little plane she wrestled her way out through the gap and was suddenly in the open ocean, her ears hurting with the pressure, a strong current pulling her. All around her she saw only Stygian milky-green gloom. Above her ... was it possible? ... she thought she saw fainter light.

She glanced down in sick horror and saw the plane sinking, sinking, sinking down to who knew what monstrous depth. She turned, and kicked for the surface. She knew she wouldn't make it. Her lungs were exploding with pain. Soon she would have to suck in that last, fatal breath. And Redmond was gone, swept away; he must be dead.

Despair grabbed her as she swam upward. She could see nothing, hear nothing but the bubbling rush of the sea. The current buffeted her. Soon she was too tired even to kick. Her limbs were frozen with the cold. She stopped moving and hung in the water, rising inch by inch. Heart bursting, lungs screaming, she surrendered. She lifted her head and opened her mouth and gave herself up to death.

But when she breathed in, she breathed in *air.*

She was on the surface, the wind knocking her

from side to side, the churning waves tossing her left and right, slapping her in the face.

Orla gasped in mouthful after mouthful of incredibly sweet salty air. Shivering, sobbing, she looked around her. The moon was still up there, still casting its placid silvery glow over the turbulent white-capped sea.

She was alive.

But where was Redmond, where was her twin?

She tried to scream his name, but all that emerged was a breathless croak. The sea was too cold, the currents too powerful, constantly dragging at her, numbing her, filling her mouth with sickeningly strong salt water.

From time to time, over the pummelling waves and the relentless power of the sea, she could make out a low shape to her left, an outline of black against the dark grey of the skies. A long way away. Two hundred yards, maybe?

It took a while before she understood what it was.

'Oh shit,' she wept with weak gratitude, spitting out water, shivering with shock and cold.

It was rocks.

It was *land.*

Minutes later, the sea flung her on to the shore. Scraped and bloodied by rocks, she lay there as the foam surged over her, trying to lift her head, failing, gulping down mouthfuls of salt. She was gagging, vomiting, coughing. Slowly, painfully she dragged herself up the beach until at last she was lying on wet sand, and the water couldn't reach her any more. Its roar, like an angry lion, filled her head. But she had survived. By some miracle, she had been spared.

Finally she was able to raise her eyes, look around her. The moon plunged behind clouds and then emerged again, illuminating the landscape. What she longed to see, prayed to see, was another form lying here – Redmond, her twin, her life.

There was no one.

Away in the distance, inland, she could see lights. A house. People who might help. But she was alone on the beach and for the first time she realized in panic that from here on she would be alone in *life* too.

She broke down and cried then, unable to believe that he was gone, that he was lost to her. How would she go on without him? Sodden, shivering, bleeding from many small cuts, she pushed herself to her feet and stood there, taking in the thundering sea, the ghostly moonlit sand and glossy-wet pebbles, the sheer vast *emptiness* of it all.

'Redmond!' she screamed.

But no one answered.

No one came.

6

Walking away from the beach felt like a betrayal, but Orla knew that if she was to survive, she would have to get out of the chilling wind that was flattening her wet clothes against her skin. And she might yet find him alive. She clung to that hope as she stumbled through the dark, trembling and falling and crying, toward the lights of the house. Her shivering had intensified, and she knew that hypothermia was setting in, it was all she could do to resist the overwhelming desire to simply lie down and surrender to the cold, to sleep and never wake again.

The massive roar of the sea sounded a counterpoint to her frenzied heartbeat as she forced herself to walk on, to survive this. She passed a stack of lobster pots, a pile of nets and old chains, ropes and weights. Tripping over something in the sand, she sprawled head-first on to a narrow walkway beside an upturned rowing boat, its paint peeling off. Using the boat for support, she pulled herself upright and staggered painfully on. Her shoes must have fallen off in the sea; when she glanced down her feet were bloodied and her tights were in shreds. Her feet were so numb she couldn't even feel the pain of the gravel biting into the soles.

Redmond.

She was at the cottage now, gulping, trying to

compose herself. An old bike was propped against the wall. There was no sign of a car. Instead of a doorbell there was a miniature brass bell suspended on a bracket, a brass gnome crouched beneath it, holding a chain. She yanked at the chain, and the bell rang.

Nothing happened. She yanked it again.

Jesus, please, please, will you open the fecking door?

It seemed like an age before she heard movement. Bolts being thrown back. Then all at once a small man was standing there. He was sixtyish, with a thick mop of springy grey hair. His face was as gnarled and weathered as driftwood. Bright hazel eyes stared out at her in surprise from under dark brows. He wore a white shirt, pulled up to his elbows to show sinewy workman's arms, red braces, and black trousers shiny from wear.

'Can you help?' said Orla in a cracked voice that was high with strain. She knew the one thing she couldn't afford to tell anyone was that she'd been in a plane crash. The flight hadn't been authorized for take-off. It wouldn't take the Garda long to realize that something was amiss, and they would be on to the English police before you could say knife. 'My brother and I were out in a dinghy. It capsized. Can you help me look for him please?'

The man stared for a long moment. Then he stepped back and said, 'Come along in.'

Orla entered the warm cottage interior. It felt unreal, this cosy normality, like a dream. A woman was watching TV at the kitchen table. The newsman was saying that British troops had sealed off the Catholic Bogside area in Londonderry after clashes with rioters. The woman looked up in wonder at this half-drowned young woman standing there dripping all over her clean floor.

'What...?' she breathed, coming to her feet.

'There's been a boating accident,' said the man. 'Cissie, get the brandy out.'

Orla was shaking her head, hard. *Brandy?* Desperation was making her eyes manic. 'There's no time for that. We have to go and find him. Fetch torches.'

'But I–'

'We haven't *time* for this. For the love of God, fetch the torches and let's go.' But she was trembling so badly that she could no longer hold herself upright. She fell forward almost delicately, and found herself on her knees with her head humming so loudly she was sure she was about to pass out. The cottage lights seemed to flicker in and out of focus and suddenly everything was very far away, even their clucking anxious voices as they got her off her knees and on to a chair.

'Get that brandy, Cissie,' she dimly heard the old man say. 'I'll go out and check the shoreline.'

Orla refocused to see Cissie crouching in front of her, watching her with concern.

'Yes, that's the thing for a shock like this.' Cissie hurried away and returned with a glass brimming with amber liquid. 'Here, here,' she said, putting the glass against Orla's lips. Orla sipped, felt it warming her all the way down. She coughed, sipped again.

'Don't you worry,' Cissie was chattering on, 'Donny will find your brother if anyone can, he knows this stretch of coast inside out. Now, let's sort you out some dry clothes...'

The old man was putting on wet-weather gear, picking up a heavy-duty torch from the dresser. 'I'll be away then,' he said, and went out into the stormy night.

Donny never found Redmond. He scoured the headland, the beach, all around to the next bay, but there was nothing, no one. He was out for well over an hour. By the time he got back, Cissie had taken Orla's wet clothes off her and dressed her in a winceyette nightie and a thick dressing gown. She had disinfected and covered the worst of the cuts on Orla's feet, dried out and untangled Orla's hair, forced a little soup down her, saying she must get warm and take some food.

The soup only made Orla gag. Her stomach was a knot of fear and dread. She could not yet comprehend the full enormity of this disaster. Could not even begin to believe that she was never going to see Redmond again. But when Donny came in, grave-faced, shaking his head at her pleading eyes, she knew that the worst had happened.

Redmond was gone.

She was never going to see him again.

It was as if the soul had been ripped out of her, right then and there.

'You'll sleep here tonight,' said Cissie, while Donny removed his outdoor gear and carried it into the scullery to dry off. 'Tomorrow, when the storm eases, Donny'll take the bike into the village and telephone the Garda. They'll alert the Coastguard.'

Orla shook her head. Much as she wanted the Coastguard searching for Redmond, she knew that it was hopeless. And she couldn't afford to alert the Garda. If they came round asking questions, she would have a hard time coming up with answers.

'It's far too late for that,' she said, and tears poured down her face as the sheer weight of it all struck home. He was gone from her: he truly was.

'Still, we should do it,' persisted Donny.

'No. It's no use,' said Orla flatly, and refused to discuss it further.

The storm raged on, making it impossible for Donny to reach the village the next day. At dawn the following day, Orla got shakily out of bed and knelt on the window seat in the spare bedroom where she'd passed a sleepless night. She stared out of the window at the waves pounding the shore beneath an angry red and purple sky, wondering where Redmond was. Given the ferocity of the storm, the current would probably have swept his lifeless body miles away.

I should be dead too, she thought. *I am a dead woman walking.*

Her mind kept returning to the crash. Fergal tapping the dial. The propeller juddering to a halt. The heart-stopping plummet into the ocean, into the grip of ice-cold waters that should have claimed her life, not just the lives of Redmond and poor Fergal.

Cissie had kindly washed out her clothes the day before, and now Orla snatched them up. Throwing off the borrowed nightie and dressing gown, she dressed hurriedly then went to the door and listened. The house was quiet; the old couple weren't awake yet. She crept downstairs and took a small amount of cash she found in the dresser drawer, then crammed her feet into a pair of Cissie's shoes. They were a size too small, and chafed her sore feet, but she was too intent on getting away to notice.

Pulling her coat around her, she silently unbolted the front door and stepped out into the blustery morning. She took up the bicycle, and started pedalling in the direction she had seen the lights of a village the night she arrived. From there, she could catch a bus to the nearest town. And then she would make her way home, to Limerick.

7

The Delaneys had started out in a modest house in Moyross. That was until Davey Delaney, tired of scraping a living on a factory floor, decided feck this and went to try his hand in London.

Old man Delaney had done pretty well there. After a spell as a bookie's runner, he'd got into scrap dealing. And as soon as the money started to roll in, he'd set up a few sidelines – hijacking goods lorries, operating a couple of illegal gambling dens, and of course running prostitutes.

It hadn't taken him long to carve out his niche among the London faces. And having established a little pocket of power for himself and his kin in Battersea, he defended it ferociously, coming down hard on anyone who tried to muscle in. He even managed to expand his territory, seizing control of a stretch of dockland across the river in Limehouse.

Life in the teeming dog-eat-dog city suited the brutal aspects of his nature. And the family thrived too. While in London, the wife dropped him some children: Tory first, then Patrick, then the twins – Orla and Redmond, then the baby of the family, Kieron. But they never forgot their roots. The proceeds of gambling, robbery and vice paid for a grand farmhouse a stone's throw from the Shannon, and his wife was always nipping across, checking on the renovations and furnishing the place.

Eventually the old man admitted to his age, decided it was time to retire, let the boys take over. They leapt at the chance. And all went well, until the apple of his eye – Tory, his eldest, his most beloved son – was cut down in his prime.

Davey was never the same after Tory's death. He withdrew to the farm, leaving the business to Pat, to Redmond and Orla. Kieron wasn't interested, he fancied himself an artist. When the family came to visit, he would sit staring at the wall, making no attempt to join the conversation. Suspecting a nervous breakdown, his anxious wife steered him to the doctors. Within a year, they came back with a diagnosis: dementia. There was no question of

Davey moving into a nursing home; he stayed on at the farm, the dream home declining with each year in fading grandeur, Davey losing his mind, his wife nursing him.

Now, Orla approached the farm. She paused outside to gaze around her. It was exactly as she remembered. Dad had been so proud of the place when he'd bought it, giving out about the thirty acres of land that came with it, and how old the place was.

Orla let her eyes drift over the stonework. It looked tired in places. But the house was still a fine big place, with panoramic views across open country towards the great grey sprawl of the river.

This was home, and she did have a few good memories of it. But oh, everything had happened here. For every good memory, there were ten bad ones.

She went to the big oak brass-studded door and pulled the bell chain. Far away in the house, she heard the thing echo and jangle.

She waited. And waited. Finally she rang the bell again.

At last, there was the sound of movement, and then her mother was standing in front of her, white hair awry, a blue-sprigged cream pinafore tied around her dumpy waist, a querying expression in her eyes and a vague smile on her lips. When she saw her daughter standing there, the smile dropped away in shock.

'Orla! God in heaven, what are you doing here?'

'Ma!' said Orla, overcome with a mixture of relief at seeing her mother standing there, so familiar, and the realization that nothing would ever be the same again. She had survived the tempest, but she had come through it alone. Every moment since had been a living hell, trying to hold it together, focusing on getting home. Now she was finally here, she lost all control.

'Oh, Ma,' she sobbed. 'He's gone. I've lost Redmond.'

8

London, 1980

'I am here to tell you that this. Just. Won't. Fucking. Do,' said a stern female voice.

Annie pulled the covers further over her head, trying to block out the world. She recognized the voice. And right now, she *hated* the damned voice too.

'Go away,' she moaned. 'Leave me the hell alone.'

'No can do,' said Dolly.

'Yes, you bloody *can* do,' snapped Annie, her head emerging from the covers.

Through gritty eyes she could see Dolly, turned out in her usual sharp-fitting skirt suit – powder blue this time – standing by the windows in the dimness of the master suite. Dolly threw back the curtains and Annie winced as light flooded in.

'*Jesus,*' she complained.

'It's eleven thirty, nearly lunchtime. You intending to just lie there in your ruddy pit all day?'

'That's the plan,' said Annie.

Dolly came over to the bed and looked down in disgust at her old mate.

'That ain't a plan,' she pointed out. 'That's a waste of a day.'

'So fucking well shoot me,' said Annie, sitting up irritably and tucking the bedclothes more firmly around her.

'Look at the state of you,' marvelled Dolly.

Annie didn't want to do that. But her eyes were irresistibly drawn to the dressing table mirror, where she could see a pale, frowning woman sitting up in bed, hair all mussed up and eyes red-raw from crying.

It was her.

And she never cried, right?

Ah, not true. This past few months since he'd left, it felt as though she'd done nothing *but* cry.

'What have I got to get up for?' Annie groaned, rubbing her eyes.

'Layla's away, I take it?' Dolly was watching her, hands planted on hips.

'Yes, she's away. In Barbados. With *him*.'

'And how's that going? The Layla thing?'

'She hates me.'

'She don't hate you. She *blames* you. There's a difference. Now shift your arse.'

Annie clutched the bedclothes tighter. 'Why did Rosa let you in?' she complained. 'I told her I didn't want to see anybody.'

'I'm not anybody, you berk, I'm your best mate,' said Dolly more gently. 'Come on. Out of that bed and get yourself smartened up, you look like an effing bag lady. I'm taking you out to lunch, then we're going to hit the shops.'

Annie put her head in her hands. The very idea of it exhausted her.

'Do I have to?' she whined.

'Yeah, if you don't want my boot up your crotch.'

Annie gave in. She threw back the covers.

'Shit,' she complained as the sunlight from the window hit her eyes. It felt like a scalpel, cutting into her aching brain.

'It's a beautiful day,' trilled Dolly, holding Annie's dressing gown at the ready.

'Oh, shut the fuck up,' said Annie, snatching it from her and heading for the bathroom.

9

Ireland, 1970

Orla told her mother about the crash.

'Ah, God,' the older woman said over and over, weeping. 'My poor boy, poor Redmond, oh dear God.'

The house was neglected inside, every surface covered in dust. The curtains hung uncleaned, the nets were grey, there was a slew of dirty crockery on the draining board. Orla knew that taking care of Pa must be hard, and it was clear that housework was at the bottom of her mother's to-do list. She supposed she should have kept in touch more, *done* more, as the only daughter, and the guilt of it added to her woes.

All she hoped was that the old couple who lived by the sea would just let the matter lie, and someone would reunite Donny with his bike that she'd left up against the post office wall in the village. He would probably mention it in the pub, tell the regulars about the girl at the door saying she'd been in a dinghy that foundered, and her brother was lost. Perhaps he would search the shoreline for a few weeks, maybe even report it to the Garda; but the only name Donny and Cissie had for her was a false one she had concocted.

No, they could not trace her here. Everyone would go on thinking her missing, dead like Redmond. So she would stay here. Why not? There was nothing else left for her in life.

Her mother was delighted when she said she would stay. Then Pa wandered into the kitchen.

'Look, Davey, our Orla's home,' said Ma.

But Davey Delaney just stared at his daughter, not a hint of recognition in his face.

'Who's this?' he asked.

'I told you, it's Orla.'

'Oh.'

Ma cast an apologetic look at Orla. 'Take no notice.'

'Dinner ready yet?' asked Davey.

'You've only an hour since had breakfast.'

'I want dinner!' shouted Davey, and thumped the table, making both women jump.

Orla's mother stood up, her mouth set in a long-suffering line.

'I'll help,' said Orla, and Ma gave her a grateful smile.

'Will you tell him about Redmond?' Orla asked

her later in the day, when Pa was napping.

'I will. But he probably won't understand – or even remember who Redmond is. Was. Oh my poor boy...' The tears started again.

A cleaner came in once a week. The woman brought a few groceries with her, did a bit of ironing, and pottered around chatting and moving the dust from one place to another. Orla kept out of sight and got her mother to sack the woman. A milkman called, and a baker. Orla hid away from any visitors to the farm – thanking God there were few – and started tidying the place up. Shattered by Redmond's death, she found solace in creating order out of chaos.

Then the Garda called. She was chopping wood when she saw the car coming up the track to the farm. Heart thumping, she ran and hid in one of the big disused barns at the side of the house until they left a half-hour later.

Only then did she go indoors.

'What did they want?' she asked her mother.

'They were asking if you or Redmond had been here lately,' said her mother.

'And what did you say?'

'Don't worry, I said neither of you had. And then they said I had to prepare myself, that there had been a flight out of Cardiff and that you both were on it, and the flight had vanished so we must fear the worst.'

So the British police had liaised with the Garda, as she had known they would, asking them to call by the house after the plane went missing, to check if either she or Redmond had shown up.

Now *that* was out of the way, Orla began to

relax a little.

Her mother was watching her face closely. 'It must have been hell for you, that plane crash.'

'It was.'

'And poor Redmond...' Her mother crossed herself and her eyes filled with tears. 'Ah, God rest him.'

'Who are you talking about?' asked Davey, wandering into the kitchen, his eyes bright with curiosity.

'Redmond,' said his wife.

The old man looked at the two women in bemusement. 'Who?' His eyes fastened on his daughter. 'Who are you?' he asked.

Orla stayed on, living in a dim twilight world of cooking and cleaning, exhausting herself so that she fell into bed at night unable to think, unable to do anything other than sleep. Her mother was sharp as a tack – although clearly ground down and aged from the burden of caring for her husband – but Pa's dementia had left him with no interest in the daily business of living. He would subsist on bread and water if you let him. Baths were things he had to be reminded to take on a fortnightly basis – Ma had to run his bath for him, then wash his reeking clothes.

Someone had once told Orla that grief had its passage of time. Nothing could hurry it. Two to five years was normal to grieve, going through all the processes of anger, guilt and acceptance.

Five years passed. The Garda, despite her fears that they might, never returned. The farmhouse came slowly back to life under her care. And still she longed for Redmond, for the presence of her twin at her side. And she felt plagued by guilt because she had lived, and he had not.

With so much time to think about it, she'd become convinced that the crash had been orchestrated by Annie Carter and her Mafia pals. She could never forget Fergal tapping that fuel gauge, wondering why it was showing empty when it should have been full. And now the only person she had ever loved in her entire life was gone. The one consolation was that she and Redmond had settled the score with that Carter bitch before they'd fled England. They'd finished her good and proper – there would have been nothing left of her but blood and guts. It pleased Orla so much to think of that. If the police had ever found the remains of her, God alone knew how they would have identified the cow.

The days dragged on, the skies sitting in a grey repressive bowl above her head as she went out to hang the washing. It wouldn't dry much today, but later she'd bring it in, hang it on the clothes horse in front of the fire.

Her life was dull too, dull like the sky. She was wearing an old cotton dress of her mother's, pulled in tight with a belt because she was terribly thin these days, as if the grief had eaten her from within. Over that she wore a faded quilted jacket – her father's – and Wellington boots that belonged to him too. They flopped around her feet, acres too big.

Orla grabbed the peg bag from inside the kitchen door and hurried out clutching the basket of washing. In the living room of the old farmhouse her parents were watching the news on TV. She'd sat with them through the latest reports about the IRA shooting dead a policeman who'd stumbled upon a bomb-making factory in a Hammersmith basement, and the scandal surrounding Indira Gandhi, who'd now been found guilty of electoral corruption. But when the newsreader announced that a Boeing 727 had crashed at the edge of Kennedy airport, killing over a hundred people, Orla had begun shaking uncontrollably. The footage of wreckage in the water had her reliving her own nightmare struggle for life, the icy sea, the plane sinking, the loss – oh God! – of Redmond.

She looked around her at the decaying farm buildings. It was hard to believe that they had been reduced to this. Her father, who'd seen to it that the Delaney name inspired fear and respect in London's ganglands, now a demented old man. Her mother, once so smart, so elegant, now worn down by the strain of caring for him. Her brothers, dead.

The Delaneys were a spent force.

And so was she.

10

Moyross, Ireland, 1973

'Jesus, I'm not sure about this,' said Pikey.

Alongside him, crouched down behind Pardew's parked car, Rufus Malone gave Pikey a scathing look.

The guy had no balls.

Things got rough, and he started to squirm like a big girl.

'Shut yer trap,' hissed Rufus.

Pikey fell silent.

Tosser, thought Rufus with a sigh. Rather than squatting here, cramping up in the freezing fucking cold with Pikey groaning on about not being sure, Rufus was wishing he was elsewhere. Time was, being a cousin of the Delaneys would have spared him this sort of crap. Maybe he ought to have stuck to the horse trading around St Mary's in Limerick. Or kept up with the serious betting on the sulky races, travelling all over Ireland having a piss-up and making a packet.

The lure of criminality had pulled him from an early age, even in the school playground where he'd pinched other pupils' marbles with his old oppo Rory. As one of the Delaney clan, he had a reputation to live up to.

Rufus was built like a rugby player. His size intimidated all but the most determined foe.

Added to that, he was fast-moving and had a shock of shoulder-length curly red hair. The hair gave him a primitive, caveman appearance. His facial features were pudgy, not distinctive, but his hard grey eyes promised trouble – and he always delivered.

He'd moved up the ranks since his schooldays. From regular appearances in the juvenile courts, having progressed from stealing marbles to robbing milkmen and grocery stores, he graduated to the district court on charges of breaking and entering. He became a master at blagging old judges with innocent looks and pleas to spare him, he would never do such a thing again, honest.

Of course, he always did.

As a result, he got accustomed to the occupational hazard of brief spells inside. Prison was his finishing school, where he brushed up against real hard cases, learned more about the ways of the world.

While frequenting the races with his old mate, sometime thief and sometime motor mechanic Rory, he encountered smoother, bigger criminals. People with connections to the provisional IRA and dissident republicans. And, of course, Dublin-based gang bosses who liked the cut of him and were impressed by his Delaney connections, thinking he'd be handy in a scrap. Bosses, middle-aged silverbacks, bulky and mean-eyed, like Big Don Callaghan, who owned Rufus's arse now – and paid handsomely for the privilege.

For the time being, Rufus was enforcer for Don's Island Field gang and he had a job to do.

The job was simple. Dispose of a bit of rubbish called Jonathon Pardew, who had been stepping on Big Don's toes. Don had wanted Rufus to include Pikey, his nephew, on the outing, so who was Rufus to refuse? He would rather have had Rory, who had grown up with him through various scrapes and was to be trusted implicitly. Rory was his companion of choice on such ventures. But he had no say in the matter.

'Look after the little tit, he's my sister's boy,' Don had said earlier in the day. 'See what you think of him, give me your opinion.'

Rufus thought that Don would not like his opinion one bit. Pikey was spineless. But he would look after the boy on this one outing, report back to Don that the kid was useless, and hopefully he would never be burdened again.

From early on in the proceedings, Pikey had been displaying nerves. While Rufus siphoned petrol from the can into a Lucozade bottle, Pikey's hands had been shaking so hard that he couldn't hold the bottle still. He'd ended up with petrol splashed all over his hand and arm.

When the bottle was full, Rufus stuffed paper into the nozzle to act as a fuse. Then they waited. Their information was that Pardew would come out of his mistress's house in the suburbs of Moyross dead on ten o'clock, aiming to get home before his old lady started playing up.

And sure enough, here he was, whistling his way down the path as happy as a lark. His breath was like smoke in the cold night air. Pardew had already survived one of Don's boys taking a pop at him. Someone had walked up to him in the street and fired a gun in his face. Or that had been the intention. The gun had misfired. The would-be assassin had been a marked man after that, showing up in the local morgue a week later.

Pardew's car wasn't flashy but it was – according to Don – armour-plated and bullet-proof. None of which was going to save Pardew's fat cheating arse on this occasion.

'You won't get him once he's in the car,' said Don. 'Don't attempt it.'

Pardew looked portly, balding and faintly yellow in the sodium glare of the street lights.

Rufus nudged Pikey hard.

It was their signal.

Pikey, hands trembling, flicked the lighter. Then he dropped it.

'Shit!' snarled Rufus under his breath.

He glanced at Pardew, who had stopped walking. He'd seen the lighter's flare. Rufus looked back at Pikey and saw that his hand was on fire.

Pikey let out a shriek.

The fire snaked rapidly up Pikey's arm and enveloped his head.

His screams were ripping through the evening air now, his skin melting like cheese on a hot griddle.

Shit, shit, shit.

Even in the midst of his panic over Pikey – Christ! Don's nephew! His fucking *nephew!* – Rufus kept a clear head.

He snatched up the lighter, lit the fuse, lobbed the bottle.

All an instant too late.

Pardew was holding a hand gun, and he was

shooting toward the flaming remnants of Pikey. Rufus felt a shot whistle past his ear, then an impact, hard as a hammer, took him in the shoulder, whirling him away, throwing him off his feet. He lay there on the tarmac, hearing the blood thundering in his ears, thinking: *Mustn't pass out.*

Christ, he'd been shot.

Through tears of agony he heard the roar of the Molotov cocktail as it went up. Pardew erupted in flames, a human torch. Rufus heard the screams, smelled the barbeque scent of cooked flesh. Pardew was sorted, done. Rufus crawled to his feet and staggered away from Pardew's car, which had been half-concealing him and Pikey.

He looked at Pikey.

Or what was left of him, anyway.

Like Pardew, he was well alight, and he wasn't going to live to tell the tale. He wasn't screaming any more: he couldn't. His face was gone, the flames had seared his features into one smeared covering of cooked skin.

That's Don's fucking nephew. Boy am I in the shit now, thought Rufus.

There was only one thing to do.

Run.

Stumbling, bleeding, he turned and did so.

11

Rory's old lady Megan took one look at Rufus bleeding and swaying in the doorway, and flipped. Five months gone in her pregnancy, she wanted no intruders in her nest. She started on about doctors, ambulances.

'You crazy?' snarled her husband as Rufus sat sheet-white at their kitchen table. 'That's a bullet wound – you want the Garda in on this? Fetch some towels, don't be a daft cow.'

Rufus knew he had done right in coming here. If there was one person he could always trust in this world, it was Rory.

His strength ebbing away with the blood pouring out of him, he let himself be half-dragged, half-carried up the stairs to the back bedroom. Agonized, he lay helpless on the bed as Rory stripped off his jacket and shirt.

'It went straight through,' said Rory, eyeing the wound, going a bit green around the gills. 'Shit, I think you'll be OK if the loss of blood don't kill you. How'd it happen?'

Rufus was half-fainting with the pain. Megan came haring in with a face like a hatchet to press towels to the wound. Rufus looked at her, then at Rory.

'I'll see to him,' said Rory, taking the hint, and she retreated.

Rory closed the door behind her.

Rufus lay back and tiredly recounted the evening's events to his pal.

'Holy shit. That twat Pikey, he was never going to shape up.'

'He won't get the chance to now.'

'Don's nephew! Holy *shit.*'

'I just fecking ran. Didn't know what else to do.'

'What else *could* you do? He's not going to come over all understanding, not him.'

Rory was dabbing the wound. The bleeding was slowing up, thank God.

'Thirsty,' said Rufus faintly.

'I'll fetch water,' said Rory, and opened the door. Megan started away from it, going red in the face.

'You been listening in?' demanded Rory.

'No, I...'

'Well *don't.* Go and get some water, he needs a drink.'

Megan went off downstairs, muttering. Rory watched her go. He stood there a moment, staring at the landing carpet, thinking that Big Don was going to want blood for this. He could understand why Rufus had come here, of *course* he could, but in doing so he'd brought trouble to Rory's door. Still, who could turn their oldest friend away?

Not him.

He went to the landing cupboard and fetched more towels. Right now, there was only one thing on his mind: keeping Rufus alive.

When at last the bleeding stopped and Rory had

cleaned and bandaged his friend's wound, Rufus lapsed into troubled sleep. Rory collected all the blood-soaked towels and went off downstairs. He loaded the dirty washing into the twin tub and made a mental note to fill it up and start it going later. Then he went through to the lounge.

'It's on the news,' Megan said, barely glancing up at him. She hugged her fat stomach, rocked in the armchair, listening intently to the radio.

And so it was. Businessman Jonathon Pardew had perished in a fire, thought to have been deliberately set by one of the rival gangs in his area. A second corpse, later identified as Peter Pike from Moyross, was also found at the scene. IRA involvement was suspected. When the newscaster went on to national news, talking about Nixon, Watergate, and the French detonating an H-bomb at Mururoa Atoll, Megan switched the radio off.

She looked up at her husband. 'What are we going to do?' she asked.

'Get the boy better,' said Rory. 'What else *can* we do?'

Rufus was feverish for days, and Rory was worried sick about him. It was lucky the wound hadn't needed stitching and that the bullet had passed through his bulk unhampered. It must have been a small-bore gun, maybe a lady's weapon, easy to conceal, and it had spared Rufus too much damage.

It took a couple of weeks before he was able to sit up a little and take some soup instead of water. After that, he healed quickly. He was strong, he'd always been fit. It helped.

Megan kept her distance from him. His presence threatened her composure, made her fearful for her own safety and that of the child she carried. Before Rufus arrived, her only concern had been whether Rory would keep on the straight and narrow with a baby on the way. Now Rufus had pitched up, she knew there'd be trouble and Rory would get dragged into it.

'Will we go for Diarmuid if it's a boy, what do you think?' she asked, trying to get Rory's mind back to where it should be.

'Huh?'

He wasn't even listening to her. His whole concern was for his friend.

'Diarmuid for a boy. Or Siobhan for a girl. Do you like those?'

'Ah, whatever makes you happy.'

If Rufus Malone dropped dead, *that* would make her happy.

She went down the shops, and Mrs Simmonds asked her if she had people staying.

'You what?' asked Megan, heart galloping in her chest.

'You got visitors? I've seen the light on in your box room, every evening. Is it your ma, come to stay to help with the baby on the way? I haven't seen her down in the shop, so. She taken up smoking, has she? She never used to smoke.'

'What?'

'I've seen smoke coming over the fence in the garden.'

'Oh! No, that'll be Rory, having a fag.'

'Is he doing the box room out for a nursery?'

'Yes, that's it, we're decorating. I have to go, I've been having twinges...' she said, picking up her shopping and rushing out of the shop.

When Rory came in that evening, his navy-blue overalls dirty and his hands caked black from being under engines all day, she was waiting for him.

'He'll have to go,' she said, straight out.

'What?' Rory was dipping his fingers into the Swarfega tin at the sink.

'Rufus. That old bat Simmonds says she's seen the boxroom light on every night, she knows someone's in there. And he's been smoking in the garden. She's seen someone puffing up smoke out there. I had to tell her it was you. Thank *God* for the high fences. *If* she knows something's going on, then others do too.'

Rory looked at her in concern. 'You didn't tell her anything...?'

'I told her we were decorating the room as a nursery, and that I was cramping and had to go.'

'Well then.'

'Well *nothing*. You know what she's like. Next thing she'll have baked a cake and she'll be banging on the door, wanting to see for herself who's in here.'

'You're fretting over nothing.'

'If Don Callaghan finds out we're hiding him here, he'll kill us both. *And* our baby.'

'But he don't know. And he won't.'

'If he–'

'He won't. He can't. All we have to do is hold our nerve, OK.'

Rory went off upstairs to see how the invalid

was doing, leaving Megan on the sofa with the news blaring on the radio. But she wasn't taking in a single word as she clutched her arms around her swollen abdomen, shielding the child within.

12

London, 1983

'Good trip?' asked Annie as Layla, brown as a berry, piled into the hallway wafting Hawaiian Tropic and dropping bags and suitcases on to the floor.

Layla was seventeen now, and just back from Christmas in Barbados with Max. Annie had spent Christmas pretty much alone. As usual.

'It was OK,' said Layla, looking at her mother with no appearance of affection. 'Um, the taxi...?'

Annie forced a smile and went out and paid the driver. Then she returned to find Rosa, their housekeeper, gabbling happily in Spanish and enfolding Layla in a welcome-home hug. She knew she didn't dare do the same. Layla would only push her away.

Rosa hurried off to the kitchen and silence settled between mother and daughter.

'All spent out then?' said Annie.

Layla shrugged. 'Just a few Barbadian dollars and a couple of cents left,' she said.

'So! How's your dad?' asked Annie, although it hurt.

'He's fine,' said Layla, her face a blank mask as she stared at Annie.

'You had a good time?' Annie was still smiling, smiling so hard her cheeks were starting to ache. Layla looked tanned and fit. Her hair was scrunched back in a ponytail, and she was wearing old frayed jeans and a white T-shirt. She looked pretty – and totally hostile.

'Yeah. It's fabulous out there.' Layla gazed around at the marbled hall, the chandeliers, as if this, her mother's home, was a dosshouse by comparison.

'Great tan,' said Annie, longing to hug her.

'Mm.' Layla glanced toward the stairs. 'Well, think I'll go on up...'

'Sure! Of course.' Annie stood there, still smiling that brilliant artificial smile, as Layla grabbed her bag and trudged up the stairs.

Annie turned and walked across to the study. She went inside and shut the door, the smile dropping from her face. She closed her eyes and groaned. Then she went over to the desk, picked up the phone and dialled a number she knew off by heart.

'Hello,' said the female voice at the other end. Bowie was singing 'Let's Dance' very loudly in the background. 'Hold on, let me just put the wood in the hole...'

'Doll?' There was a pause while Dolly shut the door.

'OK, right.' Bowie was muted now. 'That's better. Annie? How's it going?'

'Layla's home.'

'How is she?'

'Fine.'

'How's her Dad?'

'Also fine, I suppose.' Annie drew in a shuddering breath. 'It's no good, is it, Doll. This is how it's going to be, from here until eternity. She hates me.'

'I told you. She don't *hate* you, not really. She's pissed off with you, that's all.'

'She's seventeen. She's not a child any more. She ought to be able to understand things a bit better now, but she sodding well refuses to. It's not bloody fair. *He* was the one who acted like an idiot, and *I* get all the grief.'

'Tea at the Ritz on Thursday, don't forget. Our usual. Ellie's tagging along.'

Dolly and Ellie had become her personal team of cheerleaders since the divorce. Every time she'd stumbled, they picked her up again. She loved them both, very much.

Annie heaved a sigh. 'Yeah. That'll be nice.'

There was a tap at the door as Annie put the phone down. Layla opened the door, poked her head around it.

'I'm going out,' she said.

But you only just got in formed itself in Annie's brain. She bit back the words. Forced a smile.

'OK,' she said. 'Dinner's at eight ... you need some money?'

'Yeah.'

Yeah, of course you do, thought Annie. *That's all I am to you, the Bank of Mum.* She opened the top drawer of the desk, pulled out a bundle of fivers, then stood up and went over to the door.

'Thanks,' said Layla, pocketing the cash.

'See you at eight,' said Annie, thinking, *Other daughters kiss their mothers goodbye. Other daughters hug their mums and buy them little gifts and go shopping with them. Not mine.*

Layla withdrew, closing the door.

Annie tried to console herself, but Layla's return and the realization that things hadn't changed, the fear that they would never change, made her feel depressed. It was a New Year, another *fucking* year, and the same old scenario.

She told herself firmly that it was fine, they would meet up later; Rosa had cooked something special and they would have a chance to chat then. But Annie could feel desperation taking hold. Three years on from the divorce, and still she was getting the cold shoulder. She *had*, somehow, to reconnect with Layla, and starting tonight, she promised herself she was going to try harder.

But she never got the chance.

Layla didn't come home until gone ten, so Annie had to eat dinner alone.

13

Ireland, 1973

Months had passed and Megan's baby was due to drop. Rather than settling her, the imminent arrival of their first child was making her more edgy.

'It's the feckin' hormones,' said Rory, sitting on the side of Rufus's bed upstairs. He grinned. 'She's a head case. Can't think of anything but babies, nursery curtains and nappies.'

'Not bad things to be thinking about,' said Rufus with a sigh. He'd never had a serious woman in his life. He'd had a boyhood crush on his cousin Orla, ferocious in its intensity. He could still remember the way he'd felt about her. But they'd lost touch over the years.

He was feeling better now, almost recovered. A little weak, his left arm stiff, but he was well enough to get up during the day, retiring early to bed. Since Megan had marked his card, he'd been careful not to step outside in the garden, high fences or no.

He was lying low. He knew his presence made Megan nervous. And Rory too, if he was honest. If Big Don discovered him here, they would all suffer. He thought of Pikey, the poor little fool, dying in that horrible way before he'd gotten the chance to grow older and wiser. It tormented him.

'I want to see a priest,' he said. 'Light a candle for Pikey. Make my confession.'

'You can't,' said Rory, his face draining of colour at the thought of it. He was all too aware of Don's reputation. Rufus had screwed over a man who would never forget, never forgive. He reckoned Don would hunt Rufus until his dying day. He couldn't tell Rufus that, and he wondered if Rufus knew it. He was acting as if he didn't. Or as if he didn't care. But Rory had a pregnant wife, he had Megan. He *had* to stop this. 'The neighbours are going berserk with curiosity as it is, wondering who we've got in here. You daren't go out.'

'Still, I'd like to.' Rufus felt uneasy at what had happened. He felt responsible for Pikey's unhappy end, and killing Pardew had been a sin after all. He knew it was stupid, but he'd always been the same. He was Catholic, even if he was a crook. He needed to make his peace with God.

'We'll see, OK?' Rory said quickly. 'See how you feel in a week or so. Then, if we can, we'll sort something out.'

Rory went off downstairs, clutching his head as he entered the front room. *'Shit,'* he said forcefully.

'What is it?' Megan glanced up from the sofa.

Rory looked at his wife. She was still pretty, huge with the child though she was. His sweet Megan. He felt a surge of love for her, felt the need to protect her.

'Rufus wants to go to see a priest,' he said. 'Make his confession.'

Megan straightened. 'He can't.'

'I told him. He said even so, he'd like to.'

'And what did you say to that?'

'That we'd see in a little while.'

'No! It can't be done. Rory, as soon as he's fit enough to travel, he should be out of here. You're his friend. If he values you at all, he ought to realize the danger he's putting you in.'

'He should, but I don't think he does.' Rory sat down beside her, pulled her into his arms. 'I don't know what to do.'

'Don't you?' Megan drew away from him, her face hard. 'Well, I do. He's going to get us all done for if he carries on at this rate. I want him *gone*.' Her face softening slightly, she continued: 'Rory, you're a loyal man, a great friend. But there's a point where loyalty gets stretched beyond breaking. Think of me, your wife. Think – for the love of God – of your *child*.'

'I know, I know,' he sighed.

'Phone the Garda,' said Megan.

'What?' Rory sprang back from her, leapt to his feet. 'Are you mad? I can't do that.'

'Rory...'

'No! I won't hear of it. Call the police on my oldest friend? Don't ever say that again.'

And he went off out to the kitchen.

Megan sat there, alone. Her eyes drifted to the phone book. She wondered how many D. Callaghans there were in there. Not that many, she imagined.

Not many at all.

14

A week later, Rufus slipped out of the house as discreetly as he could and went to St Vincent de Paul, the nearest Catholic church. He moved up the aisle and to the side of the vast building, his footsteps echoing. The priest was at the altar, kneeling, communing with his God. Rufus felt better just for being in here. He went to the little confessional and slipped inside, pulling the door closed behind him.

He waited.

Presently, the priest came into the box next door. The screen slid back between the two compartments, and Rufus could see a shadowy figure sitting there alongside him.

'Bless me, Father,' he said haltingly. 'Forgive me. For I have sinned.'

'What is the nature of your sinning, my son?' asked the priest.

Rufus hesitated. But the confessional was sacrosanct. Any secrets divulged here would remain secret for ever.

'I have committed a terrible sin, Father. I have killed a man.'

The priest was silent. Then he said: 'Tell me.'

Rufus poured it all out. He mentioned no names, but he confessed to the killing of Pardew, and to his great remorse over the accidental death of Pikey. Even as he spoke of it, he felt lighter, better. He'd done the right thing, coming here. He knew it.

The priest told him what penance he had to perform. 'Now go, my son, and sin no more.'

Rufus emerged from the church into a soft day, all drizzle and cloudy skies, but he felt as if he was bathed in warm, forgiving sunlight. He hurried along the road toward Rory's house, but pulled up sharply when he saw the car there, and two big men standing at Rory's door talking to Megan.

The relief he'd felt since the confession deserted him in an instant. He ducked behind a high wall, but as he did he saw Megan's head turning, and her hand rising to point in his direction. The cow had seen him.

The men turned. Rufus recognized Col Ballard, one of Don's enforcers. The other man was unknown to him. In an instant, they were on the move, running out of the gate and after him.

Rufus fled. Megan had betrayed him. Not Rory, *never* Rory, he knew that.

The men chased him through the streets and over garden fences. *Jesus, won't they give it up?* he wondered, trying the handle of a door set into a garden wall. It opened and, panting, done in, still weak from his wound, he stepped into a deserted yard. On the other side of the wall he heard the pounding of footsteps, then voices. He prayed they wouldn't open the door.

'Where the feck did he go?' gasped one.

'That way,' said the other, and then he heard their footsteps running away into the distance.

He'd lost them. For a moment there he'd thought he was a dead man, yet here he was, still in one piece.

God be praised.

Rufus staggered to his feet, opened the door and ran in the opposite direction to one the men had taken. He was finished here. There was no one he could truly count on any more, not even his oldest and dearest friend.

It was time to get out of Ireland. Try his luck across the water in England. He had cousins there, they were big news in criminal circles. Best of all, Don wouldn't have such an easy time tracing him there, as he'd managed to do here.

15

Rufus found that London was ripe for the plucking. There were all sorts of scams going down. The big gangs had the town sewn up tight, there was always breaker work on offer, sooner or later everyone needed some muscle at their disposal. But when he went looking for his Delaney cousins, he couldn't find them.

Only rumours remained. That there had been a shooting and Tory and Pat were long gone. That Kieron was abroad somewhere, no one knew where. And as for the twins, they had gone home to Ireland. The irony of that didn't escape Rufus. He'd come here, they'd gone there. He'd wanted to see his cousin Orla again. Very badly. And he was disappointed.

The old Delaney manor was now under the control of the Carter mob. Even the tiny bit of Limehouse the rival gangs had been squabbling over for years had fallen into Carter hands. As time went by, he pieced together bits of the story of how that came to be.

'Christ, it was a right old bang-shoot,' said Gabby James, one of Rufus's new drinking buddies. 'Word is, Redmond and Orla stuck Max Carter's missus in the bloody crusher – she would've been squashed like a grape.'

'Would have been?' Rufus was downing a pint of Guinness.

'The Bill got to her first.'

'What about Redmond? What about Orla? They're back in the auld country, are they?'

Gabby puffed out his cheeks and shook his head. 'I heard they took a plane from Cardiff to Cork, or was it Dublin?'

Rufus thought of the farm in Limerick. 'Shannon, I would think.'

'Well, wherever. It never landed.'

'You *what?*' Rufus spilled his Guinness. He'd not had much to do with Redmond, but Orla ... ah God, there was something about Orla that had eaten into his very soul.

'It was in the papers, what, three years ago? Nineteen seventy it was. Where have you been, on the moon? They reckoned the plane crashed in the Irish Sea. No bodies were ever recovered. Not even a scrap of wreckage.'

Rufus stared into his beer, deeply troubled. He couldn't bear to think of Orla perishing that way, in the icy churning waters.

'Rumour has it that while Max Carter was away, his old lady was mucking about with some Mafia type from New York, and that one arranged the crash. Which is entirely possible, it seems to me. You don't mess around with those people, they'll have your guts.'

Rufus heaved a sigh. Jesus. Orla, gone. He looked at Gabby. 'What else do you know about the Carters?' he asked.

Gabby filled him in.

Rufus felt as if the heart had been knocked out of him. His mind was full of Orla, full of those sunlit days in the garden when they were young and carefree, when he had kissed her. Sadness gripped him to think of her gone for ever. And anger took hold as he thought of the Carters, the trouble they'd brought upon her.

But he had to keep his head down, even over here. If he was going to keep out of Don's way, it would be better not to make waves. He was safe here, and he could make a life for himself, provided he wasn't stupid. And he wasn't, despite what his cousins Tory and Pat had said.

'Rufus the DOOFUS,' they used to shout when he'd visit the farm to play. 'Rufus the DOOFUS!'

Only now he wasn't a hulking inarticulate thug of a teenager, upset by such goadings. Now, he was a man in his prime. Gang bosses saw his worth and made good use of him. He was a freelancer, a mercenary, hiring himself out to the highest bidder, with no loyalty to anyone but himself. The only gang he would never work for was the Carters. He spat on the ground every time their name was mentioned.

Once, he saw *her*, Annie Carter, sweeping out of a black Jaguar with a bulky bald-headed minder at her side. She was a stunner, he had to admit that. Dark hair falling around her shoulders, the black coat, the heavy shades, the red full mouth set in a grim line. She looked both exceedingly sexy and completely formidable.

The gangster woman.

Married to one gang overlord, Max Carter.

Then married again – to Constantine Barolli, Mafia boss. A bona fide Mafia queen.

And she looked it, every inch of it. Dangerous. Alluring. Expensive.

If she truly was behind the deaths of Orla and Redmond, revenge was on the cards. But that would have to wait. For the time being, he was keeping a low profile. Doing jobs. Breaking a leg or two. Intimidating late-payers with his fists or a baseball bat. And always a trip to the confessional afterwards. Time passed in a blur. He was enjoying the city life and the rewards that his choice of career brought him, which were plentiful.

Soon he had his own flat, more willing girls than he could handle, a nice motor. Life was *sweet.*

And then, in the way that life does, it all came crashing down on him once again.

16

1980

Rufus had been up to Chingford on a little job, chasing a late payer for one of the Pozo boys. The Pozos were Italian immigrants, avaricious loan sharks. Rufus had to wonder at people allowing themselves to become embroiled in the webs the Pozos spun. Did being poor make you stupid?

No – but he guessed it made you desperate enough to deal with scum like the Pozos. Borrow a thousand quid off them, and soon you owed fifteen hundred as the interest racked up. Six months down the line, after a few late payments, you could be looking at three thousand.

Which of course you couldn't pay back.

Then the threats started.

Big men turning up at your door with dogs snarling and straining at their leashes, taking your telly, your fridge, anything saleable. Object and you'd get a slap. Default after that, and you'd be in for much worse. Somehow, you had to get the money. So you stole it off family, or employers, or *any* fucker, you were that desperate, there were heavies after you, nowhere was safe any more.

Whatever it took, you paid up.

And, hopefully, you were wiser next time.

As always, Rufus did the job dispassionately, collected the cash, and departed. Ignored the spitting, the anguish, the tears, the occasional kick or inexpertly thrown punch from the punter under pressure. It was all in a day's work. Nothing he couldn't handle.

Soon as he was back in London, he headed for the pub.

'Heard a word on the street,' said Gabby, setting the drinks on the table.

'Oh yeah?' Rufus took his first mouthful of Guinness. Nectar.

'Someone's been asking around about you.'

His interest sharpened. 'Who?'

'It's been passed along to me by a mate or two. Some Irish called Callaghan was interested in finding you, they said.'

Rufus's stomach clenched sickly as the cold Guinness hit it. He went very still, sitting there at the table, 'Sultans of Swing' playing on the jukebox. The telly over the bar, sound turned down, was tuned into the Moscow Olympics coverage.

Everyone was going crazy because Seb Coe had won the fifteen hundred metres.

'Feck,' he said.

Rufus looked at his pal. He'd got quite matey with Gabby over the last few years, but trust him? No. He didn't trust anyone much any more. Not since Rory's missus had dobbed him in. He'd been living on his own in London, giving out nothing about his background. It was obvious he was Irish. He only had to open his mouth to reveal *that.* Fear of discovery, of Big Don Callaghan tracking him down, had made him cautious.

He'd been so *careful*. Thought he was settled, sorted, at last.

And now, this.

'You know him, this Callaghan fella?' asked Gabby.

'Maybe,' said Rufus.

'Well, go careful. Lay low a bit.'

'Thanks for that, Gabby.'

'No problem.'

They had another round, and then Rufus made his excuses. 'Got a bird waiting,' he said.

He didn't. But suddenly the pub felt too open, too exposed. Everywhere he turned, he seemed to see covert glances, people eyeing him up and then quickly looking away. Ridiculous, of course: but Gabby's news had made him edgy.

If Don caught up with him, he was dead meat.

He thought again of poor Pikey, erupting in flames like a fucking Roman candle. Damn, Don couldn't think that he'd *wanted* things to turn out that way, could he?

On the other hand, if he were in Don's shoes,

he would react the same. He would want revenge on the one responsible for his nephew's death. And the one in charge that night had been Rufus, which made him responsible for what happened. He couldn't argue with that.

'Give her one from me,' said Gabby with a salacious wink.

'I will,' said Rufus, and made his way to the door.

From the pub, Rufus headed straight for his flat. He was so jumpy now. He felt wired, as if he'd been on the steroids like so many of his colleagues, fuelled up with 'roid rage. But Rufus wasn't into all that. His body was a temple, he wasn't going to sully it with drugs. He'd even packed up the fags. He knew he wasn't the sharpest tool in the box, but his health and fitness meant a lot to him. It was his living, after all.

Instead of parking in his usual spot, he left the car round the corner, just to be on the safe side. Trying to look casual, he studied the cars parked along his road, keeping an eye out for anyone sitting in a car watching, or loitering on the street, waiting for him to show up.

Nothing. All the cars were empty, the street was deserted.

He began to calm down. *False alarm.*

Then he saw the flare of a lighter in a doorway and spotted two men, not twenty yards away, smoking, chatting in low voices, glancing around them, paying particular attention to the entrance to his block. *They were waiting for him to show up.* Rufus felt his guts clench with queasy fear. His heart started to hammer wildly in his chest.

Gabby was right. Don had found him.

Carefully, he backtracked. As soon as he was out of their sight he ran, scrambled into his car and drove, fast, away from them. He'd prepared for this. He didn't dare return to his flat now. He drove down to the warehouse near the Albert Dock, and made his way to the wall.

Removing a few of the bricks, he rummaged inside the cavity and drew out the plastic package he'd hidden there. It contained a fake passport with his picture in it, and a stash of francs. Then he drove to Portsmouth, parked up on a quiet side road, bought a foot passenger ticket and boarded the ferry to France.

17

Paris, 1983

Rufus loved France. More especially, he loved the club life along the Champs-Élysées, where he quickly found work as a bouncer. No one cared who he was here, no one knew him. It was all fine. He moved into a small flat on Faubourg-du-Roule and started dating one of the louche blonde dancers from GoGo, the club he worked in.

He didn't speak the language fluently yet, but it wasn't a barrier to him. He set himself the challenge of learning more as soon as he could. But most of the French spoke English. And everyone, from all around the globe, understood *fuck off* when a meaty eighteen-stone redhead with muscles bulging out from his suit like ball bearings in an overstuffed sock, said it.

He stayed there, enjoying *la vie Français.*

Then he got word that Don Callaghan was on his tail again and it was time to move on. In Lille he got a job as a driver, working for a Saudi diplomat who had business and property in the Loire Valley and further south.

Sometimes he thought of his old life in Ireland, of his happy childhood, of Orla his long-dead cousin. He missed the auld country. But here, at last, in the depths of France, he could at least *begin* to relax.

He was driving the boss down near the medieval town of Arles, gateway to the Camargue where the wild white horses ran. The air was hot and pungent as he steered the Rolls-Royce through fields of lavender and bright yellow sunflowers. There were roses, fields of them, ready to be made into rose oil, the costliest oil on earth, at the perfumeries of Grasse.

Rufus was sweating. He had to wear full dress uniform whenever he chauffeured the boss, who sat in the back studying papers and who never talked to him except through his prissy little translator.

He pulled into the forecourt of the hotel. Five star, of course. With a spa, a huge pool, cypresses all around the beautifully manicured grounds. The moment Rufus opened the door for his important passenger, staff emerged from the vine-covered entrance to greet the diplomat and escort him inside, to take his bags, to tell Rufus where he could park the car and where the kitchens were so that he could get some refreshment.

He had parked and was on his way round to the kitchen when something hit him, hard, on the back of the head. He reeled forward, falling on to the gravel drive, feeling the sting of pain as his skin was scraped from his palms. His head was spinning. For a moment he was conscious, rolling over, trying to get to his feet, staring up at the brilliant sky. Then everything went dark.

'Rufus! Hey, Rufus. Come on. Wake up.'

He could hear the voice – it was a man's – but he couldn't see a thing. His brains felt scrambled. The back of his head was hurting like crazy. He squinted, tried to focus. He was in a room, run-down, like one of those old *gîtes* the wily French sold on to gullible English tourists at a vast profit, as doer-uppers.

He was in a kitchen. There was an ancient stove in one corner, a sink with a dusty frilled curtain draped underneath it. There were cracked flagstones under his feet. A bare dead light bulb, the cord holding it frayed and dangerous, dangled over his head. Crumbling stone on the walls, mossy green with damp in places. And there was a small window, with thin tatty drapes pulled closed across it, so that the light level in the little room was dim, but good enough to see by. The air was cool in here, not like the dry, perfumed oven-blast of the air outside.

'What do you mean – Rufus?' he asked in his passable French. 'My name's not Rufus.'

Now he could see the bulky, dead-eyed man standing in front of him, and his blood froze.

It was Big Don Callaghan.

I'm a dead man, he thought.

Rufus struggled to orientate himself. His head ached like a bastard. But he was still alive. He tried to move and couldn't. He was tied to a chair. His feet were free, but not his hands. How long had he been out of it? Wouldn't the Saudi contingent raise the alarm, get people searching for him?

No. They wouldn't, not yet. The diplomat wasn't due to leave the hotel for three days, and during that time no one would give a fuck where Rufus was or what had become of him. When the boss was ready to check out, the interpreter would come looking for him, to ensure that the car would be clean, refuelled, and that Rufus had overseen the packing of his master's bags into the capacious boot. Everything ran smoothly around the diplomat. But not on this occasion.

Rufus thought that Don had aged badly. He was fatter, his hair thinner. Pouches sagged under his beady, spite-filled eyes. Nonetheless he exuded an air of menace – as did the two heavies who were standing on either side of him.

'That's a mighty good French accent, Rufus,' said Don. 'Impressive.'

Rufus said nothing. Dully, he peered up at Don, who was shaking his head sadly.

'I'm disappointed in you, Rufus. Poor Pete, my sister's boy, he died, and what did you do? You legged it. Didn't even pause to give me an explanation.'

Rufus said nothing.

'Her heart was broken by it. He was her only boy. Now, are you going to tell me what happened?'

Rufus still said nothing.

'OK, he wasn't exactly the cream of the crop. I know that. But I trusted you to see him right. To assess his possibilities.'

Possibilities? Rufus thought bitterly. Pikey had been useless. And he had *told* Don that, even before he'd foisted the boy on him and set the whole disaster in motion.

'What's the craic, eh? Say something, Rufe. Even if it's only bollocks.'

Rufus worked some spit into his mouth. 'The boy was a fucking washout.'

Don drew in a sharp breath. 'That's not nice, speaking ill of the dead. Boy's not here to defend himself. If he was, what a fucking fright he'd look. Burnt to a fucking cinder the way he was.'

'It was an accident,' said Rufus. 'He was a bag of nerves. He spilled the petrol. Set light to himself.'

'Yeah? But that's beside the point, isn't it. Because you were in charge. The buck stops with you, Rufus. The foreman always take responsibility for any balls-ups.'

'What do you want me to say, Don?' asked Rufus, feeling exhausted, in pain, defeated. He'd been putting this off so long, and now here it was, here it came for him. He wasn't going to walk out of this room, he knew it. 'God knows I didn't want it to happen. But it did.'

'What I want you to *say* is that you're sorry,

Rufus. That's what.'

'I *am* sorry. Jesus, he was only a kid. He should never have been there, Don, he wasn't up to it. I got shot, Pardew shot me. But I got him. I went to church when I was well enough, after it happened, lit a penny candle for Pikey's – Peter's – soul.'

'And I'll light one for you,' said Don, and nodded to the man on his left.

He was holding a petrol can.

Ah Jesus...

He took off the cap, and emptied the contents over Rufus's head. Rufus spluttered and coughed, the fumes engulfing him, suffocating him. He swallowed petrol. Spat it out, choking, gagging.

'Shit,' he shouted. 'Don, come on. You *can't...'*

'I can.' Don was taking a box of matches from his pocket. His eyes were hard, implacable. He was really going to do this. He took out a match, paused, and grinned at Rufus before moving to strike it.

That pause, that almost imperceptible second's worth of gloating time, was a mistake.

Rufus lashed out hard with his foot, catching Don in the groin. Don let out a wheezing groan, dropped the unlit match and doubled over, his face screwed up, falling to his knees in a moment of almost exquisite agony.

The heavy on the left moved in and Rufus kicked out again, aiming for the man's knee. He heard the thing pop out of its socket with a satisfactory snap, and the man fell to the floor, stumbling over his boss's huddled form.

Now the one on the right.

But this one was more cautious. This was the one who'd coshed him, Rufus reckoned. This one had the eyes of a thinker, he was not just a mound of dumb muscle. Rufus was on his feet now, crouching, still pinioned by the chair, tied to it, unable to straighten up. He turned sharply, hoping to hit the man with the chair, but it was only a glancing blow. The man reacted too quickly, bouncing back on his toes, just out of reach.

When Rufus looked over his shoulder a cosh had appeared in the man's right hand and he was swinging it viciously. The other two men were still writhing helplessly on the floor in a sea of stinking fuel. Rufus edged away from the cosh until the chair hit the sink and he couldn't go any further. If his arms hadn't been tied, he could have sorted this fucker with his fists. Improvising fast, he jammed the chair legs over the rim of the sink and used the leverage to lift both legs, pistoning them out with all the strength he could muster.

He caught the man in the stomach.

The man doubled over, dropping the cosh, retching and trying to draw breath as he clutched at his belly.

Rufus unjammed the chair from the sink rim and kicked the man in the head, hard, while he was down. Then he propelled himself towards the window, launching himself at it head-first, chair and all.

He shot through the tattered drapes. Felt the impact as his head went through the glass, the rotten frame disintegrating under his weight. He hit the ground hard, with bits of broken window raining down all around him in the dry dirt. And *still* the fecking chair had him in its grip, though a couple of the legs had broken off in the fall. He looked wildly around him, blood dripping in his eyes so that he could barely see, knowing that he had to get clear before Big Don and his men recovered their wits.

Scrambling to his feet, bent double with his arms still strapped to the chair, he ran as best he could.

He could see the hotel through the trees, about five hundred yards away. They hadn't even bothered to take him far, confident that they had him, that they would incinerate him in the old building in the woods and make their escape before anyone realized what had happened.

Expecting them to overtake him any minute, Rufus hobbled towards the driveway, hunched double under the chair's weight, bleeding, sweating, and reeking of petrol. When he made it to the entrance he toppled through the door with a crash, causing the thin receptionist to leap to his feet, hands raised in alarm, face contorted in disgust at this bloody apparition messing up his nice clean hotel. He shot out from behind his desk to stop Rufus coming any further.

'*Merde!*' cried the man, gawping at the blood dripping from Rufus on to the marble floor.

'Yeah, you got that right,' said Rufus. 'Now will you for feck's sake get these ropes cut before the people who tied me to this damned chair catch up with me?'

Something in Rufus's expression convinced the

receptionist that he'd best do as he was told. He found a pair of scissors and with trembling hands cut the ropes. To his obvious relief, Rufus was not inclined to stick around. The moment he was free, he ran out of the hotel and leapt into the Rolls-Royce. Picturing the diplomat's outrage at this disruption to his schedule, Rufus sped off down the drive. He didn't stop until he reached the border, where he abandoned the car and crossed on foot into Spain.

18

Don was still on his tail through Spain. He was pursued into Italy, then Switzerland. Rufus started to know how a fox must feel, with the hounds baying at its heels. He was being chased by an implacable enemy, and despair began to eat into him.

He became paranoid, jumping at shadows, seeing danger everywhere. He took a plane to Tenerife and worked the clubs along the Playa de las Americas for a while. He chilled – or tried to – in Bobby's Bar, drinking pina coladas, touring, lying in the sun on black volcanic ash, sometimes almost choking on the red dust that blew over from the Sahara. Maybe *that* was the place he should head for next – Africa. Get some mercenary work; there was always trouble there.

Then one of his bouncer mates pulled him to one side. 'Rufus, I've heard something...'

And there went Tenerife. The man told him that Don and a contingent of hard boys were sitting in Dublin airport ready to come and get him.

Don was never going to give up on this. Three, four, five near misses, and now Rufus was feeling truly desperate. And Christ, how he missed Ireland, his own true home. What the hell. Feck it. Don could find him anywhere, that much was obvious. So let him find him *there*, if he could.

Not wanting to go within a mile of his mother, the whining old cow, he went to the farm, the place by the Shannon where he'd played as a teenager with his cousins. Fatalism gripped him now. He'd given up caring whether he got caught; he couldn't run forever. He was tired, exhausted from it all. Rory'd been right: Don was never going to let this go. So to hell with it. Let him do his worst.

As a boy, he'd visited the farm as a poor relation. Now, as a man, he supposed he still was. He stood on the drive and looked at the big imposing stone building, the same way he had all those years ago.

'It's the proceeds of crime,' his mother had sneered whenever she and her husband and son were invited there. His mother claimed that her high-and-mighty brother Davey's branch of the family thought their poorer relatives beneath them. But Rufus suspected that she, with her make-do-and-mend life, was merely jealous of the material wealth they so obviously enjoyed, and it stuck in her craw to see it.

Once, Rufus's father had been given a chance to join the family firm, but Mother had shouted the old man down, the way she always did. As a result, they remained poor, and *she* remained stubbornly and stupidly resentful of anyone who wasn't in the same boat. 'Talk about ill-gotten gains,' she'd say. 'It's all robbed from London fellas, that place of theirs.'

But Rufus's memories of his visits to the farm were sweet. Mostly, they centred on his cousin Orla. He had never got on with Tory or Pat; they were ham-fisted thugs without finesse. Brutality came naturally to them, and they'd pushed and shoved and bullied the younger members of their family – Orla, her twin Redmond and the baby of the clan, Kieron – mercilessly.

Rufus might *look* like a wild man, but at least he had some sensibilities. The Jesuit fathers had raised him, instilled a little common decency – something that was completely lacking in Tory and Pat.

He carried on walking up the great sweeping drive toward the house, the vision of Orla as she had been that long-ago summer's day when he'd kissed her in the garden filling his mind. Sadness gripped him. She was lost to him, lost forever. Dead and gone.

He thought of her, as beautiful as any Dante Rossetti painting, with her lustrously tumbling auburn hair and her fine white skin. Her eyes, green as emeralds, always with that sad shuttered look about them.

Keep out, those eyes told the world around her. *Don't come near.*

He remembered her so well. Wished he could have seen her again, got to know her better. They had shared one illicit kiss, one juvenile embrace. He remembered how madly excited he'd been, he'd loved her with a kind of desperation. She, on the other hand, had kissed him close-mouthed, her jaw tense. Her neck under his hand had trembled and strained, and she had broken free as soon as she could.

He'd been hurt by her reticence. He'd thought his affection was returned. But no, obviously not. She'd looked at him as if he was a monster, and run off.

He'd never kissed her again.

He would have liked to show her Paris, the City of Light, the Eiffel Tower all a-sparkle. Forget Don and all that shit. But now ... now it was too late. He would never get the chance.

It was a bright sunny day, the river gleaming, the morning mist burned away by the sun. The farmhouse loomed ahead of him. He noticed that the grounds were no longer manicured, the way they'd been in the glory days when the Delaneys ruled the London underworld and the coffers overflowed. Some of the stonework was crumbling away, the paintwork was peeling. And no scaffolding up, no sign of repairs underway.

He went to the door. That was the same, though the oak had been stained to grey by the passing years; with its studded with brass stays it looked impregnable as ever. Rufus yanked the chain, and heard the bell ring in the bowels of the place. He waited. Finally, he rang again. There was no movement from within; no dogs barked; no hurrying footsteps approached.

He stepped back, peered up at the bedroom windows. He could see nothing, no movement. He walked around the side of the building. The sun beat down on him, he was sweating lightly. High summer, just like that day long ago.

And ... oh God ... she was there.

He stopped, dropped his bag and jacket to the ground in shock.

He was hallucinating. He'd wanted so much to see her again that here he was conjuring up a vision of her from his imagination. She was wearing a faded flower-sprigged tea dress, a rough windcheater over the top of it, and Wellington boots. Her hair was blowing straight out in the stiff breeze, a blood-red banner. She was hanging washing out to dry on a rotary clothes-line.

He felt his heart banging hard in his chest, felt his mouth go dry. He stood there and stared.

She was older. There was a frown line between her brows, a cobweb of crows-feet around those heartbreaking eyes of hers.

He closed his own eyes, opened them again.

She was still there. This was no illusion.

'Orla?' he said aloud.

The wind whipped the word away. She didn't turn, didn't hear. She pegged out another garment, an old woman's underwear.

'Orla?' he said, louder this time. It wasn't her, it couldn't be. This was an illusion. He'd wished it so much that he was seeing it.

She stopped what she was doing, turned her head, stared at him. For a moment her eyes widened in alarm. She looked as if she was going to run indoors.

'It's me,' he said. He let out a bewildered half-laugh. After the hell he'd been through, was this a sign of heaven at last? 'For the love of Christ, is it you? Is it really?'

'Rufus?' she asked.

'You're supposed to be dead,' he said in wonder. He walked towards her in a daze.

Orla was starting to smile. She was so beautiful. It was her, it was his Orla.

Suddenly Rufus was running, and Orla stumbled forward and they fell together in an embrace, Rufus laughing and lifting her off her feet with the joy of it.

He spun her around, roaring with laughter. 'You're alive! God be praised, you're alive!'

There were tears in his eyes as he set her back upon the ground, cupped her dear face in his big hands. He planted a kiss on her lips. As she had once long ago in these very grounds, she stiffened – but still, she smiled.

'I thought I'd lost you,' he said, and a tear of genuine emotion trickled down his cheek.

Orla gave a tight little smile. It was *her* smile, the same one she'd had as a teenager; restrained, secretive, closed-off.

'I've been here all the time,' she said.

'For how long?' To think of that! That she had been *here,* and he had been running around the world not knowing.

'Oh – years. Years and years,' she said, and there was that sadness again, as if she had been stuck here like a fly in amber, trapped against her will. 'Where have you been?' she asked.

'Long story,' he said.

'Well, fetch your bag and come inside, then you can tell me all about it.'

19

'Who's this?' Davey Delaney asked when he saw Rufus sitting in the kitchen with Orla and her mother.

'This is Rufus. You remember him, don't you? Sorcha's boy, Rufus,' said Ma.

The old man looked as though he didn't even remember Sorcha, his own sister, much less her son.

'That Sorcha! What a tongue she had on her,' said Ma.

Rufus had to smile at that. His mother *did* have a tongue on her, it lashed like a Fury's. More miserable in her poverty as the years passed, her husband dead so no longer the whipping boy for her dissatisfaction, she had taken to homing in on Rufus as a fair substitute. He found her depressing to be around, and his visits had become less and less frequent. In fact he hadn't visited her in years, and he didn't intend to remedy that.

The place was looking tired, for all the efforts that had clearly been made to spruce it up – much like the elderly pair who inhabited it, shuffling around in carpet slippers, eating crackers and cheese at the kitchen table, the old man gazing around him with an air of gentle bewilderment, the old woman living out her days in obdurate, long-suffering tedium.

'Pa's not always this mild,' Orla warned him. 'He gets a bit aggressive sometimes, a bit frustrated. You know we have guns on the farm, to see off vermin. All the farmers around here do. We have to be careful to keep the cabinet locked though.'

Rufus wondered if she was joking, but soon found she wasn't when the old man sprang to his feet one night and threw a coffee table at the TV in irritation at something the newscaster was saying. Rufus had to restrain him until Ma and Orla could calm him down, but it was startling to see and a warning that Orla's words were correct.

That first night, when the old ones went off to bed, Rufus sat there into the late evening with Orla. She got out a bottle of whisky, poured them both a measure, and sat there in her tea dress studying him.

'You look well,' she pronounced at last.

'And you.' In fact he thought she looked better than well: fabulous. 'Tell me what happened. I heard talk about a plane crash when I was in London. How could you have survived that?'

Orla's eyes dropped to the tumbler of whisky. She raised it to her lips, sipped a little.

'Redmond helped me get out,' she said in a low voice. 'Fergal the pilot was done for when we hit the sea, but we were still alive and the plane was filling with water and starting to sink.'

'It must have been terrifying.'

'It was. But Redmond saved me.'

'He got you out of the plane, got you to shore?'

Orla shook her head. 'He got me out of the plane, but I lost him after that. I swam to shore alone. I'll never forget how cold that water was. I was sure I would die before I got to dry land. Somehow, I managed it though.' Her voice broke. 'But Redmond was nowhere to be found.'

'Jesus,' said Rufus, and crossed himself.

She nodded. 'I can't talk about this,' she said.

'No. I'm sorry. It must be painful for you.'

Orla looked up with a strained smile. 'And what about you? How's the world been treating you since we last saw each other?'

Rufus thought of Pikey going up in flames, Don's unending fury. Losing himself in London, then in Paris and deeper in the heart of France, the flight into Spain, Italy, Switzerland, Tenerife – running and running until the weariness overcame him, and with it the need to touch the soil of home once more.

'I've been travelling.' He shrugged. 'Here and there, you know. Europe. Paris. You'd love it there.'

'Would I?'

'I'm sure you would.'

'Well, one day I must go.' She smiled her sad, secretive smile.

'I'll take you,' he said, looking into her beautiful eyes.

Orla didn't answer. She drained her whisky, and stood up. 'I'm off to bed. You can find your way to your room all right?'

She'd sorted him out earlier with the room he'd slept in as a boy, put clean linen on the bed, made it comfortable for him.

'Yes. Thank you.'

'Sleep well then, Rufus.'

Just like that. He sat there in the empty kitchen for a long time, wondering had he misread those smiles, her evident joy at seeing him again. Perhaps it was wrong, a sin to think of a cousin in that way, but he would be her lover in the blink of an eye, given the chance. She *knew* that. He believed that she had always known it. He finished his whisky and went upstairs to his allotted room – which took him past Orla's.

He stopped there outside the closed door, and thought, *This is stupid. I want her. She wants me. Doesn't she?*

The thought of her in there, her silken skin, her hair on the pillow, inflamed him. He'd loved her so long, mourned her, and she was *alive,* she was his. He reached out a hand to open the door. Turned the handle.

It didn't open.

The door was locked.

He stepped back in surprise.

Who the hell has a lock on their bedroom door? he wondered, frowning.

He tried once more. Yes, it was locked. And no word came from within, she didn't ask who it was, she didn't come running, throw the door wide.

Confused, he walked on to his own room.

Orla sat up in bed and watched the handle turn. Once. Twice. Her heart beating fast, her limbs frozen in fear, she clutched the sheets against her. Then she heard him move on, and go into his own room.

Slowly, inch by inch, she relaxed.

But after that, she couldn't sleep.

20

London, 1985

'I don't think I'm up to this,' said Annie to herself in the mirror.

No? Well, you've committed yourself to it now, so tough. Get on with it.

She stared at her reflection. She was wearing a vintage black lace Dior gown, with her hair swept up on top of her head. She had accentuated her eyes before she set off this evening with flicked-up black eyeliner, outlined her mouth in her usual scarlet red. She looked sophisticated, worldly. Beautiful even. But she was shit-scared.

However, when she left the powder room and re-entered the busy restaurant her fear didn't show. She sat down, and smiled across at her date. He smiled back. He was an attractive man with straight dark hair and expressive brown eyes. He wore a bespoke suit, navy blue. He looked good and smelled even better.

This was their second date. On their *first* one, he hadn't tried to so much as kiss her goodnight, thank God. On this one, he just might. Annie wondered how she felt about that. Answer – she hadn't a clue. She had met him through a connection of Dolly's. He was divorced too. And a banker, so not sniffing round after her money: he had plenty of his own. Layla had no idea her mum had been on two dates: she'd been away for the first one and Annie had made damned sure she didn't find out about this one either.

Annie had moved on, and she was proud of herself for that. After the divorce, she had crumbled. She knew she had. Good friends had helped her pull through a very tough, painful time. A time in which her daughter had completely blanked her. A time during which some days she couldn't even get out of bed, comb her hair or clean her teeth, she felt so low.

Bad, bad days.

But she'd come through all that. She had slowly, surely, rebuilt her life. Layla was nineteen now – a young woman. Things between them were still ... well, frigid would be a good word for it. Layla was polite but distant. No more, no less. She had a job in an accountancy firm, she was hyper-bright, could add a column of figures in record time.

As for Annie ... well, she'd learned to drive. Bought herself a top-of-the-range car. Treated herself to some designer gear: a few Yves St Laurent pieces, a lot of Chanel, some cunningly constructed items from Betty Jackson and Balenciaga. She indulged in high-end holidays, regularly jetted back and forth to the States, checked out the Times Square club, visited with Alberto her stepson, made something of a life for herself.

And ... she'd started dating.

She glanced at her date as he paid the bill, left a hefty tip for their waiter. No, her date wasn't mean. But he'd been rude and snappy to the poor little bastard more than once this evening, trying no doubt to impress her or maybe the other diners with his standing as a gourmand, his expectation of only ever receiving the very best. David Fairbright. Good-looking, wealthy but not mean with his money, and tall – taller than Max.

Shit, now why had she thought of him?

As they went out to the taxi, she pushed her ex-husband out of her mind.

'Nice dinner,' David said as they sat in the back of the cab on its way to Holland Park.

'Lovely,' she replied, although she couldn't even remember what she'd eaten. And his treatment of the waiter had annoyed her.

'You haven't been there before?' he asked.

'No. Never.'

Silence fell. Silence had been falling between them all evening, and it wasn't an easy companionable one either. The fact was, he didn't know what to say to her and she wasn't interested enough to come up with something to say to him. Annie suspected that he found her slightly intimidating. A lot of men did. She was wealthy in her own right, and some men – David included, she thought, for all his pumped-up self-importance and yes he *was* a bit of a bolshy git – couldn't handle that.

That, and her background. Which was colourful, to say the least.

They'd talked on their first date, about their divorces. She had mentioned Max's name. And she suspected that since then David had been doing a little homework, because he seemed a fraction cooler this time. Now that he knew about Max, and about her, she suspected their second date would also be their last.

The taxi pulled up outside the Holland Park house. Annie got out, and David did too, paying off the taxi driver, who drove away.

Annie walked up the steps to the big navy-blue double doors, getting her key out of her bag. What the hell had he sent the taxi away for? Suddenly all she wanted was for him to be gone, to just be alone.

On the step underneath the porch light, he took her hand. Then, to her surprise, he pulled her in close, and started to kiss her. He pushed his tongue into her mouth and Annie jerked her head away.

'Don't do that,' she snapped.

'Oh, come on,' he said, and she saw him smile. 'The evening's been a bit of a disaster so far, but that's no reason to call it off altogether.'

He moved forward again. This time Annie shoved him, hard, and he half-staggered down the steps and nearly fell.

'What the fuck's wrong with you?' he said, glaring up at her as he regained his balance.

'Me? Nothing. You? You're a pushy arsehole looking down your stupid nose at the entire world, and you know what? I don't like you.'

She opened the door and went inside, slamming it behind her. She wiped her mouth, irritated at him, at herself too because she'd hated him kissing her but what did she expect? Violins? Heavenly choirs? She marched across the hall and into the study, fell into her chair and picked up the phone on the desk. She dialled.

'Doll?' she asked when she heard the familiar voice on the other end of the phone.

'How'd it go?' asked Dolly excitedly. Foreigner were playing in the background, the vocalist plaintively singing 'I want to know what love is'.

So do I, thought Annie miserably. *Jesus, so do I.*

'It was horrible. He's a prick.'

'Damn. That's a shame.'

'He tried to French me.'

There was a brief silence on the other end of the phone.

'Annie, love,' said Dolly, 'you used to run a knocking shop. You were a gangster's moll, pardon me for pointing out the flipping obvious. And you married into the Mafia. And you're shocked that some guy *French kissed* you?'

'Oh fuck the men. Who cares? I'm happy enough without them.'

'You can't give up yet.'

Annie stared at the phone. *This* from a woman who, as far as she knew, had never so much as given any man a second glance.

'Tea tomorrow? The Ritz? Don't forget.'

'I haven't forgotten.'

'And listen, Ellie was telling me about this *fantastic* bloke…'

Annie let out a groan. 'Don't. I'll see you there tomorrow, OK?'

'Chin up,' said Dolly.

'Oh fuck off,' said Annie, and hung up to the sound of Dolly laughing merrily in her ear.

21

There was no mention of the locked door. After that first night, Rufus had tried twice more, then given up. Orla, though obviously pleased to have him around, continued to be restrained in her affection. Their lives settled into a routine, dull but not unpleasant, and gradually the months passed into years. Then one day, while the old folks had their breakfast, she asked him to chop some wood for the stove.

'Of course,' he said, and went outside into the brisk morning breeze. It was a bright clear day and he felt his spirits lift.

This old place was like home to him now, and he was glad to be here, glad to have stopped running at last. He found the axe in the shed and set to the job with enthusiasm, chopping the logs in two and piling them up in the store, ready for the coming autumn. It was hot work. Rufus stripped off his shirt and worked bare-chested in the sun. He'd been at it for an hour or so when Orla appeared with a cold lemonade for him.

'Thanks,' he said.

'You've done well,' she said, her eyes skimming over the pile of wood before returning to rest on him. Her gaze dipped to his chest, to the rivulets of sweat running down there. She thought he looked like some Norse giant from a fable, golden and muscular and strong.

Rufus watched her watching him. *For God's sake,* he thought in frustration. What was going on with her? She was clearly interested. He *knew* she was. Yet there had been that locked door, the cold shoulder.

'Can I ask you something?' he said, draining the glass and handing it back to her.

'Sure you can.'

'That first night I came here – and the two times I tried after that – didn't you hear me at your door?'

Orla's smile slipped. She stared at the ground. Didn't answer.

'Why d'you have to lock your door anyway?' asked Rufus.

She shrugged, looked up. 'I can't sleep without it locked.'

'Really?' This sounded strange. 'But you heard me at the door, didn't you?'

Her eyes met his. 'Yes. I heard you.'

'Orla ... why don't you leave it *unlocked,* to-night.'

Orla stared, said nothing.

'Don't you want to?' asked Rufus gently.

Orla started to shake her head, then slowly she nodded. Her fingers were clenched so hard around the empty glass that he thought she might break it.

'Leave it unlocked,' said Rufus, and his eyes held hers. 'I'll take care of you, I promise. You know I will.'

'I do,' she said. 'I know that.'

She walked away, back indoors. He watched her go. Then he started chopping more wood, with a smile on his face. He couldn't wait for the day to go, for night to come.

And now here he was, outside her bedroom door again. He knocked lightly – he didn't want to disturb the old folks – and then tried the handle. This time, it opened. He went in. The bedside light was on. Orla was sitting up in the bed, wearing a pink winceyette nightdress, the kind a granny would wear, her hair loose around her shoulders, the soft light making her glow like an angel.

Rufus closed the door behind him. He turned the key in the lock, to keep her happy. Besides, he didn't want the oldies wandering in and finding them making love. Unbuttoning his shirt, he went to the bed and smiled down at her.

She looked nervous. In fact, she looked afraid. He was puzzled. Of course she would have had lovers over the years.

'It's all right,' he said soothingly. 'I promised to take care of you and I will.'

He took a packet of Durex from his trouser pocket and placed it on the bedside table. He thought she was probably past child-bearing now, but this consideration would reassure her.

He kicked off his socks and shoes, unbuckled his belt, unzipped, slipped off his trousers and underpants. Then he slid under the sheets and cuddled up to her. She stiffened, but he drew her close, nuzzled at her neck. Tentatively, her arms went around him. He kissed her more deeply, and she pulled away.

'We'll take this slowly,' he said, although he

didn't want to. 'As slowly as you need. Don't worry about a thing. Now, perhaps we could just slip this off...?' He indicated the nightdress.

Orla nodded. He thought that she looked as if she was about to be shot, not pleasured. But she yanked the unflattering thing off, tossed it on the floor, and then clutched the sheet against her breasts.

He was almost amused by her reticence. It was like seducing a teenager, not a full-grown woman. He'd had lots of experience, personally. There'd been many women, impressed by his bulk and strength, younger ones and one particular older one, a goddess in human form, who had taught him at a very young age how to make a woman lose her mind in bed.

'And the sheet, if you could let go of that,' he said, smiling, making light of it to relax her.

Orla let go of the sheet. Rufus pushed it down to the bottom of the bed, his eyes running over her with great admiration. Where his eyes went, his hand followed, smoothly gliding across her silky white skin, lingering at the fiery red bush, progressing to her cinnamon-coloured nipples, which were hard as pinpoints on the soft small mounds of her breasts.

'I've dreamed of this,' he said with a shiver of delight. 'So many years, I've dreamed of it.'

'I know,' she said in a small voice. 'I always knew.'

'And you wanted this too,' he said. 'Didn't you.'

She didn't answer. She pulled his head down for another kiss. It became deeper, longer. Her head snapped back, but his hand was on her neck, holding her there. He came forward again. This time Orla drew away completely.

'What is it?' he asked. 'Don't you like that?'

Orla shook her head.

'OK, I won't do it. No problem.'

His kisses were lighter now, fleeting, and she relaxed a little. He guided her hand down, folded it over his erection. She flinched again, jerking her hand away. Rufus looked at her.

'You're not ready for this, are you?' he said. 'Maybe I've rushed you.'

'No! You haven't, I'm just being silly.' Her eyes were wild.

'I can wait,' said Rufus. 'I'll wait until you're ready. I don't mind.'

'No. Do it to me, Rufus. I *want* you to. Just *do* it.'

Rufus pushed her back down on to the bed, easing her thighs open. He knelt between them. As he reached for the packet of condoms he was aware of her watching him, something like panic in her eyes. He hesitated.

'Go on,' she urged him. 'Do it.'

He opened the packet and slipped the condom on. Then he lay upon her, pushing his penis down between her thighs, desire overtaking his caution, his concern. He found the place, but discovered to his dismay that she was dry. Quickly he spat into his hand and wetted his cock so that he shouldn't hurt her. Overwhelmed with his love for her, he pushed at the place eagerly, wanting her so much.

Orla stiffened.

'Relax,' he urged, kissing her mouth, her neck,

her shoulder.

Her hands were bunched into fists against his chest.

She was clenched shut – so firmly shut that he couldn't enter her.

He pushed again. It was no good. He felt his erection wilt as his mind whirled with bewilderment. She was rejecting him, her actual *body* was saying no. He looked at her face and saw that her eyes were screwed up as if she couldn't bear to even *see* what was happening to her.

'I can't breathe,' she said, shoving her fists against him, starting to writhe in panic.

Instantly Rufus withdrew, flopping back on to the bed. He threw the condom aside. He was no longer erect. He turned his head and gazed at her.

'Are you OK?' he asked.

She nodded, her arm across her eyes.

'What is it? What's wrong?'

She said nothing.

'I've rushed you,' said Rufus. 'I'm sorry. We can try again, later.'

Orla dropped her arm down on to the bed. Her eyes were wet.

'Hey. Don't cry. It doesn't matter. We'll leave it for tonight, OK? We've all the time we need, don't worry.'

'All right,' she said faintly.

'We'll just sleep together,' said Rufus. 'Nice and cosy. All right?'

Orla nodded.

'I'll turn out the light,' he said, and did so, pulling the sheets and blankets up to cover them both, snuggling in against her back. It felt so good that he almost forgot his worry at their abortive attempt at love-making. He drifted off to sleep, inhaling the sweet scent of her hair, his arm around her. When the morning light flooded in, she was no longer in the bed with him; he found her asleep on the chaise-longue under the window, wrapped in one of the blankets.

'Hey,' he said, nudging her awake. 'You OK? Why are you over here?'

Orla stretched and woke. 'It's nothing. I find it hard to sleep with someone else in the bed with me, that's all.'

But I'm not just someone, he thought, hurt. *I'm Rufus. And I thought we were childhood sweethearts, adult lovers.*

Clearly she wasn't used to sharing her life, that was the problem. He reassured himself with that thought as he left her there and padded along to his own room to shower and dress. It would all come right, in the end.

22

He left it a while, let the dust settle. He was kicking himself because he'd charged at it like a bull at a gate, he should have held back. He finished chopping the wood, mended a leaking gutter, made himself useful. Then a week later, as the evening drew in, he said:

'I thought I might come to your room tonight.

If you'd like that.'

Orla gazed at him across the kitchen table. 'All right,' she said at last.

After that, his blood fizzed with anticipation. It would be OK this time. She no longer saw him as some threatening stranger. They'd laughed and chatted together these last few days, walking the banks of the Shannon with the salty winds buffeting them, relaxing after they'd finished their chores on the farm, sitting in the shade of an old apple tree. Becoming familiar with each other after all those years apart.

This time, it would be fine.

Only it wasn't.

The same thing happened. She was so tight, he couldn't get inside her. In fact, he began to fear that if he *did* manage entry, he would hurt her badly. And that dissolved his arousal like nothing else could.

They lay afterwards, him cuddling up to her, Orla stiff as a board. In the early hours, he awoke. And she was gone again.

He fumbled for the bedside light, turned it on.

The room was empty but he could hear a distant thumping, like someone hammering a nail into a wall. He wrapped himself in a robe and went and opened the bedroom door. Instantly, the sound was louder. He went downstairs and stood in the hall, trying to place the direction of the noise.

It was coming from *outside*.

He went to the front door: it was unbolted. He opened it, stepped outside into the cool night air: out here the din was much louder. It was coming from the barn beside the house. And it wasn't hammering. It was music.

He opened the barn door and the noise almost smashed him backward. AC/DC were belting out 'Highway to Hell'. The interior of the barn was awash with brilliant strip lighting, and there was colour everywhere. At first he thought it looked like blood, but there were dark blues, indigo-deep, and fiery oranges, great swirls of chaotic colour. And there in the centre of it, the boom box perched on a chair at her side, was Orla. She was on her feet, in her nightdress, and she was feverishly daubing paint on to a big canvas set up on an easel. The scent of linseed oil and paint assaulted his nose.

'Orla?' he shouted.

She didn't turn: couldn't hear him.

He shut the door, so as not to wake the old folks.

He walked forward, switched the music off.

Orla stopped what she was doing and turned, startled.

'Orla?' he said more softly. He looked at the canvases, back at her face, then again at the canvases. They were propped up all around the walls, in colours so vivid they were shocking. And ... they chilled him, these paintings. There were swirls and huge great gouts of colour. The pictures were awash with an anguish that seemed to scream out at him.

'Sorry,' she said, turning away from him, back to what she was doing. 'Did I disturb you?'

He looked at her. Everything she did disturbed him more, every day. He was getting a sinking feeling, and that saddened him. He'd been so thrilled to see her again. But ... oh, something was wrong here. Something was terribly wrong.

'What are you doing?' he asked, although it was obvious. He stared around at the paintings, the violent clashing colours, and he thought, *My God, what is this?*

Every single painting was of a man – tall, slender, handsome and pale, with neat red hair. The man was enveloped in a swirling tornado of colours, or down a dark tunnel, falling; smiling out of a canvas here, screaming out of another one there. She was painting Redmond, her twin, over and over again, like a stuck record.

Rufus didn't know *what* to say.

He was seriously spooked. Orla's old dad had spouted nonsense ever since he'd arrived, saying things like *Redmond called today, while you were out.*

Ah yes? his wife would say, with a smile that didn't reach her sad eyes. *Is that a fact?*

But of course it wasn't. Redmond was dead, and so were Tory and maybe Pat and even young Kieron. All dead, all gone.

This is a haunted place, thought Rufus with a shudder.

'What do you think?' she asked, and her smile had a manic edge to it that unnerved him. 'Kieron was a painter, you know. Exhibited in Dublin and then in London, he was big news. Of course I don't have *his* sort of talent, but I enjoy it. Whenever I can't sleep, I come out here.'

Yeah, he thought. *If someone's in bed with you, someone you're supposed to love, you can't sleep. So you come here and do this.*

His heart felt chilled in his chest. This wasn't right. This behaviour ... it was beyond him. He couldn't understand it.

'That's Redmond,' he said at last.

'Yes.' She paused, gazing at the canvas she was working on, her eyes caressing it. 'It is.'

He moved closer. 'You're very talented,' he said. He didn't mean it. He was ... horrified. Yes. That was the word. Horrified, and trying to understand where this madness might have come from. He hated the paintings. They made him think of Van Gogh's mad desperate eruptions of colour, and of that one they called *The Scream.* These canvases were evidence of her obsession with someone, someone other than him. A dead man, someone he could never hope to compete with.

'So you don't ... exhibit?' he asked.

'No. Why would I? This is for my own pleasure, no one else's.'

'Orla.'

She was back at it again, flinging thick gobs of pure viridian green on to the canvas, smearing it about with a pallet knife. 'Hm?'

'We have to talk.'

'About what?' she didn't even look round.

'About why you tense up when I try to make love to you. About that.'

Her shoulder stiffened; there was no other sign she'd heard him.

'Orla.'

She turned to him then, brightly smiling; there was a smear of yellow ochre on her cheek.

'It'll come right in the end,' she said.

But it went on like that: nothing changed. Rufus tried to make himself useful during the long days, and every evening he sat with her and watched TV with the old ones, seeing Haughey elected for a third term as Taioseach, and Thatcher visiting Moscow.

Often he awoke to find himself alone, hearing faint the hammer-drill of Guns N' Roses or Deep Purple coming from the barn. He persisted, spending the nights with her whenever she'd allow it. But it was useless.

He'd heard of this sort of thing, he knew what it was called: vaginismus. The woman he loved, the woman he *worshipped,* had been hurt somehow in the past, hurt so badly that a normal response to a man was impossible for her.

He was going to talk to her about it. He *had* to.

But then something else happened, and that problem was pushed aside.

23

He was out in the grounds as autumn sailed in with fierce gusts of wind, wrenching the leaves from the trees. He was muffled up warm and sweeping up piles of the things. In summer, the place was marvellous, but as winter approached it was rough being buffeted by gales. The moisture from the water hit the windows, caking them so that they were diffused, and from inside it was like looking through gauze, as if you were trapped in a bubble.

It was a cosy enough bubble though. The old folks were no trouble. And Orla ... well, he loved her. They sat sometimes in the evenings when the old couple had gone to their rooms, just curled up together on the big sofa, chatting or watching TV, and he thought *This is bliss.*

Only, of course, it wasn't quite. He no longer even attempted to make love to her. He could see she hated it, that her body rejected it utterly.

So ... here they sat, like an ancient married couple, comfortable, not talking about it. But still it bothered him. He noticed things about her that worried him greatly. When she saw babies on TV adverts, she turned her head, looked elsewhere. When he kissed her, she pulled away. And he didn't even try to sleep with her any more. She didn't like it. That much was plain.

So here he was, sweeping up leaves to put into the compost bins to feed the garden next year. Killing time. Wondering, with a heavy heart, what to do.

Next year, he thought, and paused.

Would be still be here, then? He didn't think so. Some people could settle for platonic love, but he wasn't one of them. He was a passionate man. It would break his heart, but he knew that he would go, one day soon.

'Hey! Rufus, you big bazoo!'

The shouting male voice startled him out of his thoughts. He paused, looked up. No one ever came here. Oh, the grocery van called by, and the postman and the milkman, but they never actually had *visitors,* as such.

He couldn't believe his eyes. It was his old mate Rory, striding toward him. A battered Land Rover was parked up near the open gate.

'Rory!' Rufus's big face split in a grin. 'Is it really you?'

'Who else d'you think it is, feckin' Santa Claus?' Rory ran over, laughing. He looked exactly the same, a little thinner maybe, his face with a few fresh lines. Rory hugged him and they both laughed.

'Well, what the hell are you doing out here in the arse-end of nowhere?' asked Rufus, pushing his mate back a step, his brow crinkling. 'How did you know I was here?'

Rory shrugged. 'How the hell would I? I didn't. But I was down this way doing a bit of horse trading, and I remembered your relatives had this place and I wondered if they were still here, living in the grand style, and whether they could give me news of you. And here you are! Large as life and twice as ugly.'

'It's good to see you, boy,' said Rufus in real delight. 'Come away inside and let's have a drink to celebrate.'

'And how's Megan?' asked Rufus as they sat drinking late into the night. Davey and his wife had gone on to bed, and so had Orla. She had been polite to Rory, but not effusive. She had cooked them all a good dinner, then said she was tired and gone off to her room.

Rufus didn't tell Rory that he knew Megan had

betrayed him all those years ago, summoning Don's men the moment his back was turned. Only good luck and keen eyesight had saved his arse that day, and he couldn't forgive the cow for it. But it hadn't been Rory's fault.

'We split up. About a year after little Diarmuid was born.'

'I'm sorry,' said Rufus, although he wasn't. He thought Rory could do a lot better than *that* bitch.

'Don't be. It was all feckin' arguments, a living hell. I was glad to be out of it.'

'But you still see the child?'

'Ah, sometimes.' Rory's mouth turned down. 'Truth to tell, I don't see either of them very much.'

'I can't say I took to her,' admitted Rufus.

'Ah, forget her. It's good to see you again. I couldn't believe it when you just cleared off without a word.'

Rufus shrugged, his eyes averted from Rory's. If he hadn't slipped away, Don's boys would have nabbed him, and he'd be dead by now. *Thanks, Megan,* he thought. *You cow.*

'I'd outstayed my welcome,' he said.

'Never,' said Rory.

'Megan didn't want me there – and that was understandable, what with the child and everything.'

Rory couldn't deny it. 'So what have you been up to?'

'Oh, travelling, stuff like that.'

'Seeing the world.'

'Yeah.'

'Lucky bastard.'

Yeah, with Don on my tail every inch of the way.
'You?'
'Mechanic jobs, same as always. Boring, but it pays. Still doing a bit on the nags, too.'
'Drink up. We'll have another,' said Rufus.

24

'I don't like him,' said Orla as time wore on and Rory stayed.
'What?' This had come out of left-field for Rufus. *Everyone* loved Rory. He was chatty and charming. Certainly Orla's mum adored him, making no end of a fuss, and even Davey seemed to enjoy his company.
'He's a shifty little fellow,' she said.
'Rory? No, he's not. He's a bit on the loud side, I grant you, but...'
'I wouldn't trust him if I were you.'
Orla didn't trust anybody. Rufus felt the words rise to his lips and quickly stifled them. He didn't want to fight with her.
'Why not?' he asked.
'Because he's turned up here unannounced. And why?'
'I *told* you why. He's in the area to look over some horses. We used to go to the sulky races together. He loves the nags.'
'So he says. When's he going to get on and do that, then?'
'Orla...'

‘What? You’re too trusting, Rufus.’

‘I’ve known Rory since we both crawled from our prams.’

Orla shrugged. ‘I’m only saying.’

‘I don’t think your cousin likes me very much,’ said Rory as he helped clear some shrubbery with Rufus one day. He hadn’t gone off to see any horses yet. After that first mention of it, he hadn’t spoken of it again. And Rufus did wonder about that, just a bit.

‘What, Orla? She don’t care to mix much. Take no notice.’

Rufus felt embarrassed by Orla’s behaviour around Rory.

‘He’s nothing but a gobshite,’ she said when Rufus asked her why she disliked him so much.

He couldn’t tell Rory *that.*

‘If I’m in the way...’ said Rory.

‘You’re not. You’re welcome here, of course you are.’

‘What is it with you two? Are you...?’ He gave Rufus a knowing look.

‘No, we’re not. At all,’ said Rufus.

‘If I’m not welcome, say the word and I’ll go.’

‘Shut up, will you?’ said Rufus with a grin.

Rory seemed to relax then, and they carried on working side by side.

Later, Rufus wished with all his heart that he’d taken Rory at his word that day, and let him go.

25

Rufus was sleeping soundly in his bed when the light came on, waking him. Orla had entered his room and was leaning over him, her expression almost crazed, her hair tickling his face. He opened his mouth to ask what was the matter – she *never* came to his room, and he had long since ceased to expect it – but she laid a silencing hand across his mouth.

'Get up!' she whispered, her voice full of excitement. 'I've something to show you.'

Ah Jesus, he thought. It would be another batch of mad paintings. He looked at the clock on the bedside table, it was one fifteen in the frigging morning.

'Orla...' he started, pushing his hair out of his eyes, feeling exasperated, sad, irritable.

'Come *on,* sleepy. I'll show you.'

Shit, he thought. Nonetheless he stumbled from the bed, put on his dressing gown – she was wearing her winceyette nightie, he saw – anything to humour her.

She grabbed his hand, holding a finger to her lips to keep him silent.

'Come on!' she hissed.

He allowed her to lead him from the room and along the hall. More and more he was coming to realize that Orla, his precious Orla, was ... well, she was *unhinged.* Something had made her unstable. Probably poor Redmond's death.

'Listen! Here!' He'd expected her to drag him down the stairs and out to the barn, but instead she'd come to a halt outside one of the guest rooms. *Rory's* room, he realized.

'What the…'

She shushed him urgently. He could hear a voice. Like a child playing a naughty game, Orla produced a glass from her pocket and held it out to him. 'Listen,' she whispered.

'For God's sake...'

'Go on!'

Rufus let out a sharp sigh. How long had she spent doing this, suspecting Rory the same way she suspected any outsider, never mind that he was Rufus's oldest friend? For all he knew she'd been here eavesdropping every night since Rory arrived, trying to trap him in some imagined transgression.

His mood veering between annoyance and a weary sadness, he took the glass from her and placed it to the door. Instantly the muffled voice came clearer. It was Rory's voice. And he was talking to someone. He was on the phone.

'I didn't pick up the extension because I thought he'd hear the click,' hissed Orla. 'I *knew* he was up to something.'

Rufus tuned her out and listened hard to what was going on in Rory's room.

Rory sounded near to tears. Which was weird. Rory never cried. He wasn't an over-emotional man. He was always happy, always upbeat.

'Yes. I told you so, didn't I? That's right,' said Rory.

'I know. I know. And he's OK, is he? He's not hurt?' asked Rory.

'What the hell does that mean?' There was panic in Rory's voice now.

'But we had a deal!' Rory almost shouted.

'Listen,' Rory's voice was low, urgent, angry. 'I've done what I said I'd do. You have to let him go. Yes. He's here. I *told* you, Rufus is here. Now you've to let the boy go. You swear. You *have* to.'

Rory was silent for a while.

Rufus stood there, stunned. Orla was right. Rory had come here to betray him. His heart sank as he realized he'd been set up. Big Don had Rory's nuts in a vice; he'd taken his son, threatened to harm him if he didn't deliver Rufus. Caught between a rock and a hard place, Rory had gone searching for his old mate. And having found him, he'd waited, lulling the household into a false sense of security, until the time came to report back.

'You see? You see?' Orla was staring at him, her eyes sparkling with excitement.

Rufus saw. Don would come here, and that would be it. He'd be finished. And what about Orla and the old folks, what would become of them? Don wouldn't risk leaving any witnesses alive to tell the tale.

He let the hand holding the glass fall to his side. This was a bitter blow. And while he was standing there, wondering what on earth he should do, Orla pushed open the door and hurried inside.

'Orla...' he started, but she was already in the room, and Rory was there, sitting on the bed, replacing the receiver, his face a picture of guilt.

'You treacherous shit,' she spat at him.

Rory's eyes were wide. He looked at Rufus, and his cheeks burned with shame at being discovered this way.

'We heard,' said Rufus. 'That was Don, I take it?'

Rory caught his breath and seemed about to deny it: but then his shoulders slumped and he nodded miserably. 'He's got my boy, little Diarmuid. Snatched him from his mother, and then said I was to find you or else.'

'All this time,' said Rufus on a sigh, 'I've been wondering why he's left me alone. But he hasn't, has he? He's still after me.'

'Rufe, I'm sorry, I really am. The man's ill, they say. He's losing it. He told me the one thing he wants to do before he dies is to find you. To have his revenge. He's got my kid, Rufus. What else can I do?'

'I'll tell you what you can do, you worm,' snapped Orla, looming over Rory. She snatched up the receiver. 'You can call your hoodlum pal back and say that Rufus has moved on, caught a flight to the States or something. That he *was* here, but he realized the game was up and he's gone.'

Rory was shaking his head. He stood up, starting pacing back and forth.

'I can't do that,' he said. 'I *can't.* I'm sorry as hell, but I can't risk it – he'll kill Diarmuid.'

'You can,' said Orla. 'And you will.'

'No, no...'

Orla lifted her hand, and it was only then Rufus saw she was holding a knife. 'Get on the phone.

Do it.'

Rufus felt sick to his stomach. He'd been betrayed by his closest friend, and now Orla, the woman he loved, was waving a knife around like a maniac. Rory's eyes were imploring as they rested on his.

'Do it,' said Rufus.

'Rufe, I daren't...'

'Do it,' he said, and this time his voice was loaded with hurt and rage.

His hand shaking, Rory reached for the phone and dialled. They all waited, holding their breath. Then Rory stiffened.

'Don? He's gone,' he said. 'I've just been to his room and looked. Rufus is gone. He must have got suspicious and done a runner.'

There was an angry sound from the other end of the line.

'I *know* that,' Rory shouted. 'Don't you think I know that? But I'm telling you, I just checked his room and he's not there.' Rory's eyes met Orla's. She jabbed the knife at him: *Go on.*

Rufus gave her a look. *Let him speak.*

'He was talking about moving on to the States,' Rory babbled. 'He was keen on the idea, my guess is that's where he's gone. So I can't help you any more. You've to let the boy go.'

The angry voice jabbered away. Rory's eyes grew wide with panic.

'What do you *mean*, "we'll see"? I've done all I can do. Rufus has gone, that's all I know. I can't ... hello? *Hello?*'

The line had gone dead. Trembling, Rory replaced the receiver.

'He'll kill him for spite,' he mumbled, his eyes vacant with fear. 'He will. He won't let him go.'

'Rory...' started Rufus, wanting to comfort his old friend, to say that he had done what any father would have done in the circumstances, that he wasn't to blame.

But Orla moved in with the knife and before Rufus realized what was happening, she lunged hard, sticking it squarely in Rory's midsection.

Rory let out a breathless scream of pain and shock. Orla yanked out the knife, blood flying in a wide spurting arc, spattering the front of her nightdress. And then she struck again, plunging it up to the hilt in Rory's windpipe. He sank to the floor, the blade embedded in his throat, gurgling, blood bubbling and foaming on his lips. Then Rory's eyes turned up in his head and he toppled sideways, hitting the ground with a thump.

Rufus stood frozen, sick with shock, unable to believe what he had just seen. Orla had *killed* Rory. He blinked, shook his head. He couldn't take it in. He hadn't thought for a moment that she would actually use the knife or he would have snatched it off her. But she'd done it. She'd killed his friend.

Orla was breathing hard. Spattered with blood, she sat down on the bed, staring at the corpse at her feet.

Not a word was spoken for a long, long time. Rufus was shaken and filled with cold horror. He wanted to wring her neck with his bare hands. His eyes kept returning, again and again, to Rory, lying there dead on the floor.

But ... but he loved her.

Didn't he?

Then she looked up at him, and she smiled.

'You see?' she said, happy to be vindicated. 'I *told* you he was not to be trusted.'

26

When he could force himself to move, to acknowledge that this nightmare was real, Rufus went down to the barn and fetched a tarpaulin, praying that neither of Orla's parents would wake up and ask what was going on. Because what could he say? *Your daughter has just knifed my best friend?* But all was quiet, thank God.

He carried the tarp to the bedroom and was sickened to see that during his absence Orla had reclaimed her knife from Rory's throat, and was wiping it clean on the front of the dead man's shirt.

Between them, they wrapped the body and all Rory's belongings – Rufus kept the Land Rover keys to one side – in the tarp and heaved the bundle down the stairs and outside to the little stand of woodland not too far from the house. Then Rufus fetched a shovel and started digging. He'd go down four feet, he reckoned, that would be deep enough to stop the foxes getting poor Rory out again.

He dug. And he wondered if Don was going to show up at any second, thinking that Rory had duped him – which was the truth – and then the game would be up, he'd be caught.

The way Rufus was feeling tonight, he would be glad of it. He was sickened by what Orla had done, killing a man without a qualm. And he had lost the only true friend he had in the world. So if Don were to show up, yes, Rufus would be relieved. It would mean an end to all this running, all this hiding. He was tired of it. Tired of life. Tired of the whole awful, shitty mess.

He buried Rory, filled in the grave, stood there and mumbled a few words of blessing over the poor bastard. Then he went to Rory's Land Rover, which was parked up in one of the outside lean-to spaces, and moved it into the far barn, locking the door behind him so that no one could just wander in and see it there.

As he walked back to the house, he wondered what would happen to Rory's kid.

He'll kill him for spite, Rory had said.

And he might. Don was hell-bent on taking revenge on Rufus, and he'd been thwarted yet again. There was every likelihood he'd kill the boy to punish Rory. And that would be another death on Rufus's conscience.

Bone-weary in body and spirit, Rufus went back into the house. While he'd been busy at the grave, Orla had been clearing up in Rory's room. The metallic stink of blood had been replaced by the smell of pine disinfectant. Everything was clean, and tidy. It was, he thought, as if Rory had never been there at all.

They sat up the rest of the night. Rufus felt as if he

would never sleep again. Orla had changed her nightdress for a clean one, and the blood-spattered winceyette gown was soaking in the washing machine. She seemed almost chatty, sharing a glass of whisky with him.

'I told you, you see? You wouldn't listen. I'll tell Ma tomorrow that he's moved on, don't worry about it. I was right, you see. All along, I was right.'

'Yes. You were right.'

But you're not right in the head, are you?

He'd never seen a woman kill before – let alone kill so dispassionately, as if she hadn't a feeling in her entire body. His instincts had been telling him all along that something was wrong with Orla. She seemed devoid of emotion. She killed in cold blood. She painted mad pictures. She found sex repellent. She hated babies. She had no time for anyone, and seemed constantly to anticipate attack from any direction. When he looked at her face, he no longer saw her beautiful green eyes. All he saw was the chilling taint of madness.

'I'm sad that Redmond died,' said Rufus, draining his glass and refilling it. 'Because I can see what it's done to you.'

'I'm sad about that too,' said Orla. 'I'll be sad until my dying day over the loss of him.'

'Orla ... is that all it is? Is that what's made you this way?'

Orla took the bottle from him and topped up her own glass. 'What way is that?' she asked, smiling.

'Cold,' he said. *Frigid. Frigid and fucking dangerous.*

'Cold?'

'You ... don't want to make love,' he said by way of explanation. *And that's the least of it.*

Orla let loose a heavy sigh. 'Ah, are you *still* going on about that? I can't help it. I just don't like it very much, that's all.'

'Yes, but why? Have you never looked into it, asked a doctor maybe?'

'No. Because I don't have to.'

'Why is that?' He wanted to hear the truth of it. A voice inside him warned that prodding her into some sort of confession might be dangerous, but he was past caring. He'd been staying all this time, living with the constant fear that Don would show up, thinking that was the worst thing that could happen. Little did he know. Nothing could have been worse than the horror he'd witnessed tonight, the loss of Rory, the sheer God-awful weirdness of Orla.

She shrugged. 'Ah, you know. Old things.'

'What old things?'

A shrug. Her eyes were fastened on the table. One finger was tracing the grain of it, over and over again.

'Can you tell me about it?' he asked, keeping his voice gentle. 'This is me, Orla. How long have we been friends? For ever. So why not tell me what's been going on with you?'

Orla's fingernail dug into the grain, leaving a half-moon mark there. Her eyes flickered up to his face, then back to the wood.

'It's nothing,' she said. 'Old stuff.'

'Such as...?'

Again, a shrug. 'Nothing that matters any more.'

This was driving him mad. He *had* to know. 'Come on, Orla, tell me.'

Now her eyes met his. She picked up the dregs of the whisky, drank it down in one.

'Tory used to come into our room – mine and Redmond's. Pat too. He liked to watch.'

Rufus sat back with a frown. Of all the things she could have told him, he hadn't expected that.

'Come into your room...?' he queried.

'To have sex with us,' she said, and gave a tight little smile.

Rufus sat there feeling as if the marrow in his bones had been turned to ice.

'You *what?*'

'That's why I don't like it much. Sorry.'

'Orla ... for the love of God, what are you telling me? You're saying your two elder brothers abused you? Both you and Redmond?'

She nodded. And then she smiled.

'But Tory's dead, and Pat went missing long ago, so I suppose he's dead too.'

'Jesus ... Orla...' He couldn't get his head round it. Her elder brothers, who should have been protecting her, loving their sister as any brother should, had been doing that to her? And to Redmond as well!

'Don't feel sorry for me,' she said. 'It happened years ago, it's all forgotten.'

No it isn't, thought Rufus. *You're scarred right through from it, but you think you're normal. You poor bitch.*

'I had no idea.' He was thinking of the lock on her bedroom door, the clenching when he tried to make love to her, the dislike of babies. 'There wasn't... I mean, did anything happen after they'd...' He couldn't even say it. It was too monstrous, too awful.

She took another gulp of whisky. 'I thought I was pregnant at eleven years old,' she said. 'I wasn't. Which was lucky.'

'Oh Jesus. Orla...' He thanked God that Tory was dead. He wanted to dig up that bastard's bones and beat them against a wall, he felt so choked.

'You can't imagine how it was. I was so confused. This was Tory, this was Pat. They played football with us, with Redmond and me and baby Kieron, out on the lawn. Like a normal family would do, with Mum and Dad looking on. And then at night, nothing was normal. Nothing at all.'

'I'm sorry,' said Rufus, shaken. That she had been through such a hell appalled him. He wished he had known. Wished there could have been something he could have done to help her. But the façade of family life had been so smooth, so polished. And beneath it – chaos.

'Ah,' she shrugged again, poured more whisky. 'It doesn't matter. All gone. All done and dusted.'

'I want to kill him,' said Rufus.

'Too late,' said Orla.

'Maybe I could catch up with Pat.'

She shook her head. 'No. I think he's gone too.'

So they had escaped their punishment. Meanwhile Orla was having to live with their crimes every day of her life. It must have been such a comfort to her, to have Redmond at her side, understanding, knowing the hell they'd both lived through. And now she'd lost him. No wonder she kept painting those mad pictures of him in her studio.

'You must miss Redmond an awful lot,' he said.

'I do. Every day. We had a good life in London for a while,' she said, her eyes misty with remembrance. 'We ran the manor, the two of us. After Tory was gone.'

'I know.'

'Still, there's one thing that gives me comfort.'

'What's that?'

'Knowing that we finished off that bitch Annie Carter. Too bad we didn't kill her sooner, before her Mafia friends organized the plane crash, before I lost Redmond.'

Rufus frowned. What was she *talking* about? 'When was this – what year?'

'Nineteen seventy,' said Orla. 'I'll never forget it.'

But he'd seen Annie Carter long after that, when he'd been working in London's East End.

'Orla,' he said, dry-mouthed.

'Don't worry, Rufus. I'm still alive, aren't I? Feck them all. I'm alive, and they're gone, Annie Carter included.'

'She's not.'

Orla's hand paused halfway through bringing the glass to her lips. Her eyes met his.

'What?' she said.

'She's not dead, Orla. Annie Carter's alive.'

27

Orla could only stare at him.

'*What* did you say?' she asked at last. All the colour had drained from her face, leaving it sickly pale. Her green eyes were huge as they stared into his.

'I said she's alive. I swear it, Orla. She's alive.'

Orla was shaking her head. 'No! That's not possible…'

'Possible or impossible, it's the truth. She was in London and she was alive. I saw her myself at one of the clubs there. It must have been back in seventy-three or four.' Rufus looked at Orla. 'How could you not know this? Surely you have contacts ...?'

Orla sat a long time in silence, trying to absorb this shattering news. Annie Carter, alive? *Alive,* while Redmond was dead?

She was clutching at her head, shaking it. 'No, no…' she moaned.

'Orla...' Rufus stretched a hand out, seeing her pain, wishing he'd kept his mouth shut.

She twitched away from his touch. 'No!' she shouted, jumping to her feet. She started to pace around the room, swigging whisky from her glass, eyes feverish with confusion and seething hatred. 'We left the scrapyard and we got Fergal out and he flew the plane. We had to run, London was finished for us. But first I wanted to make *sure* we'd got rid of her.'

'Sorry, Orla – you didn't. Last I saw, she was alive and well.'

Orla rushed to the table and slammed her glass down, hard. Whisky slopped over the rim.

'But Redmond's *dead,'* she hissed, leaning into him, her jaw clenched with fury. 'And she was behind it, I know she was. She was having an affair with that Mafia man, Barolli – he must have taken out a contract on us to avenge her death. The fuel dial was low, that's what Fergal said. And he'd only just refuelled. Someone must have cut the fuel line. We were *meant* to die that night.'

Rufus chewed his lip. He was startled by the intensity of her anger. The news of Annie Carter's survival had made her incandescent with rage. 'Look, Barolli might well have arranged it, but it wasn't to avenge her. To please her, perhaps? She married him. Moved to the States with him.'

'No! She should have *died,'* Orla howled in his face, spittle flying. 'She was meant to *die.'*

'Orla,' he said gently, 'she didn't die. She's alive.'

Now Orla's eyes grew distant. She slumped into her seat, drained the whisky in one gulp.

'I'll kill her,' she said with flat, bitter venom.

Rufus felt a chill creep up his spine. His thoughts flew to poor Rory, lying in the grave outside. If only he could have brought himself to *believe* that she would use the knife, he would have stepped in, snatched it off her. But the truth was, he hadn't wanted to think her capable of such an act. And his reluctance to see the truth had cost Rory his life. Rory's betrayal had been motivated not by greed but by the need to protect his son. At heart he was a good and true man, undeserving of the cruel end she had inflicted on him.

'I *have* to kill her,' said Orla, her lips drawn back, baring her teeth so that she seemed almost to snarl. In that moment, she seemed more animal than human. 'She took Redmond away from me,' she spat. 'It's *her* fault he's not with me now. I want to do to her what she's done to me: snatch her family from her, hurt her so that she wishes she were dead.'

Rufus said nothing. He knew now how much she had lost when Redmond was taken from her, how deep and damaging that hurt must be. He couldn't punish the other hurt she'd suffered; Pat and Tory were beyond his revenge. But he *could* see to it that the Carter bitch got what she deserved.

'Let me help you,' he said, his eyes burning into hers. 'I swear I'll do whatever it takes.'

Orla gazed at him, her eyes mad with the hunger for vengeance. Finally, she nodded. 'Good. I'm going to destroy Annie Carter, I'll make her pay for what she's done – and then I'm going to kill her. And this time she won't get away.'

28

New York, 1988

Annie Carter was standing among the gravestones in St John's Cemetry in Queens, New York. She was holding a wreath. She came here every time she crossed the Pond, to visit the grave of Constantine Barolli. It was a hot day, New York was sweltering, baking in summer heat. Oblivious, she was staring at the elaborately carved headstone.

Here lies Constantine Barolli

Despite the heat of the day, she shivered. She could still see him in her mind's eye, so clearly – the silver hair, the dark tan, the brilliant blue eyes, a collection of sharp suits worn with elegance and panache. He'd loved her. Constantine had steadied her, made her calmer. Whereas Max... .

Ah God, what was the point of thinking about *that?* She laid the wreath of red roses and green laurel upon the grave, then straightened with a sigh. She was tired and feeling low. She'd spent much of the past week at Annie's, the club in Times Square, making sure that everything was running smoothly. Which of course it was. She needn't have bothered really. She knew she was only killing time.

Her marriage to Max had been over for eight years and her relationship with their now adult daughter was still not good. She was just wondering what to do next with her life. Pestering Sonny Gilbert was unnecessary. For the past fifteen years, gay exuberant Sonny had been in charge of operations at her New York club, and with him at the helm all her concerns were rendered superfluous.

Maybe she ought to stop coming to the cemetery. It always depressed her. It had been a long time ago, so long ago and so far away. Constantine was gone. He wasn't here.

'Hey,' said a soft male voice, breaking into her thoughts.

She turned. And there was Constantine standing there, in the flesh.

Only of course it wasn't. Miracles didn't happen. *Shit* happened. Still, her heart gave a lurch as she saw the man standing a couple of paces away, tall and handsome as ever. He was wearing a thousand-dollar suit. His fair hair was lifting slightly in the hot breeze. His laser-blue eyes were smiling into hers.

As usual he had a bodyguard on either side. Sandor, of course – Eastern bloc, huge and black-haired, with only a rudimentary grasp of English but an unswerving devotion to his boss; the other man was slightly smaller but no less dangerous. Two more heavies were waiting by a long black car. Make one suspicious move toward him, and you'd be dead before you hit the ground.

He was holding two large bunches of red roses.

On his index finger glinted a ring, the gold one glittering with diamond stars. Annie had a flashback then, men bending to kiss the hand of the godfather who would help them, grant their wishes, ease their pain – at a price.

She took a gulp of air and stepped toward him. 'Hi,' she said.

He pulled her in tight against him, hugged her. Annie closed her eyes.

'How are you, Stepmom?' asked Alberto, Constantine's youngest son.

'Fine,' she lied.

'Going home today?'

'Yeah. In...' she glanced at her Rolex, 'about three and a half hours.'

'Give Layla my love then.'

Annie sighed, thinking of her lovely, problematical daughter, still as hostile as ever, still keeping her at arm's length. Unlike his siblings, Alberto had never resented her, never shown any hostility toward her. She had never said it – she never would – but *he* had been the main reason her marriage to Max had foundered. Max had never believed that her trips to the States were purely business. He'd been convinced that she went there to see Alberto, that she was having an affair with him. Because Alberto was almost the same age as her. And because he looked so much like her old love Constantine that it hurt.

Because, because, because...

She had fought tooth and nail to convince Max that this was not true, that it was him she loved. But slowly, steadily, his insane, stupid jealousy and his refusal to believe her had gnawed away at her patience, exhausted her, eaten away at her love.

She would not be confined. She would not live in a box of his devising, watched and worried over like some bloody *possession.* When she had finally snapped and flung the divorce word in his face, his eyes had been so hard, so implacable. He had said, 'OK, that's what you want? That's what we'll do. *Then you'll be free to fuck whoever you damned well like.*'

Even now, eight years on all from that hurt, that agony, she still felt sick, dizzy and dangerously near to tears when she thought of it. It had taken her a long time to get to grips with her grief over Max.

Of course Layla blamed *her*, not him. Layla thought that if her mother had stayed in London more, there would have been no divorce.

Annie sighed heavily. She had found some comfort here in the States with Alberto, but for God's sake, how could Max have thought such an absurd thing? Alberto was not her lover, she had never wanted that. He was like a son, a little brother maybe, to her. There was nothing sexual in their mutual affection.

Looking at Alberto's face, she could see that he too had suffered. He had aged in the few years since she'd last seen him. Time and knowledge and bitter experience had carved their indelible lines in his handsome face, making it harder, tougher: more fearsome. Now he was even more like his father. He was no longer the readily smiling youthful charmer. He had become the godfather.

'Just visiting the grave,' said Annie, indicating Constantine's last resting place. 'You?'

'Yeah. I come here to see them every week.'

Alberto walked forward and laid one of the bouquets in front of his father's headstone. He placed the other one on another of the graves there. Away in the distance, Annie saw a priest walking, hurrying between the headstones.

'It's been a long time,' she said.

'Yeah.'

Sandor and the others were scanning the graveyard. They watched the priest vanish from sight, then cast around for any other movement. *Dangerous men,* she thought. Her life had been full of them. If there was one thing she hoped for, it was that Layla would one of these days – *soon,* with luck – fall for some nice straight guy. That the lure of bad boys wouldn't affect her life as it had her mother's.

'You look tired,' she said to Alberto as he straightened up.

'Do I?'

'Everything OK?'

'As OK as it ever is,' he said.

'Alberto, what is it?'

He gave a smile. 'I've been thinking, that's all.'

'About what?'

'That this whole house of cards is about to come crashing down.'

Annie looked at him in alarm.

He shrugged lightly. 'Sometime soon, I might have to take off somewhere.'

'Why? What's happened?'

Alberto's eyes were smiling into hers. 'Stepmom,

I'm a very bad man. The Feds have levelled a lot of accusations against me. And my attorneys are working hard at batting them away, as usual. But I get the feeling, the strong feeling, that before long the game's gonna be up.'

Annie stared at him, worried. 'And these accusations are…?'

'How long you got? Money laundering, evading tax, sale of stolen goods, conspiracy, racketeering … oh, and maybe murder. If they can make it stick.'

'They can't – can they?'

'They move slow. We move faster. But some day, the axe is gonna fall. Regan wants a clean sheet, and that means taking care of outstanding business. And that's people like me.'

'The murder charge...'

'It's not a charge. Not yet.'

'Is that … would that be Lucco?'

'And others,' said Alberto.

Lucco was Alberto's older brother, Constantine's eldest son. He had vanished years ago, presumed dead. After that, Alberto had taken over the reins of the family firm. Annie hated Lucco, but nonetheless she had always wondered what happened to him.

Alberto's eyes grew colder. 'Lucco had no respect for anyone, living or dead. Everything our father had worked for, *slaved* for, he would have run straight into the ground.'

And you couldn't let that happen, thought Annie.

'You know, once I thought you and Daniella...' she started.

Daniella had been Lucco's wife.

'I thought that too.' He gave a small sigh. 'But what you just said about Lucco – obviously you think I had a hand in whatever happened to him. Well, Daniella thought the same thing. She couldn't live with that. It ate at her. She's a fine, honest woman, Daniella. Not long after he went missing, she returned home. She's remarried. And she's a mother.'

'I didn't know that.'

'Another world,' he said, and gazed off across the graveyard, his eyes wistful.

Annie watched him. Maybe he was seeing the sunlit island of Sicily, his ancestral home – the lemon groves, the hot sun beating down on dusty roads and lush vineyards. And Daniella, dark-haired and lovely, laughing, kissing her husband, playing with her children.

Annie reached out, touched his arm. She didn't want to see him come to grief.

'How long...?' she asked, meaning how long would it be before the Feds picked him up and charged him.

'Months, I think. Maybe weeks.'

Annie was horrified. 'You must have contingency plans?'

He shrugged. 'Aunt Gina's gone to Sicily. But me... I'd miss New York. I was born here.'

'Better an open sky and freedom,' said Annie. 'Are you winding things up?'

'Stepmom...' He turned to her with a smile. 'Don't ask. That way you know nothing, and it'll be safer for both of us.' His gaze intensified. 'You know what I wish?'

'No. Surprise me.'

'I wish before all *that* hits the fan, you'd move on. Find a nice guy. I'll have to approve him, of course.'

Annie shook her head. 'I don't want to move on, Alberto. The fact is, I've no desire to get serious with anyone, ever again. I have the Times Square club to run, and I have Layla. That's enough.'

He was staring at her.

'What?' she asked.

'I can't believe that would ever be enough, not for you.'

'No? Well, you're wrong. Come on,' she said, reaching out to take his arm. 'Let's get some coffee, I'm parched.'

'Coffee? I thought you English only drank tea?'

Annie caught the teasing note in his voice and hugged his arm against her as they walked toward the cars. His foot soldiers followed them.

God, how could she bear to lose him? She couldn't. It hurt her even to imagine it.

'I'm becoming Americanized,' she said.

And maybe she was. Maybe London wasn't home to her any more. Back in Britain, Margaret Thatcher was in her third term as Prime Minister, and Annie sensed there was big trouble brewing. Soon it might erupt on the streets of London. But ... she knew that as long as Layla was there – no matter how cool Layla was toward her – that was where she had to stay.

'Americanized? You? I don't believe it,' he smiled.

By tomorrow she'd be back in Holland Park, in her home. With her daughter. Her heart didn't lift at the thought, even though she knew it should.

29

London 1988

They were watching Layla Carter like cheetahs about to run down an impala.

'That's her,' said the man in the driver's seat.

The two men stared out of the steamy windows of the car, parked at the edge of the park. Thin sunlight was beginning to penetrate the dull grey clouds. They'd been waiting for over an hour; she was late this morning. They'd started to wonder if she was coming at all, but it was unlike her to break her routine.

Finally, here she was. A dark-haired young woman dressed in navy shorts, white sports bra and trainers was jogging steadily around the perimeter of the park, kicking her way with long easy strides through the dewy grass, her breath pluming out in the cool morning air.

'She'll check her watch when she reaches the shrubbery,' said the one behind the wheel, his eyes on the woman. 'One, two, that's it...' The woman slowed to a walk, looked at her watch. The driver, a big man with pudgy features, the build of a rugby prop forward and a shock of long curly red hair, turned to his companion. 'See that? A creature of habit.'

'So shall I do it, Rufus? Can I?' Dickon was getting excited. The coast was clear, there was no one else about. Perfect timing. She wasn't, he was disappointed to see, that young – not as young as *he* liked them – but he was still eager to get on and do it.

'No.' Rufus savoured the sight of the woman, the feeling that she was within his grasp. His for the taking, whenever he was ready. Orla would be pleased with him, he knew it.

'I could do it now,' said Dickon.

Rufus sent him a cold glare. Dickon was a kiddy-fiddling piece of shit who was bound straight for hell, but in the meantime he had his uses.

'Not yet,' he said. 'She'll run again in a minute. Let her. Then she'll be too tired to get away.'

Layla bent double, hands on knees, until she got her breath back. She was slow this morning. It irritated her. She could feel her heart pounding, and her head was thumping too. Last night's company dinner hadn't gone well, she'd drunk too much and now she felt awful.

Looking back, she was annoyed with herself. She hadn't even wanted to attend the dinner, but she knew she had to make the effort. After all, Bowdler and Etchingham, Chartered Accountants and Registered Auditors, had given her a chance, hired her despite all the whispers about her family background: the least she could do was turn up at their annual bash. But now, she wished she hadn't.

That moron Paisley, a trainee who had joined the firm at the same time as her, had been goading her for ages. He'd started in again last night, his whip-like tongue worse than usual because of the drink. And for the first time ever – yes, probably *also* because of the drink – she had risen to the bait.

'Caught your finger in the till, did you?' he'd asked her, his face red from too many mojitos.

Layla stared down at her left hand. She had only three fingers and one thumb on that hand. The smallest digit was missing. And Paisley thought that was very funny. Paisley knew, *everyone* knew, that her family background was ... well, not exactly law-abiding. Hence the crack about the till.

She had promised herself she would never lose her temper. Never sink to that fool's level. But she was sensitive about her missing finger. Something had snapped in her brain, and she had leaned in to Paisley, ignoring his foul breath, and hissed: 'Why don't you shut up, you fool?'

It wasn't much of an outburst. Her mother would have said: 'One more word out of *you*, shithead, and you'll find your dick caught in a mincer. You got that?'

But all the same Layla had registered the shock in his eyes. It was there and gone in an instant, before he recovered his usual smirk.

She was, after all, quiet diligent Layla Carter.

As a rule, she never bit back. She did her job. She was punctilious, polite, efficient. She had to be all that and more, because of who she was, where she came from. She wasn't her mother. She wasn't Annie Carter.

Layla checked her watch again. Nearly eight o'clock. She turned and set off for the house at a fast walk that became a steady jog. Tonight, her mother would return from New York, where she'd been checking in on the club management in Times Square – and no doubt checking in on Alberto, too.

Alberto.

Layla felt her heart flip painfully at the thought of him. She could see his face in her mind as clearly as if he were right there in front of her. Her first real memory of Alberto was when she was five years old. He'd hoisted her aloft and into his arms, tossing her into the air, grinning up at her.

Her stepbrother, Alberto Barolli.

And yet, as the years passed, she had become more and more aware that he *wasn't* related to her – or at least, not by blood, which was all that mattered. Constantine Barolli, the great Mafia don, had been a widower when he met Annie. His wife Maria had died in a hit, leaving him with three children – Lucco, Alberto and Cara – and no wife.

Enter Annie Carter.

Fabulously beautiful with her flawless olive-toned skin and her heavy fall of chocolate-brown hair. How could any man resist her?

And so Layla had become 'related' to Alberto.

Only not by blood.

Into her brain came another image. It made her frown. Annie and Alberto, together. Smiling and talking in that verbal shorthand they seemed to share. Layla could understand why her father was suspicious about the relationship. He had always been crazily possessive where Annie was concerned. Sometimes, the sheer heat between her parents had been so palpable it was embarrassing. Max had gone apeshit every time Annie insisted on shooting across to New York. Claiming it was business that took her there, not the fact that *Alberto* was in New York. No wonder Dad had ended the marriage and taken off abroad.

Their divorce had left a bitter taste for Layla. As a teenager she had half-blamed herself, and even now she desperately missed having Max here full-time. It had become a source of festering resentment between her and Annie, a solid wall that had grown higher, more impregnable, with each passing year. The fact was, Layla believed that if Annie hadn't spent so much time in the States, her marriage to Max wouldn't have ended. And Layla couldn't forgive her for that.

Layla's upbringing had at times been almost unbearably lonely, with no brothers or sisters and her dad half a world away. Only Mum had been constant in her life: and Layla had pushed her away.

She hadn't offered to pick her mother up from the airport. Why should she? There was always a chauffeur-driven car, a private jet, a flotilla of minders, fixers and flunkies hovering around to attend to her mother's every wish.

Layla was nothing like her mother.

Never would be.

She thought back to all the times her mother had abandoned her, just as she'd left Max, going abroad on 'business'. Or the times Annie had sent her away, to stay with Auntie Ruthie or

Jenny and Josh Parsons or anybody, so long as she was out of her mother's way.

Growing up, Layla had always known that she came second in the great scheme of things. First came Annie's career, the New York club she owned, the business. There was no doubt about it – her mother was a cold-blooded, controlling bitch.

But sometimes – though she hated to admit it – Layla wished she could have just a fraction of Annie Carter's gloss and glamour, a little of her *chutzpah.*

She quickened her pace, broke into a fast run.

Fuck it.

She was Layla Carter. She was dependable. She was bright and honest.

Wasn't that enough?

30

Layla ran hard, feeling exhilarated and by the end of it, very tired. And it was then that she saw the big man with the mop of flying red hair coming from the edge of the park toward her, *running* toward her. And the set expression on his beefy face told her his intentions were unfriendly.

For a moment she froze in total shock.

Then, gasping in a startled breath, Layla turned on her heel and fled.

'Hey!' he shouted.

She didn't stop. Her muscles were aching, her

chest was aching with effort, but she kept her legs pumping, making for the end of the park that led out on to the road that would take her home. She could hear his heavy footsteps pounding the ground behind her, could hear his breathing. He was gaining on her.

Shit.

What the hell was happening here?

Panic made her step hard on the gas. There was no one about, no one to help. She had no option but to keep running. She could feel herself flagging though. Could feel her energy draining away. Too much heavy food and too much alcohol last night. And fear was making her chest tight. She was struggling to breathe. Fighting to draw oxygen in, feed her aching, exhausted muscles.

Run. Just run dammit.

She was fit. She was young. She was strong.

Come on. You can do it.

Layla glanced over her shoulder – and felt a bolt of terror shoot up through her entire body.

He was only a couple of metres behind her, and accelerating. He was reaching out to grab her.

Layla jinked like a thoroughbred refusing a fence, swerving left, out of his reach. He stumbled forward, swearing, wrong-footed.

She ran on, fear giving her extra speed, a voice inside her head repeating, *I can't keep this up.*

Would she make it home, get to her front door?

And – oh Christ – where was the door key? It was in her trainer where she always put it. She was going to have to stop, get it out, stick it in the lock, open the door ... and he was so close. *Too* close.

Her pulse was hammering. She was sweating and straining and her legs felt like lead. She was tired. Nearly done for. And having been wrong-footed once, he had stepped up the pace, determined not to let her escape him next time.

This was what happened to people, they were snatched and never seen again.

A memory stirred: a cellar, a knife, hostile strangers who had hurt her.

No. Not again.

He was close behind her as she tore out of the park and on to the pavement, so close that she could hear his every breath. Any minute now, and he would make another grab for her. The road they were on was lined with parked cars. If he succeeded in dragging her into a car, that would be it.

She could see the house now, the big William and Mary mansion with its dark-blue door. Lengthening her stride, she willed herself to keep going. Every step jarred her body, and he had closed the gap still further, his hand was snatching at her shoulder. Sobbing with panic, she was almost at the bottom of the steps, but he was snatching at her, she could feel his fingers on her shoulder, trying to get a grip.

Layla knew that she would never make it up the steps, would never get the key in the door.

She was finished.

Except...

She stopped dead. Dropped to her knees, curled into a tight ball. Felt a huge impact on her back, heard a loud 'Feck!' and then her pursuer went flying over the top of her.

Irish?

She couldn't even pause to consider that. Scrambling to get her trainer off, trembling fingers fumbling to fasten on the key, she saw him hit the pavement hard. There was a dull thud and she heard all the breath go out of him in one almighty *whoosh.*

Gripping the key tightly, she dropped the trainer. He was getting to his knees, cursing with a steady monotony that unnerved her. She stumbled to her feet. He was glaring at her with murderous eyes. There was blood around his mouth. He spat out a tooth, broken in the impact when he hit the pavement.

He lurched toward her, grabbed her ankle.

Layla shrieked and hit his face with the key. He let out a yell. Released his grip. She bolted up the steps, flung herself at the door. Tried to get the key in the lock. Her hands were shaking so much she couldn't get the damned thing in.

And he was coming up the steps.

She could hear him, so close now, she had nowhere left to run.

Panting like a hunted animal, she found the keyhole at last, turned the key, pushed, *shoved* the door open and fell inside, then smashed the door back, hard as she could against his body.

He was too big for her, too strong...

He was pushing the door open, she was trying to get it shut, they were both heaving and swearing and straining.

Layla still had the key in her hand. She took a sobbing breath and reached round the door and stabbed him straight in the eye with it. He screamed and floundered back, losing his footing.

Layla slammed the door shut.

Locked it. Slapped on the chain.

She slid, quivering and panting, down the wall beside the door and sat there on the cold marble of the hall with one trainer on and a bent key in her hand. He hammered on the door once, hard.

Layla scuttled away from it with a shriek of fear.

Then there was silence.

What the hell was that?

Slowly she pushed herself to her feet. She wasn't going out to collect her other trainer. No way. She limped up the stairs, shaking like an old woman, heading for the shower.

'What the fuck happened?' Dickon asked when his companion flung the driver's door open and fell into the seat.

Rufus slammed the door shut and sat there, blood trickling down his face, one eye scrunched shut.

'Little fecker got away,' he gasped, touching a hand to his watering eye. 'How does my eye look? Hurts like buggery. She hit me. Is it OK?'

'You were meant to grab her – what went wrong?'

'She was too fecking fast.' Too fast and too clever. He wasn't about to say *that*, though. He had some pride. He was mopping at his bloody mouth with a handkerchief. 'Shit, I'm bleeding.'

'She hit you, did she? So you were close enough to grab her.'

'Look,' snarled Rufus, 'it didn't work out, that's all. We'll do it next time.'

'Yeah, but next time she'll expect it.'

'Shut the feck up, will you?'

'And I tell you, *she* ain't going to be happy about this.'

That evening, Layla opened the front door, peering nervously up and down the road before venturing on to the steps. No one ran at her, no one shouted. She sprinted down and grabbed the trainer, shook the rain from it. As she did so, a tiny green paper four-leaf clover fell out, and fluttered to the ground. She picked it up. Stared at it. And then she raced inside, locked the door and put the chain on.

31

Annie Carter's old friend Dolly Farrell was in her flat above the Palermo club, court shoes kicked off, pale-pink suit jacket with the big shoulder pads flung aside, skirt unbuttoned, feet up on the sofa, taking a well-earned mid-evening break when she got the call.

'Damn that thing,' she said as the phone started ringing.

She loved her job and she'd been doing it for a long, long time. Back in the day, she'd managed all three of the Carter clubs, but these days it was just the Palermo. Her old mate Ellie Brown was in charge at the Shalimar, with her husband Chris, while Gary Tooley was overseeing the running of the Blue Parrot.

The clubs had seen their fair share of re-inventions over the years. They'd gone from old-world nightclubs to discos, and now they were lap-dancing venues. Trade was good. Because the prices were high, the punters were, on the whole, very well-behaved. But Jesus, couldn't a girl get a moment's peace...?

Dolly swung her legs to the floor, patted her big blonde (just a little grey in there now) up-do and picked up the phone. And heard Layla telling her something unbelievable. So maybe she hadn't heard her properly.

'*What* did you just say?' Dolly clamped the phone more firmly to her right ear and covered her left to stifle the din coming up from the club below, where Whitney was belting out 'I Wanna Dance With Somebody'. 'Speak up a bit Layla, can't you? The line's bad and the music's doing my head in.'

'I *said,*' repeated Layla, 'that there was a sort of incident today, Auntie Dolly. In the park.'

'Wha– An incident? What sort of incident?'

'A man tried to grab me.'

Dolly sat down sharply, her stomach tight with anxiety. She wasn't Layla's aunt, not really; Layla was her goddaughter, but she'd been calling her 'Auntie Dolly' since she was small. '*Grab* you?' she echoed, stunned.

'I got away. Only just, though.'

Dolly took a breath. 'You told your mother about this?'

'She's in the States, due home in a few hours. I didn't want to worry her.' Layla was about to mention the shamrock, but stopped herself. That was one weirdness she didn't feel inclined to share. Dolly might *really* freak out if she did.

'You told the police?'

'No.'

'You alone in the house?'

'Rosa's here.'

Like *that* was reassuring. Rosa the housekeeper was ancient, deaf and panicked at the least provocation. 'Does she know what happened?'

'I couldn't tell her that.'

'I'll give Steve a ring.'

'No. Don't. It was probably just some pervert...'

'Just some pervert?' Dolly snapped. 'And is that something to be taken lightly? I'll call Steve, he'll–'

'No. Don't. I wanted to talk to someone, that's all, so I phoned you. Please don't go calling Steve.'

Dolly rolled her eyes in exasperation. She loved Layla to bits, but the girl was so straight it made your teeth ache. She admired her for making her own way in the world, for working hard at being her own person – and putting up with the taunts that went with the territory.

It couldn't be easy for her. Layla utterly rejected the sort of life her parents led. She refused to work in the family business, even though her Dad would have liked her to. It seemed to Dolly that Layla's whole life so far had been about distancing herself from her parents. Not that surprising, given that Annie had once been in court for running a posh knocking shop. And her father was Max Carter, who was … well, never mind.

She didn't like the sound of this 'incident' one bit. Much as Layla tried to, she couldn't escape her family connections. And in her parents' world, there were times when muscle was called for. This seemed like such a time to Dolly.

'Promise you won't call him,' said Layla. 'Promise me.'

'Are you going to tell your father about this?'

'Yeah. Maybe. I don't know.'

'Layla.'

'I don't want trouble.'

Sounds like you got it anyway, thought Dolly.

'Tell him,' ordered Dolly.

'I don't–'

'Layla!' Dolly's voice was sharp. 'Wake up and smell the bloody coffee. You are who you are. Which means you got to be careful. So tell him. OK?'

Layla sighed. 'OK.'

'Tell him.'

'OK, I will.' She wouldn't.

'Be careful.'

'Yeah, yeah.'

'Night then, honey.'

'Night.'

32

'You know what, Rufus? You can be such a fucking fool sometimes.'

'I thought...' Rufus was floundering under this onslaught. She was pacing back and forth in front of him, spitting with rage. News of his failed attempt to snatch Layla Carter had not gone down well.

'I told you I'd see to this. That I would be in charge here, that *I* would decide what was to happen, when it was to happen.'

'But–'

'You've tipped them off! How could you be so bloody stupid?'

'I haven't tipped them off,' he objected. He felt wounded, through and through. His eye was smarting, he was aching all over from where he'd struck the pavement. The girl had run rings round him and now his Orla was giving out about it, like he was a moron.

Rufus the DOOFUS.

But he'd been trying to *help,* that was all.

She stopped her pacing and, breathing hard, came to a halt in front of his chair.

'Here's what's going to happen,' she said, her eyes wild with anger and determination. '*I'm* going to do it.'

'I'll come with–'

'*No.* You won't come with me. I go in alone.

And I do it, OK? I do it.'
'When?'
'Tonight.'

33

Annie Carter awoke in darkness. Pitch-black, all-enveloping. She was completely disorientated for a split second, before she got her bearings. She was in the master suite in the Holland Park house in London. And she was – of course – alone.

Into her brain came tumbling a multitude of alone-related thoughts, Alberto, Layla, Max.

She flinched.

Max.

Eight years, and it could still cut like a knife, how he'd hurt her. She threw back the covers, sat up, shutting off that train of thought. No good going there, none at all.

Something had awakened her. She pressed the button on top of the alarm clock and the dim light illuminated the dial. Two twenty-five a.m. She sat there and groaned. She'd only got home a couple of hours ago; jetlagged and exhausted, she was desperate for sleep but her brain was in overdrive, turning over problems instead of letting her relax.

Alberto.

She put her head in her hands, thinking about everything he'd told her as they'd stood together at the graveside. Was he going to vanish from her life one day soon, never to be seen again?

Give my love to Layla, he'd said when she left him.

Dammit, Annie couldn't even give Layla *her* love, let alone his. She'd flown home and there'd been no hugs, no kisses from her daughter. There never had been. Only Max got those, she guessed. It was only a guess – while Layla visited Max several times a year in Barbados, and he came to London occasionally to meet up with their daughter, Annie hadn't caught so much as a glimpse of him since the divorce.

She knew Layla blamed her. It had hurt Layla terribly, being parted from Max, but Annie had got custody and so it was a done deal. And now there was this great yawning *gulf* between mother and daughter. Annie seemed incapable of reaching across it, to touch Layla as she wished she could, to see her daughter smile at her with unguarded love instead of sullen wariness, to be vulnerable and sweet as she had been when she was a little girl.

At the moment, Layla was in the adjoining room, asleep. Or so Annie had assumed. But maybe it was Layla who'd woken her up. Maybe she couldn't sleep either. Annie felt a surge of maternal pride as she thought of how hard Layla worked, how conscientious she was. Who'd have thought a kid of hers would end up a trainee accountant? Wherever Layla had got that weird gift for figures, it certainly wasn't from her.

From Max, must be, thought Annie.

Again she felt that stab of pain. No, she wasn't going to think about him. She was *over* that. She had even dated other men since the divorce. Well, two. Just two. Disasters, both of them, and best forgotten. Her mind spun away from that and back to Layla. Her terribly strait-laced and difficult-to-know daughter, who poured all her energy into her job. Maybe Layla couldn't sleep because something work-related was bothering her? Not that she would ever confide in her mother. Her father? Yes. Her mother, forget it.

Annie thumped the pillows and lay down. Her relationship with her own mother had been unhappy. Maybe there was a pattern there? Connie Bailey had been a single mum. Her husband had taken off for pastures new, leaving her with two young daughters – Annie and her older sister Ruthie – and bills to pay. And the drink.

Oh God yes, the drink.

People were always saying, *The best years of your life, growing up, aren't they? Happy childhood years.*

Annie's childhood had been far from happy. Her mother had detested her, preferring gentle, quiet, well-behaved Ruthie.

Maybe I reminded her of Dad, thought Annie.

It was too late to ask her mum about any of that. Mum was gone.

Her memories of her mother were not fond. They were of Connie lying on the sofa, drunk out of her skull, and the rent man or the milkman or the baker or *some* fucker banging on the front door demanding to be paid.

Her and Ruthie would be cowering behind the sofa pretending they were out. There was always fear, a constant endless nagging fear, that one day they would come home and Connie would finally have downed one drink too many and seen herself off to that great ever-open bar in the sky.

Annie sighed heavily. No wonder she'd no taste or tolerance for alcohol. She had hoped for better from her relationship with Layla. But – oh, and this was hard to admit, even to herself – they didn't get on. Unable to break down the wall Layla had put up between them, Annie had lashed out in frustration, saying hurtful things – things that she didn't mean and wished she could take back.

You're always working, don't you know how to have fun?

That colour doesn't suit you.

Can't you do something with your hair?

Annie turned on to her side, berating herself.

Stupid.

She *knew* that her criticism would only make Layla withdraw further behind that big, invisible, *fucking* wall.

Clunk.

She stiffened, every sense alert.

There! Somebody was definitely moving about downstairs.

Probably it was Layla. But Layla was such a deep sleeper, usually. Even as a child, she would lay immobile all night, her bed as neat in the morning as it had been the night before. And Rosa, their ancient housekeeper, was never downstairs at night; she had her own little self-contained apartment at the side of the house.

What if it's neither of them? What if someone's broken in? suggested a tiny voice in her brain.

Her heartbeat was deafening. She wanted to

put the light on, to drive back the darkness. But that might alert whoever was downstairs if they glanced up and saw the strip of light under her door. No lights then. Instead, she reached for the bedside drawer.

Max's side.

Banishing the thought, she slid open the drawer, groped inside, felt the cold hard outline of the Smith & Wesson revolver there. It was loaded. It was an old, old gun, but effective. Scary to see, scary to shoot too. It kicked like a mule. But she wasn't going to be firing it, she just wanted to frighten the shit out of any intruder and send them running for the hills.

She sat up, mouth dry, pulse accelerating, felt in the darkness for her robe and slipped it on, belted it. Then she took hold of the gun. Barefoot, she crept to the door that connected her room to Layla's, and turned the key to open it.

She grasped the doorknob, twisted it. Pushed the door open and passed inside. She could hear more noises coming from downstairs. She knew this house, every creak, every moan it made while the wind howled around the eaves, every protest the old floorboards uttered when someone stepped upon them.

Someone was moving down there, quietly. But not quietly enough.

Still in darkness, Annie crossed to the bed. 'Layla!' she hissed, and shook her daughter's shoulder. Layla turned and Annie could see her eyes in the dimness of the moonlight opening wide, her mouth opening too. Annie clamped a hand over it. 'Hush,' she said urgently. 'There's somebody downstairs.'

Layla's whole body stiffened. Annie took her hand away.

'What?' Layla whispered, scrambling up on the bed, getting into her dressing gown.

They both heard it then.

Someone was moving.

Someone was coming up the stairs.

'What should we do?' hissed Layla.

'Give them a surprise,' said Annie with more boldness than she felt.

Layla was staring at the outline of the gun in her mother's hand. She shook her head. 'No! I'll call the police.' She started to reach for the phone on the bedside table.

Annie grabbed her hand. 'We don't have time for that. They could hear one of the extensions pick up. And if they hear you speaking, they'll know we're awake. Come on.'

Keeping hold of Layla's arm, Annie steered her to the connecting door to the master suite. They passed inside, then Annie locked that door. Which left only the main door into the hallway for anyone to come through. And they were going to be ready for that.

Annie took Layla across to the door into the hall. She tucked herself in behind it, and placed Layla behind her. She squeezed Layla's hand. And then focused all her attention on the door.

Don't come in here, she thought. *Please, please don't.*

But the footsteps were coming closer. She froze into stillness, raised the gun – and watched the doorknob start to turn.

34

Layla gave a frightened gasp. Annie felt the hair on the back of her neck stand on end. Whoever it was, they were coming in here.

Hit him with the gun or fire it?

Fire it and get herself banged up on a murder charge? No. Hit him. Hit him *hard.* She wished she had the kiyoga, the martial arts weapon Tony had given her years ago, but it was long-forgotten, in a cupboard somewhere.

Now the door was swinging inward.

The two women froze, held their breath.

A tall dark outline appeared, moving cat-footed on the floor of the master suite. As his head came into view, Annie struck out with the gun. But the intruder had fast reactions and must have sensed it coming. He turned his head away so that the weapon caught him only a glancing blow. Then, knowing they were there, he jammed his shoulder into the door, driving Annie back into Layla.

Caught off balance, Annie staggered, fell to her knees, dropped the gun.

Layla screamed as the intruder flung himself upon them. Annie, unable to reach the gun resorted to kicking out at him as hard as she could, her face a mask of terror and fury. He stumbled, crashing into Layla and sending her sprawling to the floor. When she looked up, her mother was grappling with the intruder. Wild-eyed with horror, Layla thought she saw the flash of moonlight on a knife.

The gun was lying on the floor where Annie had dropped it. As the man knocked her mother down again, looming over them both, Layla didn't hesitate: she snatched it up, and fired.

The shot was deafening in the enclosed space of the bedroom. The intruder cannoned backwards, hitting the wall and then sliding down to the floor. Layla, caught off guard by the weapon's recoil, staggered backwards, tripping over Annie's legs. Practically gibbering with fear, she groped her way upward and threw the switch.

Light flooded the master suite.

'Oh my God,' she gasped out as she stared at the man lying half in and half out of the doorway. He was dressed all in black, his head covered by a hood with slits for the eyes and mouth. There was a rip in the hood and blood was showing through where Annie had hit him with the gun. And there was a lot more blood, trickling thickly down the wall where he had collided with it when he was shot. A wet stain was spreading across his chest.

'Oh no,' said Layla, staring down at him. '*My God,* I shot him,' she wailed.

Annie was coming to her feet, half-supporting herself against the wall. She felt horribly unsteady. She too was staring at the fallen man, wondering what to do next.

Not a man, she thought. *More like a boy.*

The body was tall, but now she could see it was slender, too.

Her eyes were caught by the wicked-looking knife lying on the floor near one of the man's gloved hands.

She swallowed hard, feeling the dry heaves start at the back of her throat. Shakily, she kicked the knife away, in case he should reach out, get hold of it again. He'd come here to kill one or both of them. *Her,* of course. Layla hadn't done a thing wrong in her entire life. Whereas she ... well, she...

'Wait,' she said suddenly.

She was staring at the man.

'Wait? What do you mean, wait?' Layla was babbling in panic. 'For God's sake, Mum – I've *shot* him.' Her eyes went down to the gun, still in her hand, and she dropped it with a grimace of disgust.

Annie snatched the gun up and approached the fallen boy. She glanced at Layla, who was deathly pale, her skin coated with a sheen of sweat. She wanted to embrace her daughter, hug her, reassure her, but she stopped herself. Even now she was afraid Layla would only shrug her off, the way she always did.

She knelt at the boy's shoulder and pressed the muzzle of the gun firmly against the side of his head. Then she reached down with trembling fingers and felt his neck, searching for a pulse.

'Is he...?' asked Layla, looking like a ghost, she was so white.

'No pulse,' said Annie, feeling her stomach clench and churn.

A stranger had come in the night armed for murder. That stranger was now dead. But even in her current state of shock she knew there was something about this intruder, something wrong.

Setting the gun carefully aside, Annie started tugging at the woollen hood.

'What are you doing?' shrieked Layla. 'I can't believe this…'

'Quiet,' said Annie sharply. 'Give me a moment.'

'Mum, I've *killed* him.'

'Well, at least he hasn't killed *us*,' snapped Annie, giving the hood a final tug. It came loose, revealing a thick heavy fall of red hair.

Annie Carter slumped to her haunches and stared at the corpse. 'Holy *shit*,' she murmured.

The face of their attacker was revealed. Milk-pale, with green eyes still half-open, frozen in death. Not a man's face at all.

Layla had shot a *woman*.

Annie stared at the woman's face.

Stunned, Layla turned to Annie. 'Who is it? Mum?'

'I know her,' said Annie, dazed with shock. 'No, this isn't possible, this isn't possible.' Annie was shaking her head in disbelief. 'It *can't* be.'

'For God's sake, *who is it?*' asked Layla desperately.

Annie took a breath.

'That's Orla Delaney,' she said.

35

'Who ... who's Orla Delaney... Oh shit, I'm going to be sick,' said Layla, turning to dash into the bathroom.

Annie moved away from the body and stood staring, arms wrapped around herself, trying to stop the shaking. Every muscle in her body was trembling with the aftershock. She couldn't tear her eyes away from that face – a face she'd hoped never to see again: the hated face of Orla Delaney.

There had been a time when a gangland map of London would have shown the Richardsons and the Frasers in control of the South, the Regans the West, the Krays ruled Bethnal Green, the Nashes the Angel, while the Carters had Bow and the Delaney mob ran Battersea, with a foothold in Limehouse down by the docks.

The Delaneys made the mistake of trying to expand their Limehouse territory, which meant stepping on Carter toes. One by one the Delaneys had paid for it, too. Until all that was left were the twins, Orla and Redmond. They had targeted her, made it personal. She'd known she would never be safe while they were alive. And then finally, finally, she'd thought they were gone forever. She had believed that Constantine had finished them. A plane crash. It was in the papers. Their plane had gone down in the Irish

Sea. No survivors. That was back in 1970, a year she would never forget. Constantine had told her it was done. The nightmare was over. And she'd believed him.

But ... this was *Orla*. There was no mistaking that face.

She could hear Layla, retching weakly in the bathroom. A chilling bolt of horror shot through her as she thought of what *could* have happened tonight. If she hadn't woken, Orla would have slit her throat. And then she would have moved on and done Layla too.

Annie gave a violent shudder and thrust the images of bloody mayhem from her mind.

'What are we going to do?' asked Layla at her shoulder.

Annie half-turned. Layla's face was white and tear-stained with shock. Her eyes were darting everywhere, she was trying not to look at the corpse but her eyes seemed to be pulled back to it, time and again.

'Oh God, I did it, I shot her,' she said, starting to cry in earnest.

Annie hesitated for a moment. Then she put an arm around her daughter's trembling shoulders. 'You saved my life,' she said simply.

Layla nodded, glancing uneasily at Annie. Tonight, they were united – if only in fear and desperation. Layla stepped away, shrugging off her mother's embrace.

'What are we going to do...?' she moaned.

Try to figure out what the fuck she was doing here after all this time. How she could have survived, thought Annie.

Orla Delaney should have been long dead.

Yet here she was, dead on Annie's bedroom floor – at Layla's hand.

Annie looked at her daughter, concerned. Layla was so straight. She even *dressed* straight – all those dull beiges and pale greys. Her hair pulled starkly back, never worn loose. Her face with its constant half-angry expression, never enhanced with make-up. Layla would not raise a hand to anyone. She had fired the gun in panic, not meaning to harm, not meaning to kill. But she had. And it had shaken her to the core, Annie could see that.

'We have to get rid of the body,' said Annie.

Layla stared at her mother as if she was mad. 'No,' she said, 'we have to phone the police.'

'That's the last thing we should do,' said Annie.

'What are you *saying?*' A strained half-laugh emerged from Layla. 'She came in here with a *knife*. The police will understand...'

Annie was shaking her head.

'Understand? We're in possession of an unlicensed firearm. They're not going to understand *that*, Layla. If she'd gone for us with the knife and we'd knocked her out, overcome her, that's just about excusable in a court of law. But this?'

'No, no...' Layla was talking rapidly now. 'No, wait. We were provoked...'

'Yes. We were. But we *killed* her. With a gun we shouldn't have had in the first place. That's not reasonable force. The law wouldn't see it as such.'

'Do you think Rosa heard the shot?' asked Layla suddenly.

'No I don't. She's deaf as a post.' Annie stared down at Orla. How had she managed to get inside the building without triggering the house alarm? Hadn't Rosa set it, as she usually did?

'No, I ... I'm going to phone the police...' Layla was saying breathlessly, stumbling to the phone by the bed.

She picked up the phone and started dialling. Annie crossed the room quickly, snatched it from her hand.

'No.' She grabbed Layla's shoulder and shook her. 'You want to spend the next part of your life banged up in a cell?'

'It won't come to that.'

'Layla, honey, it *will.*' Annie stared into her daughter's terrified eyes. 'Phone the police and I promise you, one of us is going down for this.'

'One of us? *You* didn't shoot her.'

Annie shook her again. 'Listen. If you insist on doing this crazy thing, I swear I'll wipe your prints off that gun and put mine all over it. I'll say it was me who pulled the trigger, not you.'

Layla slumped on to the bed and put her head in her hands. She was quiet for long moments, then she let her hands fall into her lap. Her eyes slid to the dead woman.

'You said her name was Orla...?' she asked unsteadily. The hot iron scent of blood was making her feel sick again. She'd killed someone. She couldn't get to grips with it, couldn't begin to believe that it had happened.

Annie sat down on the bed too.

'Orla Delaney. She used to run a gang with her twin brother. I thought she was dead, years ago.'

'She was going to kill you. She really was.'

Annie nodded.

Layla swallowed hard. 'OK. So we can't call the police. What do we do?'

'We call Steve Taylor. We need his help with this. He'll clean this up,' said Annie.

Steve worked for Max on the security side of things. She knew he would report back to Max, but she didn't see what else she could do.

Layla turned to Annie, incredulous. Her mother never seemed fazed, no matter what life threw at her; she remained clear-headed, able to think things through. Confronted with a crisis, Annie Carter simply moved up into another gear – a gear most people didn't even possess.

'OK,' said Layla finally.

'Good.' Annie dialled Steve's number.

While she waited for him to pick up, Annie's eyes rested on the corpse. Once Steve got rid of Orla's body and dumped Max's gun, would that be an end to this?

Yes. It would. She told herself that, refused to even contemplate any other outcome.

This would finish it, once and for all.

Oh yeah? asked that niggling voice in her head. *But if Orla's here, if she survived the plane crash that was supposed to have wiped out the Delaney threat ... where's Redmond?*

She shivered. Orla was bad, but her twin was truly the stuff of nightmares.

'H'lo?' said Steve's voice at last, fogged with sleep.

'It's Annie,' she said, and she told him what had happened.

‘I’m on my way,’ he said.

Annie put the phone down. She went to Layla, squeezed her shoulder reassuringly.

With nothing to do but wait, they both stood in silence, looking at the body on the floor.

How did she survive? wondered Annie. She stared at the dead, glazing green eyes. *Orla, how did you do it? Or is it true that the devil takes care of his own?*

‘You don’t think this could have anything to do with what happened to me in the park, do you?’ Layla blurted.

Annie’s eyes whipped from the corpse to her daughter. ‘What?’

‘Oh Jesus, maybe I should have told you...’ Layla was clutching at her head.

‘Told me *what?*’ Annie demanded.

‘About the man who tried to snatch me.’

36

Steve Taylor, Eric and Jackie Tulliver turned up half an hour after Annie made the call.

Annie and Layla had taken the time before the troops arrived to get dressed. Layla was now sitting on her bed in the adjoining room to Annie’s, with the connecting door firmly shut. She didn’t want to look at what she’d done, she didn’t want to know about it. She was shivering with shock. She still felt sick. When she heard the low male voices mingling with her mother’s in the master suite, she glanced up fearfully at the door.

Minutes passed, though it seemed like hours to Layla.

Finally, looking pale but otherwise composed, Annie came through the door and closed it behind her. 'Body's gone. They're cleaning the room up.'

'The gun?'

'They've taken that away, and the spare ammunition.'

'What will they do with her?'

Annie looked at Layla. Usually pin-sharp, Layla was acting dazed. As well she might. And what was this about a man in the park? Layla had refused to elaborate, beyond saying that some guy had made a grab for her. She'd been in such a state that when she said she couldn't talk about it now, that it would have to wait until the morning, Annie had no choice but to back off, though her mind was in turmoil over what it could mean.

'They'll get rid of the body. It *was* Orla,' said Annie, almost talking to herself. 'She was one of twins ... Orla and Redmond Delaney.'

Annie felt as if her head was about to spin off with all the questions whizzing around in her brain. How come Orla hadn't died in the plane crash? Why had she waited eighteen years to show up here, intent on doing what she had tried and failed to accomplish back in 1970 – to kill Annie? Worst of all – where was Redmond? The thought of him skulking around London was terrifying. Shit, maybe he had planned this. Maybe he was out there right now, waiting for his twin to return. And when she didn't...

'So where's Redmond?' asked Layla. She had

never seen her mother frightened before, but she was seeing it now. 'What's so bad about Redmond?'

Annie shook her head. 'You really don't want to know.'

'What is he, some sort of freak?'

'All right! He's a pervert who loves inflicting pain. It turns him on, hurting people.'

Layla's pallor increased as Annie's words hit home. 'This is a nightmare,' she said, burying her head in her hands.

Annie sat down beside her daughter. 'No. Nightmare's over,' she said.

The truth was she didn't believe that for a minute. Orla's turning up tonight had re-awakened old traumas, old half-buried fears.

'I wish Dad was here,' said Layla.

Annie found herself wishing that, too. But only for an instant. She'd schooled herself well since the divorce. Now she was convinced of one simple fact: she could live without that bastard Max Carter.

But Orla Delaney had come back, a ghost from the past, and the vision of Orla lying dead was still stamped on Annie's brain.

How did you do it, Orla?

How?

37

'Why didn't you *tell* me?' asked Annie.

Annie and Layla were in the dining room the morning after the break-in, eating breakfast. Or at least trying to. A sense of unreality was gripping them both. Annie couldn't stop thinking, *Orla, that was Orla. And if Orla was alive ... does that mean Redmond is too?*

Perverted, ice-cool Redmond Delaney, who'd once left her for dead...

She felt a shiver take hold, had to set the cup down before the hot liquid spilled. The mere thought of Redmond terrified her. Orla's survival had to be a fluke, surely. Redmond *couldn't* have lived. Constantine had arranged things. And Constantine rarely made mistakes.

Oh no? He'd got himself murdered, hadn't he? He can't have been infallible, else he'd have uncovered the plot to kill him.

'Eat something,' said Annie. 'You'll feel better.'

Layla looked at the toast, the tea. Annie was forcing down a slice or two, sipping from the cup. Layla couldn't. She'd killed someone, shot them dead. Her mind was constantly replaying the moment the bullet hit Orla – then it would flinch away in horror. All that blood, smeared on the wall. She kept hoping that last night had been an awful dream. That at any moment she would wake up to the real world, and everything would be right again.

Reluctantly she picked up a slice of toast and started buttering it. 'I couldn't tell you about the man in the park – you were in the States,' she said.

'Bullshit. Someone tries to *attack* you and you don't call me?' Annie was incensed.

'You were due home that night, I wouldn't have been able to get hold of you. I told Auntie Dolly,' said Layla.

'You did *what?'*

'I told Dolly.'

Annie sipped her tea, trying to put a lid on her anger and the panic welling inside her. She glanced at Layla's hand, at the missing finger. Annie would never forget the despair she'd felt when her baby girl was taken from her, the horror when the kidnappers delivered her child's finger in a box. She had done things then she hadn't believed she was even capable of; there was *nothing* she wouldn't have done to get her baby back. And now someone had targeted her daughter again. That bastard who tried to grab her could have been Redmond. If he'd succeeded...

'You told Dolly and she didn't tell *me?'* said Annie.

'She wanted to tell Steve.' Layla threw the toast down on to the plate. She glared at her mother. 'Look, I'm not used to all this, I can't even think straight! But this is what you do, isn't it?'

'Meaning?'

'Meaning all *this:* lurking in shadows, getting rid of bodies in the middle of the night. I don't know about any of this, I don't *want* to.'

Annie was still thinking about Dolly. 'So how

come Dolly didn't tell Steve about this bloke in the park?'

'I made her promise not to. I didn't want to *start* anything.' Layla eyed her mother in something approaching disgust.

All her life she'd fought against being part of that world. Her mother, the Mafia queen. Her father, the gangland boss. Layla was proud *not* to be a part of that. The incident in the park had seriously rattled her. It was a reminder that the shadowy world she had resisted for so long was merely a footstep away. Her first instinct had been denial, to pretend it never happened. The last thing she'd wanted was to stir up a hornet's nest by raising the alarm.

'There was something else,' she said at last. 'Something weird. When I went out to pick up my trainer, there was a little paper shamrock in it.'

Annie hitched in a breath. *A shamrock?* She stared at Layla. No use ranting and raving. She could see that Layla was upset enough as it was. But she was going to have to do something about this, and quick.

'You know, like a four-leaf clover? Do you think there could be a connection between that and Orla breaking in here?' Layla asked. She was peering at the buttered toast as if it was going to rear up and bite her.

'It's possible,' said Annie. Orla and a shamrock – oh, there was a connection, no doubt about it.

'What should we do?'

'You have to go into work?'

Layla nodded.

'Phone in sick.'

'I can't do that.'

'You bloody well can. Until I find out what's going on here, we're not take any chances.'

'But–'

'That's not a suggestion, Layla. That's an order.'

Layla drank her tea and said nothing. Much as she resented her mother barking out commands, after what happened last night she was – grudgingly – glad to have her here, taking charge.

Annie stood up.

'What are you going to do?' asked Layla.

'This and that,' said Annie, heading for the door.

'And what does *that* mean?' demanded Layla.

'What it says,' said Annie. 'Stay here. No running around the park or anything like that.'

'I wasn't going to.'

'Good. Use the gym in the basement if you want. And there's the outside pool. Steve's left one of the boys on the door, his name's Bri. You'll be quite safe here.'

'You're saying I can't go out?'

'I'm saying it's wisest not to. Seriously, Layla: stay inside. I'll be back in about an hour.'

38

By dawn Rufus was climbing the walls of the rented flat in Islington with anxiety. Orla should have been back hours ago. The previous night she had gone to bed still angry with him. Given the mood she was in, he'd sensed that sharing a bed was out of the question, so he'd gone to sleep on the couch. At one o'clock he'd woken to find her all dressed up in black like a ninja, fired up with excitement about what she was about to do.

'I should come with you,' he'd said, worried for her.

'No!' she'd been adamant. 'Keep away, Rufus. I don't want your help, not with this. We stick to the plan, this time. No deviations.'

He nodded. He wasn't happy, but this was her quest, not his.

'If anything goes wrong, anything out of the ordinary happens, we meet back at the farm. OK?'

He wanted to kiss her, but knowing it would not be welcomed he merely nodded.

'I'll be back by six. If I'm not, stick to the plan.'

'I'll say a prayer for you,' he said.

'Don't bother,' sniffed his beloved. 'I don't need your prayers. Say one for *her,* she's the one who'll need it.'

But now it was seven the following morning and Orla hadn't returned.

Her orders had been crystal clear: *If anything goes wrong, we meet up back at the farm.* But he couldn't just go back to Ireland, not if it meant abandoning her. He *loved* her. Anything could have happened.

He got dressed, not bothering with breakfast, stuffed his gear into a backpack – safer than leaving it here in the flat– and went out and hailed a taxi that took him to Holland Park. Having paid the driver, he loitered at the end of the square. He could see the house where he'd almost caught the girl. The place was quiet, no signs of life. His car, the one Orla had taken the previous night, was parked a few doors down. It was a Fiat, bought cheaply off an East End car lot a couple of weeks ago. He strolled towards it, glancing in as he drew level. It was empty, the keys still in the ignition. He took off his backpack and carefully placed it on the front passenger seat, then got behind the wheel and closed the door, his mind in turmoil, his eyes glued to the dark blue doors of the house.

Where could Orla have got to?

Follow the plan, she'd told him. Meet up back at the farm.

But she hadn't come home to their tatty little rented flat. And the car was here, keys in the ignition. She must have done it, though. When Orla set her mind to anything – and this in particular – for certain sure, it would be done.

He thought of Rory then, mouldering in an early grave, and shuddered.

Still undecided, he sat in the car, weighing his options.

She'd be angry if he stormed in there, went looking for her.

No, he couldn't do that. He'd...

And that's when he saw Annie Carter, alive and well, exit the house, stride down the steps and across to a black Mercedes. She got in and drove away.

He was so taken aback that for a moment he was unable to think. Then he gunned the engine, and followed.

Layla remained sitting at the breakfast table, too numb to move, as her mother left the room and closed the door. She heard Annie's rapid footsteps going off across the hall.

The house settled around her, silent, waiting. Rosa was downstairs but that wasn't much comfort. Annie had questioned the old housekeeper before breakfast, and Rosa had sworn she'd set the alarm last night, same as she always did. A swift examination by Bri, the man now on the door, of the outside of the house revealed that the wires to the alarm had been cut and the lock on the basement window forced. Orla had climbed in through there, made her way to the ground floor and up the stairs.

Feeling like a prisoner in her own home, Layla went into the study and sat down at the desk, chewing her lip nervously. Shivers of dread and horror still coursed through her body every time her mind went back to last night, to what had happened.

Someone had come to kill her mother.

She couldn't absorb it, no matter how she tried.

Worse still, *she* had killed the woman, never intending to – of *course* not. Nonetheless, she had shot the woman dead.

But she was carrying a knife. A knife she'd intended using on Annie Carter.

Annie Carter... Her mother hadn't reverted to her maiden name after the divorce. She'd claimed that Bailey didn't suit her, she hated the name, it conjured up bad memories. So she'd remained Annie Carter.

Maybe she still loves him a little? wondered Layla.

She shrugged the thought aside. No. When her parents had been together, there'd been nothing but ferocious rows and ugly scenes.

Sitting in her mother's study, she wondered where Annie had gone, what she was doing that was so urgent. Feeling sick to her stomach and cripplingly anxious, she picked up the phone, called the office. As she'd anticipated, it wasn't well received. The work ethic at Bowdler and Etchingham was set in stone: illness was unacceptable.

She put the phone down and listened to the silence in the house. What had once seemed to her a comfortable home had changed overnight. The whole place now felt creepy, unsafe. Layla stared at the phone, trying to make her mind up. Finally she picked it up and made another call. This one was international.

39

Max Carter was lying in the hot sun on the terrace, wearing black Speedos and nothing else. He loved basking in the sun. It refuelled him, made him stronger. At teatime he would take a shower and dress for dinner, until then this was *his* time and he was all alone, blissfully alone at the villa with the sun warming his skin and no sound but the lap of the waves on the narrow crescent of white sandy beach.

He let his mind meander into freefall. He had a good life out here in Barbados. His villa was one of a select few situated on the west coast up near Prospect, away from the encroaching luxury hotel complexes, shaded by manchineel trees and palms. He passed his time easily, developing the odd property or two around the islands, doing a few deals, swimming off Prospect beach and target-shooting in his garden among the mango and breadfruit trees to keep his eye in.

He was living the Bajan dream of hot sands and turquoise-blue seas. And there were other diversions too, very pleasant diversions – like the women who sometimes shared his bed, but never his life. Nevertheless there were times – though he would never admit this to a living soul – when he woke up and *she* was there in his mind, even after all these years. That annoyed the hell out of him. Sex with other women shifted her image, but somehow it always returned. He'd even find himself reaching for her in the night before it hit him that she wasn't there, that they were divorced, that she was involved with another man and living half a world away.

The fact that she was so far away was a *good* thing, he knew. Their fights, his suspicion of her, her defiance – they had caused each other nothing but pain. Jealousy had made him vicious, verbally attacking her: she had retreated into coldness, had become as responsive as a block of stone.

No, they were better apart.

This was the life…

The peace was shattered by the ringing of the phone.

He got to his feet, his movements lithe and easy. With his deep tan and his muscular, compact body, his predatory hook of a nose set under black brows, his dark curling hair, he didn't look English. 'My little Italian', his mother Queenie had always called him, though he was English to the core. Even his eyes were dark – a dense yet piercing navy blue.

He went into the shade of the villa, snatched up the phone in the hall.

'Yeah?' he demanded, dragging a hand through his hair in irritation.

That was when he heard Layla's voice, high with tension. 'Dad?'

Max Carter grew still. Irritation evaporated to be replaced by concern. 'What is it?' he asked.

'God, it's so awful…' she said, a tremor in her voice as if she was trying not to cry.

'Take your time. Tell me.'

She told him.
He couldn't believe it.
Orla Delaney?
How the fuck had *that* happened?

40

Annie drove herself to the Palermo in her new Mercedes. The club was quiet at this time of day, the punters long gone. One of the cleaners, recognizing her face, opened the door for her. The interior was luscious, luxurious, and identical to the Blue Parrot and the Shalimar, her ex's two other clubs. All three were popular with the glitterati and with the big City earners. There were matt tobacco-brown walls, gold angel frescoes, gilded chandeliers, deep cosy banquettes and overstuffed armchairs, all covered in the same striking soft faux tiger skin. There was a small stage and podiums where the girls danced, and over in the far corner to the right of the long blue-backlit bar was the VIP area and the rooms where private dances took place.

She made her way through a door to the left of the bar and up a flight of stairs. Hearing voices, she stuck her head around the dressing-room door. Delight and Marlena were in there, wearing their day clothes, smoking and chatting, all day to kill before they had to get set for the evening's business.

'Hi, Annie,' said Delight, a tall voluptuous

redhead with a broad toothy smile.

'Dolly in?'

'Yep, up in the office.'

'Thanks.'

Rufus watched Annie Carter park the sleek black Mercedes and go into the Palermo. Rufus glanced at the backpack. Maybe Orla would be annoyed with him for not following instructions and heading back to the farm, but that was a chance he was prepared to take. Her anger would soon turn to joy if he could report that he had succeeded where she'd failed.

He tried to imagine the expression on her face when he told her the good news. It helped to suppress the doubts that were eating away at him. Ever since he found the Fiat sitting in the street with the keys in the ignition, he'd had a sick feeling in his gut. Why had Orla abandoned the car like that?

Rufus pushed the doubts aside, told himself to focus on the job in hand.

It was time he fixed Annie Carter for good.

Frankie Day was a forty-two-year-old junkie who spent his days picking over the detritus of other people's lives and usually coming up empty. He'd been on the streets for months, having been chucked out of the squat by his mates, who weren't exactly *princes* but were picky enough to know they didn't want to share their grand abode with filthy Frankie and his gross personal habits for one minute longer.

So, here he was. Mooching around the streets,

mugging a granny here, snatching a wallet there, doing a bit of housebreaking, nicking a few cars, selling stuff on and using the proceeds to buy smack. He'd had a decent education. He was even – in the days before drugs and drink had fucked his brains up for good – what you'd call *bright.* He'd picked up a few skills. He could get into a house and have the contents away – jewellery, cash and electrics, all easy to sell on – before you could say knife.

Oh, and he could hot-wire a car.

He *loved* hot-wiring cars.

Whistling under his breath, he was ambling along, *Nothing to see here, officer,* discreetly trying this car door, then that one, then another. One or two in every London street would be unlocked. He knew this from experience.

A group of girls passed by, got a waft of his unwashed body, looked at him in revulsion, and edged away.

Frankie didn't care.

He was on a mission.

He needed another hit.

As he moved on down the street, trying the next car door, and the next, he saw a bloke up ahead sitting in the driver's seat of a black Mercedes. The door was wide open, he had one leg out on the pavement as he leaned in, fiddling with something in there, cassette player maybe. The man glanced around.

Frankie had never seen such a long curling mop of fire-engine-red hair, especially on a guy. It was all the more striking because his skin was bleached-out white. Funny-looking fucker.

Frankie slowed his pace and watched, fascinated. Finally the man finished whatever he was doing, got out. He was big, Frankie noted, a burly geezer, not someone you'd want to tangle with. Not realizing he was being watched, he closed the car door gently. Didn't lock it.

Frankie smiled.

All his Christmases had come at once.

What could he get from selling on a hot Merc?

A fucking fortune, that's what.

The man hurried away up the street. Frankie moved in.

41

The office door was open and Dolly was sitting at her desk. She looked up in surprise as Annie appeared.

'Hello,' she said, starting to smile. 'What are–'

'Why the fuck didn't you tell me Layla'd had bother?' Annie asked, shutting the door behind her.

Taken aback, Dolly sat gawping at her.

'Well, come on,' snapped Annie. 'Why didn't you *tell* me?'

For a moment, Dolly could only stare at Annie, who'd marched in, all guns blazing, and was now leaning both fists on the desk and glaring at her.

Dolly let out a sharp breath. 'One,' she said, counting off on her pink-manicured fingers, 'Layla didn't want me to. She insisted. She made me promise not to call Steve, although I wanted to. Two,' Dolly raised another well-kept digit, 'I couldn't tell *you* because you were faffing around en route from the States as per bloody usual. I didn't think there was any possibility I could reach you. *Also* as usual.'

'Faffing around?' snapped Annie. 'I was in New York on business. That's not faffing around, that's doing a job.'

'You're a bit touchy, ain't you?'

Annie's face tightened with anger. 'For fuck's sake, Doll. If I'd known about what happened to Layla, I'd have been forewarned. I'd have been prepared for something *serious* instead of being caught off guard.'

She pulled out a chair and sat down, wiping a weary hand over her brow. She was shattered. After Steve and the boys had taken the body away in the early hours, she'd spent the rest of the night in Layla's room, neither of them getting any sleep. It had taken a lot of convincing to keep Layla from freaking out and phoning the Bill. Even now, Annie wasn't sure she'd done the right thing in leaving her, but she couldn't rest until she had it out with Dolly face-to-face.

The fact is, I could be dead, she thought. *Layla could have been hurt, taken away, maybe tortured or raped – anything. My whole world could have fallen apart. Again.*

So here she was, exhausted and edgy and anxious, trying not to think about what could have been – and failing. Because disaster could still strike. Yes, Orla was dead. But – oh, and shit she didn't want to think this, but it had to be faced –

Redmond might still be alive.

It had been a *man* chasing Layla in the park. Annie thought it unlikely that it would have been Redmond himself – Layla had described her assailant as thick-set, huge, with a wild mane of hair. Nonetheless Redmond might be the one calling the shots. And if he was, he'd be wondering where his sister had vanished to. It wouldn't be long before he'd come looking for her.

'Something serious?' Dolly was frowning at her. 'Like what?'

'Never mind,' said Annie. Part of her wanted desperately to confide in Dolly, but it was no good flapping the lip to her about this. The less people knew about what had gone on last night, the better. She let out a shaky sigh. 'How's tricks, Doll?'

'Good,' said Dolly, peering closely at her old mate. Something was up, but Annie had that familiar *keep out* expression on her face. No use pushing. If she wanted to confide, she would. If not, forget it. 'Full of loaded punters most nights, everything's fine.'

'Girls all OK?'

'One or two niggles, nothing much.'

Annie looked around her. 'This old place has seen some changes,' she said wistfully.

This was true. Back in the sixties, when it was known as the Palermo Lounge, major acts had performed there. Heinz with the white-blond hair, and the chap with the deaf-aid, Johnny Rae, and many others had taken to the stage beneath the arching red curtains with the gold MC over the centre. Then for a while – along with the other two Carter clubs, the Shalimar and the Blue Parrot – it had been a cheap strip joint, one more tasteless haven for the dirty-mac brigade. Annie had soon put that right.

In the seventies she had transformed the three clubs into discos where dolly birds bopped in white-fringed bikinis on strobe-lit podiums while the punters lounged on chocolate-coloured banquettes eating scampi or chicken in the basket with chips.

Now it was the eighties. You moved with the times or you got left behind. The Carters *never* got left behind. So the clubs offered table-dancing. Nothing tacky, not here. The clientele were wealthy City types, jaded executives, TV personalities, sometimes even film stars. Following the stock market crash last year there'd been a sharp decline in trade, but there were still enough high-flying punters to keep the clubs busy. All three venues were packed with yuppie bankers and stockbrokers every night, out for a good time and a wind-down after a frantic day's trading on the money markets. Max's clubs were giving Stringfellows a run for their money, and if they were doing *that,* then they were doing just fine.

'Is anything wrong? Anything else?' asked Dolly delicately.

Annie shook her head. 'Listen, in future, Doll, if something happens – regardless what Layla says – don't keep it to yourself. Tell me or tell Steve, pronto.'

'What about Mr Carter?' asked Dolly. 'Should I tell him too?'

Annie stood up. 'Dolly,' she said, 'shut the fuck up, will you? I'm going to borrow Tone and the car. OK?'

Dolly's mouth opened. Then she closed it with a snap as she saw the look on Annie's face.

'What?' asked Annie.

Dolly shrugged. 'I'm wondering why you need a driver, that's all. *You* drive.'

Annie stifled her irritation. She'd taken her test a couple of years after the split from Max. Maybe she'd been trying to prove she was self-reliant, that Max Carter could go and *fuck* himself.

'I think I need some muscle around me at the moment,' she said. 'If that's OK with you?'

Dolly curled her lip. 'I suppose it'll have to be,' she said. 'Won't it.'

'You got *that* right,' said Annie, just as the window exploded inward, showering them with glass and knocking them both to the floor.

42

For long moments all they could do was lie there, the wind completely knocked out of them. They could hear people yelling, out in the street.

'What the fu–' said Dolly, crawling to her feet and helping Annie get back to hers. They stared at each other in shock, then looked at the window. It had blown in, but there were still jagged bits of glass clinging to the edges of the frame.

'You OK?' asked Annie. She saw that a trickle of

blood was winding its way down Dolly's cheek.

Dolly nodded. 'Yeah. You?'

'Doll, you're bleeding.' Annie fumbled in her bag, found a tissue, dabbed at Dolly's face.

Dolly looked in surprise at the blood on the tissue. Then Annie turned and stumbled out of the door, down the stairs. Dolly followed. They threw open the double doors on to a scene of chaos. Smoke, flames, and...

'That's my car,' gasped Annie.

Or at least it had been. All that remained of the Mercedes was a blackened, mangled, smoking heap. Cars around it had caught some of the blast, too. All the windows on the opposite side of the street, where she had parked, had shattered. Glass glittered on the pavement like snow after a winter blizzard.

'Where's Tone?' asked Annie, her heart in her mouth. She'd seen him parked up in the company Jag when she'd arrived. He'd waved at her. Huge, bald and wearing twin gold crosses in his ears, he was an old and trusted friend.

Her ears were humming and she was afraid she was about to pass out.

Delight and Marlena crowded into the door behind them.

'Oh my God, what happened?' demanded Delight, eyes wide.

Annie barely heard her. She couldn't see Tony. She couldn't see the Jag. Bile rose in her throat. This wasn't the first time she'd survived an explosion. Terrifying memories came flooding back in all their sick-making, ear-shattering horror. The glass, the sirens, the screaming...

'Oh Jesus...' She couldn't see Tony *anywhere*.

'There he is!' said Dolly, pointing.

Tony was climbing out of the Jag. It was parked halfway down the street, on the other side of the road. His expression was shocked as he stared at the remains of Annie's car.

Then he spotted the women in the club doorway. After a long moment, he closed the car door and walked over.

'I thought you were parked right next to it,' said Annie, shuddering and clutching at her chest.

Beneath his usual healthy tan, Tony was looking grey.

'I was,' he said. 'I went to fill up. When I got back, someone had nicked that spot, so I parked further away. You OK, Mrs C?'

Christ will he ever stop calling me that? thought Annie. But she was so very glad to see him, she could have kissed him at that moment. The car that had taken Tony's slot was a smouldering wreck.

'I'm fine.'

'You've got glass in your hair,' he said. 'And fuck it, look! You're bleeding, Doll.'

'It's nothing, just a scratch,' said Dolly, dabbing at her face.

Annie brushed tiny shards of glass from her hair. 'Really. I'm fine. We all are.'

They were silent then, gazing around them at the chaos.

'D'you think anyone's been hurt?' asked Dolly.

'I can't *see* anyone.'

Other people were emerging from buildings, staring at the wreckage in a dazed fashion. Then they heard the sound of sirens approaching.

'Shit,' said Annie. 'That's all I need, the old Bill on my case.'

'I think I see some blood there,' said Dolly, pointing.

Annie felt her stomach turn over. Dolly was right: there was blood on the pavement. Her car had been blown up, and someone must have been standing alongside it when it happened.

'Well, now you're *definitely* going to need Tony and the Jag,' said Dolly shakily.

Tony turned to Annie. 'What, you got some bother?'

For a moment Annie felt too overwhelmed to speak.

No, no bother. Turns out this is the deal: someone tried to snatch Layla, then Orla Delaney rose from the dead and tried to knife me in cold blood, and I'm damned sure I was meant to be in my car when that bomb went off. No, Tone, no bother at all.

'That motor of yours is never going to be the same again,' said Dolly. 'I've been seeing stuff like this on the TV, you just never think...' She stopped speaking, shook her head.

'Stuff like what?' asked Annie.

'Like *that.* Car bombs. It's been on the news, haven't you seen it? The IRA. Northern Ireland.'

Now Annie really did feel sick. The sirens were getting louder, people were coming out of shops and offices, milling around, staring, fascinated and horrified at the same time. There was a flicker of flames darting from the broken bonnet of her car. Her eyes were drawn back to the pavement, to the splodge of crimson there. She shuddered and looked at Tony.

'I'm getting out of here,' she said. 'Tone, drive me back to Holland Park, will you?'

''Course,' he said.

Dolly was looking at her like she'd flipped.

'It's no good going,' she said. 'What am I supposed to say when they come in here asking questions? The Bill will trace you through the registration number anyway.'

Annie looked at the Merc's number plate. The front one was nothing but a piece of blackened metal. The one at the back was probably intact, though, and there'd be the ID on the engine. Plus her prints would be all over it – if they could still find any.

'Tough,' she said. 'Let them. If they ask, you don't know a thing.'

'Well, I *don't,*' said Dolly in exasperation.

'That's fine then, isn't it? Come on, Tone. Let's get the fuck out of here.'

43

When Annie got back to Holland Park, Bri was still there on the door.

'Hiya, Bri,' said Tony, as he followed her in, eyeing him curiously.

Bri nodded a greeting to them both. He was tall, lean, with a shaven head and a steady gaze. A man of few words but – Annie hoped – direct action.

'Layla!' called Annie, crossing the marble hallway, her steps echoing in the stillness of the house.

No answer.

'She could be downstairs in the gym,' said Annie, peering around her with worried eyes as she made her way to the basement stairs.

Suddenly she needed to know where Layla was as a matter of urgency.

This place was grand, luxurious in the extreme. It had belonged to Constantine, one of many properties he owned all over the world. These included vineyards in the Loire Valley, an old sugar plantation in Jamaica, a beachside retreat in Martha's Vineyard and a compound in glamorous upstate Montauk. When he died, all Constantine's properties had passed first to Lucco, then to Alberto, with the exception of the Upper East Side apartment, and this London house, both of which were now Annie's. Much as she loved the New York apartment, this was the place that had always felt like her true home.

Or it had done until now. After the events of the last twenty-four hours it made her feel uneasy, just being here.

Orla Delaney had made her way in here with murder in mind. Annie found herself starting at shadows. She no longer felt secure in her own home. And that explosion ... she could still hear it, ringing in her ears. The jar of the shockwave when the device had gone off kept reverberating in her bones. Her mind insisted on replaying each detail, over and over. And it was dredging up memories of that other explosion, the one in the States, that had wrecked her life seventeen years ago, the whole ghastly thing playing on an endless loop. She stopped at the bottom of the stairs, closed her eyes, gulped hard. It felt as if someone heavy was sitting on her chest.

Tony took her arm. 'You OK?'

'Yeah.' She managed to raise a smile. 'Bit shook up, that's all.'

They could hear Duran Duran blaring out of the speakers, and the treadmill humming.

That was a relief. Layla was OK, she was here, she was safe. So was Tony. Annie thought again of the panic she'd felt when there was no sign of him after the explosion.

'I thought we'd lost you back there,' she said with an unsteady laugh.

'I thought we'd lost *you.*' He grinned. 'Scared the shit out of me, till I saw you standing in the doorway.'

They crossed the hallway and pushed open the door to the gym. It was state-of-the-art, with a mirrored wall and a water cooler, cross-trainers, rowing machines, static cycles and a heavy-duty treadmill – on which Layla, hair pulled back in her usual no-nonsense ponytail, wearing black shorts and beige T-shirt, was pounding furiously away. She saw her mother and Tony in the mirror, and punched a button on the machine. The treadmill slowed, then stopped. Layla unclipped the safety tie.

Breathing heavily, she stepped off, turned down the music. She snatched up a towel, patted her face. 'Did you want me?'

'You OK?' asked Annie.

'Yeah,' said Layla.

Annie didn't think she was. Layla's eyes were shadowed, haunted. She'd done a dreadful thing last night, and Annie could see that it was tormenting her.

'What's up? Has something else happened?' Layla was glancing from Tony's face to her mother's.

'Somebody blew up my car,' said Annie.

Layla's jaw dropped. 'You *what?*'

'It went off too early,' said Annie. She thought of the bloodstained pavement. 'Maybe the bomber muffed it.'

'Thank God for that. Are you OK? The person who set it, were they ... were they hurt?'

Annie let out an irritated breath. 'Was the bomber hurt? Not that I care, but he was blown to *fuck*. That's what bombs do to people, as a general rule.'

'Right.'

Seeing the chastened expression on her daughter's face, Annie felt guilty.

'Sorry,' she said quickly. 'It was a shock. Get cleaned up and come upstairs, will you? I think we'd better talk about all this stuff that's been happening.'

Tony was looking at Annie curiously. He held up a shovel-like hand. 'Wait on. Are you telling me there's something else, apart from the car?'

Annie heaved a sigh. 'You don't know the half of it. Unless Steve's told you...?'

'He ain't told me nothing. Is this to do with Bri being on the door? What's going on?'

'Look, let's go upstairs and I'll fill in the blanks.'

'Mum...' Layla grabbed Annie's arm. Her eyes were wide with alarm.

'It's OK,' said Annie. 'Tone's sound as a pound. We'll see you up there.' She'd already decided to dig out the kiyoga Tone had given her years ago. And she had a can of Mace here somewhere.

Yeah, really effective against knives and bombs, she thought.

What the hell. Any protection was better than none.

Rufus couldn't believe it. He'd stayed to watch, from a distance. This time he wanted to see the Carter woman get what she deserved. Instead some scruffy little tit had come along, trying car doors. And it wasn't as if he could run over and stop him.

The inevitable happened. The car blew up, taking the homeless guy with it.

Boom!

That bitch must have nine lives, like a cat.

Worse, there was still no sign of Orla.

If anything goes wrong, we meet at the farm.

He clung to the hope that she was following the plan, that when her hit failed she'd hot-footed it back to Ireland. Part of him wanted to race to the farm, to see for himself that she was OK. Part of him was terrified to go there in case it would confirm his worst fears.

Either way, he was determined not to leave London until he'd finished the job she started. When Annie Carter was dead, then he would head home.

44

'The police are going to come calling over the car, for sure,' said Tony when they were sitting in the drawing room.

'So? I tell them the truth. It's all legal, as far as I'm concerned,' said Annie.

'Yeah, but someone bombed it out. They're going to wonder.'

'They can wonder. They've been wondering for years. So what?'

Tony was silent for a while. She'd just filled him in on the news about Orla, and about Layla nearly getting herself abducted in the park. Layla was chewing a fingernail, saying nothing.

Annie started ticking off items on her fingers. So long as she kept thinking, trying to reason all this out, then she wasn't panicking, she wasn't losing it – and losing it was only a heartbeat, only a single moment of lapsed concentration, away.

'Three things: Layla in the park. Orla in here last night. The car bomb today.'

'For God's sake, how can you be so damned *casual* about it?' Layla slammed her hand down on the armrest.

'What do you want me to do? Run around screaming?'

'At least that would prove you're not *totally* made of wood,' snapped Layla.

Though obviously uncomfortable about the

bickering, Tony kept quiet. It wasn't his place to interfere in Carter family business.

'Layla, honey,' said Annie more reasonably, 'we have to keep thinking here. Someone's trying to get to us. The minute we cave in, we're done for.'

'Well, *I'm* caving in,' Layla cried. 'I should be in work today, doing VAT returns, and instead I'm sitting here discussing the fact that I've murdered someone, and that someone else has just tried to murder *you*. It's *insane*.'

'Insane or not, hard to take in or not, it's *happening*,' said Annie. 'So we have to deal with it.'

'*We?* This isn't the sort of thing I deal with. I wish I'd gone ahead and called the police last night, like I wanted to. Let them deal with it.'

'That would be a bad move,' said Tony.

'Hear that?' Annie pointed a finger at Tony while staring at her daughter. 'Do you *hear* that? Those are wise words. No police. We don't *ever* mention what happened last night to the police, you got that?'

'But the car–'

'The car, that's OK. They'll trace it to me, and I'll handle it. No sweat.'

'Someone died–'

'The bastard who was planting the bomb! Good riddance!' Maybe that would be an end to it. Maybe the bomber was Redmond, and it would all be over now? But deep down Annie wasn't convinced. Bombs didn't seem like Redmond's style.

'They'll find it odd that you left the scene, won't they?'

'I panicked,' said Annie.

'You? I don't think so.' Layla folded her arms across her chest, hugging herself as if she were cold.

'Look, here's what'll happen: you'll stay off work–'

'No, I–'

'You're staying off work,' repeated Annie more firmly. 'Until we know what's we're dealing with, you're going to a safer place with secur–'

'No!' said Layla.

'I don't want any arguments about this.'

Layla was silent a moment, brooding. Her mother was repeating the same old patterns that had dogged her all through childhood. All Annie had ever done was send her away. She was an adult now, but nothing had changed: she was sending her away *again.*

'The police will come soon, won't they?' said Layla. She doubted her own ability to front this out as her mother could. She was afraid she would crumble and confess everything.

'You won't be here when they do. Which is another good reason for placing you elsewhere.'

Annie was right. Layla could see that.

'Get some stuff together, Tony will drive you, and I'll get one of the boys to stay with you. And you don't tell anyone, not even your closest friend, where you're going. OK?'

'I don't *know* where I'm going.'

'You know what I mean.'

Layla stood up. She didn't *have* any close friends. All she had were work colleagues. When she'd been a child, it hadn't taken long before the parents of other kids in her class got wind of the fact that the Carters' wealth came from disreputable sources. Inevitably the rumours would begin to circulate as the respectable parents – doctors, lawyers, academics – dug deeper. The *gang* rumours. The *brothel* rumours. So they'd steer their children away from Layla. This had gone on, all through school, through college, even into work.

'OK,' she sighed.

'Good.' Annie and Tony stood up.

Layla went to the door, and paused there.

'I suppose I ought to tell you...' she said.

'Tell me what?' asked Annie.

'I phoned Dad.'

45

'Hiya, honeybunch,' said Ellie Brown, throwing her arms wide as Layla came up the stairs to the upper floor of the Shalimar.

'Hi, Ellie,' said Layla gloomily, getting to the top stair and being enfolded in Ellie's cuddlesome perfumed warmth.

She'd seen her cousin Jimmy Junior downstairs behind the bar, where he worked tossing cocktails and flirting with the girls. He'd shot her a puzzled grin, clearly wondering what she was doing here. She was wondering *that,* herself.

'Your mum told me to expect you,' said Ellie, kissing Layla's cheek.

'Hi, Layla,' said Chris, Ellie's big, ugly but

good-hearted husband, taking her overnight bag. 'Come on in. Hey Tone. Keeping OK?'

'Fine,' said Tony, bringing up the rear. 'You?'

'Yeah, not bad.'

'Let me show you your room,' said Ellie, and Layla followed her with a heavy heart along a plainly decorated hallway. She thought how noticeable it was, the difference between the opulence of the tiger-skin-and-gold club downstairs and the austere magnolia neatness of the upper floor. But Annie was right – this place was *thick* with muscle, guarding the door, monitoring the safety of the girls who worked here. The club was *tight*.

'Here we go,' said Ellie, opening a door.

They entered a room with a double bed, dressing table, wardrobe and a small TV. Chris placed her bag on the bed, then withdrew.

'Loo's just across the hall there,' said Ellie, flinging back the curtains to let the sun in.

Layla went and peered out of the window. Below, there was a busy road lined with parked cars. Downstairs there was glamour, luxury, champagne on tap. Up here, there were no fancy trimmings. But it was neat and clean. Ellie showed her along the hall to the office, the monitor room, the girls' dressing room.

'It's like bloody Fort Knox, this place,' said Ellie with a smile. 'Nice and secure.'

Layla nodded. She knew that Ellie had once run a far more down-market establishment in Limehouse. A knocking-shop, not to put too fine a point on it. Since then she'd gone up in the world.

'Did Mum tell you what happened?' asked Layla, when they'd returned from the grand tour and Ellie was bustling around, making sure everything was in order in the bedroom.

Ellie was a big woman, stocky in middle age and comfortable with it. She wore flattering business skirt suits in peacock blue, red and purple, no accessories. It was the red today, and it suited her. She dyed her hair a fetching mid-brown and kept it tucked up neatly in a chignon. Her nails were short and well manicured. Her skin was as clear as a twenty-year-old's, her manner confident and smiling.

'Annie told me there'd been a bit of trouble and she wanted you out of it,' said Ellie. 'That's all.'

I am standing in a room over a lap-dancing club, thought Layla morosely. *I should be at work filling in tax returns, and instead I am standing in a room over a lap-dancing club.*

Grimly she remembered her mother's parting shot: 'Don't go getting all pally with the girls, OK?'

Layla thought that wasn't OK at all. She thought it was pure snobbery on her mother's part, imagining the daughter of the great Annie Carter was too good to mix with lap dancers.

'I won't be staying long,' said Layla, praying that would be the case. She was dreading having to phone in sick again tomorrow. No one was ever sick at Bowdler and Etchingham. Anyone foolish enough to take sick leave was liable to return to find their desk had been moved to a less desirable spot, their chances of promotion reduced.

'You can stay as long as you like,' said Ellie. 'That goes without saying.'

I'm going to lose my job, thought Layla. She loved her job, it defined her. She loved neat rows of figures, making columns add up. She craved order, and accountancy gave her that.

Yeah, because it's missing in other areas of your life, right?

'Telly's there if you need it,' said Ellie, desperate to break the uneasy silence. 'And there's the radio.'

'Fine,' said Layla.

She made no move to start unpacking, settle in. Just stood there, looking lost.

'Don't go out if you can avoid it, but if you do, you take Chris or Simon or Kyle with you,' said Ellie.

Layla knew Chris on sight: Simon was a blond mound of muscle, and Kyle had waved her in the door today, dark-haired and barrel-chested, with a broad smile of welcome. She rather liked Kyle.

'And you don't ever go out without telling me exactly where you are.'

'Don't tell me,' said Layla. 'Mum's orders?'

Ellie smiled but didn't answer that. 'Just ask if you need anything,' she said, going to the door. 'Oh – and Layla?'

'Hm?'

'Probably best if you stick to your room in the evenings,' said Blue, and with that she closed the door.

Terrific, thought Layla.

46

Annie was alone that evening when the police came knocking. She was just sitting there, thinking over what Layla had said before Tony had taken her off to Ellie's place.

I've phoned Dad.

Shit. If there was one thing she didn't need, didn't ever need, it was him poking his nose in.

She'd got used to him being on the other side of the world, and she liked it that way. Max had his fingers in quite a few pies still, she knew that. She couldn't avoid knowing. Layla always came home from her Barbados vacations fizzing with joy, keen to impart news of her dad.

Annie didn't want to hear any of it. She didn't want to see, either, how lit up her daughter was, how suntanned, happy, exuberant – a different girl almost – simply because she'd been in her father's company, in her father's home.

His home.

Well, that was what Barbados was these days. Max lived the life of a wealthy ex-pat, with interests in Barbados, Cuba and the Cayman Islands. He still owned the three London clubs, along with Carter Security, which was now managed by Steve Taylor. The clubs were raking in a fortune and Steve was doing well, pulling in lucrative City contracts and work all the way out to Essex.

Annie sighed. She wouldn't mind being an ex-pat herself, upping sticks to New York where her work was. But then ... you couldn't really call the club work, not with Sonny running the place so smoothly that she was left with little to do. He was a good manager, honest and diligent. Her occasional flying visits to check up on the place only served to put his nose out of joint; he took it as a lack of trust on her part, an affront to his integrity, when in fact all she was doing was trying to pretend she had a purpose in life.

In London she had nothing to occupy her besides shopping and chewing the fat with her mates. But most of the time they weren't even free. Dolly and Ellie were both busy women with responsible jobs, so she was often hanging about alone, like a spare part. She would never admit to anyone that she was lonely. And – up until these last few hellish days – she'd been bored witless, too.

It almost came as a relief when Rosa's knock interrupted her thoughts.

'Senora Carter?' The housekeeper's eyes were wide with worry in the wrinkled folds of her face. '*Polícia.*'

Here we go, thought Annie. *Eyes down, look in.*

She stood up. 'Thanks Rosa. Show them in here, will you?'

Rosa nodded. She ushered in two plain-clothes cops, one an older man, tall, dark-haired, grave-faced, with inky-brown eyes that scanned her like a computer.

The other was a young female, with honey-coloured hair scraped back to display knife-sharp cheekbones and hostile eyes. The girl didn't *look* like Layla, but something in her buttoned-up manner, her deliberately unflattering choice of hairstyle and strictly unsexy clothes, reminded Annie forcibly of her daughter.

I suppose she's here in case I faint or something, thought Annie wryly.

She thought she recognized the older detective. Could be an undertaker, a face like that, with that turned-down trap of a mouth. She hadn't expected CID this fast in the proceedings, though. She'd assumed uniforms would arrive first.

The senior man flashed his badge.

'For God's sake,' said Annie.

'Mrs Carter,' he said.

'DI Hunter! *Thought* it was you. Long time no see.'

'I had hoped to continue that absence of contact,' he said smoothly, taking a seat. 'And it's DCI now.'

'Well, good for you.'

'This is DI Duggan.'

Annie nodded to the woman. 'Haven't seen you in a long time,' she said, returning her attention to Hunter. He'd aged well. Still looked the business.

'Is this your car, registration number...' asked DI Duggan, whipping out her notebook and rattling off a number.

'It is,' said Annie.

'And are you aware that it was blown up not far from one of the Carter clubs?' asked Hunter.

'Yes.'

'You drove it there?'

'Yes.'

He stared at her. 'You left the scene.'

'I was shaken up. Had to come home.'

His stare hardened. The Annie Carter he'd known – the one he'd encountered back in the day when some nutter was wasting London prostitutes – wouldn't have been *shaken up*. That Annie Carter had been too busy throwing her weight around, leaving him and his colleagues playing catch-up while she stalked the streets that she – according to her – owned.

'No one else was in the car with you, I take it?'

'No. Nobody.'

'Yet someone was right there when the bomb exploded. And that person is dead.'

'That's terrible.'

'Isn't it. We've yet to identify the indiv–'

'As far as I could see, there wasn't much left of them. Whoever they were. Was anyone else hurt?'

'Minor injuries, which was lucky. Cuts and scratches. It wasn't a large explosive device. Only lethal at short range.'

'Did you talk to Dolly Farrell? The manager of the Palermo.'

'We did.'

'Then she'll have told you that I was with her when it went off, in the office upstairs. I didn't see anything, I was inside the club.'

'But you saw the aftermath, obviously.'

'I did.'

'And you have no idea who this person might be? The one who died in the blast?'

'None.'

'Have you anything you'd like to tell us, Mrs Carter?'

'Such as?'

'Such as – oh, let's see. How about telling us why someone would be trying to kill you?'

'There's nothing I can tell you. Nothing I know that you don't.'

'And you locked the car when you left it?'

'Yes. I did.'

'You're sure?' asked Hunter.

'Perfectly sure. This person who was in the blast,' said Annie. '*You've* no idea who he or she is?'

It couldn't be Redmond. Could it?

Hunter stood up. 'Not yet. We'll be in touch, Mrs Carter.'

'Only that might tell us something important, don't you think?' said Annie.

He paused. Seemed to count to ten. 'Our first and most urgent priority will be to discover the identity of the person who died.'

'That's a damned good place to start.'

Hunter glared at her. 'Don't give me any trouble, Mrs Carter.'

'Of course not,' she said, standing up and moving around the desk as his DI got to her feet too.

Annie escorted them to the drawing-room door and across the hall to the front door. When she opened it, Bri turned and looked at her. She widened her eyes at him.

'Thanks for coming, DCI Hunter,' she said as the policeman and his cohort went off down the steps, bypassing Bri with suspicious glances.

'We'll be in touch,' said Hunter, his eyes resting

coolly on her face.

'Look forward to it,' she said, and went back inside to make a telephone call to the States.

47

Next day everything was quiet at the house. Annie phoned Layla to check that she was OK – which she was – and then spent the rest of the day on tenterhooks, thinking *this is the calm before the storm*.

Her mind was a whirl of anxiety after another sleepless night, and when daylight began to stream in through her window she was consumed with dread. Another day of waiting. Followed by another night when she would go to bed in the master suite and think of Orla dying in there. And all the while Redmond might be out there, waiting his chance to come and get her.

She sat alone watching TV late into the evening, putting off the evil hour when she would have to go upstairs. When Rosa tapped on the door, she nearly jumped out of her skin.

'Senora,' said Rosa, coming in, smiling.

Annie was clutching a hand to her chest. She had to swallow hard to get her breath. 'Yeah, Rosa. What is it?'

'It's...' started Rosa, then someone stepped past her.

'It's your worst nightmare,' said Max Carter, coming inside, and closing the door behind him.

Annie felt her heart flip. Her chest was so tight it was a struggle to breathe. What had he just said? That he was her worst nightmare?

'You're not *quite* my worst nightmare,' she said coldly, flicking off the TV. 'You're flattering yourself. As usual.'

Max came over to the big pair of Knole sofas. He sat down on the vacant one, opposite where Annie herself was sitting. Leaned back. Studied her for a moment. 'Layla phoned me,' he said, his dark blue eyes on her face. Annie kept her expression neutral.

She'd been expecting him to arrive ever since Layla had told her she'd been in touch with him, but the reality of it was still a shock. She found herself feeling ... well, she didn't know *what* she felt.

Up to this point, contact between them had been practically non-existent. Now here he was, and his physical impact on her was no less than it had ever been. He was still a stunning man, she had to admit that. Fit lean body, black hair, dark tan, hard dark-blue eyes that gave him the flashy, dissolute air of a riverboat gambler. He was gorgeous. She could see that, could admit it to herself. And once, that might have made her weaken. But those days were long gone.

'I know Layla phoned you,' said Annie. 'She told me.'

'She said Orla Delaney broke in here.'

'That's right. She did.'

'She *said* that she shot her.'

'That's right too.'

Max frowned. 'But I *thought* Constantine finished Orla. *And* her brother, that fucker Redmond.'

'I thought he did too.'

'A plane crash, didn't you say that? Back in the early seventies?'

'Yeah.'

'But how the hell could that be? You're certain it was Orla?'

Annie took a breath. 'It was her. No question.'

'And please explain to me how you allowed my daughter to get hold of a gun, to actually *shoot* someone.'

Annie bristled at his tone. It was accusatory, to say the least.

'*Your* daughter? Excuse me – she's mine too. And it happened like this: I heard someone moving about, coming up the stairs. I got your old gun, the .45, and woke Layla. Orla knocked me flat on my arse as she came through the bedroom door. She had a knife. Layla panicked, snatched up the gun and shot her.'

'I'm not happy at any of this,' said Max. 'What sort of crap security you got here? You even switch the house alarm on?'

'Rosa did it, same as she does every night. Orla cut the wires before she got in through the basement window. And we haven't needed "security". Why would we?'

'See you've got one of the boys on the door now.'

Annie nodded. 'Steve put Bri on there.'

'And Steve cleared up?'

'Yes.'

'Where's Layla now?'

'In a safe place, until we know what's going on here. Did she tell you about the man in the park?'

Max nodded. 'Why didn't *you* tell me about that?'

'I was away when it happened.'

'Where?'

'Does it bloody well matter?'

He shrugged.

'I was in the States.'

'Right.'

'On business.'

'Oh yeah. Business.'

Annie could feel her blood pressure starting to build. Eight years apart, and he could *still* drive her mental. She stared at him, narrow-eyed.

'And how *is* Golden Boy?' he asked.

'*Don't* call Alberto that.'

'Might've known you'd leap to his defence.'

Annie released a pent-up breath. No. She wasn't going to put up with this again. No way.

'I'm not having this conversation with you,' she told him flatly.

'No?'

'No.'

Max was half-smiling, but the smile was cruel, calculating. 'So – why didn't you tell me *after* you'd come back from the States?'

Because I didn't want to speak to you or see you or even know you're breathing, she thought. *Because it hurts.*

She wasn't about to tell him *that.*

Aloud, she said: 'By that time, Layla had already told me she'd been in touch with you. I knew you'd show up.'

'And you're delighted to see me, I can tell.'

'Oh yeah. Ecstatic.' Annie smiled sourly.

'I took a ten-hour flight to get here.'

'Yeah. In first class. With air hostesses dropping their phone numbers "accidentally" in your lap, I'll bet. That must have been rough on you.'

'Is there anything else I should know about?'

'Not much. Unless you count the paper shamrock that was left in Layla's trainer. And unless you count someone bombing my car.'

'You what?'

'My car was blown up. But hey – bonus – I wasn't in it at the time. *Someone* was, though. Or at least they were near enough to get blown apart.'

Max was silent for a moment. Then he said: 'What the fuck have you been up to?'

Annie sank back in her chair with a sigh. 'Anything kicks off and it has to be *my* fault?' She shook her head and stared at him. 'You don't change.'

He stood up. 'Look, I came back to see that Layla's all right. So where is she?'

'At Ellie's place,' said Annie. 'Locked up tight.'

'I'd better get over there.'

'Yeah you'd better, hadn't you,' said Annie, and picked up the phone.

He went to the door. Paused there.

Annie looked at him. She just wanted him to go, before she lost it completely and flung a heavy object at his smug face. 'What?' she asked.

'I'm glad you're OK,' he said, and walked out the door, closing it behind him.

Annie sat there staring at the door in mute surprise. Then she shook herself and dialled her sister's number.

'Hello?' It was Ruthie, picking up at her house in Richmond.

The sound of Ruthie's voice calmed her a little. Her older sister was everything she was not. Ruthie was gentle, considerate, caring. She would have made a wonderful mother for Layla. So much more suitable than Annie was or could ever be.

'Hi, Sis, it's me,' said Annie.

'Annie. You OK?'

Hearing the smile in Ruthie's voice, she hesitated. She hated to have to do this. Ruthie had her nice safe life. She was a dental receptionist, she had a nice home, she was straight. She was also single, and Annie was convinced that she liked it that way.

'Not so good,' said Annie, swallowing hard.

'What is it?' Ruthie's voice was immediately anxious.

'Max is back.'

'Oh?' Ruthie was silent for a moment. 'That doesn't bother you, does it? I mean ... it's *over* between you, isn't it? Has been for ... oh, how long is it?'

'Eight years.' *And he can still rile me like no one else. I'm sitting here shaking like an over-excited teenager just because he's been in this room.*

'That's right. A long time.'

'Yeah, but ... thing is, Ruthie, Layla called him because we've had some trouble.'

'Trouble? What sort of trouble?'

Annie told her. And then she suggested it might be a good idea if Ruthie were to take herself off somewhere for a while.

'There's something you're not telling me,' said Ruthie.

'There is. It's about the woman who was shot,' said Annie. She hadn't told Ruthie, not even Ruthie, that Layla had fired the gun.

'You didn't *know* her, did you?' asked Ruthie anxiously.

'I did. Ruthie, it's really weird. I thought she was dead, years ago.'

'Who?'

'Orla Delaney.'

Ruthie was silent.

'Ruthie?'

'I'll pack a bag,' she said, and hung up the phone.

48

Layla was in the kitchen above the Shalimar. It was eight o'clock and the club was starting to come to life, the staff busying themselves putting the champagne on ice and making sure everything was looking glamorous for the punters. Meanwhile Layla was pouring hot water on to a pot of noodles. She really didn't think she could eat anything, not after all that had happened. But she had to try.

'Jesus, that looks grim,' said a voice behind her.

Layla stopped pouring. She turned to find a vision standing in the doorway. The woman was about the same age as her, but she might as well have been a totally different species. She was tall – taller than Layla herself, and voluptuously built. She was wearing an emerald-green silk evening gown that showed off a terrific pair of breasts. Her hair was big too, tumbling down her back and shoulders in a rich dark cascade. Her face was pale, long, her lips pouty and accentuated with scarlet. Her brows were straight dark lines above huge black-lashed eyes of a strikingly clear light grey.

'Hi,' the creature announced herself. 'I'm Precious.'

'You're *what?*' Layla was half-smiling at the absurdity.

'Precious.' The girl was smiling too, a huge megawatt grin. 'Yeah, I know. We don't use our real names here. You'll meet China and Destiny too. And a couple of others. All called Jane or Margaret or something boring in real life. But this isn't real life, is it?'

Layla blinked. 'Isn't it?'

'No, no. This is dreamland. This is where men come when they're tired of what's going on out there, and need to connect with fantasy.'

'Can I get you something...?' asked Layla, stirring her noodles, trying not to gawp.

'No, it's OK. Just having a herbal tea,' said Precious, reaching up to one of the cupboards and taking down a packet. 'That's all I ever drink, apart from a sip of bubbly when the punters are in.'

'Right.' Layla carried on stirring, still staring.

'Ellie said she had a guest staying,' said Precious, putting the kettle back on.

'Oh! I'm Layla,' said Layla, belatedly.

'Layla. That's your *real* name? That's pretty.'

'That's me. Layla Carter.' Layla took up a fork, leaned against the worktop and determinedly started in on her evening meal. 'What's *your* real name?' she asked, curious.

Precious held up a manicured finger. 'House rules. We don't use those here.'

'Oh.' Layla felt rebuffed. And wrong-footed, somehow. Not only that, she felt *plain.* She didn't wear make-up, she never had. Her fingernails were short and unpolished, and her hands were covered in paper cuts. And here was this *apparition,* so beautiful and bedecked in bright jewel colours, like a celestial being.

Precious poured boiling water on to her camomile tea. Her movements were delicate, very feminine. Layla watched her. She was almost mesmerized. She'd never even been inside one of her Dad's clubs before, in fact she'd avoided them. They were all part of that dodgy, underworld her parents seemed to operate so comfortably in. She'd certainly never seen or spoken to any of the girls who worked here.

'Layla *Carter?*' said Precious. 'Hang on a minute. Are you Max Carter's daughter? The Max Carter who owns these clubs?'

'Guilty,' said Layla. 'So ... you dance for money then.'

Precious turned to look at her; she was smiling. 'Yep. It's good, too. Well paid.'

But isn't it embarrassing? Layla wondered. *Writhing about half-naked with men watching you?*

She couldn't ask her that.

'You enjoy doing it?' she asked delicately.

'I wouldn't put it as strongly as that. It's like the song, you know the one? You keep your mind on the money.' She picked up her cup. 'Look, I have to go. Catch up with you later, yeah?'

'Yeah,' said Layla, and Precious left the room, trailing a waft of Giorgio strong enough to stun a bull.

Layla stared at her half-eaten noodles. Again the image rose in her mind – Orla Delaney, lying dead at her feet, killed by her own hand. She'd never set eyes on a dead body before. Her stomach clenched queasily and sick bile rose in her throat. With a shudder, she slung the rest of her dinner in the bin.

'Layla?' Ellie bustled into the kitchen.

'Hm?' asked Layla, wondering if she was going to hurl.

'Your dad's here.'

'Dad!' Layla ran out into the hall and flung herself into her father's arms.

'It's OK, I'm here,' said Max, hugging her tight.

Suddenly all the fear and bewilderment she'd been holding in became too much for her and she started to cry. Max's eyes met Ellie's over Layla's shoulder.

Taking the hint, Ellie heaved a sigh and left them to it. Sometimes, she found it hard to believe that soft-hearted Layla really was Annie Carter's daughter – she was nothing like her.

'It's so awful,' Layla was sobbing.

'We'll fix it,' said Max. 'Whatever it is.'

'How?' she wailed.

'Where can we talk?' asked Max, rubbing her back reassuringly.

'Oh ... in here,' said Layla, and led him into her bedroom. Max followed her in and closed the door, leaned against it. Layla sat down on the bed.

'Tell me all about it,' he said.

Layla told him, leaving out nothing. The man pursuing her in the park. The intruder her mother believed to be Orla Delaney. The car bomb.

'Mum could have been killed, you know. She was so brave and I was just ... *useless.* She could be *dead* now,' she said, dropping her head into her hands.

Her mind stalled, unable to comprehend such an outrage. All right, she couldn't relate to her, but Mum had been a constant, solid presence in her life, and to think of her gone for ever – that was too terrible to contemplate.

'Layla...' Max came to the bed and sat down beside her. He gave her shoulder a tiny shake. 'She wasn't hurt. The main thing is, you're both OK. And you're safe here.'

'Yeah.' She might well be safe here, but ... stupid as it might sound, what she felt right now was hurt. Rejected. Her mother had sent her away yet again. 'I'll lose my job if I don't go in tomorrow,' she said, wiping her eyes. 'They're laying people off, and if I don't show up–'

'Fuck the job,' said Max. 'Stay here. Just until we know what's happening.'

'What *is* happening?' asked Layla in despair.

'That's what I'm going to find out,' said Max.

49

DI Sandra Duggan was doing the door-to-door on shops and offices up and down the street where Annie Carter's car had been done. She was getting nowhere in a hurry. Nobody knew a damned thing. Nobody had *seen* a damned thing. They looked at her, saw FUZZ writ large all over her, then she flashed the badge and they thought, *I don't need this trouble.* So far everyone she'd spoken to might as well have been deaf, dumb and blind for all they'd told her.

She was tired. Her feet were aching. She was sick of looking at these people and seeing only lies and evasion staring back at her. Then she went into the charity shop and the girl behind the counter – who was tricked out in kohl eye make-up, sucking on a lollipop from a bristling potful of lollipops beside the till – said yes, she'd seen something.

Sandra nearly wept with gratitude.

'What did you see?'

'Who,' said the girl. '*Who* did I see.'

'Who then?'

'I saw Frankie.'

'Frankie?'

'Frankie Day,' smiled the girl. On her own at lunchtime, thank the Lord. No one with half a brain in here to shut her up.

Sandra wrote it down. *Frankie Day.*

‘So you know him, do you? This Frankie Day?’

‘Everyone knows Frankie,’ said the girl, shifting the lollipop deftly to the other cheek with her tongue.

‘I don’t.’

The girl laughed as if this was extremely funny.

‘But *everyone* knows him. He’s always up and down this road, all the time.’

‘Doing what?’ asked Sandra.

The girl laughed and tossed the lollipop with her tongue again.

‘Doing what?’ Sandra persisted.

The girl winked. ‘Doing the ... you know.’

‘No, I don’t. What?’

The girl made a gesture with her hand, swivelling the wrist.

‘Trying the car doors,’ she said with a sharp sigh and a roll of the eyes, as if Sandra was thick and should have known. ‘He passed by the front of the shop. Then I heard the bang. It blew out some of the windows, but this one–’ she nodded to the big plate-glass job at the front of the shop – ‘*this* one was OK. It moved in the frame, though. You know what I mean? And I went to the door to go out and see what had happened, but Martha – she’s the manager – she screamed at me not to touch it, because the whole thing was out of its frame, just hanging there. If I’d opened the door, it could have fallen out and cut me.’

‘And you didn’t see Frankie again, after that?’ asked Sandra.

‘He hasn’t been back.’ The girl frowned. ‘I don’t know why.’

Think I do, thought Sandra. ‘Can you describe

Frankie for me?'

The girl described Frankie, and Sandra made notes. 'Can you remember anything else?'

'A dark-haired woman dressed in black left the car that blew up,' said the girl, her forehead knotted with concentration.

Annie Carter.

'And then a big tall man, thick-set, with lots of this bright red hair, he went to the car and got in. I think he popped the lock. He sat in the driver's seat with the door open. And when he'd left it, Frankie rolled by.'

'And when the car blew up, you were standing here?'

'No, I was over there. By the baby clothes.'

'And you could see the car?'

'Yeah. I saw the red-haired man sitting in the driver's seat of the car after the woman with the long dark hair left it. He had the door open. Next thing I knew, he was gone, the car door was shut and that's when I saw Frankie try the handle. Then I was walking back to the till, and boom! Up it went.'

'What's your name?'

'Tracey Esler.'

Sandra made a note of that and put her book away. 'Thanks, Tracey. You've been a great help.'

Tracey beamed and held out the pot of lollies. 'Have a lollipop,' she said.

50

'Oh, fuck, it's you,' said Kath the next day when she found Annie standing on her doorstep.

She turned without a word and led the way up the hall. Annie closed the front door behind her and followed her cousin's great wallowing arse into the kitchen. Once there, Kath, who was wearing a deeply unflattering navy shell suit and greyish-white T-shirt, collapsed on a chair by the table as if the effort of opening her own front door had exhausted her. She picked up a smouldering fag from an ashtray.

Annie looked around the kitchen. Nothing ever changed here. The place was the same tip it had always been, dirty washing piled on the floor instead of in the laundry basket, unwashed cups and plates littering the draining board and filling the grubby sink. The table awash with debris from meals, toast-crumbs, a paper blazoned with the headline PIPER ALPHA TRAGEDY, dog-eared magazines and chunks of half-eaten pizza.

'Hi,' said the eighteen-year-old girl leaning against the sink. She was fair-haired, hazel-eyed and showing a big toothy overbite, dressed in skinny hipster jeans and a pink T-shirt.

'Hiya, Molly,' said Annie.

Her eyes drifted to the young man standing beside his sister. Jimmy Junior was twenty-one, and while his sister was plain and a bit goofy-looking like her mother, Junior favoured his father. He had close-cropped dirty-blond hair and a face any sane woman would fall for. His eyes were a stunning clear blue, vivid as Sri Lankan sapphires.

Annie'd always liked Junior, she'd put him forward for the bar job at the Shalimar. *I have a weakness for good looks,* she thought, and knew it to be true. But it was more than that with Junior. He was her blood. Added to that, he was a hard worker, and he had charm.

'Hi, Junior,' Annie greeted him.

He nodded.

'What is it this time?' asked Kath.

Annie turned to her cousin. Once briefly pretty in her youth, Kath had settled into her mid-forties as if she belonged there, with a disastrous poodle perm on her yellow-grey hair. Her face was red and her breath was wheezy. She knew Kath hated her and she also suspected that Kath bore a grudge against her over the disappearance of Jimmy Senior.

'There's been some stuff going down, I just wanted to tell you,' said Annie.

'What stuff?' asked Jimmy Junior.

Annie looked at him. She wondered what Kath had told the kids about their father. Had she told them he'd once been Max Carter's number one man, trusted and revered? Or had she told them the real, painful truth?

Annie pulled out a chair. She didn't dust it off, although it took an effort of will to resist the temptation. She sat down, took a breath. And told her cousin and her cousin's children about the intruder – leaving out the shooting and who she believed the victim to be – and the bomb, and the man who had tried to attack Layla.

'Holy *crap*,' said Molly when Annie finished speaking.

'I think you should all clear out for a while,' finished Annie.

'So *that's* why Layla's at the club with all that muscle hanging around,' said Junior.

Annie didn't reply to that.

'I don't run,' he said defiantly. 'Not from nobody.'

Annie looked to Kath, then Molly. 'I'm here to let you know, that's all. *I* think you'd be well advised to disappear, take a holiday, tell no one where you're going. Because they've had a serious pop at me, and at Layla too. There's no telling where they intend to stop. And you're family.'

'And if we don't?' asked Molly.

Junior crossed his arms over his well-muscled middle. 'Fuck 'em. Let 'em come.'

Annie stood up. 'Look – I'm telling you, you should go. Talk to Steve, there's a safe house waiting.'

'And if we don't?' asked Junior.

'If you *don't* ... well, keep your eyes open. Whoever they are, they're not messing about.'

Tony drove her back to Holland Park. She hadn't been indoors ten minutes when the doorbell rang. She poked her head out of the study door, expecting to see Rosa letting someone in. Instead she saw Bri doing the honours, admitting two heavy-looking faces in dark suits.

Instantly she recognized black-haired Sandor, big as a bear as he lumbered inside. He was scanning the interior, checking everything was clear. Another two men came in behind him. Then Alberto Barolli stepped into the hall.

Annie leaned against the door frame and grinned with delight. 'Shit!' she said. 'The eagle really *has* landed.'

'Hiya, Stepmom,' said Alberto, striding across to give her a hug. 'You OK here? I came as soon as I could.'

'I'm fine. There's been some trouble, though.'

Alberto glanced around. 'Layla here?'

'No, I thought she'd be safer elsewhere.' She told him about Ellie's place.

'I'd like to see her, I'll go today.'

'She'd like that.' Annie said it automatically, though she doubted her own words. Layla had been awkward around Alberto all through her teenage years. Attending school in England, she had managed to duck out of any significant contact with him. Teenage girls were funny.

When *she* had been a teenager... Annie thought back and almost cringed with the shame of it. God, she had been *obsessed* with Max. She'd hung around wherever she'd thought he'd show up. She'd literally thrown herself at him. Annie was convinced that Layla'd had a similarly massive crush on Alberto. And she wondered whether her daughter nursed an infatuation for her glamorous and dangerous 'stepbrother' even now.

'Look, I'm going to get washed up, then we'll talk, OK?' he said.

'Yeah,' said Annie, and she watched him go up the stairs to his usual room, watched the heavies disperse – and felt comforted.

51

Almost despite herself, Layla was beginning to get quite comfy at the club. Already Precious – or 'the Glamazon' as Layla secretly thought of her – had taken to coming into her room and sitting on the bed with her, just chatting. They had a connection: they'd 'clicked' straight away.

She was quickly learning a new respect for the girls who worked here. They weren't stupid, as she'd previously suspected. They weren't slappers, either. Circumstances, she found, had pushed them into this line of work. And the pay, as Precious so rightly said, was tops.

'We get all our friends – only the pretty ones, management doesn't like dogs in the club – to come in,' Precious told her. 'For that, we get ten pounds per girl. They add to the club vibe.'

'Let me get this straight.' Layla was outraged at this. 'You're saying that, if a girl's ugly, she's turned away?'

'Got it in one.'

'But that's...'

'Business,' said Precious. 'All our nice-looking mates get free drinks, too.'

Layla squinted at Precious. 'But aren't you sort of *prostituting* these girls? Your mates?'

'In what way? They're having a great night out, all expenses paid. And they encourage the male punters to buy drinks for us, and for them too, at a hefty mark-up. Everyone's happy.'

'And the men sit around ogling them – and you – like prime cuts of beef.' Layla shuddered.

'It's nature,' smiled Precious. 'The laws of attraction.'

Layla raised a doubtful eyebrow.

'And then there's the podium work,' Precious went on.

Layla was fascinated, despite herself. It was another world!

'See, we get a basic wage, but the podium pays an extra seventy pounds per dance. And it's a hundred pounds per private dance in the VIP rooms. I pull down just under a thousand a week, on average.'

'*How* much?' Layla didn't earn that in a month. 'And does anyone ever – you know – proposition you, in the club?'

'Constantly,' said Precious. 'Goes with the job.' There were voices out in the hall. 'Look, the other girls are in, it's time you met them, don't you think? Come on. Let me introduce you.'

Precious led the way out into the hall and along to the dressing room. There were two women in there. They glanced up as Precious came in with Layla.

'This is China,' she said. 'China, meet Layla Carter. Her dad owns the club.'

China couldn't speak much English. She was tiny and exquisite, with hair like a bolt of black silk, big dark slanted eyes and peachy olive skin.

'She's from the Philippines,' explained Precious. 'Every penny she earns here, she sends home to her husband and her little girl. She used to be a cleaner, but the pay was lousy.'

Layla thought about that – the reality of being parted from all that was familiar, having to clean other people's toilets to scrape a living, then the hell of realizing it wasn't enough, would *never* be enough to feed your loved ones on the other side of the world, and having to do this – table dance for strangers – instead.

'And this is Destiny,' said Precious.

'Hi,' said Layla, and Destiny smiled. She had sad eyes and seemed quiet, Layla thought.

Destiny looked older than the others, maybe in her mid-thirties, but she was still ravishing. White-blonde and deeply tanned, she looked more Scandinavian than true-blue Brit.

'They seem nice,' said Layla when Precious came back to her room later.

Layla was ashamed of it now, but she had prejudged Precious. Prejudged *all* the dancers. She'd thought they must be dense to do a job like this one. But that wasn't the case. Talking to Precious soon convinced her that there was a pin-sharp brain working away inside that beautiful head.

'They *are* nice,' said Precious with a sigh. 'I feel sorry for China, though. She'll never get out of this game. She'll always have to be funding her family.'

'What about you?' asked Layla, curious.

'Me?' Precious's eyes lit up. 'Oh, I won't be in it for much longer. Let me show you something.'

Precious ran off out of the room and returned

minutes later clutching a textbook and a large wad of paperwork.

'What's this?' asked Layla, turning the textbook around so that she could read the title.

'Clinical Psychology?' she read in surprise.

'I'm studying for my finals, and supporting myself with the dancing,' said Precious. 'I've covered bereavement counselling, now I'm doing stress management.'

'My God,' said Layla, laughing. 'You're full of surprises.'

'I'm doing couple counselling next.' Precious pulled a face. 'Maybe Destiny could benefit.'

'Why do you say that?'

'D'you think she does this for fun?' Precious got up and gently closed the door. She lowered her voice. 'She's got three kids to support. She was stinking rich once, you know. Her husband was a banker, but he lost his job.'

'That's tough,' said Layla. A lot of City jobs had gone down the drain since Black Monday, the previous October. It had hit the market like a tornado, and the fallout had dragged on and on. Fearing for her own job, she could well understand the trauma Destiny's husband had gone through.

'It gets tougher,' said Precious. 'He was full of it at first. Men are, aren't they. Their loss, he said. Firms were crying out for his sort of expertise. He'd farm himself out to small companies, give them guidance for shares or a fee.'

'Sounds a good plan.'

'Yeah, but meanwhile they're living off their savings, and he *insists* on carrying on as if he's still pulling in a fortune in basic plus a hundred grand in bonuses.'

'Ah.' Through her accountancy work, Layla had come across this sort of thing all too often. A previously wealthy, powerful man's inability to accept a lesser reality. It usually led one way: to the bankruptcy court.

'It seems even he started to wake up in the end. He said they'd sell the house. And the live-in housekeeper-nanny would have to go. And the gym memberships. Destiny agreed to it all. But when she said she'd get a job, he flew into a rage, so she dropped it. He'd handle it, he told her. He'd always managed their money, did she think he was incapable of looking after his family or something? Only the house didn't fetch nearly as much as they'd expected, and his business didn't go well, and the rental on their new flat was forever being hiked up by the landlord. But whenever Destiny voiced her concerns, her old man would go into a strop, so in the end she just kept quiet.'

'Didn't he take any financial advice?' asked Layla.

'Oh, are you kidding? He thought he was Paul Getty, he could turn shit into gold. What would *he* want advice for? After a while the moods dipped even further and he started to sink into depression, lying on the couch all day staring at the TV. Then Destiny got a call from the landlord telling her he hadn't been paid in months.'

'Jesus!'

'So Destiny pulled the kids out of their private schools and put them into the local comprehensive. Hubby went crazy, of course. But by this time Destiny'd had a gutful. She said she was going to get a job. She'd been a secretary when they first met – she was his second wife, the trophy wife, the beautiful younger one – and she said she could do that job again. He freaked and accused her of only wanting to get into an office so that she could embark on an affair. Still, she started applying, going for interviews, only she couldn't land a secretarial job, and the bills were mounting, so she ended up here.'

'And does he *know…?*'

'Don't be silly.' Precious heaved a heartfelt sigh. 'She's covering the bills, but playing it down as much as she can, telling him she's waitressing. Because the pay's so good, she's been salting a bit of fuck-you money away on the side.'

'Huh?'

'Fuck-you money. Haven't you heard that expression?'

'No.'

'It's for when she decides enough is enough, and she bails.'

'Will she bail?'

'Hard to say. She still loves him, but if she's got any sense, she'll get out of it. Her life's a nightmare, the poor cow. He barely even talks to her these days, and she's starting to suspect he's being unfaithful. Well, he cheated on his first wife, why wouldn't he do it to his second?' Precious shook her head. 'Me, I'm never getting married. Not ever. I like to steer my own ship. I don't need some gormless, arrogant git to start grabbing the controls.'

'So you're going to be a psychologist,' smiled Layla.

'Got it in one. As soon as I qualify, I'm out of here.'

'Yeah, as if I haven't heard *that* a million times before,' said Ellie, putting her head around the door.

'It's true,' said Precious, unfazed.

'We'll see,' Ellie smiled. She turned to Layla. 'You got a visitor, Layla. Your brother's here.'

52

Layla stepped out into the hall. It seemed to be packed full of tall, hard-eyed men. One of them turned around and gave her a dazzling smile. Layla felt the blood rush to her face at the shock of seeing him here. She was *blushing,* for God's sake. And she looked a mess. Old jeans and a tatty T-shirt and her hair pulled back and ... damn it, some things never changed. He had only to *smile* at her and she was ready to roll over and die.

'What the hell are you doing here?' she said.

'And hello to you too,' said Alberto.

'He's not my brother,' Layla blurted out to Ellie, who was standing there with Chris, the pair of them all expectant and deferential, as if royalty had pitched up at their door. Which she supposed it had, sort of.

'Oh?' Ellie looked uncomfortable. She knew

who Alberto was. She had known his father Constantine through her connection to Annie. And she couldn't understand why Layla was acting so bad-tempered.

Why the hell did I say that? Layla wondered in anguish. She was hotly aware of all eyes on her, of Precious pushing into the doorway behind her and ogling Alberto with great interest.

'Well, that's correct. I'm not your brother,' said Alberto, stepping smoothly forward. 'Not *technically.*' His eyes were resting on Layla's face. 'But I've always thought of you as my sweet, prickly little English sister.'

Precious cleared her throat. Layla saw Alberto's eyes slip from her to Precious, and felt her guts clench up.

'Aren't you going to introduce us, Layla?' said Precious, smiling, already extending her beautifully manicured hand toward Alberto.

'Sure.' Layla folded her arms, her face like thunder. 'Alberto, this is Precious. Precious, Alberto.'

'Who is definitely *not* Layla's brother, right?' said Precious, all smiles. 'And American, is that right too?'

'That's right,' said Alberto, taking Precious's hand. 'Hi, Precious.'

Then he turned to Layla. 'Now come here and gimme a hug, Layla. And in answer to your question, your mother asked me to come. That's what I'm doing here.'

'Oh. Dear. God,' said Precious, stretched out on Layla's bed an hour later and staring wistfully at the ceiling.

Alberto had departed, taking his entourage with him. And Precious had said there was not a single doubt about it: she was in love.

'What?' snapped Layla, sitting on the stool by the dressing table.

'Oh, come on. That man is *fabulous.*' She turned her head and stared at Layla. 'And he's not your brother? Really?'

'Of *course* he's not my brother. Not in any way, shape, or form. His father married my mother. We're in no way related.'

'Right.'

Precious was staring at Layla's face.

'What?' demanded Layla.

'You seem mad at me. Why are you mad at me?' asked Precious. This was a feature of the girl, and one of the reasons Layla had taken to her. She had this disarming, completely in-your-face and open honesty – she was so unlike Layla herself, who bottled everything up inside.

'I'm not mad at you,' said Layla.

'Well, you *seem* to be.'

'It's just...' started Layla.

'Yes?' prompted Precious. 'Just what? Is there a problem with me fancying your brother...?'

Layla jumped to her feet. 'He's not my fucking brother!' she yelped.

'Oh.' Precious sat up, her eyes fastened on Layla's face. She swung her legs to the floor. 'Oh dear. I think I've got it.'

'You've got *what?*'

'You fancy him yourself.'

'That's...' Layla swiped a hand over her scraped-back hair. 'That's complete and utter *bullshit.*'

'Is it?'

Layla's face seemed to collapse in on itself. 'Oh Christ ... no it's not. Oh damn it, I'm such a mess...'

'No you're not.'

Layla started pacing around the room. 'It's totally ridiculous. How could I be so stupid as to develop a crush on him? It's *insane.*'

'Well, I wouldn't put it quite as strongly as that,' said Precious, smiling slightly. 'How long have you felt this way about him?'

Layla looked at Precious uncertainly. She'd never shared this with *anyone.* But she liked Precious. They'd formed a bond from the instant they'd met. And ... yes, she trusted her. Precious wouldn't blab, she knew it.

'Oh shit, just about forever,' she said, exhaling sharply. 'Since I was ten years old, I think. It was so bad I was embarrassed to be anywhere near him – I was relieved to be at school in England. And whenever he came over, I did the vanishing act.' Layla looked at Precious. 'Pathetic, yes?'

Precious shrugged. 'You can't legislate for how you feel. And as you so rightly say – he's *not* your brother.'

'Oh no.' Layla was shaking her head, wagging her finger in Precious's face. 'No, I can see what you're doing. You're *doing* me, aren't you? All this psychology stuff, all this counselling hoo-ha – you're trying it out on me.'

Precious didn't seem to be listening. She had a look of excitement on her face. Her eyes were moving over Layla assessingly.

'He sees you – and he sees his sister,' she said.

'Well, obviously.'

'He doesn't see you as a fanciable woman. Well, it would be a bit of a push,' said Precious.

'What does that mean?'

'Nothing.'

'No, come on. What?' she demanded.

'I wonder why you feel the need to play down your looks so much, that's all,' shrugged Precious.

'Look, just bugger off, will you?' said Layla through gritted teeth. Who the *fuck* did this girl think she was, to say that? '*Bugger off.* Go and shake your arse in someone's face, that's what you're best at.'

Precious stood up. Though Layla was trembling with fury, she seemed unperturbed. 'Attack as the best form of defence,' she said, smiling.

'Fuck off!' yelled Layla.

Precious hadn't long gone when Layla heard the phone ringing in the office down the hall. Ellie picked up, and Layla heard her own name mentioned. She went out into the corridor, listening. Ellie was saying: 'No, no, far too poorly to come to the phone... Well, of course it's an inconvenience for *you,* and she feels terrible about letting you down, but what can she do?... A major audit?... Well, you know what a conscientious girl Layla is, she wouldn't ever want to let you down, but she's so ill... Yes, OK, I'll see she gets the message.'

Ellie put the phone down, looked at Layla. 'Sounds like your boss is a right prick!'

'Was it Etchingham?' Layla could feel her heart pounding.

'Yeah, that's the one: Graham Etchingham. Your mum must have given him this number,' said Ellie. 'Cold-blooded fucker.'

'That's my head of department. What exactly did he say?'

'He wants a doctor's certificate by tomorrow.' Ellie shrugged. 'Don't worry about it – your dad could get you ten if you wanted. Whew – talk about a short fuse!'

Layla chewed her lip. 'I'm going to lose my job,' she moaned.

'No you're not,' said Ellie, getting up to give her a hug. Layla was such a worrier: Ellie wished she'd toughen up, grow a bit of a ruthless streak like her mother. *Fuck* Etchingham. He was a tiny parasite on the arse-end of the Earth, nothing for a Carter woman to trouble herself over. Why couldn't Layla *see* that?

'Yes, I *am*,' Layla insisted, pulling free of Ellie's embrace. 'Because no one knows how long this is going to go on for, do they? I've been off three days – three days! – and already Etchingham's spitting blood.'

'Well, there's nothing we can do about it, is there?' said Ellie. 'We just have to sit tight until this resolves itself.'

Layla had her doubts that this would ever resolve itself. Ellie didn't know the whole story, the full awfulness of what had happened. All Ellie knew was that Annie had a bit of trouble. No one had told her that Layla had killed a woman, shot her dead. Layla shuddered anew to think of it. Couldn't believe it, even now. She had a terrifying sense of things hurtling beyond her control, and she hated that. She craved normality, neat rows of figures to add up and make sense of.

She craved her *job.*

53

'The police are sniffing around,' said Annie next morning.

They were in the drawing room, Max on one sofa, her on another. Only a few feet apart, but it seemed like a mile. She didn't want to talk to him. But all this shit was happening, and Layla was clearly at risk. They were her parents. They *had* to communicate, even if it was a pain in the arse.

'I'm not surprised,' said Max.

'Meaning?' she asked.

He stretched lazily in his chair. Annie kept her eyes on his face.

'Meaning you're sitting on a pile of Mafia money here, aren't you.'

Annie felt her jaw clench. 'This house is mine,' she said.

'Yeah, but it *was* Constantine Barolli's. Before he cashed in his chips.'

'What are you driving at, exactly?'

'The Bill don't ever rest over Mafia millions. They'll never let it go.'

Annie thought of standing in the graveyard with Alberto, of the things he'd told her. That he might be forced to make a break for it any time now. She knew Max was right about the cops and their attitude to people profiting from organized crime.

'And besides, there are other things,' said Max.

Annie took a calming breath. 'Can we not talk in riddles please?'

Max shrugged. 'If I say it straight, you'll kick off.'

'Try me.'

'Come on. You *know* what people are saying. Same thing they've *always* said.'

'No. I don't. Humour me.'

'OK. They're *saying* you're his mistress. And that you only have to let out one little squeak and he's over here, hanging out the back of you.'

Annie's eyes were like chips of ice. 'Alberto's my stepson,' she snapped.

Her heart was pounding hard against her ribs. She felt sick. *This* was what had broken up their marriage. *This* was the whole source of all their bitter arguments. Max had *never* accepted that her relationship with Alberto was an innocent one.

She could tell him it was until she was blue in the face: he'd never believe it. All her business trips to New York, he perceived as visits to Alberto. They weren't of course. Oh, she'd often see Alberto while she was there, but she'd rarely stayed with him. Usually she stayed at the Old-Colonial-style penthouse she owned in Manhattan. She adored Alberto. But *not* the way she had always adored Max. Which she didn't any more, she told herself. Not at all. Because he had killed her love for him stone dead.

Max gave a chilly smile. 'Looks a lot like his dad though, don't he?'

Before she knew it, Annie was on her feet, the blood singing in her ears.

'Listen up, will you? Alberto is my *stepson,*' she repeated, glaring at her ex-husband with murder in her heart.

'Sure he is.' Now Max stood up too. Annie didn't flinch – she wouldn't give him the satisfaction. They glared at each other, nose to nose.

'He *is.* And you know something else? You and me, we're *divorced.* If I wanted to sleep with *anyone,* you'd have no say in the matter. Even Alberto. Which isn't the case, which has *never* been the case, you arsehole.'

Max was silent for a moment, his eyes locked with hers.

'You know what?' he said at last.

'No. What?' demanded Annie. She could feel the heat of his breath on her face. Could smell the faint citrus tang of his cologne. She wanted, *so much,* to hit him.

'I never know whether to fight you or fuck you, and that's a fact,' he said. 'I'm leaning toward the second option, right this minute.'

This was how it had always been between them. Max was deep and dark, forever pulling strings and taking risks, determined to come out on top in anything he did; Annie was obstinate to the last, with a strong need for security and stability. She was his polar opposite. They sparked off each other, attracted, repelled.

She could feel the tug of his attraction, even now. And he could feel hers. She could see it in his eyes, the dilation of his pupils, the red-hot flash of desire evident in the tension in his body.

He started to move forward. Annie drew back her arm and slapped him, hard, around the face. Max stopped in his tracks. He rubbed at his jaw, gave her a glinting smile and stepped forward again, undeterred.

At that moment, the door opened.

'Am I interrupting?' It was Alberto.

Max looked at Alberto, then at Annie. 'You see what I mean? One little squeak.'

Alberto glanced between the two of them. 'Did I miss something?' he asked.

'No,' they said together.

'Come in,' said Annie, glad of the distraction but all too aware that this would only confirm Max's suspicions: here was Alberto, with her. She'd called for help, and he'd come running.

'Have a seat,' she said. Max sat down on the sofa opposite her. Alberto took one of the armchairs. She hoped she wasn't blushing, but she was very afraid that she was. She could see the mark on Max's face, where she'd struck him.

Fuck it. I shouldn't have lost it like that, she thought.

'OK. This putz who got himself blown up by the car bomb,' said Alberto. 'His name's…'

'Frankie Day,' said Annie and Max at the same time.

There was a silence. Annie cleared her throat, and avoided looking at Max. 'The police filled me in. They phoned, asked me if I knew him. I don't.'

'I heard it from my people on the street,'

shrugged Max. He had a network in London who usually kept him up to speed on what was happening.

'He was a hobo,' said Alberto.

'A...?' Annie frowned.

'A drifter. A drop-out. And a small-time thief. He obviously didn't rig the thing. That was down to a red-haired man spotted at the scene just after you left the car,' said Alberto directly to Annie.

'You're not telling us anything we don't already know,' said Max.

'Then where are we going with this?' asked Alberto.

'So far? Nowhere,' said Annie. 'How was Layla?'

'You went to see Layla?' said Max. He didn't look too pleased.

'Yeah, I did. And she's fine.'

'She's fucking traumatized, she's not fine at all.'

'She's a tough kid. And I left a few of my guys there.'

'That's taken care of already,' said Max. 'My boys are on the spot.'

'Still, a little extra never hurts.'

Annie looked between the two of them in exasperation. 'This isn't a contest for who can provide the best back-up,' she pointed out. 'We have to find out what's going on. Or we won't ever be able to rest.'

'You think the intruder was Orla Delaney,' said Alberto.

'I don't think. I know,' said Annie.

Max leaned back in his chair, linked his hands behind his head. 'Steve wasn't one hundred per cent sure, but he thought it was, too.'

'Well, I'm delighted he's reassured you that I'm not imagining things,' snapped Annie.

Max gave her a sour smile. 'This red-haired bloke *could* be Redmond. You thought of that? And this business with the shamrock. That says Irish, don't it. A calling-card.'

She had thought of it. And then she had tried not to. Whenever her brain did drift toward Redmond, it stalled in total panic. She had never feared *anyone* the way she feared Redmond Delaney. If he was out to get her...

'What?' asked Alberto, looking at her face. 'What is it?'

'Well, it's just ... why *Orla?*' Annie was frowning. 'Why would Redmond have left it to her to break into the house – assuming this red-headed man is Redmond. It doesn't make sense. Orla was never one to actively *participate* in the hard game.'

'She was always there to yank Redmond's choke-chain when he got out of hand,' said Max thoughtfully.

'That's it! Exactly,' agreed Annie. She glanced between the two men. 'And there's something else…'

'Go on,' said Max.

'You knew Redmond,' she said to him. 'Planting a car bomb – does that strike you as something Redmond would do, in person? He was always…'

'I met Redmond too,' said Alberto. 'He didn't seem the hands-on type.'

Annie had a vision of Redmond: the sharp Savile Row suits, the black coat, the black leather gloves;

his pale, still face that looked as if it had been carved from ivory; his dark red hair clipped sternly into submission, and those stunning, coldly staring green eyes that seemed to lance straight through to your innermost heart. She felt a shiver run through her.

'Maybe he's changed,' said Max, watching her face. 'Maybe he don't have the manpower he once had, maybe now he has to dirty his hands.'

Annie nodded slowly. Max could be right. The police said the man they were looking for was bulky and red-haired. Redmond had *never* been bulky. But maybe, in his middle years, he'd gained weight. Who knew? 'The police said Semtex was used in the car.'

'Suggesting what? IRA?'

'The Delaneys were heading to Ireland when their plane vanished,' said Alberto, thinking aloud. 'If they survived, maybe they became involved in the Irish troubles. Don't you think that's possible?'

'*Anything's* possible,' said Max. He looked at Annie. 'You've warned Ruthie? And Kath and the kids?'

'Of course.' And here they were again, plunging the whole family into crisis, forcing them to scatter. 'Junior's being bullish about it, I don't think he'll go,' she said.

'Your cousin ... Kath...?' asked Alberto.

Annie nodded.

'And Molly, her daughter. They've gone?'

'Kath and Molly have made themselves scarce, even if Junior won't,' she said. 'And Ruthie's already gone.'

'So our next move is...?' asked Alberto.

'You're the fucking Golden Boy. No ideas?' sneered Max.

Alberto stared at Max. Then he smiled, very slightly. 'Not one,' he said. 'I'll put the word out, see what I can rustle up.'

Annie felt comforted by that. She knew what a word from Alberto involved. The request for information would be passed from mouth to mouth in bars, restaurant, discos, working men's clubs, at Salvation Army hostels, on taxi ranks in high streets and outside airports; working girls shivering on the streets would pass it on to doormen; truckers in greasy spoon cafes would be notified. Everyone would be keeping an eye out, searching for the information, anticipating a rich pay-off if they passed on anything valuable.

'Did Layla get a good look at the man who tried to attack her? That could be a help,' said Alberto.

'I'll talk to her,' said Max.

The phone rang on the side table. Annie snatched it up.

Listened. Then put it back down on the cradle. She swore once, loudly.

'What?' Max demanded.

'That was Ellie. About Layla.'

'What about her? She OK?'

'She's gone back to work.'

54

Rufus was going crazy with worry. Three days had gone by and still there'd been no word from Orla.

He'd called the farm in Limerick. She should have been there by now. She'd told him that if anything went wrong, that was where she'd go. But there was no answer. Even though he'd let the phone ring and ring, no one picked up.

Knowing Orla, she was probably out in the barn, music blasting out of the speakers while she worked on those mad paintings of hers. She'd be livid, knowing that Annie Carter was alive, that her plan had failed. Maybe she was still angry with him, for letting the daughter slip through his hands. Maybe that was it: she was ignoring the phone deliberately, to punish him. Her mother was a bit deaf, so she wouldn't hear it ringing, and old Davey's mind was too far gone for him to notice.

Despite the sick dread in the pit of his stomach, he would not let himself consider the possibility that she was dead, that the Carter woman had somehow turned the tables and emerged triumphant.

After the car bomb screw-up, he had driven to the house in Holland Park. There was a burly guy guarding the front door, so he kept to the far side of the square, careful not to attract attention. It was as well he was cautious, because it was soon apparent that he wasn't the only one keeping an eye on the place. He spotted a couple of men in cars, and there were other men repairing the burglar alarm and replacing the basement window.

I'll be back by six. If I'm not, stick to the plan ... we meet back at the farm.

He remembered how insistent she had been that there must be no deviation from the plan. So that was where she would be: at the farm, waiting for him. And he would join her there.

'I will. I swear it,' he muttered under his breath.

It was a promise he intended to keep. But he wasn't going to show up empty-handed.

First he would kill Annie Carter. Then he would take a little gift for his beloved, something to prove that he had succeeded in his mission – a hand or a foot would do, or perhaps the scalp. Yes, that beautiful long dark hair would made the perfect trophy.

The Holland Park address remained heavily guarded, but Rufus had seen the daughter leave the house on the day of the bomb, he'd followed the car that took her to the Shalimar. He'd been keeping an eye on the place ever since, waiting for an opportunity. And finally he was rewarded for his patience. The girl emerged, minders all around her. And she travelled into the City. An accountancy firm, Bowdler and Etchingham. He went in, timing his entry so that he walked in with another man while the girl on the reception was on the phone, busy. Once inside, he took the lift to the second floor.

'Where's Layla's office?' he asked the first secretary he saw.

She didn't know. 'Try the next floor up,' she told him.

He did. Picked up a few leaflets from a desk and sauntered through with them in his hands. No one stopped him. He asked another girl the same question.

'Over there,' she said.

At lunchtime, when Layla Carter went out with her minders, he got one of his little helpers to leave a gift, and a little something extra in her Filofax.

55

There was an atmosphere so thick in the office that you could cut it with a knife. Resentment festered beneath the surface of every water-cooler conversation. Nobody spoke to Layla. But she was determined to tough it out. They'd mellow. She wasn't sure *Ellie* would, though. They'd got into a screaming match as Layla was going out the door.

'What harm can I come to?' Layla had demanded. 'The minute I move, an army of heavies trails behind me. Dad's boys and the Barolli boys too. They're watching me like bloody *hawks*. I'm safe as houses.'

But despite her bold words, she didn't *feel* safe.

The journey to work was taken in a limo with one of Alberto's heavies at the wheel. Another one followed her to the door. She saw a muscle-bound suit watching her from across the street as she entered the office building. Everything about the men crowding around her reminded her that she'd stepped sideways into a dark and dangerous world.

However the minute she got to her desk – the atmosphere notwithstanding – she settled down to work, and was soon absorbed, soon calmer.

So what if all the office banter seemed to be directed toward anyone but her? She was happy enough, making neat columns of figures into perfect sense.

Then Graham Etchingham, her head of department, walked by her desk, and paused.

'Have you brought in the doctor's certificate?' he asked.

Layla shook her head. 'Couldn't get an appointment. Sorry.'

'Make sure you bring it tomorrow.'

'I will,' she said, and he moved on.

He didn't ask if she was better now. Didn't give a *shit,* she knew. She was just a number-cruncher. Who could be replaced, in an instant, by some other hopeful, job-hungry number-cruncher.

Layla knew that Ellie would tell Mum. And Mum would tell Dad, and Alberto, and they would all kick off like crazy. For now, though, she was happy. She could almost – but never quite – forget what had happened, what she had done, how awful it was.

Lunchtime, she had arranged to meet up with

Precious in the park. She nipped to the shops for a sandwich and a drink, aware of the minders dogging her footsteps.

'Hey! Layla! Layla Carter!'

She stopped dead on the pavement. She wasn't ten paces from her office building. Junior was rushing toward her. Two men immediately moved in and jostled her backward; two more grabbed Junior.

'Shit!' complained Layla, dropping her pack of sandwiches.

'What the fuck?' bellowed Junior.

People were turning, staring.

'It's OK, it's only Junior,' she said quickly. 'My cousin.'

The heavies drew back. The two holding Junior dropped him. He straightened his jacket, glaring at them. 'Thank you,' he said, stalking toward Layla. 'Jesus, is this all to do with what your mum told us about? What's going on?'

He really was *very* good looking, thought Layla. And very aggressive. Very in-your-face. Which was quite attractive, in a man. Layla thought of the contrast between loud, bouncy, bolshy Junior, who always seemed such a child, and Alberto, who was so adult, so smooth, so polished – and yet so deadly. Just thinking of him, she felt her stomach contract with longing.

'What has Mum told you?' she asked him cautiously.

'That we should clear off out of it, that there's trouble. The thing with her car. And she said someone tried to nab you.'

'That's right. But you haven't gone,' said Layla.

He shrugged. 'Molls and Mum have.'

'Not you though?'

'I'm not scared of some bastard I can't even see,' said Junior.

Isn't that the scariest type? thought Layla. 'So Mum told you about the bomb?'

'Christ, *everyone* heard about that. It was on the freakin' news.'

'Well, I'd say that was pretty damned scary.'

'Look, I've got to go. Working,' said Junior, planting a smacker on her cheek. 'See ya, Layla.'

Then he was gone, surging off into the crowds. She watched him go, springing along on his toes. So bloody self-confident. Whatever Mum had said to him, he clearly hadn't been listening, or he'd be running for the hills right now.

Layla walked on, crossed the road to the park.

'Hey! Layla!' She was searching out a free seat when the female voice halted her. She turned. Four minders in eye-line. And Precious, hurrying along in jeans and a cream ruffled shirt, her hair loose and bouncing around her beautiful face, her luminous grey eyes alight with a smile.

'Hi, Precious,' grinned Layla. Precious's was only the second friendly face she had seen since starting work this morning.

Two of the minders approached, watching Precious, their hands creeping inside their jackets. Layla shook her head hard, and they backed off.

'Here's a free one,' said Precious, and they sat down on a guano-spattered bench under the shade of a tree.

'Haven't you brought any lunch?' asked Layla.

'God, no. I never eat until six. Got to watch

the body.'

'Don't be daft, you're gorgeous. Have one of these, I can't eat all this.' Layla split open the cellophane pack and handed Precious half her lunch.

'Oh, OK. Thanks.'

They ate in companionable silence. Rather, Precious ate and Layla nibbled. Then Precious said: 'Um, Layla?'

'Hm?'

'Are you *aware* that there are four men watching you?'

Layla sighed. 'My dad's men. And Alberto's.'

'Oh, that's good. They're looking out for you.'

Layla shuddered. 'I hate it,' she said.

'Is this how you always live? Under guard this way?'

'No. It isn't. It's just...' Layla stopped herself. She was in danger of saying too much. It was so easy to talk to Precious, to confide in her. And she mustn't. 'Something's happened, that's all. It's put the family sort of on red alert.'

'Ah, then I suppose all you can do is loosen up, let them carry on with their job of guarding you, and get on with your life.'

'Loosen up? How would *you* feel if someone was after you, someone you didn't even know, so you had to be surrounded by all these *people...?*'

Precious stared at Layla. 'Sorry,' she said. 'Me and my big mouth. But, well...'

'Well what?'

Precious shrugged. 'You're Max Carter's daughter. I thought you'd be used to all this shit.'

'I'm not.' Layla felt guilty now. Precious was trying to be friendly, and she had slapped her down quite hard, for the second time. Both times, Precious had hit a nerve.

'Look, I'm sorry I bit your head off,' she blurted out. 'And before, when we spoke about Alberto. Sorry.'

Layla swallowed a bite of sandwich. It was dry. She took a swig of Coke, then set it aside on the bench. She was going to have to start eating properly soon, but right now food just made her gag.

Precious waved a casual hand. 'Ah, forget it. I do it all the time. Poke and pry. And I shouldn't. People hate it. And you've been stressed to hell, I can see that.'

Stressed? She'd been going out of her mind. She still was.

'I know you were only trying to help,' said Layla.

'That's true. I was.'

'I'm sorry.'

'Forget it. It was nothing. If I'd known it was such a sore subject, I wouldn't have opened my fat gob.'

'Can I ask you something?' said Layla.

'Anything. Go on.'

'About the dancing. It's *naked* dancing, have I got that right?'

Precious shrugged. 'Sometimes. Sometimes it's a G-string, but mostly it's nude.'

'How do you *do* that? In front of strangers?'

'Easy.'

'And what about when – you know – you've got the curse?'

'That's easy too. Put in a tampon, cut off the

string. Sorted.'

Layla was silent for long moments. 'You ever been in love with anyone?' she asked finally.

'God, yes. Too many to count,' grinned Precious.

'Not punters?'

'Sometimes.' Precious's eyes grew distant. Then she turned her head and smiled at Layla. 'Not often.'

They carried on eating, and shared the Coke. After a while Layla glanced at her watch. 'Got to get back,' she sighed, 'or Etchingham's going to kill me.'

She stood up, depositing the detritus from their meal into the nearest wastebasket.

'It's been nice,' said Precious. 'We should do this again.'

'Yeah. Why not,' said Layla, feeling a little pang of something, maybe happiness, settle into her gut. Precious had forgiven her, the sun was shining, she was back at work in a world she understood. All was well *except* ... she had killed someone. The glimmer of happiness vanished in a flash.

The shooting filled her dreams, tormenting her nightly. It was there when she woke too. Occasionally, for a blissful moment, something else would distract her, but it was never long before the memory came crashing in on her again. She'd killed Orla Delaney.

As she left Precious and walked towards her office, her minders following, that tiny fragment of happiness fell away. There was danger all around the Carters, and none of them knew where it would come from next – or who was directing it.

She looked ahead, to her office block, to the third-floor window where she worked. It almost looked as though the glass was obscured. She stared, wondering what trick of the light had caused the effect. And then she realized that what she was seeing was smoke behind the glass. There was a *fire* in her office.

56

Annie was waiting at Ellie's place when Layla showed up carrying a small cardboard box containing her Filofax, her pens and a few other bits and pieces.

'What the hell's going on?' demanded Annie, stopping her in the upstairs hallway.

Layla looked blankly at her mother. This she didn't need. Not now. She could see Ellie and Chris rubber-necking along the hall. She pushed past Annie and went into her room, dumping the box on to the bed.

'I told you to stay put. Not to go wandering the streets. Not to go in to work. I *told* you.' Annie followed Layla into the bedroom and closed the door.

'Well?' asked Annie.

'Well *what?*' Layla flung her bag aside and slumped down beside her box of possessions.

Annie let out a sharp breath. 'Layla. We aren't

playing here. This is serious.'

'I realize that.'

'So, no more flouting the rules, OK?'

'No fear of that.' Layla looked up at her mother, her eyes suddenly bright, her expression brittle.

'What do you mean?'

'I *mean* I've been sacked.'

'You what?'

'Yeah. Sacked.'

'Well ... it doesn't matter. Jobs are ten a penny, you'll get another when all this blows over. Why'd they sack you?'

'Blows over?' Layla let out a sobbing laugh. 'What are you *talking* about? I shot someone, Mum. Shot her dead. You nearly died in a car bombing. Someone tried to grab me, and if he'd caught me...' She stopped, shaking her head. 'And you talk about when it *blows over!* How *can* it?'

Annie took a breath. Somehow or other, Layla was going to have to tough this out, absorb it. She'd always seemed soft, but Annie thought that deep down her daughter had a strong core. Now, she was going to have to prove it.

'Why'd they sack you?' Annie repeated, more gently.

'Because I was smoking in the office.'

'Well, there's no law against *that.*' Annie frowned. 'Since when did you start smoking?'

'I don't. That's the point. I went out to lunch, met Junior and then Precious. As I was heading back to the office and I saw smoke at my office window. By the time I got inside, and all the fire alarms on the third floor were going, people were running around shouting. A cigarette had been left smouldering in the waste bin and it caught fire. Luckily, someone spotted it quickly and put it out. But my boss, who's fed up with me anyway because of all this *shit* that's happening, because I've been off sick and I'm never sick and he thinks I'm taking the piss – he lost it completely. Said I could have burnt the whole place down, I was a fucking nuisance, and to clear my desk.'

Layla stopped speaking, seeing the whole scene again. Everyone watching. The gloating, avaricious expressions on their faces, the stench of smoke, the endless shrieking of the fire alarms, while Etchingham tore into her.

'But you don't smoke. Surely they *know* that?'

Layla waved a tired hand in front of her face. 'Oh, no one came leaping to my defence. Even the young mums who keep having time off to nurse their sick kids aren't as hated as much as I am. And that's saying something. I told Etchingham I didn't drop the cigarette in there, but he wasn't buying. He wanted an excuse to fire my arse, and he found it.'

'Does anyone else have access to your office?' asked Annie.

'Everyone. I don't lock it when I go out – there *is* no lock on my door. No one goes in there, as a general rule. But *someone* did. And they tossed a lit cigarette into the bin, and got me sacked.'

'Jealous colleague?' suggested Annie.

Layla dropped her head into her hands. 'Oh, you know what? Take your pick. They all hate me. What does it matter now anyway.'

'He's probably done you a favour,' said Annie,

wondering if someone in the office would really risk a major fire just to get Layla into trouble. Or had someone from outside the building walked into her empty office and started it?

'Thanks for that,' said Layla coldly.

'There's no security on the front door at your office, is there?'

'No. Of course not. Why would we need it?'

'Maybe to stop someone coming in off the street and setting a fire.'

Layla grew still. 'I thought it was just a prank, to get me in bother with Etchingham.'

'It's possible,' said Annie. 'But on the other hand...'

'Jesus!'

'All the more reason to stay here and stay secure, OK?'

'I'll die of boredom,' said Layla.

'There are worse things to die of.' Annie peered intently at her daughter. 'Look, I had a thought. Why don't you help Ellie out with the books?'

Layla stared at Annie. Fuck's *sake*. She had sworn she would never get involved in her parents' business, and here she was: living over the shop, and now about to do the firm's accounts. This was absolutely bloody great.

'Thanks, but I don't think so.' Layla took out her Filofax. She had contacts. She would phone around, see what she could come up with. She unfastened the Filofax and screamed when a four-leaf clover fluttered out and floated gently to the floor.

When her mother was gone – taking the shamrock with her – Layla reassessed the situation. The fire and the fact that some creep had been up close, handling her Filofax, slipping that damned thing inside it, gave her the shudders.

Much as she hated the fact, she knew Annie was right: going out to work – *any* work – was out of the question. But maybe she could do what Mum suggested, help out with the company accounts? She didn't want to. On the other hand she couldn't just sit here and wait for the next disaster to occur. This forced inactivity was *killing* her.

She approached Ellie early that evening, when the club was still empty but the girls were getting prettied up for the punters. Ellie was in the office, talking to Miss Pargeter, a dried-up old stick of a woman who came in and helped out with the bookkeeping.

'Um ... could I have a word?' asked Layla. She glanced at Miss Pargeter. 'Privately.'

Ellie moved out of the tiny office and into the hall. 'Yes, Layla?'

'I was wondering ... Mum suggested you might need some help with the accounts...?'

Ellie hadn't closed the door of the office. Miss Pargeter looked up at Layla, and in that single glance Layla saw the whole story of Miss Pargeter's life. Some of the more unkind girls laughed about her behind her back, called her an old maid. She was often seen bent double over the desk in the windowless office, scratching away at figures.

That's me, isn't it, thought Layla. *That's me in thirty years' time, an aged lady, unmarried, childless, with a hairy upper lip and nothing to live for but doing the accounts.*

'Well...' said Ellie, glancing back at Miss Pargeter. Miss Pargeter returned her attention to the page she was working on.

'Actually, no,' said Layla quickly. 'It was an idea of Mum's, but I don't think I want to, not really. Not just now. Sorry to have bothered you.'

Layla hurried back to her room.

No, she thought grimly. *No way am I becoming that.*

Precious was in there waiting for her, glammed up for the evening's trade, wearing her sapphire-blue silk gown this time. She turned from the mirror and smiled when she saw Layla there.

'Precious?' said Layla. She thought that she had never seen anyone as beautiful, as poised, as downright *fabulous* as Precious.

'Yeah, sweetie?'

Layla *almost* said what was on her mind. She felt restless and trapped. As if she was on the edge of something awful, momentous, some twisting turn of fate that was going to change everything forever. She wanted to say all this to Precious, to talk it through with her. But instead she bottled it and turned away.

'Nah. It's nothing.'

57

When Annie left the Shalimar after talking to Layla, she bumped straight into Max.

'Oh!' she said, taken off-guard. She glanced at Tony, who was hovering nearby. 'Wait in the car, Tone, will you?'

Tony went off, leaving her and Max standing in the busy street, people passing by, stepping around them.

'Has she told you about the fire?' she asked him.

'Yeah, she did. She phoned me from the office. Sounded like all hell was breaking loose. That's why I'm here.'

She told you before she told me, thought Annie, feeling the familiar nagging sensation of hurt.

'I'd warned her to stay put,' said Annie defensively. 'There was one of those paper shamrocks in her Filofax, you know. The same as was left in her trainer when that arsehole tried to get her.'

'Right.'

There was a silence. It wasn't a comfortable one.

'So,' she said brightly. 'How are you?'

Max's eyes widened. 'Christ, we're being civilized all of a sudden, aren't we?'

'I've always tried to be civilized with you, Max. Despite provocation.'

'Well don't. You spitting and yelling at me seems more natural.'

Annie stared at him. He was trying to rattle her. He loved to rattle her. And he wasn't going to succeed. But her teeth were gritted and her shoulders were tense. *Fuck* him.

'I've done all that,' she said. 'And you know what? It's not worth it.'

'Quite happy with Golden Boy then,' said Max.

'I'm not *with* Golden Boy,' she said. There was a cramp in her left shoulder. She could feel her temper starting to take hold. 'I never have been.'

'Sure.'

'Alberto's my stepson.'

'Yep.'

'And that's all,' she said. She wanted to scream it. She forced herself not to.

'If you say so.'

'I *do* say so. And actually – if I wanted to "be" with him, as you so tastefully put it, I could whistle for it. Because he doesn't see me that way.'

Max's eyes narrowed to slits. 'And how does he see you? Exactly?'

'As his stepmom. Which is what I am. Nothing more, nothing less.' Annie took a calming breath. He could do this to her, every time. Make her blind with rage, completely *lose* it. But she wasn't going to. Not this time. 'And you know what? I've had this out with you already. About a thousand times. And I am *not* doing it again. So let's get down to business, shall we? The man who planted the car bomb. Do you think it was Redmond?'

'Dunno. Bulky and red-haired, that was the description Layla gave me of that fucker in the park, and it matches what the police are saying about the bomber. But Redmond? Not sure.

Could have been.'

Annie's mouth dropped open. 'What do you mean, it *could* have been?' she snapped. 'Is that the best you can do? You've got people crawling all over this city and you say it *could* have been?'

'No other sightings,' he shrugged.

'Well, let's not wait for *sightings,*' said Annie sharply. 'Let's go to where the Delaneys are likely to be found. Their old houses, clubs, the places they controlled. What about the scrap yard, is that still operational?'

'We've covered that. The scrap yard's gone, has been for years. Everywhere's been checked out,' he said. 'No sign of Redmond. The boys have lifted quite a few stones, waited to see what crawls out from underneath. Nothing much has, except–'

'Then we're sitting ducks! If he realizes Orla's been taken care of, he's going to come in all guns blazing.'

'You going to let me finish? We've found a distant Delaney relation called Dickon. We think there's a cousin too, but we're having trouble tracking him down.'

'For God's sake, Max, why didn't you *say* so?'

Max gave a slow smile. 'Scared?'

Annie glared at him. '*Fuck* you. Of course I'm scared. I'm scared for Layla. She's already trying to break out, and it's dangerous. She has no idea what we're dealing with here – and I don't want to tell her just how sick, scary and downright bloody perverted Redmond is.'

'If he's alive,' said Max.

Annie nodded slowly. 'You know what...?'

'Go on.'

'I've got a creeping feeling. I think he is. I really do.'

'Then I guess we'd better get him before he gets us,' said Max.

58

'The IRA use this stuff,' said the portly male pathologist.

'What stuff is that?' asked DCI Hunter. He was trying not to look at the remains laid out on the table. Trying not to inhale, too. *Smoke and pork*, he thought. Hadn't he read somewhere that cannibals said human flesh tasted like pig meat? Well, it probably did, and here was the proof. Shit, it was enough to turn a person vegetarian overnight.

'Semtex. Traces of it all over the clothes.' The pathologist plucked up a detached finger with his gloved hands. He could have plucked up any other part, easily. A toe, an ear, a fragment of a cock. Lumps of shattered blackened flesh draped in charred scraps of clothing. When you pieced all the bits together, laid them out like the pathology team had, then you could see that this had once been a living, breathing person. Otherwise, you'd be hard put to guess.

'It's clever stuff,' said the pathologist, his eyes alight with interest.

'How so?' Hunter thought it was vile.

'Sniff. See? Not much odour to it.'

All Hunter could smell was scorched flesh.

'Semtex is easy to use. Very stable, unlike nitro. Gaddafi's boys out in Libya have been shipping it to the IRA for years. The Irish boys have been using it for landmines, and as a 'booster' for homemade bombs. And for little car jobs like this, too.'

'Right,' said Hunter.

'What else can I tell you? He died instantly. Literally blown apart. Not a bad way to go, actually, despite appearances. Oblivion in an instant. You found a name for him yet?'

'Frank Day,' said Hunter. DI Duggan had filled him in on the departed.

Frank or 'Frankie' Day, as he was known, had been a small-time criminal feeding a voracious dope habit. He'd been trying car doors the day the bomb went off.

He'd tried the Merc.

Boom!

No more Frankie.

Interestingly, the car belonged to Annie Carter. Who apparently had no idea why someone would want to blow her arse to kingdom come. But no smoke without fire, right? He thought of Annie Carter and along with the thought came just one word: trouble. For years she'd been skirting around on the edges of criminal gangs. London overlords like her ex husband. She had connections to the *Mafia,* for Christ's sake. But the woman was like Teflon. Nothing ever stuck to her.

So all they had to go on was the red-haired man the girl in the charity shop had mentioned. The one who'd been sitting in Annie Carter's Merc just before Frankie had gone off to knock on the pearly gates.

DCI Hunter wondered who the hell the red-haired man was.

59

'The amygdala controls emotions,' said Precious. She was curled up on Layla's bed in jeans and a sky-blue jumper, writing this down as part of her course work. Her pen was scribbling busily across the page. 'And the emotional reaction to any given situation kicks in before the intellectual...' She paused, looked up at Layla, who was sitting on the stool at the dressing table, idly staring at her reflection. 'Which I guess is why people of limited intelligence are quick to lash out.'

Layla was thinking *Amygwhat???* Precious didn't realize that she was sitting doing her homework in a murderess's bedroom. Was that why she had lashed out, killed Orla Delaney? Because she was dense? Or psychotic.

Precious was staring at her.

'What?' she asked.

'Tell me to mind my own business if you like, but why *are* you so strung out? You really need to relax.'

'I can't talk about it.'

'OK. But I can teach you something, calm you down if you want.'

'Go on then.'

'Do you know the heart-brain has forty thousand neurons?' asked Precious.

'What?'

'Every time your heart beats, it sends information to the head-brain, and that regulates ANS signals.'

'ANS?' echoed Layla.

'Automatic Nervous System.'

'You lost me back at "relax".'

'And you've *got* to relax, Layla. Look, try this. Whenever you feel stressed, put your hand on your heart, breathe slowly, and think of a happy time in your life. Give it a go now.'

'That's bullshit,' said Layla.

'Try it.'

Layla closed her eyes and put her hand over her heart. She breathed deeply, slowly. Thought of Orla Delaney, lying dead and bloody on the floor.

Her eyes shot open.

'Close 'em,' said Precious. 'Relax. Breathe. Happy times. Think of the happiest time you can remember.'

She was out on the Maria, *Alberto's yacht, on New York Sound. She was ten years old, and he was there, bronzed and godlike, telling her to watch out for the boom, and the sails were luffing, and then they spun about, into the wind, and the* Maria *shot along like a bird in flight. She'd been so happy, then. So very happy.*

'OK, you can open them now.'

Layla's eyes flickered open. She felt calmer. Her heart was beating slow and easy. She looked at Precious.

'How did you do that?' she demanded.

Precious smiled and returned her attention to her textbook. 'Simple standard relaxation technique. A child could do it. And now you can too.'

'What was that thing called again? The amyg–'

'Amygdala.'

Layla nodded and let Precious get back to her work. Had she reacted emotionally, killed Orla because she was of low intelligence? No. Of course she wasn't.

She *knew* she wasn't.

She had acted in haste and in panic, to save her mother. To stop Orla Delaney. And God how she'd stopped her. She didn't think she would ever forget the noise of the blast, or Orla flying back, or the blood trickling down the wall...

'Precious?'

'What?' Precious looked up, her dark hair falling in her eyes. She pushed it back.

God, she was beautiful, thought Layla. Precious was beautiful enough to turn a straight woman gay. And Layla remembered – painfully – that look on Alberto's face when he'd met her. He'd been bowled over, she could see that. *All* men reacted to Precious in that way. But Precious was more than just beautiful: she was warm and kind. Layla couldn't believe it, but Precious actually sought her out every day. For the first time in her life, she had by some miracle acquired a real friend.

'I've been thinking about what you said,' said Layla, 'accusing me of playing my looks down.'

Precious let out a laugh. 'No, I didn't *accuse* you

of anything. And I've already apologized. It was tactless of me, I'm sorry.'

'But you *did* say it.'

'Yeah. I did.' Precious looked concerned. 'I thought I was forgiven.'

'I'd just like to know what you meant, that's all.'

'No, no.' Precious put down her pen down. 'Let's drop this. I don't want to offend you.'

'I won't be offended,' promised Layla, knowing she probably would.

'You sure...?'

'Sure I'm sure. I want, *need,* your help with this. Go on. Tell me.'

'Well ... the hair, for a start.'

'What's wrong with my hair?' Layla patted the top of her head nervously. Her hair was long and dark brown, like her mother's. And thick, too. Mostly she wore it pulled back – no fringe – in a bun. Kept it out of the way in the office. And in a ponytail when she worked out.

'Nothing. But you just don't *show* it, that's all.'

'I can't have it dangling all over the place when I'm working,' said Layla.

'Yeah, but you never let it down, do you? Not ever.'

'Well, I...' Layla felt defensive. *I asked for it,* she thought. *And I got it, right between the eyes.* 'OK, OK. What else?'

'No make-up,' said Precious.

'I've never worn it.'

'Why not?'

'Never occurred to me, I suppose.'

'Why not?'

Layla thought about it. Shrugged.

'And the way you dress,' said Precious.

'What's wrong with the way I dress?' She studied the plain black pencil skirt and camel jumper she was wearing.

'You dress to play down your body, not flatter it. Which is – sorry – sort of odd. Wouldn't you say?'

Layla felt a flare of indignation at that. 'Well, I don't dress like a tart, if that's what you mean.'

'You don't even dress like a *woman.*'

Compressing her lips, Layla looked at the floor.

'And I just have to wonder, why is that? Do you know? Have you any idea?' Precious went on.

Layla didn't know. She'd never given it a moment's thought. She'd been busy studying, then working, and her family life, the bickering between her parents, had always been going on in the background.

'See? I have offended you,' said Precious.

'No, but I think we'd better drop this before you do,' said Layla stiffly, feeling the prickle of emotional tears behind her eyes. God, she wasn't going to cry. This was ridiculous. It was stupid to get upset over something so silly.

She stood and headed for the door.

'And your hands, what the hell happened there?' Precious called after her. 'You never heard the word "manicure"?'

'Oh shut the fuck up,' said Layla, and left the room.

Hurt as she was by the things Precious had said to her, still Layla found herself fascinated by her – and by the other girls too. There had been a time when she'd thought: *Jesus, lap dancers!* But now she knew these girls weren't fools. China was supporting her family as best she could, Destiny was holding up a faltering marriage, and Precious was paying her way through uni, plotting her escape into psychotherapy.

That night, Layla ignored Ellie's advice and went downstairs when the club was open, to take a peek at what happened down there. It was such an opulent place, like a palace, all tricked out in acres of gilt and faux tiger skin, with dark polished wood bars, cosy banquette seating areas and chandeliers dripping with crystals and tiny droplets of gold.

Away at the back of the room, behind a gold beaded curtain, she saw people moving. The VIP rooms for the private dancing were through there. Precious had told her about the private dancing.

'We have strict rules here,' she'd said to Layla. 'No touching's the most important. The girls don't touch the clients, and neither the clients nor the girls touch themselves. Let's keep this all decent. The girls dance. The client watches. That's it.'

But Ellie had warned Layla off going downstairs. 'I don't want you in the club, Layla. You'll only get some lairy banker trying to chat you up, then I'll get grief off your mum and dad. You stay up here.'

Yet here Layla was, breaking the rules. It gave her a bit of a thrill, actually. She saw Precious, long dark hair flowing, wearing a midnight-blue dress that clung to her beautiful body, go through the beaded curtain with an older man. China was at a table, chatting to a group of men and a couple of women.

Destiny was at the bar, talking to a man who a moment ago had been drinking on his own. There was a gold bucket overflowing with ice on the bar, two bottles of Moët et Chandon chilling in there. Junior, behind the bar, opened one of the bottles, poured out two glassfuls. Destiny smiled and tossed her blonde hair, looking around.

Layla sank back into the shadows by the staircase, but not before Junior's eyes met hers. He grinned and wagged a finger at her. *Naughty naughty.* He knew Ellie wouldn't want her down here.

She looked again at the beaded curtain, still swinging after Precious and her companion had passed through it. For safety's sake all the private dancing rooms were monitored from the room upstairs. She couldn't help wondering what went on in those VIP rooms. Quickly she crept up the stairs, returned to her room and closed the door. Maybe one evening she'd sneak a peek in the monitor room, take a look at what went on.

60

'You *bastards!*' shouted Dickon.

There was a rusted bridge strung between two tall unused warehouses down in a disused part of the old docks. It was this bridge that Dickon, second cousin of the Delaney twins Orla and Redmond, found himself hanging from one dark night.

He was dangling upside-down, suspended by a rope tied around his ankles. The whole black and grimy night world was whirling around him, and his head felt as if it was about to be ripped off. Up on the bridge above him were several beefy types, all suited and booted and wearing black overcoats. One of them, grinning like a pirate, was now holding a knife. Dickon could see the thing sparkling in the moonlight.

'Shit!' he yelled, and thrashed about wildly. It didn't help. His hands were bound, his feet were tied, he'd been dragged out of his nice warm lodgings and he was now dangling over this scary space like a landed cod, his thin hair blowing in the cold evening breeze. All right, he knew he was no angel. He was a small-time house burglar and sometimes – just occasionally, mind – he liked to touch up a kid or two. He couldn't help himself, couldn't be held responsible. He got these urges. He didn't deserve *this*.

Max Carter placed the knife against the rope. It was all that stood between Dickon and a high-impact headache if he should fall forty feet to the hard cobbles below.

'OK, let's get down to business,' said Max.

'I didn't do it!'

'Didn't do what?'

'If I'd known the woman was anything to do with you, Mr Carter, I wouldn't have gone near. Ask Moira! I don't do women,' wailed Dickon. '*He* wanted to get her, not me.'

Max drew a breath. 'Who's Moira?'

'My landlady.'

'Right. So where's Redmond Delaney?'

That took a minute or two to sink in. 'Redmond? What? Well ... I ain't seen him. Nobody has. Not in years.'

'Wrong answer,' said Max, and started sawing at the rope.

'Wait!' screamed Dickon.

Max stopped sawing. 'God's honour, Mr Carter, he ain't been around in years, no one's seen him, and you can *cut* that rope but I ain't seen him, that's God's truth, that is.'

'He set a bomb on a car. On Annie Carter's car.'

Dickon was shaking his head. 'No! It couldn't have been him.'

'Or you're covering for him,' said Max, handing the knife to Steve so that he could think this over. Now Steve applied himself to the rope.

'No! I ain't!'

Steve swiped the blade down, cutting into Dickon's scrawny calf. Dickon screamed.

'You tosser, you better start telling the truth or you're well and truly *fucked,*' snarled Steve, waving the knife and throwing off droplets of blood from its razor-like tip.

'I'm telling the truth! On my life!'

Max sighed and leaned against the bridge, gazing down at Dickon as Steve started sawing again. Was there anything in the world worse than a nonce?

Yeah, there was. A filthy little nonce who'd been within a hundred miles of his – admittedly adult – daughter. Like this one obviously had.

The rope was fraying now, quite badly.

'Start talking,' said Max, his mind consumed with disgust at the thought of Layla being anywhere near this scum. And that car blowing up. His wife – *ex-wife,* he reminded himself, and Layla's mother – could have been inside it. He felt rage at that, ungovernable, unstoppable. Layla being pursued through a park, barely escaping. Who knew what could have happened to her, if she'd been caught?

'I don't know nothing...' Dickon cried.

Steve sawed and the rope frayed.

'Only about Rufus Malone...'

Screaming, Dickon plunged forty feet to the cobbles below and hit them with a wet, meaty *whack.*

Steve stared down there for a long moment. Then he drew back. 'Oops,' he said.

He handed the knife to Max.

Max shook his head. 'That's a bit inconvenient,' he said, tucking the knife away. *Rufus Malone?* he thought.

'Can't stand nonces,' said Steve.

'Let's sort *that* mess out and get on to the next one.'

61

'Precious,' said Layla next day as they sat on the bed chatting. They'd made up, they were friends again.

'Hm?'

'I need your help,' said Layla.

'To do what?'

'To ... well, do myself up a bit. You know?'

Precious grinned and clapped her hands together. 'Really?'

'Yeah, really.'

Precious jumped to her feet. 'About bloody *time*,' she laughed. 'I thought you were never going to ask. Get your hair washed, I'll be back.'

Layla washed her hair and then Precious returned with a bag-load of stuff and sat her down in front of the mirror. She started pulling a broad-toothed comb through Layla's dark locks, then coating it in a strong-smelling solution.

'What's that?' asked Layla suspiciously.

'Setting lotion,' said Precious, and then she carefully wound Layla's hair on to huge rollers, put a plastic hood over her head, and told her to sit there and shut up until it was dry, and here was a magazine to pass the time.

'Jesus, is this going to take long?' complained Layla.

'You heard the old phrase about suffering to be beautiful?' said Precious with her sweet, patient smile. She settled on Layla's bed, and opened her textbooks. 'Read your magazine.'

Layla did as she was told. An hour passed, then Precious set her pen aside, took the curlers out, brushed Layla's hair through, back-combed the top, smoothed it down, doused her in hair spray.

'Don't look yet,' said Precious, teasing away with her comb.

'Gawd,' said Layla, choking.

'Patience.' Precious made a final adjustment, then turned Layla round to face the mirror.

Layla could only stare. A stranger was staring back at her. Oh, it was her *face,* but surrounding that face was a big puffy cloud of dark, lustrous hair. Rather like her mother's. Only it wasn't her mother's. It was *hers.*

'Holy shit,' said Layla breathlessly. 'Well, that's...' She stammered to a halt, unable to think of a word to describe it.

'Nice, yeah?' Precious turned and shouted: 'China! Destiny!'

China and Destiny crowded into the doorway of Layla's room. Layla noted that Destiny had a black eye that she had tried – not very successfully – to cover with make-up. Marital relations were still strained.

'What do you think?' asked Precious.

'Fabulous,' said Destiny. 'Layla, you look amazing.'

'Fab-los,' said China, nodding. 'But no...' China

made painting motions in front of her perfect little face.

'No make-up,' said Precious. 'You're right. Spoils the effect, no?'

'I don't like make-up,' said Layla. They had a point, though: her hair now looked as if it belonged on some other woman, someone glamorous, exotic. Not her, plain old Layla Carter. 'Lipstick, I hate that. Tried it once. Too *jammy.*'

'We can kit you out with a matt one,' said Precious.

Layla stood up, bewildered, overwhelmed. Peered at the stranger in the mirror again.

'No,' she said. 'I don't think so...'

Ellie appeared in the doorway behind Destiny and China.

She caught Destiny's chin in one hand as Destiny tried to turn her face away. Stared at Destiny's blackened eye. 'What the hell happened *here?* Walked into another door, did we?'

'Ellie...'

'Take a couple of days out,' said Ellie. 'You'll frighten the fucking punters, looking like that.'

'Oh, come on,' pleaded Destiny. 'I can't afford to skip work.'

'No.' Ellie released Destiny's chin with a sigh. 'But you can't work marked up either. Give it a couple of days, we can cover what's left of it then.' She turned to Layla. 'Visitor, Layla. Your brother again.'

Shit, thought Layla. Her heartbeat accelerated. She wasn't ready for this.

'How many times? He is *not* my frigging brother.'

Layla pushed her way out through the throng. Alberto was there, Sandor looming beside him.

Alberto smiled, came forward, hugged her. Seemed not to even *notice* her bloody hair, she realized. All that effort, and for what?

'Hi, Layla. How are you?'

'Peachy,' she snapped.

'Your mom told me about the business at your office. You're getting tired of sitting around here, I guess.'

'You guess correctly.'

'Can't you give Ellie a hand with the accounts?'

And do poor old dried-up Miss Pargeter out of a job she loves? 'No, I can't.'

The tetchiness of her tone was starting to penetrate. 'Something wrong?' he asked.

'Nothing.' Layla folded her arms, looked at the floor. Anything was better than looking at him, he was just too damned handsome.

'I wanted to see you, to *assure* you that we're going to sort this out.'

As if this could be 'sorted out'. She'd killed someone. Layla shuddered again at the memory.

'We're tracking down the twin, Redmond Delaney,' said Alberto. 'The woman's off the scene, but we want to be certain he is too. Until then…'

'Until then, I'm stuck here,' Layla finished for him. *Off the scene*. That was one way of putting it. Very decorous. So much better than *dead as a doornail.*

'Yeah. You are. So try not to give your mom a hard time over it. She's looking out for you, doing what she thinks is best.'

Yeah. By sending me away.

'Well...' Alberto paused. Sandor shifted subtly. Layla was still looking at the floor. 'If you need me for anything, just pass the word along.'

'OK.'

He was going. She wanted to fling herself at him, to feel his arms holding her. She remembered him lifting her up when she was little, twirling her around the room while she shrieked with laughter. She had never felt so safe, so loved, as she had in those moments with him.

But now she was grown up and her feelings were more complicated. And this was too damned *awkward.* Because she'd loved him all her life. But *not* the way he loved her.

'Layla?' he said.

Layla lifted her gaze. Alberto was staring at her. He had Constantine's eyes, she remembered them even now – eyes of a bright, armour-piercing blue. Like his father, he was tanned, strong, authoritative, startlingly good-looking – and probably had about a million women queuing up to date him.

'What?' she asked, dry-mouthed.

'What the fuck have you done to your hair?'

Layla raised a hand self-consciously to her head. 'Um, nothing. Just primped it up a bit.'

'Right.' He was still staring. 'Well ... I'll see you then. Layla?'

'Yeah?'

'It's ... nice,' he said, staring at her quite oddly. Then he leaned in and kissed her cheek.

Layla pulled back as if she'd been burnt. 'OK. Thanks,' she said, and turned quickly away, went back into her room.

Precious was there, with China and Destiny.

They were all grinning.

'What?' asked Layla sharply.

'He noticed the hair!' they chorused.

But Layla's expression was gloomy.

'So he noticed it. He'd be hard put *not* to, wouldn't he. Suddenly I've got big hair, of *course* he notices it. So what?'

'So *what?'* Precious was looking at her like she'd gone mad. She pulled Layla into her arms and hugged her. 'Layla. Honey. This is what is called *making progress.'*

62

'It's a shit-hole,' said Max succinctly.

They were sitting around the table upstairs in his old mum's place. For sentimental reasons, he'd never been able to get himself to sell Queenie's gaff; so it had stood empty over the years, serving only as a quiet, private meeting-place for the boys.

The gang was all here – what was left of it. Max at the head of the table, and that ugly little cigar-smoking goblin Jackie Tulliver on his left, with whip-thin, blond and mean-eyed Gary Tooley on his right, along with bulky dark-haired Steve Taylor.

There were others here too tonight. Alberto Barolli sat at the other end of the table, a couple of his goons close by and Sandor at the door. Annie Carter sat beside Alberto.

'It's a crappy little club in Soho. And I do mean

crappy. It's run by one of the Delaney leftovers – a cousin called O'Connor. Pretty tough bastard, by all accounts.'

'I thought the Delaney clubs were burned out years ago,' said Alberto.

'The good ones were,' said Annie.

Feeling restless, she got up and moved to the window. It was getting dark outside and the rain was pouring down, the streets were slick with it, cars hissing past, headlights flicking on. People were hurrying along under umbrellas.

'This is just a remnant,' said Max.

'The Delaneys were always aware that you did business with my family, covered the doors on our clubs in the West End,' said Alberto. 'They hated the Carters. And any of them that are left, I bet they still do.'

'Yeah, they won't be laying out the welcome mat,' said Max.

'With Dickon missing, this O'Connor could be expecting a visit,' said Steve.

'He's right to expect a visit, because he's fucking well going to get one,' said Max. 'They'll probably turn the muscle away. Even Jackie.' Max flashed Jackie Tulliver a conciliatory grin. Jackie might not be muscle, but he was brainy, and he was quick. Then Max's eyes went to Alberto. 'Might let you and me in, just us.'

'And me,' said Annie.

'You what?'

'I'm coming in too,' said Annie.

'The fuck you are.'

'The fuck I *am*. They were coming after me, remember. *Me*. And Layla. No way are you shutting me out of this.'

'Oh, for fuck's ... all right then. But you keep out of the way, let me do the talking. For a change.'

Annie gave him a smile of blinding sweetness. 'Of course,' she said.

'Now I remember why I divorced you. You drive me bloody crazy.'

Annie said nothing.

Max fixed his attention on Alberto. 'How does that grab you, Golden Boy?'

'Max!' Annie objected.

Alberto shrugged, turned his hands up. It was a very Italian – *no, Sicilian* – gesture. His eyes didn't blink as they rested on Max. 'You got a plan?' he asked Max. His expression hadn't changed. It was patient, faintly amused.

'Maybe,' said Max.

'OK,' said Alberto, and stood up. 'Shall we...?'

The following night at the door to the strip club – neon-lit and boasting the name Debbie's – a pot-bellied bouncer was trying to collar punters to go inside and drink the overpriced plonk the hostesses were passing off as vintage champagne. When he spotted them coming at him across the pavement, he disappeared inside the club.

The Carter and Barolli contingent moved inside. They handed their coats to the female cloakroom attendant. Two large men joined the pot-bellied bouncer and the three of them stood barring the way into the main body of the club. Music boomed out from within, Spandau Ballet were singing 'Gold'. There weren't many customers passing through. The place had a dead, seedy feel to it.

'You got a problem?' asked Max, all innocence. 'We're only here for a word with Benny O'Connor.'

One of the heavies sneered. 'We *heard* about you having conversations with people.'

'Yeah, and we're not happy about it,' added the bouncer.

'We're not looking for trouble,' said Max. 'We just want to talk. Me and my wife...'

'Ex-wife,' said Annie, her heart in her mouth. The atmosphere in the small, crowded lobby was thick with danger. She glanced at Alberto. He was dead calm. Then at Max. *He* seemed to be enjoying himself, the mad bastard.

'...and Mr Barolli here, we'd like a word with Benny. Clear it all up.'

A tall man in his fifties with a shock of ginger-grey hair, bushy eyebrows and the brick-red face of the perpetual drinker had emerged from the main body of the club. He was flashily dressed in a double-breasted wide grey pinstripe and an expensive pair of light grey leather shoes that looked Italian. He stood and stared with arrogant assurance at the group.

'All right. Frisk 'em – all three of 'em,' said Benny O'Connor.

It was a very thorough frisking. Annie shut her mind to it as the hands travelled up and down her body. She kept her eyes to the front, not meeting Max or Alberto's gaze. Alberto and Max were worked over too, more roughly. 'They're clean,' one of the heavies told Benny.

'Good,' he said. 'Follow me.'

Annie glanced over her shoulder as he led them through a door beside the cloakroom. Alberto's men were standing in the lobby. Steve, Gary and Jackie were there too, watching. Benny O'Connor's men were lounging against the cloakroom counter, but one peeled away from the bunch and followed them through the door beside the cloakroom. Annie caught Steve's eye as she went through it. He winked. Then the door closed on them. They were inside a Delaney sanctum, and anything could happen.

63

The office consisted of a desk and several chairs at the far end of the cloakroom. The check-in girl, a sweet-faced middle-aged woman with dyed blonde hair showing black at the roots, was in there with them, hanging up coats, storing away tickets, sometimes glancing across.

'Dora?' said O'Connor.

Dora stopped what she was doing, looked at him.

'Fuck off for a bit, yeah?'

Dora fucked off.

'Now,' said Benny, seating himself grandly behind the gargantuan desk in a big executive-style leather-backed chair. 'What can I do for you people?'

Max turned, studied the muscle-head blocking the door. Then he returned his attention to Benny.

'We're looking for Redmond,' he said.

'Redmond?' Benny's eyes were cold but his lips were smiling. 'As in Redmond *Delaney?* We ain't seen that bastard in years. Last we heard, he was missing, presumed dead. Took off in a plane and it vanished over the Irish sea.'

'Only, things have been happening,' Max went on.

'What sort of things?'

'Things like people trying to snatch my daughter.'

'Oh?'

'Yeah. Oh, and blow up my wife.'

'Ex-wife,' said Annie.

'And it upsets me, as you can imagine,' said Max, as if she hadn't spoken.

'I can understand that.'

'I'm starting to suspect that he didn't die in a plane crash. That he's alive and well and making trouble. So if you know anything about what Redmond's up to, or where he is, or who else might be behind these things that have been happening, this is your chance to tell us.'

Silence.

Benny was very still, his eyes locked with Max's. Then he slumped back in his chair and assumed an air of disappointment. He shrugged. 'Sorry. Can't help you. Don't know a bloody thing.'

'But if you did, you would tell me,' said Max.

No he fucking well wouldn't, thought Annie.

'Of course.'

'If you should hear anything, I'll make it worth your while.'

Annie turned and looked at her ex-husband.

He had clearly gone berserk. If Redmond was on the scene, it would be more than O'Connor's life was worth to say a word. Max must realize that.

'I appreciate the offer,' said Benny, very smooth. Then he turned his head and shouted: 'Dora!'

Dora reappeared through a door at the rear of the cloakroom, like a rabbit popping out of a hole. She looked at Benny.

'Give these people their coats, our business here is done,' he said, getting to his feet.

While Dora hurried off to fetch his visitors' coats, Benny swaggered around the desk and extended a hand to Max. Max shook it.

'I'll be in touch if I hear anything,' said Benny.

Liar, thought Annie. Why the hell wasn't Max grabbing this fucker by the scruff of the neck, why wasn't he making O'Connor spill his guts?

'Thanks,' said Max.

Dora handed Annie her black cashmere. Then she gave Alberto, who was standing beside the big man on the door, his camel-coloured coat.

'Thank you,' said Alberto politely.

She gave Max his. 'Thanks,' he said, and Dora went back into her rabbit-hole.

Max shrugged on his coat – and turned with a gun in his hand.

Benny's eyes popped out of his head. 'What the f–' he squeaked.

Max fired the gun. It had a long barrel, a silencer. It went *thunk,* hardly made a sound.

A neat hole appeared, ripped in the costly grey leather of Benny's right shoe, just above his instep.

Benny opened his mouth to yell in pain and Max clamped a hand over it.

'Make a sound and your knee's next. Then kiss goodbye to your bollocks.'

It had happened so suddenly that Annie could only stand and stare. She half-turned, and saw that Alberto had a silenced pistol in his hand too, and its muzzle was jammed against the slab-like neck of the heavy on the door.

'Do yourself a favour, pal,' Alberto told him. 'Don't move.'

They arranged this, she thought. *The cloakroom woman passed them the guns.*

'Holy shit...' escaped her lips.

Sweat had sprung out on O'Connor's face. It had gone redder than ever. He was trying not to shriek with pain, biting his lip to stop himself. Max was staring into his eyes, and Benny could see that Max meant every single word.

'Now, you tosser,' said Max, pushing Benny until he was bent painfully back over his own desk. 'Where's Redmond Delaney?'

'I don't know...'

'Wrong answer.'

'Well, he's *dead,* isn't he? I told you. The fucking plane vanished, and him with it.' The man was panting in distress. 'Oh *shit,* my foot.'

There was blood seeping out of the top of his ruined shoe. Annie felt faintly nauseous just looking at it.

'Those shoes were fucking horrible anyway,' said Max conversationally. 'Back to the point, yes? Redmond. Dead? I don't think so. Some people are damned hard to rub out. Like cockroaches.'

'I don't know,' wailed Benny.

'As I said, wrong answer.'

Max took aim at Benny's knee.

'No!' yelped Benny, sobbing now. 'Don't.'

'Redmond,' said Max. 'Three seconds. One...'

'I don't–'

'Two...'

'Please–'

Max took aim. 'Three...' he said.

'No! I'll tell you!' said Benny in a paroxysm of fear.

'Where is he?' said Max, pausing.

'Redmond? I don't know, but wait! Wait! His cousin – Rufus. He came over, flew in from Shannon a couple of weeks ago, they said he had Orla with him. I didn't believe it at the time. Thought she was long gone. But no one said a damned thing about Redmond.'

Max glanced at Annie. Rufus again. The same name Dickon had given up before he'd gone straight to hell. This was starting to have the ring of truth.

'This Rufus, where's he staying?'

'I don't–'

Max sighed. 'Wrong answer. Where's he staying?'

'No, he'll kill me!'

'Not if I kill you first, arsehole,' said Max, and fired the gun again.

Thunk!

A hole appeared in the other shoe, up near the big toe this time. O'Connor let out a half-stifled moan of agony. 'Shhh,' said Max, coming in close to the man's tortured face and whispering into his ear. 'We don't want to wake the neighbours, do we? Not when we're getting on so well. Now, tell me. Where is Rufus staying? And don't jerk me about, my friend. I'm running out of patience very fast here, and *you've* run out of feet. Knee's next.'

Benny, sobbing with pain, told him.

'Good boy. Was that so hard? Now go and sit in the chair. Alberto, bring your boy over and seat him here. Let's get you all comfortable, shall we?'

O'Connor could barely walk on his wounded and blood-sodden feet, so Max half-carried him round and dumped him into his grandiose chair. Alberto got the heavy into another one. Max dug in his coat pocket and handed Annie scissors and duct tape.

'Their mouths and hands – tie 'em up nice and tight.'

Annie did so, seething with anger. He should have *told* her he was planning this. Furiously she started ripping off lengths of tape, roughly gagging the two men and securing them in their chairs.

'That's good.' When both men were gagged and bound, Max and Alberto gave their guns to Annie. 'Take 'em out to Dora.'

She hurried in the direction the cloakroom attendant had vanished, and found the woman waiting outside in the alley behind the building, puffing on a cigarette. Annie handed her the guns, scissors and duct tape.

'When did Max set this up?' Annie asked.

'Yesterday,' said Dora with a quick smile.

'You're going to have to make yourself scarce.'

'All arranged. I'm gone.' Dora sniffed in disdain. 'Never did like working for that bastard anyway. He's all hands.'

Annie went back inside, through the cloakroom, into the office section where the two men were tied up and where Max and Alberto were waiting for her.

'Are we set?' asked Max.

She nodded.

'OK, let's go.'

They went out into the lobby. 'Addicted to Love' was blaring out of the club, and through a swinging bead curtain painted with dolphins they could see a tired-looking stripper bumping along in time to the music, peeling off layers for her adoring public. Max paused by the door and spoke to the Delaney heavies.

'Benny says he don't want to be disturbed for a half-hour or so,' he said. 'He's got some urgent work he wants to get through.' Max gave a shark-like smile. 'And the mood he's in, I wouldn't risk it, if I were you, or he might just decide to tear you an extra arsehole.'

The Carters and the Barolli boys departed into the night.

'I want a word with you,' said Annie to Max as they strode towards the cars.

'Save it. We've bought a bit of time, until Benny with the fashionable footwear manages to put in a call to Rufus and warn him we're on our way. Best make use of it.' Taking her arm, Max walked her to the Jag, where Tone was waiting. 'Get her home,' he said, and hustled her inside the car, closing the door behind her and hurrying away.

Fuck *you*, Max Carter, she thought.

Tone climbed in behind the wheel, and drove her home.

64

By the time they got to the Partyland amusement arcade in Southend, it was gone midnight and the whole place was in darkness, the shutters pulled down against the vandals. Everyone piled out of the cars gloved up and with masks over their faces. They paused outside the side door.

Steve stepped forward and, using a heavy police battering-ram, he broke the door in. The alarms started going, but what the hell, they'd be in and out and away before the rozzers responded.

They all thundered up the stairs and into the flat above the arcade, flicking on lights, armed with guns and baseball bats. They went from room to room, throwing open doors, looking for hiding places.

'Fuck,' said Max at last. The flat was deserted, and no sign that anyone was living there. The fridge was empty, there were no toiletries in the bathroom. Either O'Connor had lied through his teeth or somehow Rufus had been forewarned and cleared out. But there were no signs of a hurried departure. More likely the guy had never lived here; guessing that Benny would crack under pressure, he'd fed him a story about staying at this place when all the while he was holed up elsewhere.

'Let's get out of here,' said Alberto.

'Yeah,' said Max. He took one last look around

him. Turned to Steve. 'Get back here tomorrow though. Take a look, see if he's loitering.'

'OK, boss.'

'And show 'em it don't pay to fuck around with us.'

When Alberto and Max and their boys got to the Holland Park house, Annie was still up. She was waiting in the doorway of the drawing room when they came into the hall. Their faces told the whole story.

'No luck?'

Both men shook their heads.

'I could use some sleep,' said Alberto, crossing the hall and kissing her cheek. He rubbed her arm. 'Don't worry. This is just a setback. We'll find this Rufus character.'

Annie nodded, aware of Max watching them, of the tenseness in him.

Alberto went upstairs. Annie went back into the drawing room, and Max followed.

'Did O'Connor lie?' she asked him.

He shrugged. 'Who knows. Nobody's been in that place since the sodding Ice Age. What did you want to see me about?'

'I would have thought that was pretty obvious,' said Annie.

'Nope. It's not.' He glanced at the clock on the mantelpiece. It was nearly two o'clock in the morning. 'And it's too bloody late for guessing games, so whatever you've got to say, why don't you just spit it out?'

'You know something?' she said. 'You take the fucking biscuit. You really. Bloody. Do.'

'Drink?' asked Max, heading over to the big world globe containing an assortment of liquors. He selected a tumbler, poured himself a whisky. 'Oh no, you *don't* drink, do you? Can't hold your liquor. I forgot.'

So here they were again and here *he* was, helping himself to *her* whisky, offering her a drink in her own house, making her feel furious and discounted and as though *she* was the one in the wrong – the way he *always* made her feel.

She slumped down on to one of the sofas. Kicked off her shoes. Leaned back, closed her eyes. Then she said what had been boiling away in her for the last few hours.

'Why didn't you tell me what you were planning? You told Alberto. Why not me?'

Max drank some of the Chivas Regal. 'That's a very fine malt,' he said, holding the glass up to the light.

'Rosa has excellent taste in drinks. Don't bullshit me, Max. Why didn't you let me in on it? I was in shock from the minute you shot that fool straight through the foot.'

'Do you think he'd have told me a damned thing otherwise?' asked Max, coming to stand in front of her.

'You,' said Annie succinctly, 'are a complete bastard.'

'Yeah, but I get answers.'

'Actually no. You didn't. All you got was a pack of lies. Or a false trail. And who the hell is "Rufus"? That was the first time I'd heard the name mentioned.'

'Didn't it crop up back when you were all

cosied up with Kieron Delaney? You and he were quite an item once, as I recall. And Redmond... I always felt there was something there, with you and him.'

Annie sighed bitterly.

'Max, you'd suspect there was *something there* between me and the *cat.*' Annie thought of Kieron, once a promising artist but, deep down, as dangerously unhinged as the rest of the Delaney tribe. Dead now. Just as Redmond was supposed to be dead. But then *Orla* was supposed to have been dead too – eighteen years had gone by, with not so much as a whisper about her, until she showed up at Annie's house in the middle of the night with a knife in her hand. At least this time there could be no doubt whatsoever that Orla was dead. But as for her twin...

Annie thought of the paper shamrocks, fluttering out of Layla's trainer, out of her Filofax. Someone was saying *Look, I'm here. Be warned: I'm coming to get you.*

Max finished his whisky, put the glass aside.

'You cut me out,' said Annie. 'You let me go into that situation tonight and you *knew* it was going to be dangerous, but you didn't even think to warn me.'

'Didn't want to risk you signalling our intention. Things would have gotten even more dangerous if you'd given the game away.' Max gave a slight smile. 'You always were a lousy poker player.'

'And I can't drink. One glass of sherry and I'm out of it. Something else to add to my list of accomplishments, as outlined by *you.*'

'And you're a bad shot, in case you were building up to asking why I didn't get you a gun, too.'

'Thanks for that. Can't drink, can't play cards, can't shoot worth a single solitary damn.'

'And your point is…?'

'My point is, where the fuck do you get off, thinking you can treat me that way? Like the dopey little woman! You've got some bloody nerve.'

Max sat down at the other end of the sofa. 'Jesus, a man can't do right for doing wrong around you.'

'Meaning?'

'I was trying to protect you, you silly mare. That's why I didn't want you there in the first place. I said you shouldn't come along. But you insisted.'

'Christ, the word 'chauvinist' was invented for you,' said Annie.

'Some things are too tough for a woman to get involved in.'

'Bollocks.'

'Would you have used the gun?'

'Like that? No.'

'I rest my case.'

'So you didn't find him. You didn't get this Rufus.' Max shook his head.

'I'm going to bed,' said Annie, getting to her feet. 'And tomorrow I'm going to call on Dickon's landlady. What was her name? Moira?'

Max nodded.

'See yourself out,' she said, heading for the door.

Max caught up with her when her hand was on the handle. He was suddenly standing very close behind her. *Too* close. She could feel the heat coming off his body, enfolding hers. She felt one hard-muscled arm snake around her middle, pulling her hard against him. His other hand was resting on her thigh.

'What do you think you're doing?' she asked coldly.

'Feeling you up,' said Max, brushing her hair aside and putting his lips against her throat. His breath there made her shiver.

'Well *don't,*' she snapped.

'Sure?' His mouth was getting busy, and Annie was having trouble concentrating on non-arousal.

'Perfectly sure, thank you,' she said.

Max let her go. Annie thought she did very well, she didn't even stagger even though her legs felt like jelly.

'Maybe I should stop here,' said Max. 'Act as chaperone to you and Golden Boy.'

Jesus was he never going to let that go?

But she realized he was only saying it to provoke a reaction. If she were to fly into a rage and turn on him, she knew precisely how the night would end – with them having wild sex, which would resolve nothing, mean nothing. Tomorrow, she would hate herself for having weakened. And tomorrow, the same old problem would still be there. His jealousy. His need to control her. His general *craziness* where she was concerned.

Annie reined in her temper. 'Suit yourself. I don't give a toss either way. There are at least a dozen bedrooms going begging, take your pick,' she said, very casual. She wasn't going to admit, not even to herself, that the idea of him sleeping under the same roof was disturbing. It was. It really was. But she'd die rather than admit it to him.

Max was staring at her face, trying to fathom her mood. 'OK, I will,' he said. 'How about the one adjoining yours. That free?'

Annie stared at him. 'That's Layla's room,' she said.

'But Layla's not here. And as you say: plenty of rooms going begging. She can take one of the others if she comes back. In present circumstances, it's better if I stay close. Don't you reckon?'

Annie *didn't* reckon. The very idea of having him in the same *house*, sleeping, living, was bad enough. Having him in the adjoining room – that would be torment.

'Suit yourself. Goodnight,' she said with as much dignity as she could manage, and she tore out the door and up the stairs, not looking back. Not once.

Next day, the Carter and Barolli boys returned mob-handed to Partyland. There were twinkling lights that flickered and Mexican-waved like a mini Vegas all along the front of the place. Boy George's 'Do You Really Want to Hurt Me?' was blasting from the speakers – an appropriate choice, given the circumstances. There were big brightly lit clown cut-outs all over the place, vividly coloured bumper cars in a smooth-surfaced little pen, polished and ready for the day's entertainments. And cowering in the midst of them was a terrified manager who went the colour of putty when he saw the big men striding in. The only other employee was a teenage girl, doling out change to the kiddies from a booth. No evidence of Rufus Malone, anywhere.

The boys emptied the place of punters, gave a mouthy dad a warning slap, then took their baseball bats to the machines, pushing the gaily-coloured money-guzzlers over like so many heavy-weight dominoes, smashing the glass cases, until all the pops and whistles and toots and flashing lights fell silent and dark and were finally dead. Suddenly Partyland didn't look much fun any more.

After the job was accomplished, Steve and Jackie drew the manager to one side. He was quivering with fear. Jackie was blowing cigar smoke in his face, turning him a sickly shade of green. Steve loomed over him, a wall of solid muscle, his face an implacable mask.

'You see Rufus Malone around here,' said Steve, tucking a small scrap of paper into the manager's shirt pocket, 'you phone me. Got that?'

The man nodded, apparently unable to speak.

Steve patted his cheek. 'Good,' he said, and the boys left.

65

Rufus was starting to wonder what had happened to Dickon. A couple of days ago he'd vanished; no one had seen him in any of the crappy pubs he usually hung around in. But no matter. He'd seen all the men heading out and he'd got word that Partyland had been smashed up. Good job he'd fed that lie to Benny, thrown them off the scent. All those years of ducking and diving and dodging Big Don Callaghan had taught him everything there was to know about covering his tracks.

Thankfully, Big Don seemed to have given up trying to find him. Not because he'd finally accepted that Rufus hadn't intended that Pikey should fry that way. No, according to Rufus's contacts back in Ireland, the old man had forgotten about trying to avenge his nephew because he had bigger troubles to contend with. The big C – pancreatic, terminal. So instead of hounding Rufus to death he was preparing for his own demise. Too bad the bastard hadn't kicked the bucket years ago, before he dragged Rory into all this.

He thought of that night at the farm, Orla pulling the knife out of Rory's throat. He'd never have dreamt she was capable of such violence, but after the things she'd been through, who could blame her? She'd never have survived otherwise. There had been the same wild look in her eyes that night she left the Islington flat to deal with Annie Carter. When she got that way there was no stopping her...

But something had stopped her, because the hit had failed: Annie Carter was still alive. Whereas Orla...

No, she wasn't dead. She'd gone back to Ireland, as planned. She still wasn't answering his calls – he'd phoned the farm every day since she left, but no one answered. Most likely she was angry with him for not sticking to the plan, for hanging around in London. All the more reason not to show up at the farm empty-handed. She'd soon forgive him when he showed up with a little souvenir for her, a little token to remember Annie Carter by.

Meanwhile, he had a girl or two on the go here: just for sex, though there was one who was proving useful in other ways too. But it was Orla he loved.

He phoned the farm again.

No answer.

But she was there, waiting for him. He was convinced of it.

66

'OK. Let's see what we have here.' Precious had scrubbed Layla's face clean, slicked it over with moisturizer, then placed her in front of the brightly lit dressing-table mirror. Layla sat there like a prize dog at Crufts while Precious tipped her head this way and that. 'Right. What we have is good skin. Flawless, actually. Well done for that.'

Layla said nothing. If she had clear skin then it was down to genes: her mother's skin was good, too.

'Also we have a good face shape, very defined cheek bones. Those eyebrows are a bloody disaster though. Hold still.'

Precious got busy with the tweezers.

'Jesus!'

'Shut up and hold still.'

Layla yelped a lot, but by the time Precious had finished, she looked in the mirror and saw that she had nicely shaped, finely arched black brows.

'Good lips,' Precious went on. 'Got a proper little cupid's-bow mouth there, and *very* nice oval-shaped eyes. What's that colour? Brown?'

'Sort of a dark green. Like my mother's.'

'Actually, with the big hair you look a lot like her.'

'Oh, come on.'

'You do.'

'No way. She's...' Layla paused.

'She's what?' Precious leaned over the dressing table, started pulling tubes of flesh-coloured gunk out of her make-up bag.

'She's beautiful,' said Layla on a sigh. 'Absolutely bloody stunning.'

Actually Layla thought that Annie was *more* than that. In addition to her amazing looks, she had balls, real authority. Layla had seen the way grown men jumped when her mother snapped out an order.

'And you're not?'

'Of course I'm not.'

'This is what in psychological circles we call a breakthrough,' said Precious.

'A what?'

Precious squirted foundation on to the back of her hand, then began dabbing it on to Layla's face. 'A breakthrough,' she said, squinting as she worked. '*Don't* frown – those lines'll get stuck in there. A breakthrough is when you get to the nub of the problem. And that's what we've just done.'

'So what is the nub of the problem?' Layla was curious.

'Your mother.'

'My mother's the problem?' Layla tried to think without frowning. 'Well, we don't get along *that* well, but she's my mother, for God's sake and she's–'

'Stunningly beautiful,' finished Precious. 'Shut your eyes, that's right. And *because* she is so beautiful, you've never felt able to compete. So you haven't. Instead you've retired from the contest. Refused to participate. Hence the no make-up, the pulled-back hair, the sexless clothes.'

Was Precious on to something here? Was it because of her mother's looks that she'd hidden herself away? Layla was so preoccupied by the thought she abandoned all resistance and allowed Precious to proceed with the transformation unhindered.

Aside from her mother, Layla had never come across anyone so confident in her femininity as Precious. She was intrigued, fascinated by this woman who could dance naked in front of strangers and think nothing of it. Layla couldn't imagine what that was like. She longed to know how it felt.

By popping in and out of her room of an evening on the pretext of using the kitchen, Layla had discovered that the security guy on duty in the monitor room always took a fifteen-minute break at eleven. During that time one of the barmen was supposed to cover the monitors, to ensure the girls' safety while they were alone in one of the private dancing rooms with a punter. This week it was Junior who was providing the cover while the security guy took his break, and she'd noticed that he wasn't too diligent about it. Usually he'd leave the monitor room unattended while he loitered in the kitchen, making tea, or he'd be hanging around the dressing room, chatting up the girls. Tonight, she was planning to take advantage of his absence.

'Open your eyes.' Precious was screwing the cap back on the tube of foundation. Now she picked up a tub of translucent powder, opened it, and swirled a big brush around in there. 'Close your eyes again…'

The brush was applied to Layla's face. Layla sneezed.

'I'm making this nice and easy so you can do it yourself next time,' explained Precious, picking up a smaller brush and loading it with pink powder. 'Blusher,' she said, sweeping it along Layla's cheeks. Next she took out a black pencil, outlined Layla's newly defined brows. Then, using a fine brush, she applied eyeliner, sticking close to the lashes, flicking out and up at the end. When that was done she clamped Layla's lashes into a little silver instrument of torture, held them there for thirty seconds on each eye. Then applied mascara. Dusted powder over that. Then another coat of mascara.

'How much longer?' asked Layla, restless.

'Hush.' Now Precious was holding various lipsticks against Layla's skin. She settled on a wine-red one. 'That's just about the other side of the colour spectrum to your eyes, which makes it perfect.'

She painted the lipstick on with another brush, made Layla bite down on a tissue, reapplied it. Then she fluffed up Layla's hair all around her face. Finally she stood behind her, grasped her shoulders, and studied her in the mirror.

'OK. All done. What do you think?'

Layla looked in the mirror. Her mother was staring back at her.

'Holy shit!' she said, spooked.

Precious was grinning. 'Layla Carter,' she said in measured tones, 'you're beautiful.'

'Jesus H. Christ in a sidecar.'

'Stunning, yes? But we've still got work to do.'

'Like what?'

'I'm going to teach you how to achieve the same effect. What did it take, five minutes? That's all. Then we'll go and get you some make-up of your own, and some brushes – you need good brushes, rollers for your hair, all that stuff.'

Layla was still staring at her reflection, amazed.

'Oh, and we'll sort your hands out. Get them neatened up.'

'OK,' said Layla, dazed.

'And then of course, we sort out your clothes.'

'There's nothing wrong with my clothes.'

'You must be bloody well joking!'

That night Layla was hovering by her bedroom door when Kyle left his post in the monitor room. Junior wouldn't be up here for a good five minutes, and even then he'd make a detour to the kitchen first: she'd timed his comings and goings. She hurried along the hall, stepped into the monitor room, and sat down in Kyle's vacated – still warm – chair. There was an emergency buzzer on the desk, so that whoever was manning the monitors could summon assistance from the bouncers at the front of the club. It was a neat arrangement.

Layla scanned the black-and-white monitors. One of them showed an empty room with a small dark silk banquette and an area big enough for a private dance. The second showed an embarrassed young man with a happy grin on his face watching Destiny dance in a pale-coloured thong and nothing else. The third monitor showed Precious and another middle-aged man, his arms folded, watching her gyrate in front of him. He had a look about him as if he'd been hypnotized.

Layla could *see* why he was so enthralled. Precious, devoid of clothing, was performing a sinuous dance, hips moving hypnotically, her breasts swaying.

'Oh my God,' murmured Layla, fascinated.

Precious was so comfortable in her skin that for a moment Layla didn't realize that she was absolutely stark-bollock nude. But she was. Her bush was shaved, revealing everything. Her hair kept playing peek-a-boo with her breasts. Layla could only stare, transfixed. She had never seen anything so completely *seductive* in her entire life.

Maybe I'm a closet lezzer, she thought.

But it wasn't that. She had lived her life this far non-sexually, repressing any hint of the woman she truly was. Precious was right about that. She couldn't compete with her mother, so she'd never tried. But now ... she wished she could be like that, a siren, a beauty, able to summon men to her with a single glance. She thought of Alberto, just across town.

To have that power...

Wouldn't it be wonderful?

Oh, it would.

She looked again at the monitor, at Precious dancing, and then she glanced at her watch. Realized her time was up. Junior would be here in seconds. She took one last look at her friend, who possessed a secret that Layla wanted – so much – to share. How to be a woman. How to seduce.

With one last, enraptured glance at the monitor, she hurriedly got up from the desk and left the room, closing the door softly behind her.

67

'You're a crystalline winter, same as me,' said Precious. 'Thought so.'

Layla'd had her colours done. This was a strange process in Harrods, where a heavily made-up lady in glasses threw swatches of multi-coloured fabric over her shoulders and subjected her to intense scrutiny.

'No, no,' said the woman to teal, coral, peach and mustard.

'I like coral,' said Layla in protest.

'Well, don't dear. It's *lethal* with your skin tone.'

'Beige is safe isn't it?' asked Layla a bit wistfully as the colours were thrown over, this one, that one, then the next...

'Safe? We're not interested in playing "safe"! We want to find colours that will make your looks *sing.* Oh yes. Here we go. Much better,' she pronounced, as she draped Layla in brilliant fuchsia pink, deep cherry red, burgundy, turquoise, rich royal blue and vibrant, regal purple. Then she suggested lip colours, foundation, eye shadows.

Layla was relieved when they paused in Harvey Nicks' restaurant. Now she had a little purse-sized colour swatch all of her own, and a bag full of new make-up.

'I'm knackered,' she told Precious, kicking off her shoes discreetly under the table.

But Precious took no notice. 'Now we know what flatters you, we'll plough on. I could just see you in a power suit. And a red evening dress, something cut down to the waist.'

'You what!'

'Well, a bit low. Maybe not that low.'

Layla's feet throbbed. Her head was starting to ache.

'Why didn't you tell me this was going to be such bloody hard work?' she asked with a groan.

'You know what drives me absolutely *nuts* about him?' Annie asked her old mate Dolly as they sat in the Ritz taking afternoon tea – and a little champagne for Dolly, after which Dolly would probably become slightly tipsy. Or pissed as a rat, depending on her mood.

This was something they did on a regular basis. Two women who had been through a lot together, who trusted and understood each other, sitting on Dior chairs under the fabulous gold cupola of the Palm Court, listening to a gifted boy playing Cole Porter on the piano, being waited on by attentive staff in brass-buttoned tailcoats and white ties. Trying to resist going overboard on the scones, chocolate cake, sandwiches and raspberry tarts – and usually failing.

Two of the Carter heavies were sitting at a nearby table, *also* taking tea. Annie would have seen the humour of it – two big muscular guys drinking from bone china cups, their little fingers sticking out daintily as they drank – if she hadn't been so stressed out about Max being back in her life again.

'Can you guess? The thing that *really* drives me insane?' asked Annie.

'Got a feeling you're going to tell me,' said Dolly, wolfing down a finger sandwich stuffed with smoked salmon.

'The way he tries to boss me around. The way he always has to be *in charge.* Do you know how crazy that makes me?'

Dolly gave her friend a long, assessing look.

'I'm guessing that don't *always* irritate you,' she said.

'Meaning?' Annie sipped her tea with a quick, angry gesture.

Dolly let out a sigh.

'Annie. I been your mate since God was a lad, haven't I? I was a madam, in charge of a bunch of prossies. Now I'm in charge of the dancers at the Palermo. If there's one thing I know, it's *women.* What's more, I know *you.* The real problem? You're an Alpha woman. He's an Alpha man. You clash. Everywhere, I guess, except the bedroom, where he can boss you around just as much as he likes, and you love it. Am I right or am I right?'

Shit, she's right, thought Annie. Max drove her crazy out of bed. The trouble was, he'd always driven her crazy *in* it too.

'So what you going to do about it?' asked Dolly. She selected a sandwich with egg-and-cress filling, bit in.

'There's nothing *to* do, is there?' Annie turned sad eyes on her friend. 'We're divorced. It's his-tory. It's over.'

'Oh yeah. Eight years on. And how many men have you dated?'

'Hey, I've dated. You know I have.'

'Yeah. Grand total of *two*, as I recall.'

Annie pulled a face. 'And your point is...'

'My point is bleedin' obvious.'

'No, come on. Spit it out.'

'You won't like it.'

'Try me.'

'They both looked a bit like him, didn't they? Only they didn't have his balls. Or his charisma.'

Annie opened her mouth. Then she thought about it and closed it with a snap.

'And you reckon it's over,' said Dolly.

'It *is*.'

'Then why's he *still* so eaten up with jealousy over you and Alberto? Answer me that.'

'Because he's an idiot,' snapped Annie, pushing her scone aside.

'And why's he come running the instant you got trouble, fighting your corner?'

'He's not fighting *my* corner, Doll. He's fighting Layla's.'

Dolly shrugged. 'Same difference. Yours, Layla's, you're his family, both of you.'

'I'm his ex-wife, Doll. I'm nothing to him any more.'

'Oh sure. I believe *that*. Would he pick up the sexual side of things if you let him?'

Annie sat back as if Dolly had struck her, her eyes widening in outrage. Dolly gave a laugh.

'Oh, come on. This is *me*, remember?'

Annie shifted uncomfortably in her chair, thinking of the way he'd held her. The heat of his body, so hard against her own. It had shocked her, him doing that.

'Yeah, I think he would. But I'm not going there.'

'Although you'd like to…?'

'I *can't,* Doll. I can't go through all that again. He broke my fucking *heart…*' Annie's voice trailed off. She blinked, swallowed. 'I don't know,' she said quietly, after a long pause, 'I just can't *think* how to convince him that there's nothing between me and Alberto. That Alberto isn't Constantine. That he never will be. It's useless.'

'This ain't the Annie Carter I know, talking like this, like some *loser.* You got a problem, you find a way through it or around it.'

'Easier said than done, in this case.'

Dolly sat sipping her tea, eyeing Annie assessingly.

'You think you might want him back?'

'No. No way!' Annie shuddered at the memory of the fights, the bitterness, the accusations. Would she really want to put herself through that again?

'Because I think you could have him. If you played your cards right.'

'Doll, he wants to keep me in a box. And I can't do that, I can't live within limits that he sets.'

'That's not an option. He's going to have to be made to see that.'

'He's a fucking dinosaur.'

'But sexy as hell, yes?' Dolly smiled.

'Jesus. OK. Yes.'

'*Now* we're getting somewhere!'

68

After meeting with Dolly, Annie went on to the Hart household, where the late and unlamented Dickon had his lodgings. The minute she stepped into Moira Hart's abode, a shabby little Victorian terrace in a long row of identical houses, Annie knew the score straight away.

Girls scuttled on the stairs, looking her over. There was a grim-faced bruiser in shirtsleeves and braces sitting down the hall. Moira herself, a tall, bulky middle-aged brunette in a big-shouldered white silk blouse and a tight red skirt, eyed her with suspicion.

'You say you're a friend of Dickon's?' she asked, leading the way into an untidy sitting-room. Tony followed behind Annie, and Moira kept shooting him worried glances. 'Well where *is* the little git? He owes me rent money.'

'Dickon's left the area. He owe much?' demanded Annie.

Annie could see Moira thinking of the true figure, then doubling it. 'A ton,' she said.

The doorbell rang. There was movement in the hall, footsteps on the stairs, activity above their heads.

Oh yes, Annie knew this place. She knew it of old.

'Trade good?' she asked.

'Trade? What trade?'

'The *knocking* trade.'

'Don't know what you mean.'

'Don't you? Only I reckon this is a whorehouse, am I right?'

Moira looked from Annie to Tony and back again.

'I don't want no trouble,' she said.

'And you won't get it, not from me. You know Rufus – friend of Dickon's? Does he come here? Seeing the girls? Visiting Dickon maybe?'

'I think you ought to leave.'

'I think you'd better answer the question,' said Annie.

Moira glanced at Tony.

'Tone, why don't you give us a moment,' said Annie. 'Wait in the car, yeah?'

Tony gave Moira a look and went outside into the hall, shutting the door behind him. They heard the front door open, then close.

'Now it's just us girls, how about a straight answer?' Annie suggested, pulling out her purse. 'Can I square up Dickon's rent for you?'

Moira's eyes were on the purse. Her tongue flicked out, moistening her lips. 'Yeah, that'd be good.'

'OK, I'll do that. In fact, I'll double it. Two hundred sovs. Just tell me if you've seen Rufus.'

'What you think I am, some sort of grass?' Moira sneered, coming in close to Annie. Moira was bigger than her, by six inches. And wider by a mile.

Annie stared at her steadily. 'You want to answer the question?'

'Tell you what – I don't.'

Overhead, some ancient bedsprings were getting a workout.

Moira stepped in even closer; she snatched the purse from Annie's hand, and started rifling through it.

'Think I'll just take the two hundred,' she said, a twisted smile on her face.

'I don't think you should,' said Annie.

'Oh yeah? What you going to do about it?'

Annie brought her hand up out of her pocket, flicking the metal kiyoga open. She hit Moira's nose with it, and Moira collapsed to the floor. Blood gushed out like a torrent. Moira started babbling. Annie knelt down and grabbed a handful of her hair and pulled her bloodied face back with a yank.

'Shut up,' she said sharply. 'Keep yapping and you'll get another one. Now, unless you fancy spending the next decade in a dentist's chair – Rufus Malone. You seen him in here?'

Moira burbled something.

'Speak up,' said Annie, shaking the woman's head around like a marionette's.

'I *said* he's been in here,' Moira sobbed. 'My fucking *nose.*'

'Describe him.'

'Um ... well he's big, and he's got this curly red hair. He visited a couple of the girls for a shag, got his old man polished up and then fed them stupid lines about weekends in Paris. Oh shit, that *hurts.* Silly cunts believed him, too, until they compared notes.'

Annie stood up.

'Where's Rufus now?' she asked the woman at her feet.

'I don't know. God's honest, I don't,' said Moira, blood all down her front and dripping on her hands as she pawed at her face.

'You better not. I find you've been lying to me, I'm coming back.'

'I *don't know.*'

Annie counted off two hundred, dropped the notes on the carpet. Then she put the kiyoga back in her pocket, went to the door, sent a sweet smile to the man sitting at the end of the hall, and left the building to report back to Max and Alberto.

69

'Is that it, do you think?' Precious wondered aloud, linking an arm through Layla's.

They were standing outside Rigby & Peller, bristling with a ton of bags. They'd been in there over an hour, and Layla had been hoiked about, measured, assessed, and fitted out with more underwear than seemed strictly necessary. She'd been wearing the wrong bra size since puberty, she now realized. Her bras had flattened her breasts instead of accentuating them. Now Layla felt as if her chest entered a room about ten seconds before *she* did.

'Jesus, there can't be *more,*' said Layla.

She was worn out. Trailing sundry minders behind them – and that got on her nerves, having them following her around all the time, she *hated* it – they had been in and out of so many boutiques that she was dizzy. Taking Layla's colour swatch with them, they'd bought daywear, casual weekend wear, and finally evening wear, and more shoes than anyone could ever possibly need.

'Oh, you look fabulous in that,' the sales assistant had said when Layla stumbled out of the umpteenth changing room that day.

It was unnerving, seeing her mother every time she checked herself in the mirror, instead of the usual plain don't-look-at-me Layla.

God I really do, she thought.

'She'll take it,' said Precious.

Rufus watched the two women from a little distance away. He would have moved in and snatched the Carter girl then and there, but the two minders who were sticking to her like glue didn't strike him as amateurs. He ducked into a shop doorway as one of them glanced his way. No, these were definitely pros. They were watching the crowds, forming a barrier of muscle around the Carter girl and the other one. They'd spot him coming long before he had a chance to get in close enough to do anything. He watched covertly as the two women were escorted to their car, ushered inside.

Rufus smiled to himself as the car drove away.

It didn't matter.

'Of course, your big problem is deportment,' said Precious, when they were back at the Shalimar.

Layla sprawled on the bed. 'Huh?'

'The way you carry yourself.'

'What's wrong with the way I carry myself?'

'Everything. You look as though you want to disappear into the wallpaper.'

Maybe I do, thought Layla.

'So here's what you do. You don't slouch. You don't cross your arms over your body – that looks very defensive.'

'Jesus.'

'You don't stare at the floor. I saw you in the hall with Alberto, having a conversation with the floorboards. That's not on.'

'Well what *should* I look at?'

'Someone looks at you, you look back at them. Make proper eye contact. Look them in the eyes, and smile.'

'Holy shit, how much *more...?*'

'One final thing. Making an entrance. You know about making an entrance?'

'Yeah. You come in the door.'

'Don't be flippant. It's called the nailer, and it's called that for a good reason. Watch, I'll show you.'

Precious stepped out into the hall, closing the door after her. Then she came back in, looked at Layla, smiled her gorgeous wide-mouthed smile, and closed the door by leaning against it. She stood there for a moment, pinning Layla with the warmth of her smile, then she stepped forward, away from the door, and walked into the room.

'You see?' she asked Layla. 'That's the nailer. Try it.'

Layla crawled from the bed and did it. Went out

the door, came back in. Leaned against the door. Looked at Precious.

'Smile,' said Precious.

Layla smiled.

'No, that's a *grimace* not a smile. Go out and try again.'

Layla did.

'Better,' said Precious. 'Needs work, but definitely better. Now we're going to have to think about accessories.'

'Holy shit, how much more–' said Layla.

'Come on! On your feet, Layla Carter. We're not done yet. I haven't spoken to you about compliments, have I?'

'What about them?'

'How to accept them.'

'OK. How?' No one had ever complimented her. She did accounts. She worked, and when she wasn't working, she worked out.

'Graciously. Don't deflect them. Say 'thank you', as if compliments are your due.'

'I never get compliments.'

'Trust me – you will now.'

That evening, while Precious and Destiny and China were working downstairs in the club, Ellie waved Layla to her office.

'Your mum's on the phone,' she said.

Eagerly Layla took the phone. She was looking forward to telling Annie about her shopping trip, about what a total delight it was spending time with Precious. She opened her mouth to speak.

'What do you think you're playing at?' demanded Annie.

'Wha–?' Layla froze.

'You were out shopping with one of the girls this afternoon. For fuck's sake, Layla. Will you be told?'

Layla felt her heart sink. All the fun of the day was gone in an instant.

'I had Dad's people with me,' she said, instinctively folding an arm protectively across her middle, then catching herself. Was it any wonder her deportment was defensive?

'They shouldn't have let you go out like that, it was stupid. I'll be having a word.'

Layla said nothing. She stared at the floor.

'Layla?' said Annie.

'What?'

'We've been talking about it, and we think it's time for you to come home. Your Dad's here, Alberto's here. This is the safest place for you to be now. Where we can keep a closer eye on you.'

Come home? Layla stared at the phone. She'd been having the time of her life here at the club with the girls. She'd never known what it was to have friends until now. The last thing she wanted to do was leave.

But Dad was in Holland Park, and she loved spending time with him.

And Alberto was there too. Which sent a shiver through her. She wanted to see him, of course she did. But she was anxious about it, too. She was always hyper-aware of her own mortal failings around the godlike presence of Alberto. Despite Precious's tutelage, she was afraid of making a spectacular prat of herself.

'I don't know...' she said, angry at herself, aware

that she'd fucked up. Going back to work, shopping with Precious – she'd brought this sudden recall down on her own head.

'Tone's going to come and get you tomorrow morning at ten. OK?'

'Oh, for fuck's sake, Mum. What if it's *not* OK?' she asked irritably.

'Tough. Be ready, and don't arse about in the meantime. No more trips out. I don't want to hear that you've been seen out on the town tonight. Because if I do, there'll be trouble.'

Layla heard the click as her mother hung up the phone.

'Bollocks!' she shouted, and tossed the receiver back on the cradle.

Ellie was staring at her. 'Bad news?' she asked.

Layla took a breath. 'I'm going back to Holland Park tomorrow morning at ten. Orders from my mother – otherwise known as She Who Must Be Obeyed.'

'Well, that'll be nice, won't it?' said Ellie, adopting a cheery tone in the hope of wiping that unhappy expression off Layla's face.

'Oh yeah, fucking fantastic,' said Layla, and stormed off to her room.

70

'Oh shit! Oh no! Oh *fuck!*' Benny O'Connor cried out when he saw Max Carter coming toward his hospital bed.

Benny was in a small side room on his own, and Max thought that this was convenient. At the nurse's station he'd told them he was Benny's brother, and they had directed him to Benny's room. Max pushed the door closed behind him and lunged forward, snatching from Benny's hand the button that would summon a nurse.

Benny fell back on the pillows. His injured feet were concealed beneath a cage that had a hospital blanket draped across it. Sweat popped out on Benny's face as he stared at the darkly grinning man looming over him.

'Hi, Benny,' said Max, setting down a bag of grapes. 'How's the feet?'

'What do you want?' said Benny, panting with fright.

'For you to stop making a noise would be a good start.' Max sat down cosily on the edge of Benny's bed. 'One more peep out of you and there could be a terrible accident before those nurses out there can reach you.'

Benny lay back, eyes wide with terror. He believed it.

'Now, where were we?' Max gave it some thought. 'Oh yeah. You were telling me about

Rufus. Who came over from Ireland with Orla. That right?'

'I told you, he's staying in the flat above Partyland.'

'Only he wasn't. The place has been empty for ages. So that was a cold trail. And I don't like cold trails, Benny. Cold trails upset me. I want to know where Rufus is.'

'But I thought he was *there.*'

'Really?' Max was casually lifting away the blanket from the frame protecting Benny's feet. Underneath it, both feet were bandaged up like a mummy's.

'What are you doing?' whined Benny.

'Just checking. That must hurt like a bastard.'

'Wha–?'

Max slapped a hand over Benny's mouth and then pushed his thumb hard up against where Benny had taken the first shot in the foot. Benny went puce, sweat erupting on his brow. A low groan of anguish seeped out of him.

'Tell me where Rufus Malone is,' said Max, turning his attention to the other foot.

Benny mumbled against Max's hand.

Max lifted his hand. 'What?' he asked.

'I don't *know* where he is. I swear, I thought he was there,' sobbed Benny.

'Oh dear,' said Max, and slapped his hand back over Benny's mouth. Benny writhed, but couldn't get away. Max pressed hard on the other foot. Blood sprang up, tinting the bandages bright red.

'Mmph,' said Benny.

'Pardon?' Max lifted his hand.

'I don't know where Rufus is,' panted Benny.

'Oh Jesus, please believe me. He told me Partyland. I heard a rumour that he had a place out on the marshes, but I don't know where exactly.'

Max looked at Benny, who seemed to be on the verge of puking his guts up. Then he got to his feet. 'Eat your grapes,' he said. 'They're good for you.'

With that, he left.

Staff Nurse Julia Foster was irritable. She'd come on duty at six a.m., thinking she'd have time for a nice cup of tea, catch her breath, have a bit of a natter, then on to business. But her schedule was already fucked. Thanks to pea-brained Susan Challis, who'd let in some total stranger last night because he claimed to be Bullet Case's brother.

Shootings were always reported to the police, even if accidental. This one didn't *look* accidental, but Bullet Case – Benny O'Connor – claimed it was. That was all he would say on the matter. That it was an accident, over and over again.

Now here the police were, crack of dawn, bending her bloody ear. All because Susan had been duped by someone who wanted to get at Benny. So instead of enjoying a cup of tea Nurse Foster was listening to DCI Hunter giving her all kinds of grief over the hospital letting in strangers to see gunshot victims.

'But he insists he's not a victim,' she told Hunter, who was staring at her in an unfriendly fashion while DI Sandra Duggan stood alongside him, taking notes.

'So he says,' said Hunter. It annoyed him that, despite threats concerning the dire consequences of impeding police investigations, Benny wouldn't say another word.

'Maybe you should have left someone here to keep an eye on him, if it was going to be a problem,' said Julia, neatly shifting the blame. She was desperate for a fag and wished Hunter and Duggan would sod off.

Hunter gave her a pained look. 'We're stretched to our limits. No one's available.'

'That's not my problem.'

'Can you describe the man who claimed to be his brother?' asked DI Duggan.

'No, I can't. My shift has only just started. The staff nurse on duty was Susan Challis.'

'Her contact details?' asked Hunter.

'I'll get them for you,' said Julia eagerly, grateful to offload Hunter on to the moron who'd caused the problem in the first place. Maybe then she could have her tea and a smoke, and get on with the day's work undisturbed.

'We're going to miss you,' said Precious, as Layla picked up her bag at ten a.m., ready to be collected by Tone. 'Shit, *I'm* going to miss you. I really am.'

Layla could see that Precious meant it. She opened her arms.

'Come here and give me a hug,' she said. 'Please.'

Precious hugged her, hard. 'Right,' she said, smiling. 'Remember: that old Layla who wanted to be invisible, she's gone. This is the new you. Got that?'

Layla nodded. She glanced at the dressing-table

mirror. The apparition staring back at her bore no resemblance to the old Layla. She was wearing a black power suit with big shoulder pads and a neat little flick-out skirt on the jacket, to emphasize the dip of her waist. A white shirt under it, clinging to the curves of her breasts. Her hair was big, a dark cloud around her artfully made-up face. Her tights were black and sheer. Her shoes were black courts, with vertiginously high heels. You had to walk differently in heels like that, with a feline sway.

'Stare back and smile, remember?' said Precious, giving her friend a peck on the cheek.

'Stare back and smile,' repeated Layla.

China stuck her head round the door. 'You going, yes?'

'I'm going, yes,' said Layla, and China hugged her too.

'Tone's here,' said Chris, looking in.

'Where's Destiny?' asked Layla.

'Not in yet. Troubles at home,' said Precious.

'Give her my love,' said Layla. She felt depressed and anxious all of a sudden.

'Head up,' said Precious, blinking hard, tilting Layla's chin. 'Now. Go out and slay 'em. OK?'

'I will.' Layla hesitated. 'You'll come and see me, won't you?'

''Course I will. Just give me a bell.'

'Oh, blimey,' said Layla, shuddering.

'Nervous?'

Layla nodded.

'Think of it as a performance. Some nerves are good.' Precious turned her with her hands on Layla's shoulders. She gave her a salutary slap on the rump. 'Now go on. Knock 'em dead.'

71

Annie walked into her bedroom late that morning and found Max standing inside the door, in jeans and shirt-sleeves, looking around.

'What are you doing in here?' snapped Annie, pulling up short.

Max nodded to the doorway. 'This is where it happened, right? Where she got shot?'

Annie drew a steadying breath. He'd startled her. Wrong-footed her, the way he always did. She didn't like him being in here. It was too close, too intimate. She didn't trust him.

Yeah? she thought. *Or is it that you don't trust yourself?*

'This is where Layla shot her,' she said.

The wall beside the door was unmarked. Everything was spotless. No blood, no indication that the plaster had been repaired where the bullet hole had been. It was as if Orla had never been here at all.

Max studied Annie's face. 'It must have shaken Layla up pretty badly,' he said.

'It did.'

He nodded, was silent. Peering intently at the floor, the wall. 'So it was Steve who cleared up.'

'Yeah, he did. I told you. With Eric and Jackie.'

Downstairs in the hall there was movement, people coming in the front door. Annie and Max went out on to the landing and looked over the rail. Tone was there, carrying a bag in. And behind him came a woman – an impossibly chic, gilded creature in high heels and a tight-fitting big-shouldered power suit. This gorgeous creature was primped, manicured, looking around her through stylish shades, which she now, very slowly, removed.

'Holy *shit,*' said Annie.

'What the fuck?' said Max.

'Layla?' popped out of Annie's mouth unbidden.

Then she was hurrying down the stairs, crossing the hall. Tony was on his way back outside, passing Bri on the door. Both men had done a noticeable double-take when they had set eyes on Layla. Now it was Annie's turn.

'What have you done to yourself?' she asked out loud.

Layla took a half-step back, floundering for an answer, then she saw the broad smile on Annie's face. She was clearly delighted.

'You look *fabulous,*' she said, moving forward to hug her. Then she held Layla at arm's length and studied her properly. 'My God, did you do this all yourself?'

'With a little help from a friend,' said Layla, swallowing her nerves, staring into her mother's eyes as per Precious's instructions, and smiling.

'Shit, they should give that friend a medal!' said Annie. '*Look* at you.'

'Dad!' Layla's eyes had moved past her mother. Max was coming down the stairs, crossing the hall, staring at her as if she was a stranger, half-frowning.

'Christ, what have you done?' he asked, hugging her.

It wasn't exactly a compliment, but Precious had forewarned her that her father might react to her transformation with dismay rather than with pleasure.

'You're his little girl,' Precious had explained. 'Of course he doesn't want to see you as a grown-up woman. What father does? You think my dad would be happy about what I do? He'd throw a fit.' If was the first time Precious had mentioned either one of her parents.

'The girls gave me some tips to update my look,' said Layla.

'Update it?' Max echoed. 'You're unrecognizable.'

'Don't listen to him,' said Annie, putting an arm around Layla and hugging her close. 'You look fantastic. Oh – while I think of it, your dad's in your room. You'll have to take one of the others.'

Max stood speechless, gazing at the two of them. His wife – *ex-wife* – and his daughter. They were more like sisters. Each cut from the same glamorous, expensive cloth.

Layla was bathed in her mother's warmth, revelling in it. She didn't care about the room. If Dad was taking the adjoining room to Mum's, wasn't that a good sign, a sign that they might even – miracle of miracles – perhaps one day get back together?

For once in her life, her mother approved of her. Max was put out. She could see that. But Precious had been confident that he'd come round when he'd had time to adjust to the fact that she was no longer the boring little Layla he had once known.

She'd made her entrance. It was all going well, much better than she had hoped for. Annie was smiling at her in something like wonder. Max was half-smiling too; he wouldn't be a problem. And then Alberto stepped out of the study, and she felt her heart stop dead in her chest. For a long moment, she couldn't breathe. She just stood there, and waited.

His eyes swept over her and then away. He seemed to not even *see* her.

'Hi, Layla,' he said, and turned straight to Max. 'We might have another lead on this Rufus Malone,' he said.

Annie was watching Layla's face. She saw the way her cheeks flushed, the hurt in her eyes.

Oh, so that flame's still burning, she thought.

'Where?' asked Max.

'Essex.'

Max's attention sharpened. 'Out on the marshes?'

'You know about it?'

'Something O'Connor said. You get an actual address?'

'Yep.'

'Then what the fuck are we waiting for?'

Leaving Tony and Bri on guard, Max, Alberto and Annie – despite Max's protests – shot off out the front door, leaving Layla standing there alone in the empty, echoing hall.

All that effort, all that *work*. And he hadn't paid the slightest attention.

'Welcome home,' she said glumly to herself. Alberto hadn't even *noticed* what she looked like.

That *bastard.*

She angrily kicked off her heels, snatched them up, and trudged up the stairs.

It had become a daily ritual for Rufus, phoning the farm. He'd let it ring and ring until he couldn't stand it any longer, then he'd hang up.

But today, after two rings, someone answered. His heart leapt with hope.

'Yes?' It was Orla's mother, her voice quavering. She gave a thick-sounding cough.

'Mrs Delaney? It's Rufus – put Orla on, will you?'

'She isn't here. She hasn't been back since the pair of you left .... oh, when was it now? I can't think straight at the moment– I've been in bed with the flu all week. I still don't feel right. I tell you, I've been laid low, Rufus. Really bad.'

'She hasn't come back then?' he asked, his stomach twist in sickening dread.

'Back from where...?' Another hard cough; this one rattled on. When she finally recovered her voice, Orla's mum said: 'Where'd the pair of you go to in such a hurry, anyway?'

'No matter,' he said, and put the phone down.

So she wasn't at the farm, waiting for him.

He didn't think the Carters would hold her, locked up in a basement somewhere. Hold her for what? To what end?

Which left only one other option. The worst one, the one he couldn't bear to face.

Orla, dead? Truly gone from him forever?

Rage surged through him at the thought, rage against the Carter bitch and all her kin. He knocked over the table, scattering cups and plates, smashing them on the floor. Then he stood, panting, remembering that last night in Islington, Orla's excitement as she'd set off on her mission to kill Annie Carter. How much it had meant to her, making that bitch pay for the hurt she'd caused.

Part of his mind still flinched from accepting that she was dead. How could she be? He'd thought her dead once before, only to discover that she'd survived, against all the odds.

Drawing comfort from the thought, he began putting the final stages of his plan into action. He'd already set things in motion, ensuring that a nugget of information was dropped into the right ear. All he needed to do now was prepare a little gift to welcome his guests on their arrival.

72

The place was way out in the marshes. There was nothing for miles except endless mudflats, the salty stink of washed-up seaweed, and the eerie cry of curlews. It was a dilapidated old shack, long abandoned by the look of it, and there was a rusted hulk of a barn at the side. Once a farmer might have lived here, tilled a meagre field or two, grazed his sheep on sea grass and samphire. Now, there was nothing. Not even a car.

'Looks empty,' said Max, getting out of the driver's side. Alberto got out of the front passenger seat and stood there, surveying the area. Two of his men including Sandor clambered out of the back. Two of Max's boys were up ahead, in another car. They piled out, and Annie got out with them. They closed around her. They were mob-handed. They were all armed. She looked at Max, at Alberto. Looked at the house.

'Let's see,' said Alberto.

They approached the house. There was no cover, which was worrying. Any moment, Annie expected to hear the crack of a pistol-shot as they were fired on from the building, but nothing happened.

A marksman in there could finish off the lot of us, she thought.

It wasn't a comforting notion.

She watched Max go round the back of the place with his boys, watched Alberto and Sandor go to the front. Max went to the door, standing to one side of it to offer no target for anyone inside. She felt her skin crawl as her brain offered up possible outcomes to this. Someone could be crouching in there, hiding, waiting for them to try to come in.

Annoyingly, Max's boys were crowding around her, keeping her at a distance, keeping her protected. She was trying to see past a ton of muscle, and not managing very well. But she was on the corner of the building so she could just see Max at the back door, and Alberto, about to launch himself and Sandor into the front.

Max paused at the back door. It was hanging loose on rusted hinges. As the breeze sighed, it made a noise like something freshly dead coming back to life and crawling out of a grave. There was a window beside it, filmed with dirt and caked from the salty breeze. He could just about see through it into the room beyond. There was an old table, a few chairs. It was habitable, almost. Then he glanced down, his eye drawn by something on the ground. Something green.

A paper shamrock.

His eyes flicked up, heartbeat accelerating. The shack appeared to be empty. He strained, trying to see more clearly – and then he saw it. On the interior handle of the front door, there was something hanging, with wires embedded in what looked like putty.

Max turned, shouting to the group of men around Annie. 'Bomb! It's booby-trapped, don't touch the front door.'

Annie turned and shrieked: 'Alberto! Don't!'

Alberto's hand was outstretched, about to open the front door. He froze.

73

They drove back to the Holland Park house, passing the watchers in the car outside. There were other cars parked up in the square, vans, too. Annie moved anxiously into the hall, calling Layla's name.

It had been a trap. A lure. And maybe, Annie had been saying all the way home from Essex, maybe it had been a diversion, too.

'They've already tried to grab Layla. This could have been a set-up to get us out of the way, so that they could take another crack at her.'

'Tony's with her. And Bri's on the door. And others, out in the road. They'd need a fucking army to get through that lot,' said Max.

Annie wasn't convinced. She was deeply shaken by how close they'd come to disaster today. Maybe Rufus and Redmond *had* an army.

'Where is she? Layla!' yelled Annie.

Layla didn't answer.

The big house was silent.

No Rosa.

No Tony.

And no Layla...

'Mum?' She came out of the drawing room, frowning at Annie, who was wild-eyed with panic, at her dad, at Alberto, Sandor and the others. They all stared back at her, speechless.

'Fuck's sake, why didn't you *answer* me?' said Annie sharply, but she rushed forward and grabbed Layla in a hug, taking the sting out of the words. For once, Layla allowed the embrace.

'I was on the phone,' she said.

'Who to?'

'What is this, twenty questions?' Layla pushed free of her mother in exasperation.

'Don't dick me around, Layla. Who were you talking to?'

'A friend, that's all.' Annie kept staring at her. Layla threw back her head. 'All right, I was talking to Precious, one of the girls at the club. And before that I spoke to Junior.'

Annie shot a look at Max, then back at Layla.

'Did you tell either one of them where we were going today?' she asked.

'Of *course* not. I don't blab, you should know that.'

It was true, thought Annie, she *should* have known that. Layla, unlike many women, was entirely capable of keeping her mouth shut.

Running an agitated hand through her hair, Annie said 'Sorry. It's been a day and a half, that's all. Think I'll go up and take a shower.'

As she headed upstairs, Max came and gave Layla a hug. She didn't push *him* away, Annie noted as she reached the landing and looked down. She paused there, unnoticed.

'You OK?' he asked.

'I'm fine.'

'OK,' he said, and patted her head like she was five years old, and went off toward the kitchens.

The heavies dispersed. Layla turned back toward the drawing-room door.

'Layla?'

Alberto was standing right beside her.

'What?' she asked, still hurt from earlier in the day when he had practically fucking well *ignored* her, after she had tried so hard to impress him.

'Can we have a word...?'

Something going on there, thought Annie, watching the pair of them from up on the landing. *Something serious.* She wasn't sure how she felt about that. Happy or sad. If that was the direction

Layla wanted to go in, well, it wasn't going to be easy for her, that much was for sure. Alberto had big trouble coming, she knew that. She wished she hadn't felt the need to bring him in on this; she knew he had enough on his plate, that she had only made matters worse for him. Sighing, she carried on to her room.

Layla's heart had picked up speed. She led the way into the drawing room and Alberto followed, closing the door behind him. Layla sat down on one of the big Knole sofas, and Alberto took off his coat, tossed it aside, and sat on the opposite one. He leaned back in the chair, raising his arms over his head, stretching, rubbing at the nape of his neck. Layla found herself having to suppress a moan.

He looks tired, she thought. She was used to seeing Alberto as all-powerful, able to solve any problem, able to handle anything, however tough, however dirty. Like her dad, he sometimes came across as frightening, aloof, invulnerable. But now she saw that he was exhausted. That his muscles were aching. That he was human.

'What happened?' she asked, watching his face. 'At the Essex place?'

'It was rigged. And we got another four-leaf clover to add to the collection.'

'Rigged?'

'With an explosive device.'

Layla's eyes widened with fright. And all the time she had been sitting here, unaware. She swallowed hard, tried to compose herself. But the thought of Alberto hurt was excruciating. She remembered Constantine, his father. She'd adored him. And he had died in an explosion.

'Your dad saved my life today,' he said.

'Well, that's ironic,' she said with forced lightness, 'given that Dad seems to think you've *ruined* his.'

'Your mom,' said Alberto, nodding.

'You know he thinks there's been something going on between the two of you. He's always thought so.'

'I'm aware of that, yes. And it's crazy. You know, if he really wanted me out of the way, all he had to do today was keep quiet. I was about to open a door with a bomb attached to it. But I guess he couldn't sink that low. I also guess he wishes he could have.'

'He doesn't think straight where Mum's concerned,' said Layla, shuddering at the image he'd just conjured up.

'Crazy, uh?'

'Yeah. Crazy,' she agreed.

A silence fell, broken only by the ticking of the clock on the mantelpiece. Alberto was staring at Layla.

'What, have I got a spot on my nose or something...?' she asked, half-laughing, horribly self-conscious. She knew that if Precious could see her now she'd be pissed off. She wasn't acting as she should – cool, alluring. Oh, she knew she looked fine. Her hair was puffed out, voluminous, framing her carefully made-up face. She still wore the white silk shirt above a tight-fitting black pencil skirt, with nude sheer tights and high heels. Precious would have approved of her appearance. But she was finding it incredibly awkward, sitting here talking to him.

'You look ... so different,' he said, his eyes moving over her.

Layla could hardly breathe. 'In what way?' she asked, her voice sounding tight and unnatural to her own ears.

He hesitated for a moment. 'You don't look like my little sister any more,' he said at last.

Layla took a gulping breath. So he wasn't completely blind, after all. Merely distracted.

'Alberto – I'm *not* your sister. I never have been. I never will be. My mother happened to marry your father once upon a time, that's all.'

His eyes held hers. 'This is going to take some getting used to.'

'Is it?'

'Mmm.'

'Do you think you *could* get used to it?'

'Let's wait, shall we? And see.'

74

Next morning Layla was up early, in the pool doing laps. Alberto had gone out. Annie was passing Max's room on her way down to breakfast when she caught sight of him in there, combing his hair in the mirror. It was still damp from the shower. He'd changed his shirt. Curiosity got the better of her. She approached the half-open door, and knocked. Max turned.

'Something I can help you with?' he said, tossing the comb down on the dressing table.

Annie walked into the room, pushed the door closed behind her.

'Yeah. There is, actually. You can answer a question.'

'Shoot.'

'Why didn't you let Alberto open that door?'

Max stared at her, said nothing.

'Well?' she prompted.

Max came over to where she stood. Looked hard into her eyes. She caught a fragrant whiff of his skin: clean, male, mingled with the tangy lemon scent of his cologne.

'You know what?' he said at last. 'I nearly did.'

'But you didn't. You had the chance to get rid of him, if you hate him so much.'

'And I didn't,' he said.

'Why not?' Annie was staring at him as if trying to see inside his mind. She couldn't, of course. She had never been able to do that. Max was unfathomable. 'He's my lover, according to you. You keep taunting him and you hope – what? – that he'll lose it, fight you? Alberto's the most restrained person I know, but I tell you, if he did lose it, you might be sorry. Don't be fooled by that cool exterior of his.'

Max's face had grown still as a rock while she spoke. His jaw was tight. 'But he won't lose it, will he? Because he don't want to upset *you.*'

'So we have stalemate. And that doesn't answer my question. You had the chance to finish him. You didn't take it. Why not?'

Max shrugged and turned away, hunted around

for his shoes.

'I don't know. Maybe because of his father.'

'His *father?*'

Max sat on the bed, started putting his shoes on. Annie went and stood in front of him, watching.

'Constantine and me, we were in tight together for years. We shared a lot.' Max tied his shoelaces then looked up at her face. 'Come to think of it, we even shared *you*, didn't we.'

'I thought you'd let that go.'

'I have. He's dead, after all. And I,' he tied his other shoe and stood up, 'am still here.'

Annie stepped back a pace. 'And so's Alberto,' she reminded him. He wasn't the only one who could goad people.

And he's getting involved with Layla, she thought. She wasn't about to tell him that. He'd blow a fuse. But she couldn't suppress a smile.

'What?' asked Max, irritated.

'You're such a maniac,' she said.

'Oh?' He moved closer to her. Now he looked downright angry.

'Men,' she sighed. 'You miss things, don't you. So single-minded, so fucking focused – and you don't see the bigger picture.'

'And what is the bigger picture?' he asked, his eyes moving from her eyes to her lips then back again.

'Nothing. It doesn't matter.' She turned away, went to open the door.

'Yeah, it does.' He grabbed her arm and turned her toward him. Their bodies touched. His arm went around her waist and held her there. Annie bunched her fists against his chest.

'So come on,' he murmured from inches away. His breath brushed her lips. 'Tell me.'

'Alberto's not interested in me,' she said, gazing into his dark blue eyes. 'He never has been. There's someone he *is* interested in, though.'

'Oh? Who?'

Annie shrugged and looked away. Every pulse in her body was beating hard, making her breathless.

'Who?' he repeated, easing her in even tighter.

'I don't know her,' she lied. 'But I think it could be serious.' That much was certainly true.

Oh, Layla, I hope you know what you're doing.

'But you don't know who she is.'

'No.'

'Yeah you do.' He was staring into her eyes.

'No. I don't.'

'You're such a useless liar,' he said, and kissed her.

Annie jerked her head away. *'Don't* do that,' she said.

Max's eyes were smoky with lust. 'Why not? I want to. And *you* want me to.'

'Oh, you know that, do you?'

'Yeah I know it. Like I know you've been bored out of your mind.'

Annie's mouth twisted in a sour smile. 'You know that too?'

'Yep. Why don't you give it up, shove off to the USA, go and stay in New York.'

'Maybe I don't want to.'

He shrugged. 'Your club's there.'

'And my club manager, who doesn't need me

peering over his shoulder. Aren't you going to point out that Alberto lives there...?'

'It *is* a point.'

'And that I could go there and "be" with him, as you so tastefully put it?'

'Yeah. Why not?'

Annie wrenched herself free of his embrace. Now her eyes were full of fury. 'You utter shit,' she said. 'I've just told you. He's interested in someone else. Not me. *Never* me. So why don't you shut. The. Fuck. Up.'

She pushed past him, went to the door into the adjoining master suite, opened it, stepped through it and turned the key sharply in the lock.

'Bastard,' she muttered, enraged, and went and flung herself on to the bed. He was never going to let it go. He was *always* going to throw it in her face. He was a nightmare and she was out of it, and she should be *glad*, because he was–

With a crash the door that linked the master suite to the room next door suddenly flew inward, juddering. Max walked in.

'Don't do that,' he said, coming over to the bed. 'Don't walk away.'

Annie sat up, stared at the open door, the shattered lock. 'You've broken my bloody door,' she told him.

'Fuck the door,' said Max, and striding back to the door, he wrenched it off its hinges and flung it on to the carpet.

Annie started to laugh.

'Now what?' asked Max, returning to the bed and glaring down at her.

'You're such a bloody head case,' she said. She hadn't laughed like this in ... oh, about eight years.

'Stop laughing,' he said, pointing a finger at her.

She couldn't.

'This isn't funny,' he said.

'Yeah, it is.'

'Shut up.'

Annie couldn't.

'That's it,' he said. 'I am going to *shut* you up.'

Annie's eyes were streaming with mirth. She stared up at him. 'Don't you *dare* touch me,' she warned him.

'Oh, that's it. *Now* you've done it,' he said, and got on the bed and grabbed her.

Annie just laughed all the more: she couldn't seem to do anything about it.

'Stop it,' he said, and kissed her.

Annie pulled her head away. 'Did I ask you to kiss me? I don't think so.'

'Shh,' he said, and kissed her, harder, deeper.

Annie stopped laughing, gave herself up to the kiss. What the hell. She could be dead now. She *ought* to be. At any moment some new threat could present itself, and this might never again be possible.

This was just as wonderful as she remembered. Eight long dry years, and he was back, and Dolly was right, he could drive her crazy out of bed but for sure he could drive her crazy *in* bed, too.

He was driving her crazy now, unzipping her dress, yanking it off her.

'That's a very expensive dress, could you be careful with that,' she managed to gasp out.

'Shut up,' he ordered against her mouth, pulling off his shirt. 'Where's the catch on this damned thing?' he asked, kneeling, tossing her on to her front and examining the clasp on her bra. 'Oh right. Got it.'

He rolled her over on to her back, pulled her bra off, threw it on to the floor. Then paused, gazing hungrily at her naked breasts.

'That's...' said Annie, feeling almost light-headed as she watched him. She'd stopped laughing.

'What? An expensive bra? Couture, is it?' His hands went to her breasts, smoothing over them, making her shiver, making her nipples spring into life.

'As it happens, it is.'

'Right. What about these?' He was pulling down the matching pants, tossing those aside too.

'They're *extremely* expensive,' said Annie faintly, feeling the hot pulse of desire start as he knelt there, staring at her. 'And you know what?'

'No. What?' he was unbuckling his belt, unzipping his jeans, pushing them down on to his thighs along with his underpants.

'Oh...' said Annie as he got between her legs. The hard length of his cock touched her there, where she was most sensitive.

'Come on. What?' he said, looming over her.

'I really hate you,' she murmured.

'Hate away,' he said, and entered her almost roughly.

'I can't believe I just did that,' she said a while later, yawning, lying perfectly relaxed against his chest.

'Actually,' said Max, turning toward her, 'I think you're about to do it again…'

They did it again. Annie screamed in orgasm this time, and lay sweating and panting in his arms afterwards. She felt as though she'd been picked up and flung against a wall. But that was nothing new. Max *always* made her feel that way.

'Now I'm sore,' she complained mildly.

'I'm not,' said Max, and she thumped him.

'I have to get off this bed while I can still walk,' she moaned, not wanting to.

She just wanted to lie there with him, to cling on to the dream. That they were lovers. That he wasn't a jealous maniac. That there wasn't danger lurking round every corner. That Layla wasn't going to come looking for her soon, only to find her parents tangled together in bed, like guilty teenagers enjoying their first fuck.

That thought made her sit up and scoot to the edge of the bed. She looked over her shoulder at him. God, he was gorgeous.

'What am I doing? I swore I was never again going to get into this,' she said, clutching her head. 'I *promised* myself I wouldn't.'

'Come back to bed.'

'No!'

75

Annie told Layla at breakfast next day that she was going back to Ellie's. She'd discussed it with Max and Alberto, she said, and it seemed the safest option.

'*What?*' asked Layla. This was ridiculous. She was feeling like a ping-pong ball, being batted back and forth without any say in the matter.

'You heard. I think we were premature in bringing you here,' said Annie. 'I've talked this over with your father and he agrees. There's safety in numbers you know. Anyone out to get you at the club would have to get past a lot of security, and you're room's up on the first floor...'

'My room here's on the first floor,' Layla pointed out.

She didn't mention that Dad had taken her room, the one adjoining the master suite that Annie occupied. She wasn't sure how she felt about that. For so long she'd prayed for her parents to get back together, and now ... maybe it was finally happening. Or maybe it wasn't. She didn't want to get her hopes up only to have them dashed.

'I'm sorry about this, honestly I am. But since the business with the shooting, and then the way we were all lured away ... I just don't want you put at risk, that's all. The decision's made.'

'And if I disagree...?' asked Layla.

She wouldn't. She was rather keen to get back to club, truth be told. She was getting on better with Mum these days, and she was impressed by the way Annie had handled herself throughout this fraught situation; but she was also missing the girls. Missing Precious, in particular.

Layla gave in. 'OK then. Why not?'

'Good...'Annie paused. She'd been about to say 'good girl', but that no longer applied. Layla was a woman now.

So here Layla was once again, turning up at the club. Ellie and Chris welcomed her with open arms.

Precious was ecstatic to have her back, hugging her, hitting her with sultry waves of Giorgio.

'How's tricks?' Layla asked her that evening.

'So-so.'

'I haven't seen China yet. Is she in?'

Precious frowned. 'She's a bit down, poor love. Her daughter's ill. They don't think it's serious, but she's going out of her mind. Tia's on the other side of the world, and she's here. It breaks her up.'

'And Destiny?'

'That bastard's beating her up again. Why she stays with him is a mystery to me. The first mark on her face hadn't even had time to heal before he added a second one, so she's still off work and I'm doing double time. We've got a couple new girls in too. Sapphire and Opal.'

'How's the studying going?'

'I'm well into stress management now.'

'I could do with some of that.'

'Remember the heart-brain exercise. You got problems?'

'Some. And Alberto... I don't know.'

'He likes the new look?'

'I think I've bewildered him. He's having to reassess.'

'Well, that's good.'

'I'm not sure. Is it? God, what am I doing? Do I really want this? I feel as if I'm going crazy.'

'Positive thinking,' Precious reminded her.

'Hm,' said Layla.

The evening passed, with the steady boom of music from the club below keeping Layla company in her room while she read a book. Feeling restless, at eleven o'clock she went along to the kitchen to make a drink. Tony and Chris were playing cards at the table. Of course – it was breaktime, Chris was supposed to be filling in for Kyle or whoever was on duty tonight. Grabbing the opportunity, Layla snuck into the monitor room with her mug of tea in her hand.

The two new girls – Sapphire, a statuesque Nigerian, and Opal a tiny blonde, were working two of the private dancing rooms downstairs, entertaining two middle-aged men. And there was Precious, dancing for a man in his twenties who had a large, embarrassed smile on his face.

Layla watched for a little while, then stole along the corridor to her room before Kyle's fill-in or Kyle himself returned.

Alberto showed up at noon the next day, surrounded by his usual phalanx of heavies led by

Sandor. Alberto stepped into Layla's room, and closed the door to give them some privacy.

'Is something wrong?' she asked anxiously. 'Are Mum and Dad OK?'

'They're fine. Still fighting, but fine.'

He was silent, staring at her face.

'So what brings you here?' she asked.

He leaned against the door, folded his arms and stared at her.

'You're not my sister,' he said.

Layla swallowed hard. 'No. I'm not.'

'And I'm not your brother.'

'No. You're not.'

'So what the hell *are* you?' he asked.

'What?'

He shrugged. 'Look, you've moved the parameters of my world. I don't know what the hell to make of you right now. If we're not related–'

'Stop *saying* that. Of course we're not related. We never have been.'

'Which leaves us ... where?'

'I don't know,' said Layla. Her heart was thumping.

'Then I think it's time we found out exactly what our relationship is. This *new* relationship, I mean. Don't you?'

Oh Jesus. This was all moving faster than she had anticipated. Well, in fact she had anticipated a big fat nothing. That he would still see her as his little sister, that he would be unable to move on from that mindset. Instead, thanks to Precious's intervention, Alberto seemed to be assimilating this new set-up with frightening speed. Was she ready for this? No. She wasn't.

'In that case, what do I call you?' she asked brightly, defensively.

'Huh?'

'Should I call you something different? How about Albie?'

'What?'

'Bertie, then?'

'I will kill you,' he said, starting to smile.

'Alberto then,' said Layla.

'That's fine with me.' He looked at her dubiously. 'So. Layla. This is damned awkward. But if you want to, I guess we could date.'

Layla gulped hard. 'In the middle of all this?'

'Why not? Yesterday I could have died. That kind of puts things in perspective.'

'Jesus, don't say that.'

'It's the truth. And it's made me think.' He looked at her, and there was a flicker of uncertainty in his eyes. 'Maybe we should be grabbing life's chances, not letting them pass by.'

'Dating? I don't know,' said Layla. It seemed weird. She'd wanted this, had tried for it ... she just hadn't expected to succeed with such phenomenal speed. Now she was feeling the old Layla inside her, backing away, saying, *No, let's not do this.* She knew damned well that he was more than she could handle. He was an upfront, in-your-face American, and she was a tight-arsed insular Brit. He was so bent he could see round corners and she was so straight it was ridiculous. But for God's sake, *she* had started this. Not him.

'If you don't want to–'

'No! I mean, I do want to.'

He nodded slowly. 'Good. So ... how about the

day after tomorrow?'

Layla was sitting on the bed when Precious came in.

'You're quiet in here,' she said.

'Alberto thinks we should go on a date,' said Layla.

They stared at one another. Then suddenly they both shrieked and hugged one another.

'Oh Jesus, oh God help me, I'm not sure about this,' said Layla, laughing.

'Hey, it's a date, that's all. I wonder though, is this a London date, or a Manhattan date?'

'What are you on about?'

'Alberto's a Manhattanite. And in Manhattan, men and women date several people at a time, not exclusively, until they decide they're ready to date just one person seriously.'

Layla's face fell. 'You mean this is a casual thing for him? Not serious?'

'I don't know. Why don't you ask him?'

'I can't ask him that!'

'Well, I would. After all, he's one of the most gorgeous men on the planet.'

'Oh shit. You're not helping.'

'There's only one other problem.'

'What?'

'What the hell are you going to wear? When is this date happening?'

'Thursday night. You think the red dress is too much?'

'*Way* too much. The guy's in shock as it is, let's not push him over the edge just yet. Shopping. Tomorrow.'

76

The following evening, Layla was having another exciting night of telly and bed when Ellie tapped on her door. 'Phone for you, lovey. It's Mr Barolli.'

Ellie went off into the kitchen. Layla gave the luscious red box in the corner of her bedroom a gleeful glance as she hurried out to take his call – inside was the most stunning gown. Her and Precious had shopped for and bought it this afternoon. She'd tried it on three times since she'd got back to Ellie's place.

'That's a hot date gown if ever I saw one,' said Precious when Layla tried it on in the boutique.

And it was– a sheath of pure cream silk, bias-cut, that skimmed over her body as if made for it.

Grinning, she hurried along to the office, picked up the phone.

'Hello?' Her mouth was dry but she was smiling.

'Hey, Layla,' said Alberto. 'I just wanted a word.'

It was eleven o'clock at night. Couldn't this have waited until morning? 'About what?'

'This date thing.'

'Oh yeah. That. Precious said I should ask you something about that.'

'What?'

'Is this a Manhattan date, or a London date?'

'Layla...'

'Hm?'

'I don't want to be dishonest with you.'

'Well, that's good.' Her voice remained calm, but Layla was thinking *what is this?*

'Things are happening. Things you don't know about, things I can't tell you.'

Layla stared at the phone.

'Layla,' he went on, 'I wasn't thinking straight yesterday. I can't get involved with you right now. It wouldn't be fair.'

Layla's smile died on her lips.

'Layla? You still there?'

She took a breath. 'So this is a kiss-off, is that it? You're giving me that old "'It's not you, it's me" line. Is that right?'

'No. Not at all.'

'Oh come on.' She felt as if he'd cut her heart out. Her laugh was brittle with pain. 'You said you were going to be honest.'

'I'm being honest, Layla. I can't get into this. For your sake.'

Her innards were churning with the intensity of her hurt and disappointment, she could feel her eyes brimming with tears.

'You cruel bastard,' she said shakily.

He was silent for a moment. 'Yeah. That's me.'

Layla put the phone down. Her whole world was collapsing around her. That awful night when she'd shot Orla, the red-headed man who'd pursued her, losing her job, the fire in the office, and now ... ah fuck, now Alberto had blown her out. After all that trying, all that hard work, it had all come to nothing.

'Everything OK?' asked Ellie, standing in the open doorway with a steaming mug in her hand.

'Fine,' said Layla, brushing quickly at her eyes.

Ellie looked at Layla. She could see that things weren't fine, far from it, but it wasn't up to her to pry into Carter business. 'I'll be downstairs if you need anything,' she said, and went off along the hall.

Layla came out of the office, trembling, swiping angrily at her tears. She passed the monitor room: it was empty. She stumbled inside. She wanted to talk to Precious, but of course she was busy downstairs. Perhaps she'd be able to see her on the monitors...? Kyle was on his break, it was quiet in the monitor room, dark, Kyle's fill-in was nowhere to be seen. She heard the loo flush along the hall.

Feeling as if someone had scooped out her insides and filled the void with anguish, Layla slumped into the chair and stared sightlessly at the screens.

Alberto had dumped her, even before anything had begun.

She couldn't *believe* it.

Tomorrow, Precious would come hurrying into her bedroom all fired up for the big night, and Layla would have to tell her that he'd called it off.

'Bastard,' she muttered, rubbing her hands over her face. Why couldn't he have said this at the start? Instead of giving her hope, only to dash it away.

She stared at the screens with sore bleary eyes. Wished Precious was up here with her, so that she could talk to her, cry on her shoulder.

There was Opal, gyrating in a silvery bikini in

front of a man with the flushed face of a heavy drinker.

On the next screen was China, topless and sinuous, wearing a dark-coloured G-string, her long black hair swirling around her semi-nude body as the grinning man on the couch watched her.

Layla, trying to choke back tears, looked at the third monitor. She hitched in a startled breath as every nerve in her body froze into ice. The man in the private dancing room was standing up, not sitting down. He was bending, leaning over something on the floor.

Layla blinked, squinted, trying to see what was going on. Nothing seemed very clear in black and white. She was sure something was on the floor. She thought she could see something pale, maybe skin. She thought she could see dark hair. She thought – oh *shit*, she thought that what she was looking at was *Precious*.

For a long moment Layla felt glued there, unable to move, unable to even *think*.

Precious was on the floor.

And now the man straightened, and looked up.

'Jesus...' said Layla faintly, shrinking back in the seat, her skin crawling as she saw that it was *him*. The big shock of lightish hair that she knew was red. The pale face, the cold eyes.

Layla felt her body dissolve in terror.

It was the man who'd pursued her through the park. The man who had almost – *almost* – caught her. He was in there, with Precious – and Precious was lying on the floor.

Layla stumbled to her feet, a thin cry of horror

escaping her. She looked at the door, thinking *help, someone help.* Where the fuck was Kyle, shouldn't he be coming back any minute now...? Shouldn't someone be standing in for him during his break? Frantically she looked at the desk, the notepads, the pens, dirty cups, sweet wrappers, the *buzzer.* The buzzer to summon help to the private rooms from the front of the club.

'Oh Christ,' said Layla, and hit the buzzer hard, knocking cups over, cold tea spilling across her hand, the desk, the papers on it. She didn't even notice, she just kept her hand on it, jamming it hard into the sodden desk.

Suddenly Junior was in the doorway. 'What's going on?' he asked, then his eyes flicked to the monitors. He saw what was happening on the third screen, and went a sickly shade of grey. 'Oh shit,' he gulped.

Layla looked again at the screen. *Forced* herself to look.

The man was gone.

Now there was only Precious, lying on the floor.

77

Layla couldn't remember running along the corridor, hurling herself down the stairs. The club was thrumming to a loud disco beat and she ran straight through the centre of it, grabbing Ellie as she went, trailing Junior behind her.

'Precious!' she screamed to make herself heard above the noise. Ellie looked at her in bewilderment, not knowing what the hell she was talking about. Punters were looking, half-smiling, they didn't have a clue. 'The man in with her, she's on the floor, it's *him!*'

Doormen from the front were already hurrying through, alerted by the buzzer. They raced through the main body of the club, Kyle among them, and went through the gold bead curtain and into the narrow corridor where the three private dancing rooms were located.

Chris was first through the door, Kyle piling in after him.

The red-haired man was gone.

There was only Precious, lying there, naked, blood-stained and groaning.

Layla hesitated at the doorway, in a state of shock. Then she saw the two men staring down at Precious and she felt something erupt in her head.

'Give me your jacket,' she said to Kyle. When he hesitated, she yelled: 'Jacket– NOW! Don't look at her. Keep away from her.'

'Layla...' started Ellie, reaching out.

Layla shrugged her aside. Grabbed Kyle's jacket, draped it over Precious, concealing her bruised, bloodied body from view. She looked up at Chris. 'He didn't go back through the club, did he?' She was panting, trembling, her eyes flicking from Chris's shocked face to Precious, and oh shit, all the blood, she could hardly make out Precious's face, there was *so much blood.*

The men looked blankly at each other. Ellie

shook her head.

'Then he must have gone down the corridor and out the fire exit at the rear,' said Layla. 'Get after him!'

Chris, Junior and Kyle turned and raced along the corridor and out into the alley.

'I'll call an ambulance,' said Ellie, dashing off.

'What's happening?' Opal was at the door, letting out a shriek as she saw Precious lying there. 'Oh my God...'

Layla fell to her knees beside Precious. She was moving a little, and moaning softly. Her eyes were rapidly being reduced to slits, swelling up where he'd hit her. Her lip was split, it looked as though he'd knocked a couple of teeth out. Precious's exquisite nose was crooked and bloody. Layla thought with a stab of ice-cold rage that it must be broken.

There was a lot of blood coming from a wound on the back of Precious's head, where Layla guessed she had collided with the edge of one of the wall-mounted speakers when that bastard whacked her face. 'Blame it on the Boogie' was still thumping out of the speakers, adding a surreal note to the proceedings. Layla thought of the sheer brute size of the man, and of Precious's sweetness and extreme femininity, and felt sickness choke her.

Precious's eyes were half-open, maybe she could see Layla. She doubted it, but she spoke to her anyway, tried to offer reassurance.

'It's going to be OK,' she said, taking hold of Precious's hand. She saw that three of the nails there were snapped and bleeding, where she had tried to shield herself from attack. 'You're going to be fine. Help's on the way.'

Opal was starting to cry hysterically.

'Get her out of here,' said Layla. 'That's not helping.'

Chris, Junior and Kyle returned. Chris looked at Layla and shook his head.

The men escorted Opal out of the door, and Ellie came back in, shutting it firmly behind her.

'She going to be all right?' Ellie asked anxiously. She was looking at Layla like she'd never seen her before.

My God, thought Ellie, seeing the way she was snapping out orders, taking control. *She* is *Annie Carter's daughter after all.*

'She's going to be fine,' said Layla, and silently thanked God when she heard the siren.

78

Rufus thought they were all silly cunts, except Orla. She was different, a princess. Yes, she'd killed Rory, but she'd done it out of loyalty to him. She was damaged, poor love. The other women, they couldn't hold a candle to her.

It was so easy to charm them into dropping their pants.

A night in a plush London hotel, that was a favourite. Or a mini-break. *Then* they thought you were serious about them, they started thinking engagement rings, shit like that. Which was a laugh. All he was serious about was causing the Carters maximum pain. Two weeks had gone by since Orla broken into the Holland Park house. Two weeks and not a word from her. He'd been in denial before, but now he knew that Orla was gone. That the Carter bitch had killed her.

Layla went with Precious in the ambulance. She sat there holding her hand but keeping out of the way of the paramedics who were busy working on her.

'What's her name?' the younger of the two asked, while shining a light into Precious's bruised and slitted eyes.

I don't know, thought Layla, and wanted to weep. 'She's known as Precious.'

He looked at her sharply. *'Known as?'*

'They don't use their real names at the club,' said Layla. 'In case someone tries to target them. Some weirdo.'

But some weirdo had done that. Targeted beautiful, sweet, bright Precious.

This is all because of me, thought Layla.

The ambulance tore through the night streets of London, and Layla could not avoid thinking, *This is all my fault.*

'Call Mum and Dad, tell them what's happened,' she'd said to Ellie before she left the Shalimar, and Ellie promised that she would. Neither Dad's men nor Alberto's seemed to be about, and that bewildered her, but right now she didn't care, she was too frantic about Precious. 'Tell them it was the man from the park.'

Once at the hospital, Precious was quickly transferred on to a gurney and rolled away into the bowels of the place for treatment. Layla wandered into the waiting room and sat down with a thump, feeling all the desperate strength that had sustained her through this ordeal suddenly deserting her.

Don't mix with the girls, Annie had told her.

She'd thought that was snobbery.

She should have known better.

Annie hadn't been protecting *her* with that order. She'd been protecting the girls.

She dropped her head into her lap, feeling the dizziness and clammy sickness suddenly overwhelm her. The blood seemed to roar in her ears as she relived it all. The panic, the fear, Precious on the floor covered in blood.

That *bastard.*

She felt so furious, so nauseous, that she wanted to pound someone until they died, preferably *him.* To make him suffer as Precious was suffering now.

'Are you a relative?' asked a female orderly, coming in and sitting beside Layla, a clipboard and form at the ready.

'No. A friend.'

Some friend. It's my fault this happened to her.

'And her name is...?' The orderly clicked her pen, held it at the ready.

'Precious. She's called Precious. She works at the club, the Shalimar. I don't know her real name. The girls don't use their real names. If you phone there, ask for Ellie, she'll fill you in on the details.'

'You got the number?'

Layla gave it to her. She was useless, hopeless,

but the one thing she could do without any trouble at all was remember numbers. 'Is she going to be OK?'

'The doctors are with her now,' said the woman. She stood up, and left the room.

Layla sat there, waiting. A constant procession of misery passed by in front of her: a mother clutching a child's teddy and weeping into her husband's shoulder, an elderly couple fretting over an ancient mother who'd been rushed in with chest pains, a solitary girl who had the gaunt look of a druggie, hunched in her seat, bloodstains on her grubby T-shirt, sobbing quietly.

'Layla? Honey?'

She looked up. Annie was there, with Max.

Layla stood up and practically fell into her mother's arms. Annie clutched at her, held her steady.

'It's Precious,' she said, unable to hold back the bitter tears of grief and remorse.

'Shh,' said Annie, rocking her.

'It's *my fault,*' Layla sobbed. 'You told me. You told me not to get involved with the girls, you *said* that, and I thought you meant I was too good for them or something. But you weren't. I can see it now. You didn't mean that at all.'

'It's going to be all right,' said Max, rubbing her back.

'I made friends with her,' said Layla shakily. 'And now she's in bits.'

'Someone must have seen you together,' said Max.

'We were together a lot,' said Layla. 'Anyone could have seen us. Oh *shit*, I've been so stupid.'

'You shouldn't have come here on your own,' said Annie.

'There was a mix-up over whose shift it was,' said Max grimly. Someone was going to get their arse kicked over that.

'I just didn't have time to think about it,' said Layla.

Alberto appeared in the doorway.

Layla took a halting breath, tried to stop the flood of tears. Annie gave her a handkerchief.

'I've had a word with one of the nurses,' said Alberto, glancing between Annie and Max. 'They're taking her up to surgery.'

'They say what the damage is?' queried Max.

'A lot. That guy had himself a real bang-shoot with her. Broke some ribs, her nose and her jaw, and there's a head wound – they're worried about internal bleeding.' His eyes met Layla's, and slid away.

Layla wiped her eyes, pulled free of Annie's embrace.

'I was in the monitor room when it happened,' she said, struggling to regain control. 'I saw him. It was *him*, Mum – Rufus Malone. *We have to get him.*'

79

At three o'clock next morning, Annie, Max and Alberto were at the Holland Park house. They'd brought Layla home from the hospital, after a lot of protesting on her part.

'I can't go. I want to be there when she comes round from the surgery,' said Layla.

'She won't come round until tomorrow morning at the earliest. Get some rest, and we'll come back then,' Annie insisted.

So they'd returned to the house, and Annie had put Layla to bed.

Layla had been convinced she wouldn't – couldn't – sleep. But she did. She was beyond exhaustion, and Annie had only to sit with her for ten minutes before she was dead to the world. Then she'd crept from the room, and joined Max and Alberto downstairs.

'Malone can't be doing all this on his own,' said Max.

Annie rubbed her eyes. She was tired out, deeply upset by Layla's distress. She wanted this bastard found, and found fast. But it was like chasing a shadow. Somehow he was constantly evading them. Max had a point. He must be getting help. Help from close quarters.

'Who though?' she asked. 'One of the girls?' She thought of Layla, the way she'd – much to her mother's surprise – fitted in at the club, even made friends. It made her skin creep to think that someone could have been in there, assisting Malone.

'She made any enemies at the club?' asked Alberto. 'Someone there dislike her enough to help this guy?'

Annie shook her head. 'I don't think so.'

Apart from those two significant lapses, she thought that on the whole Layla had been following her instructions and keeping a low profile. And she wasn't the type to get into catfights.

Then she thought of Ellie. There'd been trouble with her in the past. Once, she had been a Delaney insider. But that was a long time ago. Since then Ellie had become her *friend,* she couldn't even begin to believe that Ellie would have helped bring all this down upon them.

'What about the guy who was supposed to be watching the monitors. What was his name, Kyle? Where did Chris and Ellie find him? Did they check his references?'

'Kyle was on his break. Eleven to eleven fifteen. And of course he was checked.'

'Don't they have someone covering?'

'Junior was standing in for him.'

'Junior?'

'Your cousin's boy?' said Alberto.

'And he was meant to be in there watching the monitors?' Max stared at her face. 'So where the fuck was he? It was Layla who saw what was happening, raised the alarm – not him.'

'He went to the loo,' said Annie irritably.

'What, he couldn't go before his watch, or wait fifteen minutes?'

'Layla said he looked sick as a dog when he came back to the monitor room and realized what had happened,' said Annie.

'Oh yeah?' Max said, fixing her with a hard stare.

'Meaning?' she snapped.

'Meaning, come *on*. Junior works there. He knew Precious was friends with Layla, and we *all* know this was a warning to Layla, to us, a little demonstration how easy it was for him to break through our security, that next time it would be–'

'Max...' Annie didn't want to go down this route, to start doubting everyone.

'Don't "Max" me. Layla's minders told me Junior showed up outside her office, the day of the fire. You know what I think?'

'I don't *want* to know what you think.'

'I think that little fucker's helping Rufus Malone. Remember when you went to Kath's, to warn them there was trouble? His mum and sister took off, but he insisted on staying. Why d'you suppose that was? Because he had a job to do.'

'No.' Annie was shaking her head. She liked Junior, she trusted him. 'He's one of our own, he wouldn't do this.'

'Annie, Kath hates your guts, she always has. She's probably been poisoning the kid against you since he was out of nappies.'

'Is that true?' Alberto asked her.

Annie took a breath. Looked at Max, at Alberto. Then she nodded. Her heart was heavy. She was praying this wasn't true. That their suspicions were wrong. She'd nurtured that boy. Given him money, gifts, even found him the job at the Shalimar. No, there was no way he'd do a thing like this.

Max stood up. 'I'm off to bed. Early start tomorrow. Going to pay Junior a visit.'

80

'We've had an order from on high,' said the super, putting aside his *Sun* newspaper.

DCI Hunter was wondering why he'd been summoned to Cyril Armitage's office first thing. Had to be something big, to get the guvnor into work this early.

On high had him worried. But Hunter said nothing, just took a seat and waited.

The day before, he'd laid it out for Cyril. Told him about the gunshot vic in the hospital, a leftover from the old Delaney mob, who'd had a visit from someone claiming to be his brother. Though the victim was still refusing to cooperate with inquiries, Staff Nurse Susan Challis had given Hunter a description that closely resembled Max Carter. Whose ex-wife Annie had recently had her car blown up with Semtex – an explosive favoured by Irish extremists – planted in her car by a redheaded man.

'They're saying we should step back from this whole Carter thing,' said Cyril.

Hunter stared at the Detective Chief Superintendent, a big corpulent Yorkshire man, with thin greyish hair scraped back from his brow and a face like a hatchet. The two men had worked together for years. Whether things were going well or badly, Cyril always appeared the same. But today ... something was different.

'Step back?' Hunter looked stunned. He *was* stunned. He'd been planning to haul Carter in for questioning later today, and now they were trying to yank him off it. 'Who's "they" anyway?'

'The people who pay our fucking wages,' said Cyril.

'If they pay our wages, they should realize that we have to dig around in things. We can't just "step back" when there are car bombs going off and people getting shot.'

Cyril leaned forward, two meaty fists planted on the desk. His man boobs, clad in tight white cotton, leaned forward too.

'This isn't a *request,* David. These are orders. Let the Max Carter thing go. Stand down.'

Hunter crossed his arms, shaking his head.

'And don't shake your bloody head at me! I told you, this is non-negotiable.'

'I'd like something more solid than that.' Hunter watched his boss curiously. 'What is this, the secret bloody service or something?'

'Or something, yes,' said Cyril.

'You're kidding me.'

'Does this face say "kidding"?' Cyril sat back in his chair, letting out a sharp sigh. 'Look. I'm telling you this because you're a good bloke. I've had orders to leave this alone or it could compromise an ongoing investigation.'

'A British investigation?'

'Why do you ask?'

Hunter shrugged. 'Annie Carter's living in a

house that she came by through marriage to an Italian-American "businessman". And that businessman's son is over here at the moment, staying with her.'

'You know, you'd make a fucking great detective,' smiled Cyril.

'Is it something to do with that?'

'I'm not at liberty to say.'

'Christ, is it FBI?'

'You didn't hear that from me.'

'They're closing in on the son, I suppose – Alberto Barolli.'

'He's the main man now. The godfather. They've got a good case together and they reckon they could put him away for good.'

'Shit.'

'And they don't want *you* arsing it up,' said Cyril, nodding.

81

When Layla got back to the hospital next morning with two heavies dogging her every move, she found that she was not the only visitor waiting to see Precious.

A middle-aged and very ordinary-looking couple were waiting at the nurses' station outside the Intensive Care Unit. As Layla approached, the nurse behind the desk was filling them in on the progress of someone called Amelia who had come out of surgery a few hours earlier.

'The surgeon set her wrist, nose and jaw, taped up her three broken ribs. The laceration on her scalp was just a flesh wound, but there was mild concussion. The surgeon was concerned about internal bleeding, and there was some, but that's been stopped. Four broken fingers...'

The woman started to cry. Her husband patted her arm.

'She's very bruised and sore, and groggy,' said the nurse more gently.

'Excuse me,' said Layla. 'Are you talking about Precious?'

'I'm talking about Amelia Westover. I'm sorry, are you a relative?' asked the nurse.

The woman turned and looked at Layla with Precious's light-grey eyes. 'Precious? That's my daughter's nickname, I always called her that when she was little,' she said. 'Do you know her?'

'Yes, she's my friend,' said Layla. She felt tears start in her eyes. *Amelia,* she thought. Precious suited her *so* much better.

'You're Layla? She mentioned you on the phone. Said she met you at the accountancy firm where she's been temping. You're one of the trainee accountants, isn't that right?'

Layla could only nod. There was no way she could tell these people the truth.

'We got the call from the hospital and came down on the train.'

'From where?' asked Layla.

'Durham. We're going in to see her,' said Precious's mother, reaching out to squeeze Layla's hand with thin cold fingers. 'You can come in with us, if you'd like to?'

'Thanks,' said Layla.

'How did this happen?' asked Precious's father.

He looked shattered, but there was anger in his eyes, as if he wanted to lash out, pay the world back for what had happened to his daughter. Layla didn't blame him.

'I don't know,' she lied, feeling like shit. These were good, decent people – what did they know of the sort of scum her daughter had been mixing with? They didn't know that Precious was paying her way through college by private dancing. They thought she worked in an office. Well, let them go on thinking that. She wasn't about to enlighten them.

'We don't generally allow more than two people at the bedside,' said the nurse.

'I won't stay long,' promised Layla, and they were buzzed through.

It was worse than Layla had expected. All the bruising was coming out now, so that the semi-mummified creature in the hospital gown on the bed bore no resemblance to Precious. A drip and an IV were attached to her arm. A bank of monitors was positioned beside her bed, machines bleeping, reporting vital signs. Her nose was packed and taped up. Bandages encircled her head. Her jaw was twice its normal size. Her eyes were slits in two blackened swellings. Both hands were splinted.

'Oh, Amelia!' cried her mother.

'Can she hear us?' her father asked the nurse.

'Yes, she can. Talk to her.'

Precious's eyes flickered open, briefly, then

closed again. *Could* she hear them, did she even know they were there? Layla drew back from the bed, feeling that she was intruding on a private family moment. She wanted to talk to Precious, but with her parents there, she knew she couldn't.

'Look, I'll come back a bit later,' she said, but they weren't listening, they were too busy focusing on the wreckage of their daughter.

Layla crept from the room. She sat outside in the waiting area, her father's two goons on either side of her, too shaky to move. It felt as if she was either going to throw up or sob her heart out. She remained there for hours.

Later she felt strong enough to go back in. The nurse was saying relatives only again.

'I'm her friend,' protested Layla. 'Come *on*.'

But the nurse wasn't having it. Layla sat back down in the waiting room with the goons, and waited for another hour until Precious's parents returned.

'Hello,' she said, standing up. 'They won't let me in to see her. They're saying relatives only.'

'Come in with us,' said Precious's – *Amelia's* – mother. Catching sight of the two big men looming on either side of Layla, both of whom had stood up with her, she looked puzzled. 'And these are your brothers...?' she guessed.

'Yeah,' said Layla, because there was no way she could explain what her two-man escort *really* was.

'I'm glad you're here,' said Precious's father. 'There was something we wanted to ask you.'

'Oh?'

'The police were saying she had a job in a nightclub of some sort.' He was frowning. 'She never mentioned anything about that to us. Did she say anything to you about it?'

Layla thought quickly. 'She did a couple of nights a week behind the bar at the Shalimar,' she said. 'You know, just to make a bit of pin money to pay for textbooks and stuff.'

Dad's brow cleared at this. Mum visibly relaxed. Layla could feel the relief seeping from both of them. She felt ashamed, lying to them this way.

'They're saying that's where this happened,' said Precious's father.

'She's going to be a psychotherapist,' said her mother.

'I know, she's so bright.'

'Why would anyone want to hurt her this way? I just can't...' Her voice faltered and she struggled to blink away the tears.

Layla felt sick. If not for her, this would never have happened.

The nurse hurried across to them. 'You can go in now,' she said.

This time, Precious was conscious. Her parents hogged the bedside, and Layla stood to the side, waiting for her moment. Precious's bloodshot eyes fastened on hers now and again, while she talked in a painful mumble to her folks.

After half an hour – it felt even longer to Layla – the Westovers said they were going down to the coffee shop to get a drink and something to eat, because Dad had to take his pills. Promising to hurry right back, they finally left the room.

82

As soon as they were alone, Layla drew closer to the bed. Precious's eyes were shut. Just the act of conversation had exhausted her.

'Not too much longer now,' said the nurse, looking in on them. 'She's very tired.'

Layla nodded, pulled up a stool, touched Precious's hand. Her eyes opened. Rested on Layla's face.

'I guess I've looked better, yeah?' she asked, and her mouth twisted, showing in painful detail the split lip, the gap where her tooth should be.

'You'll look better again,' said Layla, shrugging it off as if it was nothing, but it broke her heart to see Precious brought this low. 'Um, so your folks don't know about the work you do at the club?'

'Jesus, no,' she mumbled. 'You haven't told them?'

'No. The police mentioned the club to them, but I said you only worked behind the bar a couple of evenings a week,' she said.

'Good.' She swallowed hard.

'They told me you work at my old firm, doing the filing.'

'Oh. Yeah. Well, it just came to mind. I didn't want to get into your dad owning the club and me meeting you there. They would *die* if they knew what I really do.' Precious let out a cough.

'You want a drink?'

A nod. Layla held up the paper cup with the straw so Precious could take a sip.

'Amelia, huh?' asked Layla, putting the cup aside.

'Don't. If you make me laugh, I will crawl from this bed and lamp you. *Everything* hurts.'

'You'll feel better soon. You want me to bring you anything?'

'No...' she winced, seemed to hold her breath for a moment. 'There's nothing I need. Only to get out of this bloody place.'

'Here–' Layla took out a notepad and pen and wrote down her number at home in Holland Park – 'I'll leave this with you. Give it to your parents, tell them to ring me if you need anything. Now, before I go…'

'Hm?'

'...I need to know anything you can tell me about the man who did this. Anything at all you can think of.'

'Oh no...'

'Please, Precious, you have to try.' Layla took a calming breath. This was so hard. 'I think ... I think he did this to you because you're a friend of mine.'

Precious showed no surprise at this. A tear slipped from one bruised corner and slid down into her dark matted hair. 'He beat the crap out of me, didn't he,' she said. 'What else is there to tell you.'

'Was that the first time he'd been in? The first time you'd seen him?'

'No. He's been a few times.' She closed her eyes, as if they felt heavy.

Layla reached out and gently rubbed her hand, trying to comfort her. But much as she wanted to reassure Precious, she could feel the hairs on her neck pricking at the news that he'd been in the Shalimar, he'd been that *close,* and she hadn't even realized it. 'Come on, Precious. It's okay. You don't have to tell me anything else if it upsets you.'

'Yeah. I do.' Precious's eyes flickered open. 'His name's Rufus.'

'Rufus Malone,' said Layla.

'You know him?'

'I know *of* him.'

'He showed up a couple of weeks ago. You know I told you about China, how she's supporting her family...?'

Layla nodded, wondering what China had to do with Rufus Malone.

'Things are really bad for her. Her daughter's sick, her parents are old. Plus they're on the other side of the world. And she isn't making enough.'

'I know. You told me.'

'What I *didn't* tell you was that she's playing the long game. She's been having sex with the clients, if they look flush, but refusing to take their money. She's hoping to hook a millionaire, and you do that by *not* appearing grasping.'

Layla was puzzled. Her heart went out to China, caught in such a trap. 'But what's this got to do with you and...'

Precious coughed, harder.

Layla lifted the cup and straw to her lips again. Precious drank, then sank back on to the pillows with a sigh.

'I was getting short of money too,' said Precious.

Shit! thought Layla. 'You didn't...'

Precious swallowed painfully. 'I did a dance for Rufus in the VIP rooms. He asked me how much for sex. I said he couldn't afford me, and he said that he could. He had this wild-man vibe about him. He was solid, like a rugby player. Wild long red hair. Dark grey eyes. And ... he was sort of charismatic. He had this charming way about him, and this Irish accent. So I named a price. I wasn't serious though, not really.'

Layla felt sick. 'How much?'

'A grand.'

'Don't tell me: he said yes?'

Precious nodded and closed her eyes.

'Only you couldn't do it on club premises,' said Layla, 'because Ellie would never allow it. So where did this happen? Where did he take you?'

'He took me to Blakes – Anouschka Hempel's place.'

'He did what?' Layla knew of the hotel. It was *the* place to see and be seen right now, stuffed full of movie stars and royals.

'We had a night in one of their best suites. And he paid up, too. A thousand pounds. And he said he'd be back to see me at the club. I didn't believe him, of course. But he did come back. He came...' Precious's voice broke ... 'and he did this.'

'When you were together, I suppose you talked about your life, your friends…?'

'He wanted to know all about me.' Her mouth twisted with bitterness. 'He asked about my friends ... he did seem particularly interested in you, but I thought it was because of your dad being Max Carter. You know what it's like when the champagne's flowing – I spilled my guts, I told him everything he wanted to know.'

'He used you,' said Layla. 'To get to me.'

'Yeah, I know that *now.*' Precious sobbed. 'He beat me up, Layla. He *beat me up*. And you know what he said before he did it?'

Layla shook her head.

'He said, "Now I am going to hurt you, Precious. First you, then Layla Carter, then Annie Carter and Max Carter too. I'm sorry as hell about it, but I need to send a little message to the Carter clan."' She winced again. '"Tell them this is from me," he said. "From Rufus Malone." Those were his exact words.'

83

Junior wasn't at his usual digs, so Max went with Tony to the safe house in Ilford where his mother and sister were staying. Molly opened the door to him, looking sullen.

'Junior here?' asked Max.

'Who is it?' called a female voice from the bowels of the house.

It was Kath, Annie's cousin – Max knew that foghorn voice of old. Then Junior came clumping down the stairs.

'Who is–' he started, then froze mid-step when he saw Max standing there with Tony, a bald-headed three hundred pounds of muscle, right behind him.

'Yeah, it's me,' said Max. 'Having a cosy family visit, are we? Come on outside, I want a word.'

But instead of doing as he was told, Junior hopped over the newel post and took off up the hall to the back of the house.

Max let out a curse and shot off after him. He shoved past Molly, who responded with a string of colourful swear words in protest. Then he ran along the hall, into the kitchen. He had a quick impression of Kath sitting fat and shabby at the kitchen table, yelling something at him, but he was focused on Junior, who had flung the back door wide and was now legging it away down the garden.

Junior had youth on his side, but Max was in far better physical shape. He charged after the youngster, who was halfway up a six-foot fence when Max caught him and dragged him off.

'You little *fuck,*' snarled Max. Junior's reaction to the sight of him had told Max everything he needed to know.

Junior was scrabbling to get his footing when Max swung him against the fence. All the breath went out of him in a loud *humph* as he hit. Max hauled him away, then slammed him against the fence again. A neighbour's dog was going berserk on the other side of it, barking its head off, drowning out whatever Junior was shouting at the top of his lungs. Wrapping an arm round Junior's head, Max clamped him in a vice-lock until he stopped shouting and started to turn purple.

'Boss,' said a voice at Max's shoulder.

Max glanced back. Tone was standing there, sunlight glinting off his bald pate and the crucifixes in his ears. A gurgling noise was coming from Junior.

'He can't breathe,' said Tony gently, looking around, making sure his boss was secure, that no one was on hand to witness or try to interrupt proceedings. He nodded toward the back door of the house.

Max could see Kath standing there, mountainous, pallid and frozen with fright. He looked at Tone, and felt calm descend once more. He released Junior.

The boy drew in a strangled breath and slumped back against the fence, his eyes closed.

Max gave his face a slap. 'Why'd you run, you little shit?' he asked.

'What?' Junior was gasping, his colour returning to normal. He was clutching his throat. His eyes flickered open and he stared at Max in abject fear. 'You ... you fucking nearly *killed* me.'

'Hey! I didn't kill you. Don't make me reconsider that decision. Tell me what's going on. All this crap that keeps happening to my family, turns out you've been on hand every time.'

'I can't... I don't...' said Junior.

Max grabbed the front of Junior's shirt and yanked him in close. 'You better start talking, arsehole, because I am all out of patience with you. What's the deal between you and Rufus Malone?'

'Dunno what you're on about – I've never heard of him!' Junior was regaining a bit of his usual cocky belligerence.

Max stared at him. 'Don't bullshit me. That name rang a bell with you – I can see it in your eyes. So, Rufus Malone – tell me about him.'

'I don't–'

'You're helping him!' Max yelled.

'I'm not.'

Max saw red again. 'You lying little prick,' he said, and slapped Junior, slamming his head against the fence. A trickle of blood came out of Junior's nose, and he started to shake.

'You think I'm stupid?' Max demanded. 'Malone knew it was safe to do Precious in the VIP room because you'd told him what time Kyle took his break. You'd told him there'd be no one in the monitor room to put a stop to it. You didn't bank on Layla stumbling in there, did you?' He grabbed Junior by the hair. 'And the day of the fire at Layla's office – you were there. Did *you* set that for him?'

'No! No!'

Max drew back his fist.

'Wait! No! Don't.' Junior took a gasping breath. 'Look,' he said desperately, 'I didn't know he was going to put her in hospital, for Christ's sake! I thought he was going to give her a slap, that's all.'

'You gutless bastard. He put that poor bitch in intensive care. What do you think he'd to Layla, or Annie, given half a chance?'

'I didn't think he'd go that far, I swear it.' Junior was gasping, struggling for breath, he was shaking so hard. 'He just paid me ... paid me...'

Max was watching Junior with disgust. 'Yeah, for what?'

'He wanted me to do him a couple of favours in return for cash,' Junior managed to get out. He looked at Max and sneered. 'Mum's right. Your old lady *is* a stuck-up cow. She deserves some shit, always swanning about like Lady Muck. Rufus got me to do a couple of jobs, that's all.'

'What jobs?' asked Max.

'Nothing major. Little things. I put the paper thing in Layla's Filofax, and chucked a lit fag in the bin at her office. He told me it was a wind-up, nothing *serious.* And I thought, why not?'

'Why *not?'* echoed Max. He pushed Junior hard against the fence, crushing him. 'You miserable, ungrateful little turd. Annie thinks the *world* of you.'

'Ow ... don't...' Junior pleaded, his face screwed up in pain. Seeing the murderous look on Max's face, his cocky bluster dissolved into nothing. There were tears in his eyes now; he looked scared to death.

Max thought of Layla's mate Precious, laid up in a hospital bed. It was terrifying to think that Malone had been in the same building as Layla, being helped by this treacherous little tick. He yanked Junior away from the fence.

'Come on, you,' he said, and dragged him back up the path to the house.

'You can't do this,' complained Kath, chins wobbling in indignation at the kitchen door. 'You can't come in here and start knocking people about.'

'Get out of my fucking way,' said Max.

Kath took one look at Max's expression and

stood aside. But Molly was in the kitchen too, and she flung herself at Max with a shriek. Tony moved forward as Max fended her off, but it gave Junior just the chance he needed.

'Fuck it!' said Max loudly as Junior tore along the hall and out the front door.

Tony moved to follow, and Molly started throwing useless punches at Max's head. Kath joined in, shouting and screaming: it was bedlam. Max grabbed one of Molly's flailing arms and dragged her off down the hall after Tony.

The front door was wide open. Out on the road, Junior was behind the wheel of a cheap car, swerving away from the pavement with a squeal of tyres. The engine was revving hard as he shot away.

Tone was off down the path and throwing open the Jag's door. Max stopped and pointed a finger at Kath. She flinched away from him.

'Stay here,' he warned. 'If I hear you've been mouthing off to anyone, you're in trouble.'

Then he hauled Molly out to the car, threw her in the back seat, ran round to the front passenger door and climbed in. Tony hit the accelerator, and the Jag roared into life.

84

After leaving the hospital, Layla went shopping. She wanted to buy something nice for Precious. Her two bodyguards trailed her around Bond Street as she struggled to find a suitable gift. Godiva chocolates? No good, the poor cow couldn't eat solids yet. But later, she'd buy her some of those.

After much deliberation, she arrived at the solution: a pretty pink cropped cashmere cardigan to keep her warm when she was well enough to sit up. Precious was tough, she would heal fast.

Pleased with her purchase, Layla had the goons drive her home to Holland Park. As she hurried into the hall, passing Bri standing stony-faced on the door, Annie came out of the drawing room.

'Hi,' said Layla.

'Come in here, Layla,' said Annie.

What now? she wondered. 'But I need a shower...'

'It'll only take a moment. Please, come in here.'

Curious, Layla did as she asked. Her mother had stepped back inside the room, and as Layla passed her she closed the door behind them.

'Has Dad seen Junior?' she asked, dumping her bags on the sofa and sitting down.

'What?' Annie looked blank. She sat down too, on the sofa opposite.

'Was Junior helping Rufus Malone?' said Layla,

barely able to get that name out without a strong surge of disgust and hatred. 'Was Dad right?'

If Rufus had caught her, would he have done to her what he'd done to Precious? Or worse? She shuddered every time the thought crossed her mind, and it crossed her mind a lot. As for Junior, she couldn't believe it. Would he really do that, betray them that way? They were *family.*

'Oh,' said Annie, rubbing a hand distractedly through her hair. 'Your dad's not back yet, I don't know how it went with Junior.'

Layla pulled out the cardigan. 'I got Precious this, do you think she'll like it? Fuschia pink, she loves that colour, she's a crystalline winter same as me, and it's cashmere, soft as–'

'Layla. Honey...'

Layla stopped. She was staring at her mother's face now. A chill of fear settled in her midriff.

'What is it?' she asked.

'I got a call from Mr Westover.'

'Who?'

'Precious's dad.' Annie took a breath. 'He said ... she died an hour ago.'

Layla's face was a frozen mask.

Annie swallowed hard. 'I'm so sorry. He said the internal bleeding had started up again. That it was bad. Really bad. They did everything they could, but they lost her on the operating table.'

'But she can't have *died,*' said Layla, letting out a wild laugh of disbelief. She was holding Precious's present in her hands. She had been speaking to Precious only a few hours ago. Sure, she was a mess, but she was talking, she...

And now here was her mother, saying that she

was dead.

'This can't be,' said Layla, the cardigan falling from her hands. She stood up, shaking her head. 'He must have got it wrong, he must have misunderstood...'

Annie stood up too. She grabbed hold of Layla's shoulders and looked her in the eye.

'Layla,' she said, and her voice was full of compassion. 'He didn't misunderstand. She's gone. I'm sorry.'

Layla looked blankly around. She was silent, taking it in. Then her eyes fastened on to her mother's face. 'Dad's going to get him, isn't he? He's going to get Rufus Malone?'

'He is. He will,' said Annie, watching her anxiously. 'I know what a terrible shock this is for you. Is there anything I can do, honey? Anything I can get for you?'

Layla shook her head. 'No, I ... think I'll go up and take a shower, I want to be on my own for a bit.'

'Sure. Of course.'

Annie watched her daughter go. Her heart ached for Layla. She'd lost friends herself, dear friends, she knew how it hurt. She looked at the fuchsia cardigan, left there on the couch. Then she picked it up and put it away, out of sight. She knew her daughter would always hate the thing now. That it would forever symbolize the loss of her friend.

Layla showered, tied her hair up in a knot, and dressed in jeans and a white T-shirt, hardly noticing what she was putting on. Then she sat on the bed. She didn't feel she could face going downstairs again, seeing the pity in Annie's eyes. But she was restless, grief-stricken, trying to take in what seemed like some sick joke: *Precious is dead.*

Thoughts of Precious kept popping into her head. The incisive, intelligent Precious she'd got to know. She could picture her now, laughing and smiling and doing her fantastic private dance. And then it hit her: she would never see her laugh or smile or dance again. *Precious is dead.*

Barely knowing what she was doing or where she was going, she snatched up her bag and headed downstairs, stopping off in the kitchen. Rosa was saying *Hola, Layla, can I help you?* But no one could help with this. Shaking her head, Layla returned to the hall and crossed to the front door. She wanted to walk, to feel the air on her face with no *fucking* minders to tell her where to be, what to do. She wanted to flee this whole terrible situation, run away from her own torment. She slipped outside, but Bri was barring her way.

Shit, why can't they leave me alone?

'It's OK, I'm just going out.'

'Going where? With who?' asked Bri.

'Um...' *Please go away, please leave me alone, can't I just be alone for five minutes?* 'Mr Barolli's car's picking me up at the end of the square,' she said.

'Nobody told me.'

'I'm telling you now, OK?' she snapped.

He nodded, but still looked unsure. She went outside and down the steps, aware that he was following her. As she walked off along the pavement, she could feel Bri's eyes on her, tracking her movements. But she was out, free, alone.

Except her mind was still full of turmoil, rage, disbelief.

Precious is dead.

It couldn't be. Not just like that. It *couldn't.*

She walked fast, aware of watchers parked in cars, her father's people. She hurried along, head down.

Precious, dead.

No. Please no.

She walked, faster, faster, out of the square and away. She half-wondered if Bri would come after her, check that she really was being picked up. Her breath came in ragged gulps. She was aware that she was crying, but only vaguely, and she was alone.

Would he come now, would he try to snatch her again? Rufus Malone, the bogey-man, the one who was always hidden, the one who'd tried to blow up her mother, to kill Alberto. He would have hurt her if he'd caught her, maybe as bad as he'd hurt Precious. All this bastard knew was death and destruction.

'Bring it on, you scum,' she muttered furiously under her breath. She could outrun *anyone,* she was fit and she was strong and she would kill him, *kill* him, avenge Precious, she would do it, yes she would.

She stopped walking. People were passing her on the pavement, casting curious glances at this tear-stained girl. Cars were driving by, taxis, vans. She felt her heart pounding thickly in her chest, felt *consumed* by the need to lash out, find him, hurt him.

Come on, you fucker. Here I am. Come and get me. It's me you want. Not Precious. Me. So bring it on.

She stood there, and looked around. Traffic. People. Cars. Vans. And ... oh. One long black car with tinted windows pulling in, swerving to the pavement, blocking her progress.

Was this him?

She was out in the open and she was alone.

Easy meat.

Only not so easy. Her detour to the kitchen had netted her a fourteen-inch knife and it was in her bag right now, so let him try it, let him just *try.*

She looked at the car, at the blank black windows. Clutched her bag tighter against her.

Here it came.

This was *it.*

An electric window at the back of the car hissed down and a man's face was there.

'Layla? What the fuck?' said Alberto.

Layla stared at him. For a moment, so great was her grief and distraction, she didn't even know him.

'What are you doing out here?' he asked.

Layla felt herself dissolve, standing on the pavement holding her bag with the knife in it. 'Precious is dead,' she said helplessly, and then the tears came, great wracking sobs that shook her entire body. Suddenly she was bent double, howling with grief.

Alberto was out of the car in an instant, holding her, stopping her from falling to the pavement. He pulled her in tight against him.

'Shh, baby,' he murmured, kissing her hair. 'Come on. Get in the car. Everything's going to be all right.'

She was safe, bundled into the car, enfolded in luxury, leather, and Alberto's arms.

'Drive,' he said to Sandor.

Everything was going to be all right, Alberto kept telling her over and over, kissing her eyes, her flushed, tear-stained cheeks, her hair, while he hugged her tight.

But it wasn't.

Layla knew it was never going to be all right, not ever again.

85

Sandor drove them to Claridges in Brook Street. Layla, dazed and bedraggled, crossed the reception area with Alberto and stood silent as they got into the lift. Only when they were upstairs and the butler was leading them through a pair of huge rosewood and brass doors did she look around her and think *What am I doing here?*

They went on into a drawing room with sofas grouped around an original fireplace in which a real fire crackled and burned with a rosy glow. There were thick rugs, polished wooden floors, sunflower yellow on the walls, mirrors, big glossy plants, oil paintings. She gazed up at the barrel-vaulted ceiling, then out of the big French doors at the terrace, laid out with chairs, table, everything one could possibly need or want. Beyond, there was a rooftop view of the heart of Mayfair.

'Shall I pour the champagne, sir?' asked the butler.

'No. Thank you. I'll see to it.'

The butler departed.

Alberto took off his coat and watched her as she stood taking it all in.

'I didn't know you had a suite here,' she said, slumping down on a damask-covered sofa.

'I stay here sometimes. In the circumstances,' he said, picking up the chilled bottle of Laurent-Perrier from the ice-bucket, 'it seemed a better idea than taking you home. You know how to open champagne? You twist the bottle, not the cork.' The cork popped obligingly out, and Alberto filled two flutes.

'I don't think I can drink anything,' said Layla.

'Yeah, you can,' he said, and brought the two glasses over, placing them on the table in front of the sofa. 'Take a sip. I'm going to ring your mom, let her know you're OK.'

He went off into another room. Layla was shivering now. She realized she must have been in a state of shock, causing her mind to take off, out of her control. She opened her bag, saw the knife. Precious was dead. Would she, *could* she, have used it? She'd already crossed a line; already killed someone.

Shuddering, she reached for the champagne and sipped it. It was fresh, light, and warming. She sat back, nursing the glass against her chest, and closed her eyes.

'Your mom's fine with it,' said Alberto, coming back into the room, startling her. 'Apparently Bri told her I picked you up at the end of the square.

He didn't believe you when you told him you were meeting me, so he followed to make sure you were OK.'

Layla nodded, sat up straighter, sipped a little more champagne. 'I can't believe she's dead,' she said in a small voice.

'I'm sorry,' he said, and sat down beside her, taking her hand.

Layla would rather have fallen apart in front of *anyone* than Alberto. His hand was so big and warm. Hers felt frozen. He smelled so good, too – that expensive cologne he always wore. She glanced at him. He was watching her with those light laser-blue eyes. He was tanned from the American sun. He loved the water as much as she did. He had raced a yacht in the Americas Cup, he was a skilled yachtsman.

He was just so damned *gorgeous*, she couldn't cope with this. She was devastated over Precious, couldn't take it in. She must look a mess right now – she could almost hear Precious lecturing her about reverting to her old shabby Layla ways: no make-up, hair scraped back.

'Why'd you bring me here? Why not take me home?' she asked him, more to fill the silence than because she wanted an answer.

Her glass was empty. Alberto leaned over, grabbed the bottle, refilled it.

'It seemed better, that's all. There are some things we haven't discussed, things we need to talk about, and I didn't want to do that with your parents in the next room.'

'Oh.' Layla took another swig of the champagne. It was working, soothing her, relaxing her.

She had stopped shivering.

Except now she was thinking of how he had blown her out. Recalling the excitement when Precious's plan had worked so beautifully, followed by the bitter, horrendous disappointment when he had called to cancel. What did he think she was, some sort of lame charity case? Was he doing this because he felt *sorry* for her?

She swigged back the champagne, emptying her glass again.

'Steady with that,' he said.

'Why? Are you frightened I'll show you up?' she snapped.

'No.' He was half-smiling. 'I'm frightened you'll puke all over this couch.'

'Are you going to refill this?' She thrust the empty glass at him.

'Not yet, no.' Gently he took the glass from her hand and set it beside his. Then he turned to look at her. 'We have to talk. Seriously.'

'I can't *talk*. I can't even *think*,' she moaned, rubbing a hand tiredly over her eyes.

'Layla. Pay attention.' He opened his mouth to speak, then sat back with a sigh. 'Shit. This has happened at the worst possible time.'

'What has?'

'You and me.'

'There *is* no you and me. You made that perfectly clear on the phone, remember?'

He didn't reply to that. Instead he said: 'You know you asked me if it was going to be a London date, or a Manhattan one?'

'Yes.'

'Well, it made me think. Layla ... I've known

you almost since you were born.'

'That's an exaggeration.'

'Only a slight one. How old are you now? Twenty-three?'

'Twenty-two.'

He groaned. 'Layla, I'm thirty-nine years old. That's…'

'I can do the maths.' Oh, she'd done the maths, about a billion times. 'I know all that. And I don't care.'

Alberto was shaking his head. 'You know what I am.'

'I don't *care* about that.'

'Hear me out, OK? I want to give you the full story. When I got back from Essex, after your dad saved my life – and I'm telling you, if he could see us now, he'd reconsider that decision in a heart-beat – it blew my mind when I saw you. You'd changed so much.' He paused, half-smiling, and ran a hand through his hair. 'When you were a little girl, you were always searching me out – you loved to be around me. Then you hit puberty and you couldn't get far enough away from me. Suddenly you appear again and it's, like, *Pow!* When I saw you that day in the Shalimar, when you'd changed your hair, it was as if I was seeing you for the first time. *Everything* was different, everything was altered. Not just the way you looked, the way I felt about you.'

'I couldn't deal with it when I was younger,' said Layla. Her voice shook. 'I'd get embarrassed around you. I felt awkward. And I don't think I can cope with you blowing me out now, either. I've had a tough day. So if you're going to do it, let's get it over with and then forget it, OK?'

'Shit, will you shut up? I'm laying myself on the line here. It would *never* be a casual Manhattan dating thing with you, Layla. I don't want to date anyone else, I have no plans to do that. But this...' He raised a hand, waving it in the air. 'All *this* has happened at a bad time. That's why I cancelled. I can't ask you to commit yourself to anything with me, not now. It wouldn't be fair. So I have to say, if you want to date other people, then that's OK.' Alberto sat back, ran a hand through his hair. 'Fuck it. No, it's not. It's not OK at all. But it'll have to be. Because I can't ask anything of you.'

Layla was watching him, her mouth half-open in shock.

'Well, say something,' he prompted.

Layla closed her mouth with a snap. Sat back. Thought about what he'd just said.

'I don't want to see anyone else,' she said at last. 'I couldn't.'

'Oh.'

'Oh? Is that all you can say?' Layla jumped off the couch and glared down at him. 'Look. If you're talking about laying things on the line, then here it is. Flat out. I've been in love with you for ever. Like *always.* So don't dance around me, don't give me excuses. Don't tell me what an old man you are, or that you're in a dangerous line of work, because I don't give a fuck about any of that.'

Alberto was silent. Abruptly, he stood up. Grabbed her arm, pulled her in tight against him. Layla's eyes opened wide. She was suddenly painfully aware of their closeness, of his strength. That people were in awe of him; that he was the god-father. Golden, beautiful, powerful and deadly Alberto. She was in awe of him too. She always had been. Maybe that was the problem.

'You know what?' said Alberto, close enough for his breath to tickle her cheek.

Layla gulped. 'What?'

'You talk too much. You always have. But you want to go on chewing this over, fine. Only let's take it somewhere more comfortable.'

Layla felt her heartbeat pick up. She was staring into his eyes.

'Like ... where?' she asked.

'Two bedrooms. One through there, one through there.' He indicated two doors. 'Pick one.'

'Wait a minute. So you've skipped the date and now you're going straight on to the *seduction?*'

Alberto gave a smile. 'Time's a little tight.'

'What *is* it? What's going on?' Now he was frightening her.

Alberto bent and picked her up in his arms. Layla let out a small shriek of surprise.

'No more talk,' he said. 'Which one?'

'That one,' said Layla, throwing caution to the four winds.

86

'There's something you forgot to tell me,' said Alberto.

'I thought you said no more talking?' sighed Layla.

It was nearly an hour later. She didn't want to talk or even think. This was ... heaven. She was lying naked in a four-poster bed in a sumptuous suite, and Alberto was here beside her. What else could anyone possibly need?

Precious.

Her heart seemed to contract and her stomach turned over.

Oh God. Precious was dead. It was as if the earth had shifted under Layla's feet. Her friend, the one real friend she had, was dead, and now... Alberto had seduced her. She thought of Precious, beautiful, laughing, generous and bright. If she could see Layla, lying here with him, she'd be cheering. And maybe, somehow, she could. Who knew?

Layla felt her eyes fill with tears, but she blinked them back. She turned, cuddled in close against his chest, feeling his warmth, his strength.

'It would have helped to know you were a virgin,' he said.

'Oh.' Her eyes flickered open and she stared at him. 'That.'

The reason she was still a virgin was because no one had ever come close to Alberto, in her eyes.

She'd had a few dates, but they'd gone nowhere. Maybe she was just that dull, old-fashioned thing, a one-man woman. She'd felt the same way about friendship. It had to be the real deal or she didn't want to know.

Precious had been the real deal. Now she was gone.

'I wasn't expecting this,' she said. 'And by the time I could have told you, well ... it was too late.'

Alberto turned toward her, propping himself up on one elbow, running a hand down over her face, brushing back her loose dark hair. His eyes met hers.

'I'm so sorry about your friend,' he said. 'From what I saw of her, she seemed a very special person.'

'Yes. She was.' Layla's eyes filled with tears and he pulled her close, held her.

'Shh,' he murmured against her hair and she sobbed helplessly, the grief overflowing again in an unstoppable tide.

'Don't worry,' he said, kissing her brow. 'The bastard who did it – we're going to get him. OK?' He pushed her head back, looked at her tear-drenched face. 'Layla. You believe me?'

Layla gulped, wiped at her eyes. 'Yes,' she said. 'I believe you.'

If anyone could catch that bastard, it was Alberto – and her dad.

Layla stiffened.

Oh God. Dad.

What would *he* make of this?

No. She couldn't think about that yet. Her mind baulked at the very idea of explaining this to him. She gazed at Alberto. Couldn't believe he was here, like this, with her. But he was.

'I love you,' she said, linking her arms around his neck. 'Kiss me.'

Alberto kissed her, long and hard and slow. His hand dipped lower, cupping her breast, his thumb rubbing slowly, maddeningly, over the nipple, teasing it into hardness. Layla groaned.

'Did I hurt you?' he asked, his hand dipping lower, lower, until she gasped.

'No. A bit.' It *had* hurt, but she had been tense, expecting it to. It wasn't his fault. And as he had just pointed out, she hadn't told him she was a virgin, and she should have.

'It'll be better this time,' he said. 'Lie back…'

He was caressing her gently, firmly, until she was liquid with longing, gasping with need. Then he mounted her again and she felt him, amazingly hard but silken, pushing into her easily this time, filling her. She clung to him, ecstatic. Nothing had ever felt so right.

'Jesus,' he moaned against her neck, thrusting desperately. His eyes met hers and he kissed her, their tongues playing. 'Jesus, Layla...' he gasped against her mouth.

'I love you,' she panted. 'Alberto, I love you so much.'

'I know,' he said, and came, pushing into her so hard she could barely breathe. 'Oh, Layla, baby, what the hell are we going to do…'

About what? she wondered.

There was joy in her heart, and overwhelming sadness ... and now there was fear, too. Not for herself, but for him.

87

So the game was up. Kath the mother had phoned him in panic, the fucking idiot.

'Help us! Carter's here and he's beating up Junior. You said he wouldn't get into trouble over this, you *promised.*'

As if he'd lift a fecking finger on Junior's behalf. The little cunt was caught: no use to him now. It was time to up the stakes. No point pussy-footing around. He had one loyalty, and that loyalty was crying out for vengeance.

Vengeance is mine, sayeth the Lord.

Well, today vengeance would be Rufus's, too. He'd waited too long for this. With Orla dead, what did he have to lose? It was time to get on and do it, and then at last he'd be revenged and his poor beloved could rest in peace.

88

Tone picked up Junior's car within the first quarter of a mile. It was a ratty little Ford in graphite blue, old and rusted, billowing out grey smoke from the exhaust, leaving a trail that made the job easier. He followed it through traffic, edging ever closer.

'Don't lose him,' said Max.

'I won't.'

Max glanced at Molls, now crouched silent in the back seat. 'He been seeing much of this bloke, this Rufus?'

Molls shook her head.

'The truth,' said Max sharply.

She gulped fearfully and nodded. 'Yeah. A lot.'

Max felt the rage rise up again, nearly choke him with its ferocity. This was Annie's cousin's boy, someone she'd looked out for since he was a kid, furnishing him with jobs and no doubt with extra cash when he needed it.

He stared at Molly in disgust. He barely knew this girl, or her brother. Kath, the mother, was dog-rough; Max didn't even want to *look* at her, never had. He reckoned Molly was cut from the same mould as her mother. She could pull men now, but what few looks she had would quickly fade, the same way her mother's had, helped along by booze or drugs or binge eating till she ended up the spitting image of Kath.

'Fuck!' said Tone loudly as the lights changed. He slammed on the brakes. Molly slipped off the back seat and thumped to the floor. Junior's old Ford was chugging away into the distance.

'Jump the lights,' said Max.

Tone didn't question it. He edged out, jerking the Jag to a halt when a car shot past within inches of the front bumper.

'Holy *shit!*' yelled Molly, scrabbling back up on to the seat.

Cars honked their horns. There was a squealing of brakes, accompanied by yells of fury. Tone put his foot down and the Jag shot through the steadily moving line of traffic across the junction, at the head of which was the old blue Ford.

Cutting in and out of the traffic, Tony continued edging closer to the little car up the front. At the next set of lights, Junior pulled away again. Max didn't have to say a word this time, Tone put his foot to the floor. Then he spotted the cop car parked up at the side of the road, and stopped.

'Fuck,' said Max.

The lights changed. Tone took off again, full-speed, edging up as Junior came within distance. They were three cars behind, then two, then one. Then the lights again. This time Tone ignored them. Brakes squealed, horns tooted, people shouted and screamed. No one got killed, but it was only by luck. Tone was on Junior's bumper as he headed over the North Circular. Soon as he came off it, Junior pulled the car to the side and with a chirp of brakes parked it nose-first against the nearest pavement. Then he tumbled out of the driver's-side door, and ran.

Max was out of the Jag before Tone brought it to a halt. He hit the road and was off along the pavement after Junior. Thirty paces and he came to a brick wall. He was trying to hurl himself over it when Max caught up and dragged him down. Junior started yelling.

'Shut up,' snapped Max, shaking him. 'We've got your sister in the car. You want her to come to grief? Keep *that* up and she will.'

Junior shut up.

Yeah, he thought a lot of his family, Max could see that. Shame that familial loyalty didn't stretch to Annie. He knew his ex-wife was a crazy, maddening cow, but that had never stopped him loving her one hundred per cent.

He gripped Junior's arm and marched him to the Jag. Then he threw him in the back with his sister, and Tone drove them all to Holland Park.

89

Annie was in the study when she heard the doorbell ring. Rosa was down in the kitchen, chances were she wouldn't even hear it. But Bri was there on the door, he'd get it. She'd just got off the phone to Alberto, who'd rung in to say he had Layla with him, she was safe. She was worried for Alberto, but at a loss to know how she could help him. Soon, he'd warned her, he was going to have to run.

Christ, Alberto, please don't leave it too late, she thought, shuddering. She went to the window, looked out. There was a van out there, a black van, it had been there for a couple of weeks now; people coming and going around it, workmen she had supposed. But now ... she wasn't so sure.

She felt bad about having called him. He shouldn't be here, helping her. He had enough on his plate as it was. She shouldn't have asked him to come.

When the Feds took Alberto, she knew the

whole edifice of his organization would come crashing down. Without his rigorous control of the streets, Queens, New York would be a zoo again, wide open to any little tosser with attitude. She thought of Naples, where only recently a whole host of Mafia godfathers had been arrested. Shortly after their trials and convictions, the police authorities had found themselves unable to cope with the sudden outbreak of criminal chancers running wild.

Alberto's charmed life would be over. No more summers in the Hamptons, no more polo at Cowdray Park or in Argentina or Callien in the South of France, no more champagne and chukkas, no more racing in fiendishly expensive yachts, no more private jets and politicians and high-ranking policemen seeking favours from the don.

All that would be at an end.

Instead, there would be prison, for a lot of years.

Annie stood up. It was too painful to think that Alberto, her stepson, her friend and supporter over so many years, would be lost to her.

Would Max finally believe *then,* when 'Golden Boy' Alberto was behind bars, that there was nothing between them? She thought of Layla and Alberto. Thought of the transformation her daughter had undergone, and the way Alberto had looked at her.

Annie sighed. She didn't want that pain for Layla. She wanted a straight, uncomplicated man for her. Not Alberto, who could be gone at any moment. But it wasn't her decision to make. They were together, right now. It was out of her hands.

She went over to the door. Bri had let someone in. Who? He should have been tapping on the study door by now, letting her know who was calling. She opened it and glanced out into the hall – and froze.

Bri was lying on the floor by the closed front door. He was on his back, and he was twitching.

'Bri–' Annie was stepping forward, her heart racing.

That was when she saw the big man with the shock of red hair step out from behind the staircase.

She spun round, almost fell back into the study, slammed the door, ran for the desk. He was there, flinging the door open, sending it crashing it on its hinges. Shaking, terrified, she fumbled opened the top drawer, grabbed the can of Mace. Somehow she held it ready, stared at Rufus Malone standing there in the open doorway.

He moved like an athlete, surprisingly light on his feet for a man that size. The long, curling red hair gave him a wild appearance. The dark grey eyes were cold. He was wearing jeans and a white shirt and a beige corduroy jacket that seemed too tight, stretched across his bulky frame. He was carrying something in his right hand: a black plastic item the size of a small transistor radio, with two buttons on the front.

He smiled almost gently as he pressed one of the buttons.

There was a sharp *zapping* sound. Two electrical probes shot out of the thing on wires and hit Annie like a thunderbolt.

Next thing she knew, all the strength went out

of her. Her fingers went numb. She dropped the Mace. Instantly, she collapsed in a heap, every particle of her body short-circuiting.

Taser, she managed to think.

The shock danced all over her skin and nerves like a firestorm. Suddenly, nothing worked. Her limbs were dead weights, and the greater part of her brain seemed to be in the grip of a detached paralysis. She lay there, aware that her legs and arms were trembling but unable to stop it. She was breathing, but it felt as if someone else was doing all the work.

How many volts did those things carry? She'd read once that it was fifty thousand, which – if you were unlucky and had other health issues such as an undiagnosed heart condition – could kill you.

She wasn't dead. Neither was Bri. But they were both about as useful right this minute as a couple of babes in arms.

Rosa, she thought, and screamed out the housekeeper's name.

The sound that emerged was a tremulous whimper. What good could Rosa do anyhow? Nothing except get hit by that thing herself – and she was frail and old, the shock would most likely kill her.

Rufus pocketed the taser gun in a businesslike fashion, then came around the desk, bent and hefted her over his shoulder. She felt one of her shoes drop from her foot. Her brain was disjointed, sluggish to respond, firing a few synapses here and there.

He was going to carry her out the front door?

But there were men watching the house. Max's men. They would see, they would come and stop him. And what could have been a curse could now turn into a blessing. Those men in the black van, the ones she believed were watching Alberto's every move, would now come to her aid.

Wouldn't they?

Rufus was out in the hall now, stepping over Bri, who was still shaking and helpless on the floor. Opening the front door, he casually hefted her in a fireman's lift down the front steps. *Someone* was going to stop him.

She tried to see, tried to look around, but the world was upside-down and she couldn't move her head, couldn't move *anything.* She could see a car, and that was one of Max's men in the driver's seat. Why wasn't he moving, why wasn't he seeing this and hurrying towards them? His eyes were closed. Whether he was just asleep or had been zapped like her, she didn't know. He wasn't coming to anyone's rescue, that was for sure.

Shit.

As if this was a normal everyday event, Rufus Malone opened the back door of a car, and unloaded her across the seat. She lay there, thinking *How long until this wears off? Until I can move again?*

She had no idea.

Rufus got behind the wheel. No one stopped him. No one lifted a finger. He drove off, clipping the wing of the car parked in front of him. He didn't stop. He kept going.

'You *see* that?' asked the man in the black van.

'What?' said his companion, a squat little guy with a squint and a pair of headphones more or less permanently attached to his bald head. He was thinking about lunch. His stomach was growling. He was bored to hell with this gig.

'That guy carrying Annie Carter out the front door,' said the one who'd been looking out of the black-tinted windows at the street. He was bored too, and the scene he'd just witnessed had enlivened his day.

'You're joking, right?' The man with the headphones knew his colleague for an inveterate practical joker. He'd been on the receiving end of a few of his pranks. He hated practical jokes.

'I'm not joking. Brought her down the steps over his shoulder. Big man, red hair. Light cord jacket, jeans. You know what's even weirder? No one tried to stop him.'

The little man took off his headphones. 'Serious?'

His colleague nodded.

'Better phone it in then.'

90

They were in the back of the car, Sandor at the wheel. Heading to Holland Park.

'Alberto,' said Layla.

'Hm?'

'You keep saying that you can't start anything

now, and then what do you do? You *start* something.'

He looked at her. 'Are you sorry?'

'No. Of course not,' she said, the memory of the past few hours bringing heat to her face.

'I shouldn't have done it,' he said, shaking his head almost sadly. 'But ... I wanted to.'

'Well, it's too late for all that now. So will you please tell me what's happening?'

'Things might be catching up with me.'

'What things?'

Alberto stared at her. 'Layla. You *know* what I am.'

'You mean ... the police?'

'I mean the FBI.'

Layla went pale. 'Oh.' She sank back against the upholstery, anxiety clamping her chest. She swallowed hard. 'How long…?'

He shrugged. 'I don't know. Soon.'

Layla sucked in a panicky breath. They'd only just found each other. And here he was, telling her that he could be snatched from her?

'Then we have to get away. Go somewhere. Anywhere.'

'I'm not leaving yet, not with you and your mom in a fix.'

Layla stared at the face she loved so much. Strong, tanned, sometimes fierce, sometimes gentle. She *couldn't* lose him. Not now.

'Look, Layla, when I go, I go alone,' he said.

Layla opened her mouth to speak, then closed it again. She felt a wave of hurt hit her, snatching her breath away. *He didn't want her with him.* She would go to the ends of the earth for him, but he didn't want that. She shrank from him. He'd used her. And now he was telling her this.

'But...' she started, then stuttered to a halt. She was shocked, bewildered. 'Didn't that ... didn't that mean anything to you, this afternoon?'

Alberto turned his head and looked at her. Then he looked away again. 'We had sex, Layla. It was good, but it was sex. That's all.'

Layla gasped as if he'd punched her.

Alberto suppressed a sigh. This was so hard. It was crucifying him, but he knew he had to do it – make her let go, make her despise him, if he could. It would be cruel to do otherwise.

'Do you know how many women throw themselves at me in the space of a year?' he asked her.

'I don't...' she said, faltering.

'Dozens.' He glanced at her face. It was a picture of distress. Quickly he looked away. He couldn't afford to weaken. Not now. 'This afternoon was nice. Let's not read too much into it though, OK?'

Layla could only stare back at him blankly. *Nice?* She couldn't believe he was saying these horrible things, not to her. He was making his feelings very plain, though. He was going to take off somewhere, and she wasn't invited along for the ride.

'You heartless bastard,' she said, blinking back tears.

'Yeah. That's me,' he said, and for the rest of the journey they didn't say another word.

91

The instant Max got to Holland Park, he knew something was wrong. Paul was asleep in his car. And Bri opened the front door looking as if he'd been dragged through a hedge. He was sweaty and pale.

'What's up with you?' said Max, marching Molly inside while Tony followed on with Junior. 'And I just passed Paul, he's *asleep* out there. What the fuck's going on?'

'Something happened, Boss.' Bri's speech was laboured, disjointed.

'Where's Annie?' demanded Max.

'Let me *go,* will you?' whined Molly.

Max gave her a shake. 'Shut up, you.' He turned back to Bri. 'What's happened?'

'Sorry, Boss. Nothing I could do. Bastard came to–'

'Who?' A hot bolt of panic shot through Max's gut.

'Big guy, long red hair. Hit me with a taser. Didn't see it coming. Went down like a sack of shit. Couldn't move.'

'Where's Annie?' Max repeated, his mouth going dry.

'He took her. Zapped her – carried her out. I couldn't stop him.'

'What's going on?' asked Alberto, catching the last few words as he came up the steps, Layla trailing behind him.

'That's what I want to find out,' said Max, thinking fast. Bri had seen Rufus Malone, he was certain of that. And Malone had snatched Annie.

Layla was surging forward, her face twisted with anxiety. 'What's happened? Where's Mum?'

For Layla's sake, Max knew he had to clamp down the panic rising in him. He couldn't allow his fear at the thought of what that bastard might do to Annie spiral out of control. Looking his daughter in the eye, he told her, 'We're going to find her.'

The colour drained from her face and she sagged a little, as if she might faint. 'It was him, wasn't it? He's been here. Oh my God, no!'

'Don't wor–'

'Don't worry? Precious – the girl he beat up at the club – she died today, Dad. She *died.* And now he's got Mum.'

'We'll get her back,' said Max.

'We will,' said Alberto, taking Layla's arm. She flinched away from him. Max looked at them both. He had never seen Layla react like that with Alberto before.

'Don't *touch* me,' she snapped.

Max gave a nod to Tony to follow with Junior, and he hustled Molly into the drawing room. Alberto and Layla followed.

'Go and check Paul's OK,' Max flung back at Bri.

Bri hurried to obey.

'Precious told me...' Before she died. Layla took

a breath and started again.

This day had been horrendous, exhausting. She couldn't remember ever having a worse one. It was agony and joy and terrible disappointment, all churning together. Her head hurt. And her heart ached too – both for the loss of Precious and at the painful discovery of how little she really meant to the man she loved.

Do you know how many women throw themselves at me in the space of a year? he'd asked her. Like she was just one in a long line of easy lays. Nothing special. To be used, and discarded.

Now she couldn't get her mind off the image of her mother, *her* mum, being held by that bastard Malone. She couldn't stop thinking about the things a man like that, a man who would happily beat a woman to the point of death, could do to her mother.

'Take your time,' said Alberto. 'Just breathe steadily.'

She thought of Precious and her heart-brain exercise, and wanted to weep all over again.

'Precious told me that he beat her up to send a message to us, to the Carters,' she said. 'And now he's got Mum...'

Max was standing by the mantelpiece, Alberto alongside him. Shooting Junior a venomous look that should have killed him on the spot, Max growled, 'If he hurts her, you will pay the price.'

'Look, all I did was little things, I told you. He just paid me.'

'If you wanted or needed money, why didn't you talk to Annie? She'd have given it to you like a shot.'

'Oh yeah,' sneered Junior. 'Lady Bountiful, the great Annie Carter.'

'You little shit.'

'And you won't touch me,' said Junior with sullen resentment. ''Cos if you did, *she'd* throw a fit.'

Max was across the room in a second, yanking Junior to his feet by his shirtfront. 'Yeah? Well, she's not here. I am. And you, boy, are starting to get on my fucking nerves.'

'Where would he take her?' asked Alberto of no one in particular.

Max glanced at Alberto, then shoved the quivering Junior back down on to the sofa.

'Who knows,' said Max. 'Not Partyland. The place on the marshes? Would he go back there?'

He might have taken her to the nearest quiet place, killed her and buried the body, thought Max. *She could be dead already.*

That thought filled him with anguish. He'd returned only for Layla's sake, and it had shocked him to discover that his feelings for Annie, even after eight years apart, were as strong as ever. He wanted, needed, loved her.

Whatever had gone on between her and Golden Boy in the past – and he was starting to think he'd been wrong about that all along – he no longer gave a shit. She was his. He was hers. But had he come this close, only to lose her?

'We have to check every place we can think of,' said Layla. She was staring at Junior in disgust. She felt sick to her stomach at what he'd said. 'So you *helped* that awful bastard? Against us? Against your family?'

Junior squirmed, shrank into his seat.

'Oh God, I can see it now. That night when he hurt Precious,' she said, advancing towards him, 'you were skulking in the toilet because you couldn't face looking at those monitors, seeing what he was going to do. You didn't even have the balls for that.'

Junior looked up at her, his face red with shame.

'Look what I did was *nothing*. I just started the fire in your office and a couple of other little things. It was money for old rope. I didn't know he'd actually *kill...*' He hesitated.

'Her name's Precious,' Layla said through gritted teeth. 'You let him beat Precious to a pulp. You let him kill her.'

'I didn't know he'd go that far! I swear it.'

'No? But if you'd stuck around in the monitor room and you'd *seen* how far he was going, would you have tried to stop him? I don't think so. You're a coward and a bloody traitor.'

Max was watching Molls throughout all this. She was staring at the floor. Her cheeks were pink. He went and stood in front of her. He was getting a strong feeling about sneaky, goofy-looking little Molls. She looked up, then quickly away, her eyes darting sideways.

'Where would he go, Molls?' Max asked her, his voice low and dangerous. 'You got any ideas?'

She shrugged, hugging her arms around her body as if she was cold.

'Where?' repeated Max.

Molly said nothing.

Max reached down and yanked her upright.

She let out a yell.

'Hey!' said Junior, jumping to his feet.

Alberto placed a hand on Junior's chest. 'You want to start something?' he asked, and Layla was struck by his voice – so cold. She looked at him. This Alberto was frightening. His gaze as he stared into Junior's eyes was lance-like, threatening as a viper's. Suddenly, she felt she didn't know him at all.

'Where's he going to take her?' hissed Max into Molly's face. 'If you know something, you better start talking, or Junior here's going to get the kicking of his life. Christ knows, it's way overdue.'

Molly said nothing. Tears were trickling down her face.

'Fine, have it your way,' said Max.

He grabbed Junior, starting frog-marching him toward the door.

'No!' howled Molly. Layla came to her feet, distressed. Alberto shot her a quick look. *Shut up,* his eyes said.

Max was at the door, holding a struggling Junior.

'All right, I'll tell you what I know,' said Molly. 'Just don't hurt him, OK?'

'I'm not making any promises,' said Max. He shoved Junior back on to the sofa. 'Go on then,' he said to Molly.

Molly pulled her hands down over her face, wiping her tears away. She cast a wild look at Junior, then at Max and Alberto.

'I knew Junior was in the money all of a sudden,' she started unsteadily. 'So I ... I just wanted to find out where it had come from. I knew he hated having to take money off Annie, he'd said so to me often enough, so where was he getting it all? Anyhow when I heard him on the phone talking to someone he called Rufus, I thought it might have something to do with it. Then Rufus came to the house when Mum was out. And while him and Junior were talking in the kitchen, I was in the hall, listening.'

'You sneaky little cow,' said Junior angrily.

'Oh yeah? Well, you could have cut me in on it,' returned Molly.

'For what? It was me he wanted to help him out, not you.'

'Cut the yap and go on,' said Max.

'Then ... then I heard them coming out into the hall. I ran up the stairs and into my room so they wouldn't know I'd been listening. Junior went into the upstairs loo, and I crept out on the landing and heard this Rufus guy pick up the phone in the hall. He said a name, I think it was Dickon.'

Max exchanged a look with Alberto. They knew Dickon.

'Rufus was telling Dickon that when he got the chance he was going to do the Carter bitch out at the Essex place, on the marshes.' Molly looked around at them all. 'And you know what? I thought that just about served her right, because she's looked down on my mum all her life. She's always had everything, and my mum had nothing.'

There was a long, deadly silence. Then Layla reached out and grabbed Molly's arm, shook her.

'Is this the truth? Or is it just another set-up, another trap?' she demanded.

Alberto and her father had been led there once

before; *this* time, they might not be so lucky.

'No! I'm telling you the truth. That's what I heard.'

Max was silent, watching her, weighing it all up. Then his eyes went to Alberto. 'Get some of the boys to check out the amusement arcade, in case this *is* another false trail.'

Alberto's eyes were flinty. 'It's done,' he said. He glanced at Molls, back at Max. 'We have to risk it,' said Alberto.

'Yeah,' said Max. 'We do.'

92

Annie felt sick with fear and she was fighting flat-out hysteria. Time had passed, and it was all a blur, a horrible nightmare. She kept telling herself this couldn't be happening. But it was.

The taser-blast meant she'd been unable to move to begin with. She knew she was lying in the back of a car, and she could see the night sky, street lights, and buildings that were at first familiar and then unknown.

Within half an hour her arms and legs were tingling. She started tentatively moving her limbs, wondering whether she could throw open the door, jump out. There was a chance she'd be hurt, given the speed he was driving, but what other option did she have? Nauseous and terrified, she resolved that if she got the slightest chance, she would take it.

But her chance never came.

He stopped the car in a quiet side road, threw open the back door.

'Wait!' she managed to gasp out. 'Just wait–'

'Shut up,' said Rufus, and slapped duct tape over her mouth to silence her.

Then he bound her hands and feet, and put a sack over her head. Mould and dust filled her nostrils as he hauled her bodily out of the car. Swaying sickly as he carried her, Annie heard him open doors, then she was thrown painfully down on to cold ridged metal. The impact knocked all the breath out of her. Metal doors slammed shut.

It was an effort to breathe when every fibre of her being was screaming out a message of panic, nevertheless she forced herself to keep thinking. She must be in a Transit van, something like that. An engine started up, and the van lurched and began to move.

To hold the fear in check and keep herself calm, she tried not to dwell on thoughts of where Rufus Malone was taking her, what he would do to her when they got there. Instead she filled her mind with thoughts of Layla, of Alberto, and lastly of Max. She was still in love with him. Had never been *out* of love with him, not even when he was at his most vicious and bitter.

Now, she was never going to see him again.

This was it. This was the end.

93

Hunter had been about to head home when the Super called him into his office.

'Had a call from the boys who are watching this mob guy,' Cyril told him. 'They saw a bloke come out of the house carrying Annie Carter over his shoulder. Stuffed her in the back of a car, drove off.'

'Over his shoulder? Was she unconscious?'

'Looked like it, they said.'

'Do we have a description of this man?' asked Hunter.

Cyril flipped his notepad open. 'Beige cord jacket, jeans. Big bastard, built like a rugby player. Long curly red hair.'

'They get the registration number?' Hunter was thinking that the description Cyril had just given sounded very much like the guy who had bombed out Annie Carter's car a couple of weeks ago.

'They did. And we found the car, abandoned in a lane in Essex.'

'Prints?' he asked.

'Yep. And we've got a match on the system: Rufus Malone. Irish hard case, been all over the bloody world by all accounts. Done time in his youth, nothing recent.' The Super blew out his cheeks. 'This is a criminal act – an abduction.'

Hunter looked at him. 'But we've been warned off. We can't touch this.'

'We can't let our citizens be snatched off the street, either.'

'Out of the house, anyway.'

'You know what I mean. The car's a rental, we're waiting for further verification on his ID with Avis.'

'But we can't get involved.'

'No. Technically speaking, we can't.'

94

A fear had been eating at Annie, chiselling away at her composure, ever since Orla Delaney had bludgeoned her way back into her world. She had tried not to voice it aloud, because that would make it real and even more terrifying. But that fear was enveloping her now, snatching the breath from her throat, stealing away what little composure remained to her.

That fear was...

Oh shit, no, I can't think it, I mustn't...

That fear was that *he* would be waiting for her at the end of this journey.

Redmond Delaney.

If Orla was alive, then he could be too. She shivered as the words trickled through her mind, corrosive as liquid poison.

No, Redmond was dead. He was *meant* to die.

But then – so was Orla. And she had come back from the grave, started up this whole mad thing that was now playing out to its bitter end.

Annie closed her eyes, tried to blank the fear out. But it was too strong.

Maybe she was the one who was meant to die. Maybe, after all these years, Redmond was finally going to have his revenge.

95

'He gave false ID,' said the Super. 'To the car hire people. Banged it up a bit too, they're not happy.'

Hunter leaned back against the closed office door and gazed out through the half-open Venetian blinds at the darkening sky and the drizzling rain, seeing nothing.

'Funny-looking fucker. Like the Wild Man of Borneo,' said the Super.

Red hair, same as Orla and Redmond Delaney, thought Hunter.

'You got the word out on the ports and airports?' he asked.

'Of course. But both you and I know it's easy enough to sneak in and out from a quiet spot on a dark night, pay a skipper, no questions asked.'

'Any relatives, known associates...?'

The Super flicked open a page on the pad in front of him on the desk. 'Benny O'Connor – your gunshot victim. I sent a couple of the lads over to the hospital to question him and at the mention of Rufus Malone he started singing like a ruddy canary. Sounds as if he's a very frightened man. He says Rufus has been in the UK two or three weeks; told Benny he was staying at an amusement arcade in Southend called Partyland and then at another place out Essex way.'

'And...?' prompted Hunter.

'Partyland, it turns out, has had a visit from some hard boys. They wrecked the place.'

Hunter nodded. 'Someone else is looking for Rufus Malone.'

'Looks that way.'

'I'm thinking Max Carter; that would fit with the description the nurse gave of the man who assaulted O'Connor. What about the Essex address?'

'O'Connor reckons it's a derelict property. Claims he doesn't have an actual address.'

'Can we get a fix on that?'

'I think we should try. And there's another person of interest we're on the lookout for – name of Dickon, nasty little tit with a record as long as your arm, but we can't find him. Hasn't been seen in any of his usual haunts and his friends claim they've no idea where he's got to. And there are still some Delaney family members in Ireland. Living at a place called Fallowfield Farm in Limerick. Maybe this Rufus could be thinking of making his way there? I dunno. This goes beyond making waves for the American boys, don't you think? This is about tracing an abducted woman, a British citizen.'

96

They were heading for Essex. Steve was driving, with Max in the front passenger seat. Layla was crammed in the back between Alberto and Sandor, and she was thinking she might choke from all the testosterone floating about in here. The mood in the car was grim.

'Layla?' said Alberto quietly.

She didn't answer: she stared out at the encroaching night.

'Oh for God's sake,' he muttered.

Layla turned a freezing glance on him. 'What?' she hissed.

'Can we try and behave like grown-ups?'

Layla's eyes flashed with temper. 'Oh sure. You'd love that, wouldn't you. Sorry – I wasn't aware I was being juvenile.'

'Well, you are.'

Layla leaned forward and said for his ears only: 'My dad would *kill* you if he knew what you did to me.'

Alberto opened his eyes wide. 'Yeah? He'd better just get in line. We made love. Get over it.'

'Made love?' Layla gave a low, bitter laugh. In a fierce whisper she went on: 'We *had sex* because I was upset and you took advantage of that. You used me. Then you dumped me. I apologize if I don't like that.'

'Jesus, don't we have more important things to

think about right now?' asked Alberto in exasperation. 'Look – I did you a favour. Believe me, I did.'

'A *favour?* No, you did *yourself* one,' said Layla. She closed her eyes and moaned softly. 'Oh God. He could kill her, couldn't he? She could already be dead. She might not even *be* at this place.'

'Talking like that won't help.' They knew at least that Annie wasn't at Partyland; that had been checked out. Their only hope was that Malone had taken her to the place out on the marshes. If not, they were stumped. And Annie was finished.

'*Don't* tell me what I can and cannot think. You might boss everyone else around, but not *me*, OK?'

'What's going on?' asked Max, turning in his seat. He looked at Sandor, sitting there like a slab of rock, then at Alberto, and finally at Layla.

'She's upset,' said Alberto smoothly, his eyes holding hers.

Max reached back and took her hand. 'I said this was a bad idea. I told you not to come.'

'I *had* to come,' said Layla. Her brain kept presenting her with nightmare images of Precious, beaten to death. And the same man had Mum now. 'For God's sake, how could I not? Anything could happen to her, I *have* to be here.'

Max and Alberto exchanged a look. They both thought that Layla would be in the way, a liability; that they might have to waste time protecting her, when they ought to be able to focus on getting Annie out of danger. They had told her as much before leaving London. But Layla was having none of it.

'What's going on with you two?' asked Max, his eyes moving from his daughter to Alberto and back again.

'Nothing,' she said.

'Nothing? You sounded like you were ripping lumps out of each other a moment ago. You had a fight?'

Layla stared hard at Alberto, who returned her look coolly.

He'd kill you if he knew, her eyes said.

Yeah? Alberto's gaze said. *So do it. Tell him.*

'It was nothing,' said Layla, dropping her eyes to her lap. 'Really, nothing.'

Max looked at Alberto. Something was going on with these two.

'I'd take a dim view of anyone upsetting my daughter,' he said to Alberto.

'Of course,' said Alberto.

'So don't,' said Max.

'Wouldn't dream of it.'

'Good,' said Max, giving Alberto one last thoughtful look and Layla's hand a brief squeeze before he turned to stare ahead again.

'Can't you go any faster?' Layla asked Steve.

'We'll get there,' he said.

'Yeah. In time for *what?*'

97

Annie couldn't quite believe it when the van finally came to a halt. Her mouth was bone-dry. She was so cold that she shivered constantly, and so frightened that she was barely keeping a grip on herself any more.

She heard movement at the front of the van. Apart from the clicking of the engine cooling down, she could hear little else – only the faint sighing of the wind. The roar of the engine, that noisy nightmare, was finished.

All was quiet.

Then suddenly there was dim light through the mouldy-smelling sacking covering her head as the back doors of the van were thrown open.

Annie stiffened. She could just about see his outline against the square of dying daylight. She couldn't speak, couldn't even try to reason with him, her mouth was still taped. He stood there, looking in at her. Then he ... what was he doing? She strained to see through the weave of the sacking.

He was taking something out of his jacket pocket.

Oh shit, please no.

It was the taser gun.

Annie squirmed, trying to get away. Useless. Hopeless.

But it wasn't the taser. This time, it was a

cosh. He leaned in, and a jagged knife of pain exploded in her head. After that, there was nothing.

98

Consciousness returned slowly, dimly, as if through a dreamlike gauze. Annie was lying on something hard and smooth. No, not lying. She was leaning forward, and her back ached. Her head hurt. Her fingers felt wood. The darkness returned, and then it receded again. This time she felt she was sitting. Definitely sitting, on a chair.

More darkness.

Her eyes flickered open.

Slowly it all came back to her. Everything. Walking across the hall, Bri twitching and writhing on the floor by the door, seeing the big man coming toward her, running for the study to get the Mace spray. The taser gun. The journey, the cosh...

Her head really *ached,* and she was now ... where? She hadn't a clue. But she knew she was still in danger.

'So when are you going to admit you're awake?' asked a voice.

Someone poked her arm, hard.

'Annie Carter? You're awake. Come on. No play-acting now.'

Slowly, she lifted her head. It felt impossibly

heavy. A stab of pain hit her behind the eyes, then settled into a steady, nagging ache on her left temple. She raised a shaking hand, ran her fingers over the lump there. She blinked, looked around.

She was sitting at an old dirty table. There was a lantern at the far end of it, the flame flaring and smoking, throwing up quavering shadows. The room in which she found herself was nothing but a shell, with exposed beams and grimy walls, and now she could smell – her nose wrinkled – salt water and decaying seaweed in the air.

Rufus wasn't in the room. So where the hell was he? She'd heard him speak to her, but that could have been minutes or hours ago. He was somewhere close by, he had to be, ready to fry her brains again with that damned taser.

She was glancing around now, coming back to full awareness. Her eyes were wide with terror as they moved, searching for a weapon. There was nothing in this room except the table, the chairs.

Was this the place on the marshes?

Her eyes flew to the front door. There had been explosive rigged there last time she was here, but there was nothing now. The other door had a filthy window beside it. It was hanging loose, slightly ajar, on rusted hinges.

That was how it had been when Max spotted the bomb in here.

She could get out. Make a run for it. She braced both hands on the table and pushed herself upright. Then a wave of giddiness hit her and she fell back into the chair. Her head was spinning from the after-effects of the cosh and the taser.

Oh shit am I going to be sick ...? she wondered.

She tried to breathe deeply, easily, but the sudden realization of her own weakness panicked her, sent her heart rate into overdrive. She couldn't afford to be weak, not now. But she was.

Then Rufus Malone entered the room, and she knew her chance had passed.

Too late.

Too late for *anything*.

99

Annie felt her insides shrivel with fear when Rufus came in. In his muddy hands he was carrying a bottle of whisky, two tin mugs and a torch. She saw that he wore rubber boots, and they were mud-covered too.

His eyes met Annie's as he sat down in one of the chairs across the table from her. He put the torch on the table, unscrewed the bottle and slopped the liquid into the two mugs.

'Let's have a drink, Mrs Carter,' he said in a broad Irish drawl.

He pushed one mug in front of Annie, swallowed his own in one gulp.

'Sheesh! That's good whisky,' he said. He fixed her with an intense stare. 'So come on now. Where's my girl, eh? Where's Orla?'

Annie looked back at him. 'What?'

'Orla. Orla *Delaney*. She came to do you, didn't she. And you know what? I haven't seen her since. The plan was she had a plan – that she was going to finish you. Slit your throat. Only she didn't, because *you're* still alive. And she hasn't gone back to the auld country, as we agreed. So where is she? What's happened to her?'

Annie's heart was beating hard. 'There was a break-in at my house. Was that her? Was that Orla?' She took a gulping breath. 'But how could it be? I thought Orla took off years ago. Got lost. Or died. Or something.'

Rufus was staring at her.

Careful, she thought.

'That was her,' he said. 'Last I saw of her, Orla was alive and well.'

'Well, if it *was* her, she just knocked out the alarm, broke the basement window. She must have decided not to go any further.'

'But why would she do that?' asked Rufus.

Annie took another breath. Her chest felt tight with terror. 'Maybe she thought she couldn't go through with it. Perhaps she could see what an evil thing it would be, to do something like that.'

Rufus nodded slowly. 'Knowing Orla? Unlikely. So I'm thinking you did something to stop her.'

Not me, thought Annie. *Layla stopped her.*

And now Orla was out in the English Channel somewhere, being nibbled by crabs and fish, tossed and swept by deep underwater currents. She was gone for good this time.

'I never saw her,' said Annie.

'You're a liar,' said Rufus. He tipped his head at the mug in front of her. 'Drink up.'

'I don't...'

His eyes were hard. 'I know you don't. There's *nothing* about you I don't know. Drink it.'

Annie picked up the glass, sipped the liquid. Then without warning Rufus leaned across the table, grabbed her neck, tipped her head back, and forced the mug painfully against her lips. The whisky gushed into her mouth, burning, choking her. She swallowed convulsively. Felt it forge a molten path all the way down to her stomach.

'*Shit,*' she spluttered, turning red in the face.

'I *said, drink it.* Don't play with it.' He was pouring out another mugful. 'Now this one,' he said, lifting it to her mouth.

'No...' Annie couldn't get her breath.

But Rufus forced her head back, and she choked as the whisky filled her mouth again. She swallowed. Gagged. She was going to be sick, but that was good, wasn't it? Get it out of her system, because this was going to make her drunk very fast, and ill even faster.

She had no tolerance for alcohol. Never had. First there had been the revulsion over her mother Connie's drinking, then the realization that she personally could not drink at all. A doctor had told her she was extremely sensitive to it. Some people were. She hated the taste, and a single glass of fairly low-proof wine was enough to make her feel drunk.

This was forty per cent proof whisky.

This was going to knock her out.

This was *poison* to her.

'And again,' said Rufus, pouring her another. He winked at her while she sat there choking and retching weakly. 'It's for the best. Orla can't finish this, so I'll have to. And this will deaden the pain.'

Pain? The pain of what?

100

'There it is,' said Steve. 'Look, there's a light. Someone's inside.'

They'd stopped the car, steered it off the road and into a little stretch of woodland where it couldn't be seen from the lane. Everyone piled out. The night air smelled brackish and damp. Layla shivered.

'Too risky taking the car any further,' said Max. 'Better on foot from here on in.'

Alberto and Sandor were unloading things from the back of the car. To Layla, it looked like military gear. She nearly lost it when they started handing around sets of gloves and black goggles.

'What are those?' she asked.

'Night sights.' Max, Steve, Alberto and Sandor were putting them on.

'Don't I get a pair?'

'No, honey, you don't. You stick close to Steve. Wherever he goes, you go. Steve – you watch her. Layla – you stay with Steve. And when he tells you to do something, do it. OK?'

Suddenly their goggles were glowing red. It was surreal. Then Alberto started handing round guns.

'Jesus,' she said.

'Watch it. I can hear an engine,' said Alberto.

They could see headlights, coming along the lane. As one they moved back, away into the woods. Max pushed Layla down on to her knees beside him.

The car shot past their hiding-place and carried on along the lane.

'Come on,' said Max. 'Let's get up there.'

101

Annie didn't know how many whiskies she'd drunk. She'd lost count after seven. She only knew that she was drunk. She felt an almost detached interest in this unfamiliar phenomenon. Her head seemed to float above her body like a helium-filled balloon. Her limbs had become loose, disjointed. There seemed to be no coordination between her brain and her arms and legs any more.

And now he was forcing yet more whisky into her.

'*That's* the way, Mrs Carter, get it down the little red road,' he said.

It burned her, choked her, her stomach churned and rebelled. But he held her head back. Rivers of it ran out the sides of her mouth, spilled over her clothes, on to the cold flagged floor beneath her feet. But most of it, she swallowed. She had to. She thought that if she didn't, he would find some other way of getting it down her. Maybe a rubber tube straight into her stomach. She didn't want that. This was bad, but that would be a damned sight worse.

God, I'm going to be so sick in the morning, she thought. *If I live that long. Which I won't.*

That thought brought both pain and rage with it. Never to see Layla again. Or Max. If she wasn't sitting in a chair, she would be falling over. She felt so hot, so dizzy, disconnected from reality. Maybe dying wouldn't be so bad. Maybe in fact Orla could tell her about it. Maybe Orla was going to come staggering through that door, fresh from the sea, dripping and dead, crustacea hanging off her tattered flesh, starfish in what remained of her hair...

Oh, she was drunk.

She looked around her and Rufus wasn't there any more, he'd gone outside again.

And Rufus was right: drunk was *good.*

Whatever happened now, she wouldn't feel it very much at all.

That was when the door opened.

102

It wasn't Rufus who'd come in. Was this what happened when you were drunk – and Annie was very drunk indeed – did you start to hallucinate? She'd heard of the DT's, had seen her mum in the grip of it once or twice.

So yes, she was imagining things. Because there was no way that *Redmond Delaney* could be standing there. He'd died in a plane crash. He couldn't be alive.

Could he?

This was weird stuff. Seriously weird. Annie squinted at this thing that must have been conjured up by all the whisky she'd had shoved down her throat. There was no way this could really be Redmond. But ... he looked *older.* He was still pale, still handsome, those jade-green eyes set in that long, sober, ascetic face, but there were a few wrinkles now, and his hair was a little less brilliant in its redness even if it was still neat, close-cropped to his skull.

Of all the Delaney clan, Redmond had always been the neat one, with an ingrained elegance. Pat had been a great untidy, shambling brute, Tory had been much feared before someone decided to shoot him dead, Kieron had been the pretty one, the baby of the family. Annie didn't think that any one of the others could hold a candle to Redmond for sheer good looks – or the devastation he could wreak when he set his warped mind to it.

This isn't Redmond, she told herself. *This is the drink. That's all.*

'Mrs Carter,' he said, seeing her sitting there at the table.

Annie recoiled. *Was* she imagining this? Somehow her brain had furnished her with an older image of the Redmond she remembered. And *now* the thing was talking to her in Redmond's voice.

Oh shit, what is this?

Annie's eyes slid down. Oh, now this was the

weirdest thing of all. This imaginary drink-induced Redmond was wearing a white collar, a bright gold pectoral crucifix, and a long dark robe. *A soutane,* wasn't that what they called it? She wasn't sure. She felt terror shake her then, felt like a rat when a terrier has it caught helpless in its jaws. Drink-sodden or not, this was real enough to feel like the worst threat she had ever faced.

'God bless all in this house,' said Redmond, his green, green eyes smiling with all their old cruelty and cold calculation straight into hers. He made the sign of the cross in the air.

This Redmond Delaney was a *priest.*

103

'You're not real,' said Annie, shaking her head. 'You're *dead.*'

Redmond was moving forward, coming over to the table. He tilted his head to one side, stared down at her. 'Am I, though?' he asked her tauntingly.

'You're dead,' she repeated. 'I'm drunk, and you're dead.'

'Some people are hard to kill,' said Redmond.

Hadn't Max said something very like that? And maybe he'd been right. Perhaps Redmond was here, alive.

Or maybe not.

'You died years ago,' said Annie. She wanted to

believe it. Wanted to know that this was just the drink, summoning up old demons.

'Oh, the plane crash?' Redmond's eyes were mocking. 'You think I'm that easy to rub out, Mrs Carter? I survived it.'

Just like Orla, Annie thought. She didn't say it aloud, didn't dare: she didn't want to fasten his attention on Orla, on what had happened to her, because then...

Then I'll be finished.

But it was all right. Because he wasn't real, she was imagining this, it was OK. Her brain told her it was real, that he looked like a living, breathing man, but her brain was awash with alcohol. The danger here was *Rufus,* not Redmond.

But he looked so *real...*

'And you know what happened, after I survived that crash, Mrs Carter?' he asked.

His voice was just the same, with that cool southern Irish lilt. Annie shook her head.

'I decided that Orla and I ... ah, it was a painful decision, you know, but I decided that I wasn't going down the criminal path after that. I knew Orla would, but I didn't want that. I felt – and this may sound strange to you Mrs Carter,' he said with a wry half-smile, 'but I felt I'd been spared for a reason. Orla would never understand that, so I had to keep apart from her. I didn't want to go down evil ways any more. I wanted to make changes.'

It was a big bloody change all right. Annie looked at this apparition and now she *knew* it was all in her head. Redmond was evil to his bones; he didn't have it in him to change.

She stared up at him, the dim light from the lamp hollowing out his cheeks and his eye sockets, giving his pale skin an eerie, skeletal patina. He looked like something other worldly, something spectral and terrifying. She shivered hard.

Like someone walked over my grave, she thought.

'And that's what I did,' he went on, his eyes burning cold fire into hers. 'I repented, Mrs Carter. Like you should repent.'

'Me?' Annie blurted out.

'You have blood on your hands,' he said.

Annie looked down at her hands, clasped there on the table. In the lamp's glow, for a moment they were *red*. She drew in a gasp of horror, sickness rising into her throat – she could almost *smell* the blood.

She blinked.

And then they were just her hands again, no blood, nothing. She closed her eyes and groaned. When she opened them, he would be gone. She knew it.

Please God let him be gone.

Almost frightened to, she opened her eyes. And he was still there, watching her.

'Confess,' he said silkily, moving closer. 'Confess your sins to me, Mrs Carter.'

'I don't have any,' she gulped, her head spinning. *He isn't real,* she told herself. *Like the blood wasn't real.*

'We all have sins,' said Redmond, and he reached across the table and laid a hand on her head.

Annie flinched. His hand was warm. It was *Real.*

No. Not real. Couldn't be. False, like the blood.

He let his hand rest there. 'I absolve you, Mrs Carter,' he said softly, and his hand pressed down, harder. She felt as if she was being hammered down into the chair, such was the pressure of his hand lying there on her head. Annie screwed her eyes tight shut and prayed for this to be over. *Not real, he's not real, he's NOT REAL...*

After what felt like an eternity, his hand lifted. Annie sat there, hunched, shuddering, clutching her arms around herself. Slowly, she dared to open her eyes.

There was no one there.

She let out a hard breath of relief and slumped forward on the table. She'd imagined it.

Then there was a noise at the door. She was so gripped with terror that she let out a whimper. He was coming back, Redmond was coming back to get her...

But it wasn't Redmond. It was Rufus.

'Come on, Mrs Carter,' he said. 'It's time.'

104

They were close to the building now, its black outline stark against the night sky. The flickering light of a lantern showed shapes and shadows moving around inside. They could hear voices. Steve had one hand on Layla's arm; while the rest of them could see perfectly in the dark with the army-issue night-sight goggles, she was stumbling on the uneven ground, and her guts were twisted with anxiety.

If Mum was really here, was she still alive?

'Do you think Rufus has got her in there?' she whispered to Max.

'No talking,' he said.

The voices in the shack were getting louder. A man's voice – and a woman's.

Rufus had yanked Annie from her chair and was holding her upright, but she could barely stand. Her head was spinning and she thought she would throw up any minute. The room was careering around her. Rufus gave her a violent shake, and her feet went from under her. She hit the hard flagstones, but felt no pain.

Anaesthetized, she thought. She had a mad urge to laugh.

Grabbing her arm, he hauled her roughly to her feet.

'Come on,' he said.

And he snatched up his torch from the table and dragged her outside.

105

It was a cold night but Annie barely felt it. She stumbled along beside Rufus, him lighting their way with the torch. She was cocooned in a soft blanket of booze. Then he dragged her off of a rough driveway and the light of the torch showed a stretch of grass. There was a misty rain falling. The smell of the sea was stronger out here, and she could hear the faint offshore tolling of a buoy. It was all like a dream. At any moment she was going to wake up in her bed in Holland Park.

But she knew she wasn't.

Rufus came to a halt. As Annie stared down at the cone of light thrown out by the torch, a chill of fear began to penetrate the alcoholic haze. There was a spade thrust upright into newly turned soil. There was a mound of freshly dug dark earth. And there was a hole. The torch swung further over. The hole was deep. Four, maybe five feet.

Her heart froze in her chest.

This was what Rufus had been doing out here, when he'd come into the building with dirt on his hands and mud on his boots. He'd been digging.

Torchlight illuminated his face and she could see that he was grinning.

'Yes, Mrs Carter. It's a grave. Ah, let's be more specific. It's *your* grave.'

He shook her again. Annie gave a weak cry and fell to her knees in the dirt. The light was on her now, blinding her. She saw him move, fumble in his pocket. She saw the taser. She was right beside the grave he'd dug. She heard the horrible thing crackle and hum as he switched on the power.

He's going to zap me and throw me into the grave, she thought in horror. *Then he'll fill it in.*

Rufus was going to bury her alive.

106

'Mum! That's Mum, I heard her voice, he's got her!' cried Layla.

She broke free of Steve and stumbled forward in the dark, running toward where Annie and Rufus were, beside the grave.

With the benefit of the night-sight, Max saw Rufus stiffen. The beam of the torch swung their way. Annie was on her knees. Rufus was raising the device in his hand, pointing it down the torch's white beam at Layla who was running straight at him, uncaring, thinking only of getting to her mother.

'Mum!' Layla ran to Annie.

'Get back, get away from him,' said Annie, her words slurring.

Shit, thought Max, and raised the gun, taking aim. But he couldn't get a clear line of sight. Layla was between him and Rufus. And Rufus was about to shoot her dead.

'Hey!' shouted Alberto, off to the left, trying to draw fire.

Rufus paused. The light from the torch swung out to the left, then back. It was the moment Max needed. He moved aside, took aim. Then he became aware that there was something digging hard into his ribs: it felt like a gun.

'Let's all just drop the weapons now, shall we?' said a deep Northern Irish voice in his ear.

'Who's there?' demanded Rufus, the torch's beaming flashing wildly about.

The shot was almost deafening in the deep country silence. Rufus reeled back, clutching at his shoulder, staggering, dropping the thing in his hand – not a gun, Max noted, what the hell was that? There were other men here now, four of them, big hooded bruisers, all armed. Rufus collapsed to the ground.

Slowly, Max dropped his gun, took off the goggles and let those fall too. Alberto, Steve and Sandor did the same. The four hooded men snatched up everything. The man who had jammed his pistol into Max's side went over to where Rufus lay, gasping, on the ground. Max watched him in the faint light from Rufus's fallen torch. He had a stick and leaned on it heavily as he walked. Max thought he looked very ill, like he had something going on inside, a cancer eating him. He'd been a big man, you could see that, but the flesh had dropped from his bones and he was thin across the shoulders now.

'Rufus,' said Big Don Callaghan, looking down at the man on the ground.

Max could see that Rufus's eyes were open, staring up at the man who'd shot him.

'Don,' said Rufus, panting. He almost seemed to be grinning. Then he winced, stiffened. 'Ah, you just couldn't let it go, could you?'

'And why would I? Little Peter lying in a cold grave, burnt to a cinder.'

'I did penance for Pikey, Don,' said Rufus, fighting to get the words out.

'Not penance enough,' said Don, leaning

heavily on his stick. 'But now you have.'

And he raised the pistol in his hand and shot Rufus straight between the eyes, three times.

107

Now what? wondered Max. These Irish had the drop on them. They had the guns, the sights. He looked over at Layla, hugging Annie to her. Fuck's sake. There was nothing he could do. If the frail old geezer with the stick wanted no witnesses, they were all toast.

Max started walking toward Annie and Layla. To his surprise, the men with the guns let him.

'She OK?' he asked his daughter.

'I'm absolutely *fine,*' slurred Annie.

Max glanced at her curiously. She sounded drunk, but that couldn't be. Then he stood over Rufus. He was dead, no doubt about it. He turned and looked at the man who'd shot him.

'I've no quarrel with you,' said Big Don Callaghan.

Close to, by the light from the torch, Max could see that he had the pallor and sunken cheeks of the terminally ill.

'Nor me with you,' said Max, moving in front of Layla and her mother.

Don looked down at Rufus. 'It's done now. Finished.'

With that, he walked away from the man he'd been chasing for fifteen years. Soon his hobbling form merged with the shadows of the night. His men followed. Then they were gone.

Annie was stumbling upright. She nearly fell again. Max grabbed her, stared at her face.

'For fuck's sake,' he said. 'Are you *drunk?*'

'That does appear to be the case,' she said, and started weaving her way unsteadily back toward the building.

'Whoa!' Max caught her arm as she tottered sideways and almost went down again.

'Redmond's in there,' she said, pushing him away.

'What?'

'Redmond.' Annie stumbled to the door. 'He's a priest.'

'Redmond Delaney?' Max followed her. Drunk? She was pissed as a *rat.*

'He's in here, he was talking to me...' Annie all but fell through the door.

The lantern was still burning, its flame flickering, on the table. The whisky bottle, nearly empty, was there, and the two tin mugs.

'He's...' she started, then she stopped dead.

Redmond wasn't there.

He'd never been there at all.

She turned unsteadily. Grabbed the wall and held on.

'Honey, you're drunk. Come on,' said Max, going back to the door.

Annie stood there, alone and swaying, staring around at the room where Redmond had talked to her, absolved her of her sins.

Max is right, it didn't happen, it was just the drink...

And then her eyes fastened on something on the table just beside the lantern. There was a faint golden glint there. Annie lurched over and groped along the table, supporting herself. She reached out and picked the object up, held it in the palm of her hand and stared at the gold crucifix. It was Redmond's pectoral cross. The mark of the priesthood. She felt gooseflesh break out on her arms. Felt the hairs on the nape of her neck stand up.

Oh my God. I didn't dream it, she thought. *He was here.*

A faint breath of air wafted over her face, and she looked up.

The door at the back was hanging wide open, admitting the salty sea breeze. *Not a dream then. Not the drink.* Her hand folded over the cross, and she slipped it into her pocket.

'Come on,' said Max, reappearing in the front doorway. This time she went with no argument.

'Where's Alberto?' Layla was outside, fretfully sweeping the torch around the area. She couldn't see him. She couldn't see *Sandor* either.

'Dunno,' said Max, none too bothered about it. He took a firmer hold on Annie, who was staggering about like someone caught out in a high wind.

'But ... we have to find them. We can't leave without them.'

'Yeah,' said Max. 'We can.'

And then Layla looked at her father's face and she understood. Alberto had vanished into the night and he wasn't coming back. He was *gone.*

She swept the torch around again.

There was no one there.

Alberto was gone, with faithful Sandor at his side.

He'd evaded the Feds and now he would simply slip out of the country and disappear. Layla was overcome with anguish as the magnitude of it hit home. She was never going to see him again. *Never.*

And then they saw the flashing blue lights and heard the sirens. The police had arrived.

'Fuck it,' said Max tiredly. 'The cavalry's here.'

108

Annie didn't remember going home. All she knew was that she woke up one morning in her own bed, and her head hurt like hell, her eyes felt like they'd been scrubbed with Brillo pads, and her mouth was dry as the Gobi desert.

'What the...' she moaned, turning on to her back, her eyes flickering open and then instantly closing again as the sunlight pouring through the window scoured her retinas.

Fumbling, barely awake, she sat up, forced her aching eyes open and squinted around her. Yes, she was home. And she was – as usual – alone. And ... oh now she was going to be sick. She stumbled from the bed and went to the bathroom and threw up. Then, groaning, she cleaned her teeth, rinsed her mouth, took two paracetamol out of the medicine cabinet and tossed them down with a glass of water, and tried not to look at the mess in the mirror. She failed. There was a large bump on her brow. The cosh. She fell back into bed, and was soon asleep again.

'Is she going to be OK?' asked Layla anxiously.

'She had a skinful, that's all. She'll be fine,' said Max.

They were in the drawing room, Layla sitting on the sofa, Max pacing up and down.

'That bastard *forced* booze down her,' said Layla. 'She *never* drinks. She hates it. She's not used to it.'

'Yeah, well, he won't be doing that to anyone else.'

Layla watched her father stalking around like a caged tiger. She'd seen a different Max these past few days, a tough and terrifying Max. *Thank God he's on my side,* she thought. She wouldn't ever want to be one of Max Carter's enemies.

'I thought we'd lost her,' said Layla in a small voice. 'Maybe we should have taken her to hospital? That bump on her head...'

'The police doctor said she was OK,' said Max.

Layla fidgeted uneasily. 'I feel bad, you know.'

Max stopped pacing. 'About what?'

'When you two split up. Divorced. I was so rotten to her.'

'Ah, forget it.'

'Sometimes it seemed as though she didn't love me. She never *showed* it much.'

Max looked down at her in surprise. He shrugged. 'Of course she loves you, don't be daft.' He paused. 'You know what? She was never very close to her own mother, Connie. That old bag hated her. Loved Ruthie, but hated Annie. So she never got any hugs or any "I love you" off her own mother. Maybe that just seems normal to her.'

Layla listened closely to this. 'Perhaps that's it,' she said.

'Yeah, I'm sure of it,' said Max.

'I thought we were done for when the police showed up,' she said.

Me too, he thought.

In fact it had all turned out better than expected. Big Don Callaghan had taken the guns and night sights, so there was no evidence that Max and Steve were involved in anything but an honest and unarmed mission to get Annie out of trouble. All in all, it had worked out well. There had been a trip to the station, and a long night of interviews and making statements while Annie was checked over. But that was it. No charges, nothing.

'About Alberto...' she said.

'Yeah, what?'

'Where would he go, do you think?'

'I've no idea,' said Max.

109

Annie woke again, just before four in the afternoon. Her head was still thumping, but the sick queasy sensation had passed. She crawled from the bed with an effort, bundled her hair up in a clip and took a long, hot shower. Then she cleaned her teeth again, brushed out her hair, and paused beside her pile of clothes on the chair. She bent, fumbled in her jacket pocket – and there it was: Redmond's cross. She *hadn't* dreamed it.

She took it back over to the bed with her, tucked it under her pillow. Then she fell back across the bed, and went back to sleep.

When she next woke up it was to find Max over by the window turning on a small table lamp and pulling the curtains closed against the dark night sky. She glanced at the clock. Eleven thirty. She'd slept right through the day and now she felt ... mostly better.

He turned back to the bed and saw her watching him. The door between their adjoining bedrooms was still, she saw, lying on the carpet.

'Hi,' he said, and came and sat down on the bed.

She closed her eyes, opened them again. 'Did all that really happen?'

'It happened. But it's over. You're home.'

'Where's Layla?'

'She's here. She's safe.'

'Is Paul OK? And Bri?'

'They're fine.'

'Alberto?'

'Gone.'

Annie stared at him. 'Gone? Gone where?'

'Over the hills and far away.'

Annie was silent, watching his face. 'He didn't come back with us?'

'No. He didn't.'

She'd more or less passed out once the police arrived on the scene. Apart from a few lucid moments at the station, she'd missed most of what went on. Now she felt sadness grip her at the thought of never seeing Alberto again. But he'd got away, that was all that mattered. 'He's given them the slip then.'

'Them?'

'The Feds.'

'Jesus, you sound just like a Mafia widow.'

'Well, that's what I am. Did you two plan it?'

'What do you think?'

'I think you did.' Annie shook her head slowly. 'Talk about hidden agendas. Alberto wanted out, and you wanted to help him because it would get him away from me. Right?'

'That's the way it's worked out,' said Max.

Annie's mouth curved in a tired smile. 'You think you're so smart. But I'm telling you, you've read this so wrong.'

'Oh? Enlighten me then.'

'You've been watching the wrong woman. I *told* you it was someone else, not me. Didn't I?'

'You did.'

'Then why didn't you believe me?' she said almost sadly. 'Why do you *never* believe me?'

Max stared into her eyes. 'You really want to know?'

'Yes. I really do.'

He shrugged, frowned. 'Because Alberto is Constantine's double. And because you went with Constantine when you should have waited for me. Searched for me. Not just given me up for dead.'

Annie slumped back on the pillows.
'You never forgave me for that, did you?'
'I tried to. I wanted to. I couldn't. And then you kept finding excuses to nip across to America. Seeing *him* every time you were there.'
'My stepson.'
'Constantine's double.'
'Oh, Max.'
'Don't "Oh, Max" me. What the hell was I supposed to think?'
'You were supposed to trust me,' said Annie. 'I was your *wife.*'
'Women love whoever they're with.'
'*What?* How can you say that?'
'Fuck's sake, my own mother did. She played around all the time. Led my old dad a dog's life.' Max got to his feet and started pacing.
Annie just sat there and stared at him in silence. He'd never told her that before. And it explained so much.
'I didn't know that,' she said at last.
'Well, now you do.'
Annie took a breath. 'You had me followed. Have you any idea how much that hurt me?'
'You went off with another man after I went missing. Have you any idea how much that hurt *me?*'
'I believed you were dead. It broke my heart, but I believed it and I had to come to terms with it. Don't forget, when Layla was kidnapped, it was Constantine who got her back for me. And all right, Alberto looks like his father,' sighed Annie. 'But I was never interested in Alberto, Max. Not like that. And *he* was interested in

someone else entirely.'

'OK then. Come on. Tell me. Who?' Max came back to the bed, sat down again.

Annie took a breath and braced herself for the fallout. 'Layla.'

Max's face froze. 'What?'

'She's in love with him. I think she has been for years.'

'What?'

'This is going to break her in two, him just taking off like that.'

Max stared at her, assimilating the facts. Coming back to the house yesterday with Layla, Alberto taking her arm, her hissing *don't touch me,* then the two of them arguing in the car. Shit! Annie was right. He could see it now.

'I'm going to kill that cocky bastard,' said Max.

'Too late,' said Annie. 'He's gone. And I bet even you don't know where his final destination is.'

'No. But if I did, straight up, I would go there right now and blow his fucking brains out. You don't think that they've...'

Annie tried hard to suppress the smile, she really did. It tickled her greatly to see Max Carter, feared gang lord and general hard case, behaving exactly as any doting father would on hearing the news that his daughter wasn't his innocent little girl any more.

'What? That they've made love? Yes, I think they most probably have.'

Max looked as if he was about to implode.

'Well thank God he *has* gone. She can't go getting involved with a freaking *Mafia* boss, is she crazy? And what about the age gap?'

'The age gap's about eighteen years. And *our* age gap is about eleven, which isn't so very different.'

Max had a horrible thought. 'You don't think he's knocked her up, do you?'

'Oh God,' sighed Annie, leaning back on the pillows.

'What? *What?* Well he could have. Couldn't he? That *does* happen.'

'I doubt that she's pregnant.' *And if she was, she'd give you a grandchild you'd dote on forever,* thought Annie. *Would that be so terrible?*

'Thank Christ for that.'

'I think Alberto would have been careful.'

'Don't! Don't even go there.' Max was furious.

'Max.' She caught his hand.

'What?' he snapped.

'Please – don't have a go at her. She's heartbroken as it is. She was already in bits over losing her friend, Precious. She's had enough. Don't hurt her any more.'

And there's Layla downstairs, wondering if her mother loves her, he thought.

His little girl, Layla. Now she was a woman. And she had chosen Alberto, but he'd run out on her. Annie was right. Layla would need them both to be strong for her.

He leaned over and kissed his ex-wife briefly on the lips. 'Just rest now,' he said, and went to the door on to the landing. When he opened it, Layla was standing there.

110

'Can I see her?' she asked her father.

Max glanced back at Annie, who was smiling.

'Don't tire her out, that's all,' he warned, kissing Layla's cheek and going off downstairs.

Annie opened her arms. Layla hesitated, then ran across the room and flung herself on to the bed, hugging her mother fiercely.

'I love you, Mum,' she said, and started to cry.

'Hey, don't. Don't! What's all this for?' said Annie, feeling tearful too. She kissed Layla, gathered her into her arms. 'Shh, don't cry.'

'I thought I'd lost you!' Layla sobbed. 'I've been such a complete cow to you ever since you split with Dad, and I thought I'd lost you, that it was too late, that it would never be all right between us.'

'It *is* all right between us.' Annie pushed Layla back a little. 'Look. I'm here and I'm fine. See?'

Layla wiped shakily at her eyes. Her face was soaked with tears.

'I've never been so frightened in my entire life,' she said, shivering as she thought of it all. 'I don't know how you got through it, I really don't.'

'Well, I did. And so did you,' said Annie, smoothing back her daughter's hair with loving hands and smiling into her eyes. 'I like your hair down like this, it suits you. And that lipstick's nice, what shade is that?'

'Hot pink. I suppose it's all over my face now, and I bet my mascara's shot.'

'Just a bit,' said Annie.

Layla managed a laugh at that. She scooped a tissue from the side table and tried to compose herself. 'I'm such a wimp,' she sniffed, looking at Annie lying there, who had been through hell but seemed so composed. Her mother was strong as a rock, she admired her so much.

'Dad told you about Alberto?' she asked.

'Yeah. He did.'

Layla clutched at her mother's hand. 'I don't know if I can stand it. Him being gone. I really don't.'

Annie said nothing as Layla started to cry again.

'I'm in love with him, Mum,' she managed to get out.

'I know.' Annie pulled her back into her arms and held her tight as she sobbed.

Abruptly, Layla pushed herself free. 'You know?'

'Honey, it was obvious.'

Layla wiped her eyes. 'I'm never going to see him again. Am I?'

Annie compressed her lips, shook her head slowly. 'No. None of us are.'

'Only,' Layla gulped, 'I don't see how I can live without him.'

Annie hugged her again.

'You'll live without him,' she murmured against Layla's brow. 'You can do it. And you know why you can do it?'

Layla shook her head.

'Because you have to.' Annie wished she could

take Layla's pain away, but she couldn't. She was going to have to work through this, learn to bear it. 'I'm still here, and so's your Dad.'

But he'll be going soon.

Annie didn't say it. She didn't even want to *think* it. But she knew that it was true.

Layla's eyes drifted over to the connecting door, lying there on the carpet. She started to smile. 'Dad, right?' she said, looking back at Annie.

'Got it in one.'

'Do you think you and he...?' Layla hardly dared hope.

'No. I don't.'

111

The police called by a couple of days later.

'Just a courtesy call,' said DCI Hunter, when he and Annie were settled in the study at the front of the house. From her seat behind the leather-bound desk Annie could see out of the window. The black van that had been there for weeks was now gone.

'Where's DI Duggan?' asked Annie.

'Other duties. I thought I'd drop by to check that you're OK,' he said.

'As you can see, I'm fine.'

'What was it all about?'

'I've no idea.'

Hunter looked at her sceptically. She looked

right back at him. He was a handsome man, but so dour-faced.

'Tell me something,' said Annie.

'Go on.'

'Did you ever get back with your wife? I notice you don't wear a wedding ring any more.'

'No, I don't. And I didn't. The job, you know. It makes married life difficult.'

'Shame.' He looked like a man who needed some lightness in his life. She pushed away from the desk and stood up. 'Well, it's nice of you to call, DCI Hunter, but I have to go out, so if that's all…'

'Yes, I think that about covers it,' he said, and stood up too. 'And Mrs Carter...?'

'Hm?'

'Your stepson. Alberto Barolli.'

'Yeah, what about him?'

'No idea where he is right now, I suppose?'

'None whatsoever,' said Annie.

Hunter gave her a sceptical look. 'That's exactly what I thought you'd say. Well ... try to keep out of trouble in future. If you can.'

112

Tony drove her to the Palermo, where Dolly was downstairs checking the bar takings.

'Hiya, sweetheart,' she said, greeting Annie with a distracted smile.

'How's tricks?' asked Annie, hauling herself on

to a bar stool.
'All fine. You?'
'Great. I'm officially returning your driver and your car.'
'Oh?' Dolly's blue eyes were shrewd on Annie's face. 'You sorted out your bother then?'
'Think so.'
'Max still here?'
'He is.'
'Staying?'
'Shouldn't think so.'
'If you asked him to stay, I bet he would.'
'Well, I'm not asking. He's got his life, I've got mine.'
'Yeah, but you ain't got *much* of a life, have you?'
'Meaning?'
'Meaning all you ever do is spend money and do lunch.'
'Maybe I'll open another club. Another Annie's. Here in London.'
'Well, if you need a manager,' Dolly winked, 'call me. OK?'

Leaving Tone and the company Jag to Dolly, Annie took a cab on to the Shalimar to see Ellie.
'Hey!' said Ellie, hurrying forward to give her a hug. 'How are you?'
'I'm fine,' said Annie, as Ellie ushered her into the kitchen. They sat down at the table.
'And Layla? I sort of miss having her about the place.'
'She's fine too.'
Ellie's smile faded away. 'Terrible business about

Precious, wasn't it? Poor girl. It's the funeral on Friday.'

'Ellie, I want you to fire Junior's arse.'

Ellie looked taken aback, then she shrugged. 'If you say so. He hasn't shown up for days and I don't think he's going to, so it's a bit of a moot point.' Ellie stared at her old mate's face. 'You don't think he was *involved* in what happened to Precious, do you?'

'Up to his neck. So if he shows his face…'

'Consider it done.'

Maybe Max had already seen to this. Kath and Junior and Molls would no longer be welcome in this town. She'd tried her best for them, but look how she'd been repaid.

'The police called, said the bloke who'd done it had been found.'

'Yeah, shot dead,' said Annie. 'Seems he'd upset someone else, and they got to him.'

'Is that so?' Ellie's eyes were like saucers in her plump, pretty face. 'Well, good riddance to bad rubbish, I say.'

'The other girls OK? This must have been a horrible shock for them. Layla told me to ask after Destiny and China.'

'China's cleared out.'

'What, gone?'

'Back to the Philippines. I reckon what happened to Precious scared the crap out of her, and her daughter Tia's not well. She might come back, but my feeling is she won't.'

'And what about Destiny?'

'Jeez, that blew up in a big way. The husband wasn't satisfied with beating the living daylights out of her – he started in on the kids too. That finally brought her to her senses – she's moved them out of the family home and into a women's refuge. She's still showing up for work, but I don't know for how long. He's been turning up at the door here, making a nuisance of himself.'

Annie thought of her own heartache over Max – and Layla, mourning not only the loss of her friend but of Alberto too.

She heaved a sigh. 'Ellie, do you sometimes think that men are just too much trouble?'

'Hell yes.' Chris passed by the open door, saw the two women sitting there, gave them a smile. 'But not my Chris,' she added.

Annie left her there, and took a taxi home to Holland Park. She needed to phone Ruthie, give her the all-clear.

113

Annie offered to go with her to the funeral, but Layla refused.

'No, it's OK. I can do this on my own.'

And she could. She took the train up to Durham, booked into a hotel overnight. Next morning she dressed carefully in her black power suit, added a chunky necklace, black courts, put her hair up in a neat French pleat. Checked herself in the mirror. Added pillar-box red lipstick, smoky black eye shadow and a lot of mascara. Checked herself again. Yes, she looked the business.

Precious would be proud.

At ten thirty she took a taxi to the church. They were handing out black-edged booklets as she went in the door, with *Amelia Westover* picked out in silver on the front cover.

Amelia Westover!

Precious suited her *so* much better.

There were a lot of mourners, a lot of school friends by the look of it, university types, aged uncles and aunts. Settling herself in at the rear of the church, she saw Mr and Mrs Westover up at the front. Mrs Westover was in bits, and Mr Westover looked gaunt with grief.

Then the organ music changed tone, and the pall-bearers brought in a mahogany coffin laden with white lilies.

Precious is in there.

But she wasn't. Precious was gone, out into the stars.

Layla felt tears choke her. She put her hand over her heart, did the heart-brain exercise the way Precious had taught her, and grew calmer.

Precious wasn't in there.

She was gone, she was free.

Later, she shook hands with the Westovers. They seemed so devastated she almost started crying all over again.

'Oh! It's Layla, isn't it,' said Mrs Westover, looking at her with Precious's heartbreakingly beautiful eyes.

'I thought I'd come,' she said.

'We're so glad you did, dear.' Mrs Westover turned to a woman beside her – a sister, Layla thought, the same bone structure, the same stunning eyes. 'This is Layla,' she told her.

'Did you know Amelia well?' asked the woman, trying to smile.

'No, not very well,' said Layla, thinking of Precious, the Glamazon, the most fabulous creature she had ever clapped eyes on. 'But she was my friend,' she said with pride.

114

'But you can't let him go,' said Layla.

She was back at home in Holland Park, in the study with Annie. And Max had just told them both that he was flying out to Barbados tonight. He was upstairs now, packing.

'Layla, it's his decision,' said Annie. 'Trouble's over. He can do whatever he wants.'

Layla eyed her mother intensely. 'Ask him to stay,' she pleaded.

Annie sat back in her chair. Her heart felt bruised, the way he'd come right out with it: 'I'm going. See you.' *Bastard.*

'The funeral went off OK?' she asked.

'Don't change the subject! Yes, it was fine. Bloody horrible, but a nice funeral. *Please* ask him to stay.'

'No,' said Annie. 'I can't. Now drop it.'

'Are you going to at least get the door fixed before you leave?' asked Annie.

She had wandered upstairs and was now leaning against the wall in the adjoining room to the master suite, watching Max fling things into his bag.

He paused, glancing over at the door, still lying there on the carpet.

'No,' he said, and grinned. 'Keep it there as a little reminder of me.'

I don't need reminders, thought Annie. *I'll never forget you, not as long as I live.*

But she couldn't say it. She was obstinate, true, but he was the one who'd hurt her, not the other way around. All his pain had been whipped up out of his past experiences and his own fevered imagination. She'd done nothing wrong, had nothing to apologize for, all the blame was on him.

'Did you sort out the Kath business? And Junior and Molls?' she asked.

'They've been told to fuck off, if that's what you mean. And word is, they have.'

'Good.'

Silence fell. He tossed in a shirt, the dark-blue one the same colour as his eyes.

'Well ... I hope you have a good trip,' she said.

'Thanks.' He looked at her. 'I will.'

He's not even going to kiss me goodbye, she thought.

Well, fuck him.

'See you then,' she said, and left the room before she broke down and cried.

When she woke next morning, he was gone.

115

New York, A month later...

Annie had put feelers out. As well as scouting for premises around Covent Garden in London, she was considering locations for another Annie's club in New York. She was there now, with Layla, and right this instant she was standing in Times Square with Sonny Gilbert, her manager, looking up at the frontage of the club there.

'Maybe the red's a bit dated – what do you think? Time for a refurb?' she asked him.

She'd been impressed with Max's three clubs in London; they were classy.

Max.

No. She wasn't going to think about him.

Sonny puffed out his cheeks. He was a tall thin man with a bald dome of a head, thick glasses and eyes that twinkled through them as he spoke. He folded his arms and gave it some thought.

'Mm, dunno. I'm still liking the red.'

'Maybe alter the italics on the lettering? What about Gothic?'

'Nah, too *Interview with a Vampire*. You read that?'

'No.' Annie never had time to read. Layla loved books: she didn't.

She thought of Layla, who'd said she was going shopping today. All in all, she thought that Layla was coping with her anguish over Alberto. She was covering it up well, anyway.

'I thought maybe the background would be better dark blue, or burgundy?' she suggested.

'Hm. Not sure.'

Annie turned to Sonny in mild exasperation. He had this whole place running like a Swiss watch and he didn't like changes. But fuck it, *she* was the owner.

'I'll get some design people in, put some ideas together,' she said.

'Yeah, fine. You're the boss.'

Oh am I? For a second there, I thought you *were.*

Sonny went back into the club. Annie hailed a cab, and returned to her apartment.

Layla had been shopping in Bloomingdales on 59th and Lexington. She came out of the store laden with bags, and into the gusty street. People poured along the busy sidewalks, yellow taxis moved in droves through the multi-laned street. The sheer *activity* in New York had come as a shock to her: she hadn't visited since she was a child.

She was on her way to meet her mother at the apartment overlooking Central Park, and looking forward to it in a way that she never would have guessed at a year ago. Annie had become her friend as well as her mum now. Since that business with Orla Delaney and Rufus Malone, Layla had come to treasure her.

She was, she supposed, fairly happy. Mum was keeping busy, but then Mum usually did. And she ... well, she shopped. She hadn't thought about finding another job, not yet, she was just keeping Mum company, looking at possible venues for the new club.

She was happy enough.

As long as she didn't think about him.

Then she didn't feel happy at all.

So she shopped, and lunched and ... she caught a glimpse of herself in one of Bloomingdales' exquisitely dressed shop windows, and paused. She was elegantly groomed now – as Precious had taught her to be. She was wearing a black cashmere coat with a thick faux-fur collar. Black leather boots. Her hair was loose, glossy: her Gucci shades were big and dark.

I am turning into my mother, she thought. And once that would have appalled her; now she just felt proud. She turned away from her reflection, moved into the milling crowds, and a man came out of nowhere and bumped hard up against her.

Her bags went flying. She let out an 'Oh!' of shock and staggered back. She had a quick impression of a middle-aged man, grey-haired, instantly forgettable. He scrambled around, picking her bags up.

'Sorry, lady,' he said, and thrust them into her hands.

'Wh–' she started, but he was gone, vanishing into the crowds.

She looked down. He'd put something else into her hand too: a piece of paper. Frowning, she stared at it. Then she closed her fist over it, stepped to the edge of the sidewalk, and flagged down a cab.

116

Annie went pale when Layla showed her the small square of paper.

'It was weird, Mum. This guy bumped into me outside Bloomingdales, knocked my bags everywhere, then he gave them back to me and he gave me this, too. Next thing I knew, he'd disappeared.' She squinted over her mother's shoulder as Annie sat at the table. 'It looks funny. Letters, numbers, I don't know what the hell it is.'

'Oh shit,' said Annie.

'Do you know what it means?' Layla dragged out a chair, sat down, peered at her Mum's face in concern.

Annie looked at Layla. 'I know what it means. I know what it is.'

'OK, what is it? Come on.'

'It's a *pizzino.* Caesar's code.' And she hadn't seen it in a lot of years. Not since Constantine.

Who would use the same code that Constantine had always used? She stared at it, started to shake her head.

'Get me a pencil and paper,' she said. 'Hurry up.'

Layla did so. They sat at the table and as she scribbled on the paper, her pen moving faster and faster, Annie talked.

'This code is over two thousand years old. It was used by Julius Caesar. Each letter of the alphabet becomes a number, and you add three. So A is one, plus three, which equals four, B is two, plus three, that's five, and so on. Constantine reversed it for numbers.'

Layla watched, fascinated, as Annie jotted stuff on to the paper.

When she'd finished, Annie sat back and stared at it.

'Oh. Dear. God,' she said. 'These are map coordinates.'

'What?' Layla demanded.

Annie looked at her daughter and suddenly she started to laugh.

'Honey– It's a grid reference. Alberto's telling you where he is.'

117

Whoever said it was better to travel hopefully than to arrive was obviously barking mad. Layla felt as though she had been travelling for about a year, first shuffling in airport queues, then on a five-hour flight, then another airport, *another flight,* then a water taxi, then a sea plane. Now a dust-covered cab with a smiling man in a loud shirt at the wheel was bumping her along an unmade-up road. She was so exhausted she could barely keep her eyes open.

'Do you know how many islands there are in the Caribbean?' Annie had asked her excitedly before she left New York. 'There are *thousands.*

Saba and St Eustatius, the Virgins, then there's Andros and North Bimini in the Bahamas, and–'

'And your point is...' interrupted Layla impatiently.

'My point is, a person could lose themselves there and never be found. You could stash your money in Belize or Panama, get yourself a luxury yacht, live on it, cruise around. Get lost *for ever.*'

Layla had been looking at the maps, she knew Annie was right.

I would kill for a shower, she thought. She felt grubby, sweaty. It was so hot, there was no air-conditioning in the taxi. She peered outside, blinking with gritty eyes, and saw an azure sky, a stretch of white beach zip past, people strolling, no hurry, no problems, palm trees bent nearly double by the breeze, and the sea. She stared at it, a vast shimmering turquoise expanse that she longed to dive into to cool down.

The taxi came bumping to a halt. She fumbled for her purse, paid the driver. Clambered from the car while he went round the back and got her case out of the boot. The warm breeze tossed her hair into her eyes. She dragged it back, looked around her. There was nothing here.

'Hey!' she said to the driver. 'Where...?'

But he was already back behind the wheel, slamming his door closed, gunning the engine, driving away in a cloud of dust. That was when she saw the huge black-haired man standing near a rickety pontoon, wearing shorts and a green polo-shirt. He saw her, and came lumbering over to pick up her case.

'Miss,' he greeted her.

Layla felt like she wanted to kiss him. 'Sandor! Hi.'

'This way,' he said, and she stepped out on to the pontoon over the swirling sun-speckled clear waters, tiny bright fish dancing inches below her feet, Sandor following on behind. The taxi roared away.

Layla looked ahead, shielding her eyes from the hot glare of the sun. There was a forty-foot schooner moored out in the deeper waters of the bay. And there was a man stepping out of a small rowing boat at the end of the pontoon. He was wearing cut-off denim shorts, nothing else. His blond hair was bleached almost white by the sun and the wind, and his tall muscular frame was tanned and fit. He gazed along the pontoon, saw her standing there. His laser-blue eyes met hers, and Alberto started to smile.

Layla smiled too, her heart beating very fast. It was him. It really was.

She began to walk toward the man she'd loved all her life.

Then she broke into a run.

118

Not fifty miles from where his daughter was being reunited with Alberto, Max Carter lay in blissful ignorance in the sun on his Bajan terrace, wearing black Speedos. He loved lying in the sun.

It refuelled him, made him stronger, and he was soaking it up, making the most of it, because he'd decided that he was going back to grey blustery England soon, see that crazy bitch Annie again, why not? Put her out of her misery.

He missed her.

That was what he'd been trying so hard to blank from his mind these last eight years, with the heat and the women and the easy-living style of the Caribbean. The fact that he missed his ex-wife. And ... he could see now that he'd been a fool. He'd allowed his jealousy and his deep insecurity where she was concerned to run riot. Maybe he would tell her that, but he didn't think so. Keep her on her toes.

Treat 'em mean, keep 'em keen.

Wasn't that what his old man had told him? Oh yeah, and *Keep 'em well fucked and poorly shod.* That was another favourite of his.

Fat chance of keeping Annie Carter poor, she liked the high life too much for that.

He was drifting off into a light doze, perfectly relaxed, when someone kicked his sun bed, hard.

'What the *fuck?*' he asked, springing into a sitting position.

Someone was standing over him, blocking out the sun. He squinted, unable to see a face.

'Is this all you've got to do out here? Lie in the sun all day?' demanded a very familiar female voice.

'Well what would you *like* me to do?' he asked her. He could feel a grin forming on his face: couldn't stop it.

'You could say hello, that'd be a start.'

He grabbed her hand and yanked her down so that she was sitting on the sun bed in front of him.

'Hey!' Annie protested, suddenly on his level. 'Not so rough.'

'You want me to say hello or don't you?' he asked, looking her over. The dark green eyes, the mouth that was now beginning to smile. Her long dark hair was moving gently in the breeze. She was wearing a cream linen sun dress, and a large gold cross he hadn't seen her wearing before glinted in the valley between her breasts. 'Why didn't you tell me you were coming?'

She shrugged. 'Wanted to surprise you.'

'Missed me, yeah?'

'Not especially.'

He raised his eyebrows. 'Really.'

'Yeah, really.'

Max stood up. Reached down, pulled her to her feet and into his arms.

'You're hot,' she murmured, feeling it radiating from his sun-heated skin. She twined her arms around his neck. Later, she was going to have to break the news about Layla joining up with Alberto – she knew he was going to be spitting mad about it – but for now she just stood there and enjoyed the feel of his arms around her.

'So are you,' he said, running his hands down over her body. 'Let's go inside, where it's cooler.'

He picked her up.

'What the *hell?*' protested Annie.

'Ah, shut up,' he said, and took her into the villa.

Annie shrieked with laughter as he tossed her

on to the bed.
'Bastard,' she said, opening her arms.
'Bitch,' said Max, and kissed her.

The publishers hope that this book has given you enjoyable reading. Large Print Books are especially designed to be as easy to see and hold as possible. If you wish a complete list of our books please ask at your local library or write directly to:

Magna Large Print Books
Magna House, Long Preston,
Skipton, North Yorkshire.
BD23 4ND

This Large Print Book for the partially sighted, who cannot read normal print, is published under the auspices of

THE ULVERSCROFT FOUNDATION

THE ULVERSCROFT FOUNDATION

... we hope that you have enjoyed this Large Print Book. Please think for a moment about those people who have worse eyesight problems than you ... and are unable to even read or enjoy Large Print, without great difficulty.

You can help them by sending a donation, large or small to:

The Ulverscroft Foundation,
1, The Green, Bradgate Road,
Anstey, Leicestershire, LE7 7FU,
England.
or request a copy of our brochure for more details.

The Foundation will use all your help to assist those people who are handicapped by various sight problems and need special attention.

Thank you very much for your help.